A HAUNTED HOUSE

Virginia Woolf was born in London in 1882, the daughter of Sir Leslie Stephen, first editor of *The Dictionary of National Biography*. After his death in 1904 Virginia and her sister, the painter Vanessa Bell, moved to Bloomsbury and became the centre of 'The Bloomsbury Group'. This informal collective of artists and writers which included Lytton Strachey and Roger Fry, exerted a powerful influence over early twentieth-century British culture.

In 1912 Virginia married Leonard Woolf, a writer and social reformer. Three years later, her first novel *The Voyage Out* was published, followed by *Night and Day* (1919) and *Jacob's Room* (1922). These first novels show the development of Virginia Woolf's distinctive and innovative narrative style. It was during this time that she and Leonard Woolf founded The Hogarth Press with the publication of the co-authored *Two Stories* in 1917, hand-printed in the dining room of their house in Surrey. The majority of Virginia Woolf's work was first published by The Hogarth Press, and these original texts are now available, together with her selected letters and diaries, from Vintage Classics, which belongs to the publishing group that Hogarth became part of in 1987.

Between 1925 and 1931 Virginia Woolf produced what are now regarded as her finest masterpieces, from *Mrs Dalloway* (1925) to the poetic and highly experimental novel *The Waves* (1931). She also maintained an astonishing output of literary criticism, short fiction, journalism and biography, including the playfully subversive *Orlando* (1928) and *A Room of One's Own* (1929) a passionate feminist essay. This intense creative productivity was often matched by periods of mental illness, from which she had suffered since her mother's death in 1895. On 28 March 1941, a few months before the publication of her final novel, *Between the Acts*, Virginia Woolf committed suicide.

VIRGINIA WOOLF

A Haunted House

The Complete Shorter Fiction

EDITED BY
Susan Dick
WITH AN INTRODUCTION BY
Helen Simpson

VINTAGE

19

Vintage
20 Vauxhall Bridge Road,
London SW1V 2SA

Vintage Classics is part of the Penguin Random House
group of companies whose addresses can be found at global.
penguinrandomhouse.com.

 Penguin
Random House
UK

Text by Virginia Woolf © Quentin Bell, Angelica Garnett
and Julian Bell 1917, 1919, 1921, 1923, 1942, 1944, 1973,
1977, 1985
Introduction and notes © Susan Dick 1985
Introduction © Helen Simpson 2003

First published in Great Britain by The Hogarth Press in 1985
First published by Vintage Classics in 2003

www.vintage-books.co.uk

A CIP catalogue record for this book is available from the
British Library

ISBN 9780099442165

Printed and bound in Great Britain by Clays Ltd, Elcograf S.p.A.

Contents

Contents

Introduction

If you read only one of Virginia Woolf's short stories, make sure it is the first-published, 'The Mark on the Wall'. Though not necessarily the best – indeed, like most of her short pieces, it is not really a story at all – it is an extraordinary flight where she writes for the first time with real freedom and pleasure.

An unfettered revery, 'The Mark on the Wall' holds, glancingly, everything which fascinated her. From the depths of an armchair, the first-person voice – stimulated by a mark on the wall which may be a nail, a leaf, a snail – follows in a few pages the fluid associative movement of the mind towards pleasant tracks of thought and consolatory narcissistic reflections; gives a sensuously imagined picture of the afterlife as a giant garden; conjures 'an intoxicating sense of illegitimate freedom' from Victorian traditions and masculine values as embodied in Whitaker's Table of Precedency; traces the progress of trees from forest to wooden ships or furniture; and speculates on the nature of matter; 'thus, waking from a midnight dream of horror, one hastily turns on the light and lies quiescent, worshipping the chest of drawers, worshipping solidity...' Here is the precursor of the experiments which are to fill her future novels, where the writer will evaporate and condense solid objects over her literary bunsen burner in solutions of time or light. Woolf is fascinated by entropic states, by what time does to matter, and by time itself, its elasticity, how it can be speeded up or made to dawdle.

Why, if one wants to compare life to anything, one must liken it to being blown through the Tube at fifty miles an hour – landing at the other end without a single hairpin in one's hair! Shot out at the feet of God entirely naked! Tumbling head over heels in the asphodel meadows like brown paper parcels pitched down a chute in the post office! With one's hair flying back like the tail of a racehorse. Yes, that seems to express the rapidity of life, the perpetual waste and repair; all so casual, all so haphazard...

Woolf's writing shows for the first time in this story its fantastic drag-onfly quality – hovering and then leaping, defying gig lamp chronology, spending a page on an instant then hurtling through several centuries in the space of a paragraph. Here too for the first time her extraordinary syntax is given free rein, the long fluid sentences endlessly bifurcating, the host of semicolons leading down the garden path; then there is her refusal to close off possibilities; or to follow a straight line; and the darting down avenues and green lanes of thought and so on into mazes; with you, the reader, running after her breathless and delighted. This sense of freedom and playfulness in 'The Mark on the Wall' expresses itself in exclamations, lists, metonymic encapsulations, dabs of colour and jottings and fragments linked by the indispensable semicolon, shaping itself towards a quite new prose medium.

'I'm very glad you liked the story,' Woolf wrote to David Garnett. 'In a way it's easier to do a short thing, all in one flight than a novel. Novels are frightfully clumsy and overpowering of course; still if one could only get hold of them it would be superb. Anyhow, it's very amusing to try with these short things.' She was to continue using 'these short things' as places of freedom where she could experiment with narrative technique and limber up for her novels. Most of her short fiction was written in the seven-year period from 1917 (after that she was to aver-age one short piece a year till the end of her life). It is no coincidence that 1917 was also the year that Virginia and Leonard Woolf set up the Hogarth Press. Their first publication was a volume containing two stories, one by each of them, Virginia's being 'The Mark on the Wall'. She set the type by hand herself. For the first time she did not have to consider pleasing any publisher – she was the publisher.

'I shall never forget the day I wrote "The Mark on the Wall",' she wrote, years later to Ethel Smyth, 'all in a flash, as if flying, after being kept stone breaking for months.' Stone breaking was what novel writing felt like to her at this point – she had published *The Voyage Out* in 1915 and was working on *Night and Day*, following the traditional novelistic conventions of the time with increasing dissatis-faction. It was only in *Jacob's Room* (1922) that she at last broke free, making use of the experimental narrative and prose techniques she had been exploring in her short pieces.

Monday or Tuesday, the only collection of stories and sketches that Virginia Woolf chose to publish, appeared in 1921. It included 'The Mark on the Wall,' as well as impressionistic pieces like *Kew Gardens* and lyrical mood poems like 'A Haunted House'. The phrase 'Monday or Tuesday' appears again, as part of her thoughts on a possible new approach to writing novels, in her essay 'Modern Fiction' – 'Examine for a moment an ordinary mind on an ordinary day. The mind receives a myriad impressions – trivial, fantastic, evansescent, or engraved with the sharpness of steel. From all sides they come, an incessant shower of innumerable atoms; and as they fall, as they shape themselves into the life of Monday or Tuesday, the accent falls differently from of old.' Very short, strongly visual, the stories in this collection give most of their emphasis to descriptions of light and its effect on colour and shade. Indeed, they are more paintings than stories. When Roger Fry wrote in praise, she replied, 'I'm not sure that a perverted plastic sense doesn't somehow work itself out in words for me.'

Virginia Woolf was not the only artist after some new form of expression. These stories have something in common with Ezra Pound's belief that the poet should concentrate on 'that which presents an intellectual and emotional complex in an instant of time' and with prose poems like T.S.Eliot's 'Hysteria', seeming to aspire to the condition of painting. Painting itself, of course, was at this time in a state of seismic transition. Roger Fry's Post-Impressionist exhibition at the Grafton Galleries in 1910 had proved enormously influential in all branches of the arts. When the short story writer Katherine Mansfield saw Van Gogh's paintings there for the first time, she described how she had learned from them 'something about writing . . . a kind of freedom – or rather, a shaking free'.

Virginia Woolf first met Katherine Mansfield in 1917, and almost immediately took her long story *Prelude* for the Hogarth Press. She was six years older than Katherine, who was to die in 1923 at the age of 34. When she died, Virginia wrote in her diary, 'I was jealous of her writing – the only writing I have ever been jealous of'. For much of the six years they knew each other they were wary and distant – yet whenever they met, Virginia recorded deeply interested and useful exchanges about writing.

'We have got the same job, Virginia,' Katherine wrote to her in 1917, '& it is really very curious & thrilling that we should both, quite apart from each other be after so very nearly the same thing. We are you know; there's no denying it... Yes, your Flower Bed (*Kew Gardens*) is very good. There a still, quivering, changing light over it all and a sense of those couples dissolving in the bright air which fascinates me'.

They *were* both after the same thing – a new sort of prose, a translucent medium capable of intensity and lyricism, an escape from stolidity and superficial detail. (Virginia Woolf wrote that what appalled her was the 'narrative business of the realist: getting from lunch to dinner: it is false, unreal, merely conventional'.)

'People have never explored the lovely medium of prose,' wrote Katherine Mansfield in her Journal, 'It is a hidden country still – I feel that so profoundly'; and again, 'I want to write a kind of long elegy . . . perhaps not in poetry. Nor perhaps in prose. Almost certainly in a kind of special prose'. Virginia Woolf too wrote of the need for a special prose somewhere between prose and poetry – characteristically at more length – 'For though English poetry was a fine potentate – but no, I dare not breathe a word against English poetry. All I will venture is a sigh of wonder that when there is prose before us with its capacities and possibilities, its power to say new things, make new shapes, express new passions, young people should still be dancing to a barrel organ and choosing words because they rhyme,' she wrote in her 1920 review of Logan Pearsall Smith's anthology *A Treasury of English Prose*.

They were moving towards writing in a more condensed, elliptical, fragmentary way, cutting explanation and padding. Both women were very interested in the newly translated Russian writing which was appearing during the time of their friendship, writing which startled with its apparently random or inconclusive quality. (Katherine Mansfield helped the Russian émigré S.S. Koteliansky with his translations of Chekhov's letters; Virginia and Leonard Woolf published several Russian translations in collaboration with Koteliansky, including Chekhov's Notebooks in 1921.) Reviewing Constance Garnett's translation of Chekhov's *The Bishop and other stories* in 1919, Virginia wrote, 'We are by this time alive to the fact that inconclusive stories are legitimate; that is to say, though they leave us feeling melancholy and perhaps uncertain, yet somehow they provide a resting-point for the mind – a solid object casting its shade of reflection and speculation'. (The title and mysterious obliquity of one of her own best stories 'Solid Objects', published in *The Athenaeum* in 1920, draw on this thought.)

The modernist short story form was from the first characterised as inconclusive or random. Galsworthy wrote of Chekhov that he was 'all middle, like a tortoise'. When Virginia Woolf met Thomas Hardy in 1926, she described him chuckling about some new short stories by Aldous Huxley – 'They've changed everything now ... We used to think there was a beginning and a middle and an end. Now one of those stories came to an end with a woman going out of the room.' Chekhov's stories do have beginnings and ends, it is just that these are transparent, implicit (Chekhov himself claimed that whenever he finished a story, he cut the first and last paragraphs). Katherine Mansfield's stories are similarly shaped; a major part of their effect lies in their form, the arch they describe. Conversely, Virginia Woolf's short pieces really are all middle like a tortoise; she is not interested in the arch of a story.

'Mrs Dalloway in Bond Street' was written in the summer of 1922, and by the autumn Virginia Woolf was writing in her diary that the story had 'branched into a book'. Even so, she sent it off for magazine publication, noting, however, that 'Mrs Dalloway doesn't seem to me to be complete as she is'. How different this is, how exactly the opposite of the experience of a natural short story writer like Katherine Mansfield, who noted of her story 'The Daughters of the Late Colonel' (1921), 'Even dear old Hardy told me to write more about those sisters. As if there was any more to say!'.

It is fascinating to read 'Mrs Dalloway in Bond Street' alongside the first section of the novel *Mrs Dalloway*. The very first sentence disconcerts – 'Mrs Dalloway said she would buy the gloves herself.' What, not the flowers? The flowers for her party, towards which the whole novel leads? And to make such a point of buying gloves – the mood is suddenly more old-fashioned. Then where, in the novel, she has 'a touch of the bird about her, of the jay, blue-green, light, vivacious, though she was over fifty, and grown very white since her illness,' in the story she appears as a charming woman, poised, eager, strangely white-haired for her pink cheeks.' The story has a more garish tone altogether, and the character of Mrs Dalloway appearing here is almost a parody, a broad satirical outline of the woman described in the novel. The novel's prose is far more complex, subtle and beautiful than the story's. Virginia Woolf has reworked it with great energy, making endless qualifications and calibrations of meaning and a myriad minute and essential modulations of tone and register. It is a perfect example of how she needed space in which to linger and expand, unlimited acreage ahead of her and no constraints.

On finishing the novel *Mrs Dalloway*, Virginia Woolf did not cut off from it immediately. While considering her next novel, *To The Lighthouse*, she found herself wanting to write a series of character sketches to illustrate what she termed 'the party consciousness', she was still fascinated by the culminating party in *Mrs Dalloway*, 'I must write a few little stories first and let the Lighthouse simmer,' she wrote. In 'The New Dress', 'Happiness', 'Ancestors', 'The Introduction', 'Together and Apart', 'The Man Who Loved his Kind', and 'A Summing Up', she tries out a whole gallery of new characters, and although these stories appear to be winding down from the effort of writing *Mrs Dalloway*, they are also warming up for the next novel. They approach certain themes and subjects which will be vital to *To the Lighthouse* – the infuriating self-pitying killjoy in 'The Man Who Loved His Own Kind' has something of both Charles Tansley and Mr Ramsey about him, while 'Ancestors' has that novel's central elegaic drive, a woman remembering with a violent sense of loss her dead parents, her starlit childhood, how 'She had read all Shelley between the ages of twelve and fifteen, and used to say it to her father, holding her hands behind her back, while he shaved'.

The same impulse took her once she had finished *To the Lighthouse* – even as she revised its final pages she records how 'as usual, side stories are sprouting in great variety as I wind this up: a book of characters...'. And while preparing to start writing *The Waves*, she once again limbers up with some short pieces 'Slater's Pins Have No Points' is one of them – 'Every morning I write a little sketch to amuse myself'. Little again! 'These little pieces in "Monday or Tuesday" were written by way of diversion; they were the treats I allowed myself...' Virginia Woolf wrote to Ethel Smyth. She usually does refer to her sketches and stories as 'little' rather than 'short', as games or indulgences she allows herself, areas of free play in between the real business of novel writing.

' "The Unwritten Novel" was the great discovery, however. That – again in one second – showed me how I could embody all my deposit of experience in a shape that fitted it – not that I have ever reached that end' she continued to Ethel Smyth in the same fascinating letter of 1937. 'But anyhow I saw, branching out of the tunnel I made, when I discovered that method of approach, *Jacobs Room*, *Mrs Dalloway* etc – How I trembled with excitement.' 'The Mark on the Wall', written in 1917, was where she claimed she first wrote freely, 'all in a flash, as if flying'; but she ascribes more importance to 'An Unwritten Novel', which she wrote some three years later. This is at first puzzling, as it is definitely more interesting than successful as a story.

The first-person narrator sits opposite an unhappy-looking woman in a railway carriage, and spends the journey trying to 'read' her, constructing a background for her, deciding that she is called Minnie Marsh and, childless, is visiting her bullying matriarch of a sister-in-law in Eastbourne. At the end of the story the woman gets off the train at Eastbourne, where she is met by her son, so the narrator knows that all her guesswork was mistaken. She follows them in imagination down to the sea, ending on an ecstatic note with, 'If I fall on my knees, if I go through the ritual, the ancient antics, it's you, unknown figures, you I adore; if I open my arms; it's you I embrace, you I draw to me – adorable world!' It would all be more convincing if the guesswork about the Minnie Marsh character were not so snowed under by class detail – umbrellas, the whiff of beef from the basement, 'crusts and cruets, frills and ferns' – there is even a commercial traveller with a comic name. At no point does the reader feel anywhere near the inner life of the miserable-looking woman in the railway carriage; by the end of the story, indeed, they may well feel that Minnie Marsh is just an excuse, and that they have instead been bamboozled into reading all about the narrator.

The sense of liberation Virginia Woolf experienced seems to have been more to do with the feeling of having discovered a 'method of approach' leading towards the sort of novels she wanted to write. It is the way in which it is told that is the most interesting thing about this story – in a sort of speedy dashing shorthand, with quick sketches and guesses and retractions, dodging and darting around and pointedly ignoring the tyranny of 'and then...and then...and then'; asking questions and not waiting for answers, dizzying the reader with sudden elisions and allusions and swoops of movement – 'Now, eyes open, she looks out; and in the human eye – how d'you define it? – there's a break – a division – so that when you've grasped the stem the butterfly's off – the moth that hangs in the evening over the yellow flower – move, raise your hand, off, high, away. Hang still, then, quiver, life, soul, spirit, whatever you are of Minnie Marsh – I, too, on my flower-the hawk over the down – alone, or what were the worth of life?'.

In 'An Unwritten Novel', she saw 'how I could embody all my deposit of experience in a shape that fitted it'; and that shape was to be the novel, not the short story. 'The truth is that one can get only so much into a story; there is always a sacrifice' wrote Katherine Mansfield. 'One has to leave out what one knows and longs to use.' Virginia Woolf was determined not to leave anything out. Her writing is reflective, complex and subtle, full of literary and historical references and echoes.

She wanted a form that would allow for this and that would hold all she had experienced; on the other hand, she was not prepared to use the novel as a Victorian portmanteau, throwing in everything indiscriminately. 'Why admit anything to literature that is not poetry – by which I mean saturated?' she wrote. 'Is that not my grudge against novelists? that they select nothing? The poets succeeding by simplifying: practically everything is left out. I want to put practically everything in: yet to saturate.' And so she did.

HELEN SIMPSON, 2003.

Editor's Introduction

The works collected in this volume cover the entire range of Virginia Woolf's writing career. The earliest story, 'Phyllis and Rosamond', dates from 1906, just two years after she had begun to publish short essays and reviews in the London journals. The last sketch, 'The Watering Place', was written less than a month before her death, on 28 March 1941, and is probably the last work of fiction that she completed.

Virginia Woolf's shorter fiction has never been collected in a single volume before. To read the works straight through in chronological order is to follow the amazing evolution of her genius as a writer. Her desire, as she described it in 1908, to 're-form the novel and capture multitudes of things at present fugitive, enclose the whole, and shape infinite strange shapes'[1] led her to experiment throughout her career not only with the novel, but also with various forms of short fiction. Commenting again in 1917 on how 'frightfully clumsy and overpowering' the novel was, she added, 'I daresay one ought to invent a completely new form. Anyhow its very amusing to try with these short things . . .' (LII, 167).

Because she was continually experimenting with narrative forms, Woolf's shorter fiction is extremely varied. Some of her shorter works, such as 'Solid Objects' and 'The Legacy', are short stories in the traditional sense, narratives with firm story lines and sharply drawn characters. Others, such as 'The Mark on the Wall' and 'An Unwritten Novel', are fictional reveries which in their shifts of perspective and lyrical prose recall the autobiographical essays of some nineteenth-century writers, De Quincey in particular. Still others, which could be called 'scenes' or 'sketches', probably owe a debt to Chekhov, who helped us to see, Woolf remarked in 1919, that 'inconclusive stories are legitimate'.[2] In some works the narrator functions as a perceptive observer of the external scene, while in others the narrator dramatises from within the minds of the characters, their perceptions of themselves and their world. And in the reveries, it is the narrator's subtle scrutiny of her own thoughts that shapes the narrative.

As this brief description suggests, the line separating Virginia Woolf's fiction from her essays is a very fine one. I have included in this collection only those short pieces that are, to my mind, clearly fictions, that is, works in which the characters, scenes, and actions are more imaginary than they are factual, and in which the narrator's voice is not necessarily identical with the author's. This has meant the exclusion of a number of works which closely resemble her fiction: biographical portraits, such as 'Old Mrs Grey' and 'Eleanor Ormerod', and personal essays, such as 'To Spain' and 'The Moment: Summer's Night'. I have, however, included several fictional works – 'A Woman's College from Outside', 'In the Orchard', and 'Three Pictures' – that have been published previously in collections of her essays.

The first four works in the collection could be called apprentice pieces. In them Woolf tries her hand at creating characters and situations, and she begins to develop a distinctive prose style and narrative voice. In each the narrator focuses on the relationship of the central characters – all of whom are women – to their particular society. Phyllis and Rosamond, like the elusive Miss V., live in contemporary London, while Joan Martyn's journal takes us back to fifteenth-century Norfolk. 'Memoirs of a Novelist', in which Woolf creates a reviewer, a biographer, and a novelist, gives us a picture of one woman's life in Victorian England. The latter work in particular reflects Woolf's continuing interest in the role of the biographer.

With 'The Mark on the Wall', Woolf entered into an important new stage of her writing career. She wrote it in 1917 while she was completing her second novel, *Night and Day* (1919), the long work she later called her 'exercise in the conventional style'. 'I shall never forget,' she told Ethel Smyth, 'the day I wrote The Mark on the Wall – all in a flash, as if flying, after being kept stone breaking for months.' About two years later she wrote 'An Unwritten Novel' and discovered, she later said, 'how I could embody all my deposit of experience in a shape that fitted it' (*LIV*, 231). These two experimental works, along with six others and four woodcut illustrations by Vanessa Bell, were published in *Monday or Tuesday* (1921), the only volume of stories and sketches that Virginia Woolf published.[3]

Woolf complained in her diary that the critics failed to see that she was 'after something interesting' in *Monday or Tuesday*.[4] She was more perplexed than discouraged, however, and the following year she published her first experimental novel, *Jacob's Room*, the book that prompted T. S. Eliot to congratulate her on having 'bridged a certain gap which existed between your other novels and the experimental prose of *Monday or Tuesday*'.[5] As soon as she had completed *Jacob's Room*, she began to outline her next book which might be called, she wrote, 'At Home: or The Party'. 'This is to be a short book,' she continued, 'consisting of six or seven chapters each complete separately, yet there must be some sort of fusion.'[6] The first 'chapter' she listed here was 'Mrs Dalloway in Bond Street', the short story that would soon 'branch', as she put it, 'into a book' (*DII*, 207).

This story marked another important stage in Woolf's development, for it was in writing 'Mrs Dalloway in Bond Street' that she first found a way to place her narrator within her character's mind and to present that character's thoughts and emotions as they occur. James Joyce's use of interior monologue in the opening sections of *Ulysses*, which she was reading while she worked on this story, probably contributed to her presentation of Clarissa Dalloway's inner life, but the seeds of her new method were clearly sown in 'The Mark on the Wall', 'An Unwritten Novel', and other early stories.

She put aside her plan of writing a series of separate 'chapters' and wrote *Mrs Dalloway* (1925), which has no chapters at all. Once this was completed, she began quickly to write a group of eight stories (beginning with 'The New Dress') which were all set at Mrs Dalloway's party. In each of these she presents, from the perspective of one or two characters, the subtle tensions that distinguish 'the party consciousness' (*DIII*, 12). She had modified her earlier plan and now thought her stories might become a 'corridor' leading to a new book.[7] As soon as she had finished the last of these, aptly called 'A Summing Up', she began her next long work, *To the Lighthouse* (1927). In this book she made brilliant use of the narrative method these stories had helped her to perfect.

Between 1917 and 1925, Virginia Woolf completed twenty-five stories and sketches, as well as three novels, a book of essays, and numerous reviews. During this extremely fruitful period, her short fiction was often a testing ground where she experimented with narrative techniques that she would use and develop further in her longer fictions. The stories in *Monday or Tuesday*, like those written immediately before and after *Mrs Dalloway*, reflect the many ways that she was freeing herself from conventions, both of method and thought, and discovering the narrative voice that would be distinctly her own.

She would never write so many works of short fiction in such a brief period again; she completed seventeen stories and sketches during the next sixteen years. These were written intermittently and often as a way of relaxing, or of amusing herself. 'Moments of Being: "Slater's Pins Have No Points"' was a 'side story' that sprouted, she said, as she was completing *To the Lighthouse* (DIII, 106). 'The Lady in the Looking-Glass: A Reflection' and 'The Fascination of the Pool', both written in May of 1929, must have lightened the 'great pressure of difficulty' she felt as she contemplated her next book, *The Waves* (DIII, 229). Some of the stories and sketches written in the thirties, such as 'Three Pictures', 'The Shooting Party', and probably her comic 'Ode', grew out of actual scenes or anecdotes. Her range of characters expands in the later stories to include an inscrutable naval officer, a tiresome but untiring do-gooder, a Pentonville butcher, a social-climbing jeweller, two old ladies who preside gleefully over their family's decline, unhappy wives with self-absorbed husbands, and even a rambunctious dog. In these stories as in the earlier ones, memory and imagination often provide the characters with a means of escape from disappointing lives.

Most of the late stories, beginning with 'The Duchess and the Jeweller', are stories she had drafted at an earlier time and now revised for publication. She records in her diary with obvious pleasure the fee she is paid for each of these. And though she may refer to some of them dismissively as 'pot boiling stories for America' (LVI, 252), her typescripts and the stories themselves show that she put as much work into these as into any of her other writing. She could never, she reflected late in her life, be accused of glibness: 'I feel in my fingers the weight of every word,' she wrote, 'even of a review' (DV, 335).

I have found it impossible not to wonder, especially in the dead of night, what Virginia Woolf would have thought of this collection. Had she lived to publish the volume of her shorter fiction which she and Leonard Woolf had discussed, she would probably not have included in it all of her previously published works,[8] nor all of her unpublished pieces. It is probable that she would have revised the works she decided to reprint from *Monday or Tuesday* and from periodicals, and certain that the unpublished stories and sketches would have undergone extensive revision. Also she would probably have arranged the stories and sketches differently, not in chronological order as I have done, but in a form which would embody, as many of the individual works do, the special rhythms of her own mind. In deciding to mix the unrevised stories and sketches with those which Virginia Woolf had published, rather than to group them in a separate section, I have viewed these works as documents that will best enrich and inform the context in which the more polished stories and sketches are read when they are placed in close conjunction with them. The previously unpublished works also give us further evidence of Woolf's determination never to stop experimenting with new subjects and new narrative methods. Like the many other manuscripts published since her death – the holograph drafts of *To the Lighthouse* and *The Waves*, earlier drafts of *The Voyage Out (Melymbrosia)* and *The Years (The Pargiters)*, the typescripts of *Between the Acts*, *Moments of Being*, essays, diaries, letters, and more – these unpublished works, and those long out of print, now read with the familiar stories and sketches, will surely deepen our appreciation of this remarkable writer's achievement.

NOTES TO INTRODUCTION

Place and date of first publication has been given

1. *The Letters of Virginia Woolf*, ed. Nigel Nicolson (London: The Hogarth Press, 1975–80), I, 356. Hereafter *L* I-VI.

2. 'The Russian Background' in *Books and Portraits*, ed. Mary Lyon (London: The Hogarth Press, 1977), p. 123.

3. *Monday or Tuesday* contains 'A Haunted House', 'A Society', 'Monday or Tuesday', 'An Unwritten Novel', 'The String Quartet', 'Blue & Green', 'Kew Gardens', and 'The Mark on the Wall'.

4. *The Diary of Virginia Woolf*, ed. Anne Olivier Bell (London: The Hogarth Press, 1975–1984), II, 106. Hereafter *D* I–V.

5. Quentin Bell, *Virginia Woolf: A Biography* (London: The Hogarth Press, 1972), II, 88.

6. The holograph of *Jacob's Room*, III, 131 (Berg Collection).

7. 'Notes for Stories' in *Notes for Writing*, holograph notebook (Berg Collection).

8. In his Foreword to *A Haunted House and Other Short Stories*, Leonard Woolf explains that he has excluded 'A Society' and 'Blue & Green' from his collection because Virginia Woolf had planned not to reprint them in the collection of short stories she had contemplated bringing out in 1942. In 1931, she told Ethel Smyth that 'Blue & Green' and 'Monday or Tuesday' were 'the wild outbursts of freedom, inarticulate, ridiculous, unprintable mere outcries.' '. . . thats mainly,' she said earlier in the same letter, 'why I won't reprint' (*L* IV, 231).

9. Not included in this volume are Virginia Woolf's unpublished juvenilia, as well as 'A Cockney's Farming Experiences' and its unfinished sequel, 'The Experiences of a Pater-familias', both written by Virginia Woolf when she was ten

years old and published by Suzanne Henig, San Diego State University Press, 1972. Neither have I included the incomplete works by Virginia Woolf that have survived and that appear to be fragments of short fiction. A list of these can be found in Appendix D.

Editorial Procedures

The publication history of Virginia Woolf's shorter fiction is unusual and complex. Of the forty-six works published here, only eighteen were published during her lifetime. These are the eight stories and sketches included in *Monday or Tuesday*, nine others published separately in periodicals, and one published in a miscellany.[1] Leonard Woolf included eighteen works in *A Haunted House*, published three years after his wife's death. Six of these are from *Monday or Tuesday*, seven from periodicals, and five had not been published before. Another collection, called *Mrs Dalloway's Party* and edited by Stella McNichol, was published in 1973. This contains seven stories: four from *A Haunted House*, one from a periodical, and two that had not been published before. Three other stories have been published separately in periodicals since Virginia Woolf's death, and another was included by Leonard Woolf in *The Death of the Moth*. Seventeen of the stories and sketches included in *The Complete Shorter Fiction* have never been published before.

The editorial procedures followed in establishing the texts of these works have had to be varied according to the kind and amount of material available. I shall describe these procedures below. My aim has been to present a clear text of each story and to explain in the textual notes that accompany the stories the origin of that text.

Monday or Tuesday, Virginia Woolf's only collection of stories and sketches, ran to ninety-one pages and was too ambitious an undertaking for the newly established Hogarth Press. Leonard Woolf has described in *Beginning Again* how 'with considerable hesitation and certainly foolishly' he engaged a jobbing printer named F. T. McDermott to print it. The result was, Woolf says, 'one of the worst printed books ever published'. He recalls in rueful detail the day that he helped McDermott print *Monday or Tuesday*:

I went down and helped him to print the beastly thing. I have never seen a more desperate, ludicrous – but to me at the time tragic – scene than McDermott printing *Monday or Tuesday*. He insisted upon printing the woodcuts with the letterpress. The consequence was that, in order to get the right 'colour' for the illustrations, he had to get four or five times more ink on his rollers than was right for the type. His type was soon clogged with ink; but even that was not the worst: he got so much ink on the blocks and his paper was so soft and spongy that little fluffy bits of paper were torn off with the ink and stuck to the blocks and then to the rollers and finally to the type. We had to stop every few minutes and clean everything, but even so the pages were an appalling sight. We machined 1,000 copies, and at the end we sank down exhausted and speechless on the floor by the side of the machine, where we sat and silently drank beer until I was sufficiently revived to crawl battered and broken back to Hogarth House.[2]

It is not surprising to find that *Monday or Tuesday* contains many typographical errors, especially in the punctuation. Most of these were corrected in the first American edition, published (without Vanessa Bell's woodcuts) by Harcourt, Brace and Company in November of 1921. I have used this edition here, as it appears Leonard Woolf did when he reprinted six of the stories in *A Haunted House*. A few misprints persisted or were introduced into the American edition and these have been silently corrected.[3]

Three of the stories included in *Monday or Tuesday* had been published before: 'The Mark on the Wall', 'Kew Gardens', and 'An Unwritten Novel'. I have compared the versions of these reprinted in *Monday or Tuesday* with the earlier ones and have included comments on Virginia Woolf's revisions in the notes.

In editing all the stories published during Virginia Woolf's lifetime I have compared any holograph or typescript drafts which have survived with the published texts. There are substantive differences between the drafts and the published versions of each of the stories; I have assumed that, except in the case of obvious errors or the imposition of various printing-house styles, these differences are the result of her revisions. Thus I have reprinted the published texts of these stories rather than her typescript drafts.

A comparison of the holograph draft of a story with a subsequent typescript or typescripts reveals a process of revision which one sees continuing in the printed text. I can illustrate this with a passage from 'A Woman's College from Outside'. In the holograph, Virginia Woolf wrote: 'Now smooth and colourless, reposing deeply they lay surrounded supported by the bodies of youth, recumbent or grouped at the window; pouring forth into the garden this bubbling laughter. Irresponsible laughter. Laughter of mind and body; life itself; floating away rules, and discipline, immensely fertilising . . .' She introduced a few changes into the typescript: 'lay surrounded supported' became 'lay surrounded, lay supported' and the comma after 'rules' was removed. In the printed text one finds additional changes which further affect the rhythm of the prose: '. . . pouring forth into the garden this bubbling laughter, this irresponsible laughter: this laughter of mind and body floating away rules, hours, discipline: immensely fertilising . . .'

Often a passage which she has revised in holograph on her typescript will have undergone further revision in the printed text. For example, in the earliest typescript draft of 'The Lady in the Looking-Glass: A Reflection', we find this sentence: 'Here she was, just in the corner of the looking glass.' In the later, revised typescript, this sentence has become: 'Suddenly here she was in the looking glass' followed by 'It made one start' added in holograph. In the printed text this passage has been revised again: 'One must imagine—here was she in the looking-glass. It made one start.'

In most instances there are some substantive and accidental differences between the texts published during her lifetime and those reprinted in *A Haunted House* and *Mrs Dalloway's Party*. I have assumed that the texts published by Virginia Woolf have the greater authority and have presented these texts here.

Examples of the kinds of variants I am referring to are found in 'Moments of Being: "Slater's Pins Have No Points"', which was published in *Forum* in 1928 and reprinted in *A Haunted House*. When reprinting the story, Leonard Woolf used the typescript rather than the version which appeared in *Forum*. The differences between the two indicate that Virginia Woolf made revisions in the story that do not appear on her typescript. For example, after typing the story, she decided to place the Craye family home in Salisbury rather than Canterbury. She cancelled the first reference to Canterbury in the typescript and wrote Salisbury above it, but neglected to change the second reference to Canterbury, four lines down. The omission is corrected in *Forum*, but remains unchanged in *A Haunted House*.

Another example of this kind of variant is found at the end of the story. Virginia Woolf appears to have had second thoughts about the ending. The penultimate paragraph of the typescript, which is also the one in *A Haunted House*, differs from the version in *Forum*. In the typescript Virginia Woolf wrote:

Julia blazed. Julia kindled. Out of the night she burnt like a dead white star. Julia opened her arms. Julia kissed her on the lips. Julia possessed it.

The revised *Forum* text reads:

She saw Julia open her arms; saw her blaze; saw her kindle. Out of the night she burnt like a dead white star. Julia kissed her. Julia possessed her.

The text reprinted in *A Haunted House* also contains errors which are either the result of misprints or of Leonard Woolf's misreading of the typescript. For example, at the end of the fourth paragraph, Virginia Woolf added in holograph 'that lingering, desiring look'. This passage appears in *Forum*, but in *A Haunted House* 'desiring' is rendered 'driving'. Later in the story, the sentence which reads in both the typescript and *Forum* 'She would have considered the comparison very seriously . . .' is printed in *A Haunted House* as 'She would have considered the comparison very furiously'.

In editing the texts of all the stories published during Virginia Woolf's lifetime, I have corrected obvious misprints and used standard British spelling throughout.

In editing the texts of stories that were published after Virginia Woolf's death, I have, whenever possible, gone back to her holograph and typescript drafts and made new transcriptions of these. The differences between my transcriptions and those made by previous editors are usually small ones, and generally I have not commented on them in the notes.

The stories in this group that were published by Leonard Woolf in *A Haunted House* present some unusual problems, for he was no common editor. He says in the Editorial Note to *The Death of the Moth* that during Virginia Woolf's lifetime he always punctuated and corrected obvious verbal mistakes in his wife's manuscripts before they were published. He continued to edit her work in this way after her death. Generally it is possible to distinguish his spidery handwriting from hers and to tell when he has written in ink over revisions she had made in pencil, and when he has introduced changes of his own. I have tried to distinguish his revisions from hers, to include only hers, and those of his that are obvious corrections; when I am in doubt as to the origin of a revision, I have included the change.

The state of the drafts of the previously unpublished stories varies a good deal. Six are holograph drafts which, though they contain revisions, are nevertheless first drafts. A comparison of the first drafts of other stories with subsequent typescript drafts shows how carefully Virginia Woolf revised her narratives. Though the basic situation in a story or sketch would remain unchanged, the phrasing would undergo extensive revision. The first draft of a story appears generally to have been written quickly and to be a very rough outline of what, after numerous revisions, would become the finished draft. The reader should keep in mind when reading all of the previously unpublished stories, and especially those which exist only in holograph, that though they are complete in the sense that they are whole narratives, they have not undergone the rigorous final revision Virginia Woolf would have given them had she decided to publish them herself.

The texts of the unpublished pieces presented in this edition make no attempt to reproduce the stages of revision reflected even in what appear to be her final typescripts. The holograph revisions, frequently made in several kinds of ink or pencil (thus suggesting that they were made over a period of time), have been incorporated into the text without comment. Cancelled passages have not been reproduced, though some are given in the notes. Misspellings have been corrected and abbreviations, such as ampersands and contractions, have been written out. I have standardised the spelling of words that Virginia Woolf spelled variously (such as 'tomorrow' and 'today', which she sometimes hyphenated). Unless otherwise indicated, square brackets have been reserved for editorial use and their particular function within each story explained in the note.

The idiosyncrasies of Virginia Woolf's punctuation in the holograph and typescript drafts indicate the speed with which she wrote and typed. She often omits quotation marks either at the beginning or the end of a quotation and she frequently neglects to use commas to introduce or close a quotation. I have added both quotation marks and commas where common practice is to use them, and I have placed punctuation according to standard British usage. Though she generally does not enclose a character's thoughts within quotation marks, she is not consistent in this. I have included quotation marks when she appears to intend their use and omitted them when she omits them. She also sometimes omits a closing parenthesis or a second dash, where dashes are being used in pairs. I have added these, along with apostrophes and hyphens where necessary, since their omission seems not to be a matter of style.

Some of Virginia Woolf's unconventional habits of punctuation do affect the rhythm of her prose. She often uses colons and semicolons where another writer might choose either a comma or a full stop. Unless these appear to be errors (for example, a semicolon placed at what is clearly the end of a sentence) they have been left as they are. Also, occasionally words within a series are not separated by commas. Sometimes their omission reflects her haste, but in other instances she seems to be aiming at a specific effect, as in the conclusion of this sentence from 'Happiness': 'So if one were being pursued through a forest by wolves one would tear off little bits of clothing and break off biscuits and throw them to the unhappy wolves, feeling almost, but not quite, secure oneself, on one's high swift safe sledge.' Passages such as this have not been changed. In editing all of the stories I have silently corrected obvious errors, but I have not attempted to impose 'correct' punctuation on them. When I have felt that punctuation is neeeded for the sake of clarity, I have enclosed it within square brackets.

Practical considerations have made it impossible to record all of the variants in the stories. I have included in the notes the most extensive and significant variants and I have listed in Appendix C the existence and location of holograph and typescript drafts, for the information of those who may wish to study these. I have presented the last revised draft of each story or sketch, as I have presented the last revised text of the works that she published, on the assumption that these are the best versions and the ones that embody Virginia Woolf's latest (though not necessarily her final) intentions.

I have arranged the stories in chronological order and have given in the notes whatever textual and biographical evidence I have found to support this arrangement. A story whose first draft was written several years before the final draft, is arranged according to the date of the latter (an example of this is 'The Shooting Party', first written in 1932 and then revised for publication in 1937). Unless otherwise indicated, the typescripts referred to in the notes and appendices were typed by Virginia Woolf.

The notes also annotate any quotations or other references that seem to require it. I have generally not attempted in them to relate the stories to Virginia Woolf's other published works, but it is hoped that the information they supply will prove useful to those readers who may want to explore further the important place the shorter fiction has in Virginia Woolf's canon.

NOTES TO EDITORIAL PROCEDURES

1. The latter is 'A Woman's College from Outside' which appeared in *Atalanta's Garland: Being the Book of the Edinburgh University Women's Union* (Edinburgh: The University Press, 1926). The collection also included two previously unpublished sketches by Katherine Mansfield. The publication history of each of the stories can be found in the individual notes and in Appendix C.

2. *Beginning Again: An Autobiography of the Years 1911–1918* (London: The Hogarth Press, 1964), pp. 239–240.

3. I have found only two substantive variants that are not clearly corrected misprints: at the end of 'The Society', '"It is too late," I said' became in the Harcourt, Brace edition, '"It is too late," I replied' and in 'The String Quartet' the phrase 'old, jolly fishwives' became 'jolly old fishwives'.

Early Stories

Phyllis and Rosamond

In this very curious age, when we are beginning to require pictures of people, their minds and their coats, a faithful outline, drawn with no skill but veracity, may possibly have some value.

Let each man, I heard it said the other day, write down the details of a day's work; posterity will be as glad of the catalogue as we should be if we had such a record of how the door keeper at the Globe, and the man who kept the Park gates passed Saturday March 18th in the year of our Lord 1568.

And as such portraits as we have are almost invariably of the male sex, who strut more prominently across the stage, it seems worth while to take as model one of those many women who cluster in the shade. For a study of history and biography convinces any right minded person that these obscure figures occupy a place not unlike that of the showman's hand in the dance of the marionettes; and the finger is laid upon the heart. It is true that our simple eyes believed for many ages that the figures danced of their own accord, and cut what steps they chose; and the partial light which novelists and historians have begun to cast upon that dark and crowded place behind the scenes has done little as yet but show us how many wires there are, held in obscure hands, upon whose jerk or twist the whole figure of the dance depends. This preface leads us then to the point at which we began; we intend to look as steadily as we can at a little group, which lives at this moment (the 20th June, 1906); and seems for some reasons which we will give, to epitomise the qualities of many. It is a common case, because after all there are many young women, born of well-to-do, respectable, official parents; and they must all meet much the same problems, and there can be, unfortunately, but little variety in the answers they make.

There are five of them, all daughters they will ruefully explain to you: regretting this initial mistake it seems all through their lives on their parents' behalf. Further, they are divided into camps: two sisters oppose themselves to two sisters; the fifth vacillates equally between them. Nature has decreed that two shall inherit a stalwart pugnacious frame of mind, which applies itself to political economy and social problems successfully and not unhappily; while the other two she has made frivolous, domestic, of lighter and more sensitive temperaments. These two then are condemned to be what in the slang of the century is called 'the daughters at home'. Their sisters deciding to cultivate their brains, go to College, do well there, and marry Professors. Their careers have so much likeness to those of men themselves that it is scarcely worth while to make them the subject of special enquiry. The fifth sister is less marked in character than any of the others; but she marries when she is twenty-two so that she scarcely has time to develop the individual features of young ladydom which we set out to describe. In the two 'daughters at home' Phyllis and Rosamond, we will call them, we find excellent material for our enquiry.

A few facts will help us to set them in their places, before we begin to investigate. Phyllis is twenty-eight, Rosamond is twenty-four. In person they are pretty, pink cheeked, vivacious; a curious eye will not find any regular beauty of feature; but their dress and demeanour give them the effect of beauty without its substance. They seem indigenous to the drawing-room, as though, born in silk evening robes, they had never trod a rougher earth than the Turkey carpet, or reclined on harsher ground than the arm chair or the sofa. To see them in a drawing-room full of well dressed men and women, is to see the merchant in the Stock Exchange, or the barrister in the Temple. This, every motion and word proclaims, is their native air; their place of business, their professional arena. Here, clearly, they practise the arts in which they have been instructed since childhood. Here, perhaps, they win their victories and earn their bread. But it would be as unjust as it would be easy to press this metaphor till it suggested that the comparison was appropriate and complete in all its parts. It fails; but where it fails and why it fails it will take some time and attention to discover.

You must be in a position to follow these young ladies home, and to hear their comments over the bedroom candle. You must be by them when they wake next morning; and you must attend their progress throughout the day. When you have done this, not for one day but for many days then you will be able to calculate the values of those impressions which are to be received by night in the drawing-room.

This much may be retained of the metaphor already used; that the drawing-room scene represents work to them and not play. So much is made quite clear by the scene in the carriage going home. Lady Hibbert is a severe critic of such performances; she has noted whether her daughters looked well, spoke well[,] behaved well; whether they attracted the right people and repelled the wrong; whether on the whole the impression they left was favourable. From the multiplicity and minuteness of her comments it is easy to see that two hours entertainment is, for artists of this kind, a very delicate and complicated piece of work. Much it seems, depends upon the way they acquit themselves. The daughters answer submissively and then keep silence, whether their mother praises or blames: and her censure is severe. When they are alone at last, and they share a modest sized bedroom at the top of a great ugly house; they stretch their arms and begin to sigh with relief. Their talk is not very edifying; it is the 'shop' of business men; they calculate their profits and their losses and have clearly no interest at heart except their own. And yet you may have heard them chatter of books and plays and pictures as though these were the things they most cared about; to discuss them was the only motive of a 'party'.

Yet you will observe also in this hour of unlovely candour something which is also very sincere, but by no means ugly. The sisters were frankly fond of each other. Their affection has taken the form for the most part of a free masonship which is anything but sentimental; all their hopes and fears are in common; but it is a genuine feeling, profound in spite of its prosaic exterior. They are strictly honourable in all their dealings together; and there is even something chivalrous in the attitude of the younger sister to the elder. She, as the weaker by reason of her greater age, must always have the best of things. There is some pathos also in the gratitude with which Phyllis accepts the advantage. But it grows late, and in respect for their complexions, these business-like young women remind each other that it is time to put out the light.

In spite of this forethought they are fain to sleep on after they are called in the morning. But Rosamond jumps up, and shakes Phyllis.

'Phyllis we shall be late for breakfast.'

There must have been some force in this argument, for Phyllis got out of bed and began silently to dress. But their haste allowed them to put on their clothes with great care and dexterity, and the result was scrupulously surveyed by each sister in turn before they went down. The clock struck nine as they came into the breakfast room: their father was already there, kissed each daughter perfunctorily, passed his cup for coffee, read his paper and disappeared. It was a silent meal. Lady

Hibbert breakfasted in her room; but after breakfast they had to visit her, to receive her orders for the day, and while one wrote notes for her the other went to arrange lunch and dinner with the cook. By eleven they were free, for the time, and met in the schoolroom where Doris the youngest sister, aged sixteen, was writing an essay upon the Magna Charter in French.[1] Her complaints at the interruption – for she was dreaming of a first class already – met with no honour. 'We must sit here, because there's nowhere else to sit,' remarked Rosamond. 'You needn't think we want your company,' added Phyllis. But these remarks were spoken without bitterness, as the mere commonplaces of daily life.

In deference to their sister, however, Phyllis took up a volume of Anatole France, and Rosamond opened the 'Greek Studies' of Walter Pater. They read for some minutes in silence; then a maid knocked, breathless, with a message that 'Her Ladyship wanted the young ladies in the drawing-room.' They groaned; Rosamond offered to go alone; Phyllis said no, they were both victims; and wondering what the errand was they went sulkily downstairs. Lady Hibbert was impatiently waiting them.

'O there you are at last,' she exclaimed. 'Your father has sent round to say he's asked Mr Middleton and Sir Thomas Carew to lunch. Isn't that troublesome of him! I can't think what drove him to ask them, and there's no lunch – and I see you haven't arranged the flowers, Phyllis; and Rosamond I want you to put a clean tucker in my maroon gown. O dear, how thoughtless men are.'

The daughters were used to these insinuations against their father: on the whole they took his side, but they never said so.

They silently departed now on their separate errands: Phyllis had to go out and buy flowers and an extra dish for lunch; and Rosamond sat down to her sewing.

Their tasks were hardly done in time for them to change for lunch; but at 1.30 they came pink and smiling into the pompous great drawing-room. Mr Middleton was Sir William Hibbert's secretary; a young man of some position and prospects, as Lady Hibbert defined him; who might be encouraged. Sir Thomas was an official in the same office, solid and gouty, a handsome piece on the board, but of no individual importance.

At lunch then there was some sprightly conversation between Mr Middleton and Phyllis, while their elders talked platitudes, in sonorous deep voices. Rosamond sat rather silent, as was her wont; speculating keenly upon the character of the secretary, who might be her brother-in-law; and checking certain theories she had made by every fresh word he spoke. By open consent, Mr Middleton was her sister's game; she did not trespass. If one could have read her thoughts, while she listened to Sir Thomas's stories of India in the Sixties, one would have found that she was busied in somewhat abstruse calculations; Little Middleton, as she called him, was not half a bad sort; he had brains; he was, she knew, a good son, and he would make a good husband. He was well to do also, and would make his way in the service. On the other hand her psychological acuteness told her that he was narrow minded, without a trace of imagination or intellect, in the sense she understood it; and she knew enough of her sister to know that she would never love this efficient active little man, although she would respect him. The question was should she marry him? This was the point she had reached when Lord Mayo was assassinated;[2] and while her lips murmured ohs and ahs of horror, her eyes were telegraphing across the table, 'I am doubtful.' If she had nodded her sister would have begun to practise those arts by which many proposals had been secured already. Rosamond, however, did not yet know enough to make up her mind. She telegraphed merely 'Keep him in play.'

The gentlemen left soon after lunch, and Lady Hibbert prepared to go and lie down. But before she went she called Phyllis to her.

'Well my dear,' she said, with more affection than she had shown yet, 'did you have a pleasant lunch? Was Mr Middleton agreeable?' She patted her daughter's cheek, and looked keenly into her eyes.

Some petulancy came across Phyllis, and she answered listlessly. 'O he's not a bad little man; but he doesn't excite me.'

Lady Hibbert's face changed at once: if she had seemed a benevolent cat playing with a mouse from philanthropic motives before, she was the real animal now in sober earnest.

'Remember,' she snapped, 'this can't go on for ever. Try and be a little less selfish, my dear.' If she had sworn openly, her words could not have been less pleasant to hear.

She swept off, and the two girls looked at each other, with expressive contortions of the lips.

'I couldn't help it,' said Phyllis, laughing weakly. 'Now let's have a respite. Her Ladyship won't want us till four.'

They mounted to the schoolroom, which was now empty; and threw themselves into deep arm chairs. Phyllis lit a cigarette, and Rosamond sucked peppermints, as though they induced to thought.

'Well, my dear,' said Phyllis at last, 'what do we decide? It is June now; our parents give me till July: little Middleton is the only one.'

'Except –' began Rosamond.

'Yes, but it is no good thinking of him.'

'Poor old Phyllis! Well, he's not a bad man.'

'Clean sober, truthful industrious. O we should make a model pair! You should stay with us in Derbyshire.'

'You might do better,' went on Rosamond; with the considering air of a judge. 'On the other hand, they won't stand much more.' 'They' intimated Sir William and Lady Hibbert.

'Father asked me yesterday what I could do if I didn't marry. I had nothing to say.'

'No, we were educated for marriage.'

'*You* might have done something better. Of course I'm a fool so it doesn't matter.'

'And I think marriage the best thing there is – if one were allowed to marry the man one wants.'

'O I know: it is beastly. Still there's no escaping facts.'

'Middleton,' said Rosamond briefly. 'He's the fact at present. Do you care for him?'

'Not in the least.'

'Could you marry him?'

'If her Ladyship made me.'

'It might be a way out, at any rate.'

'What d'you make of him now?' asked Phyllis, who would have accepted or rejected any man on the strength of her sister's advice. Rosamond, possessed of shrewd and capable brains, had been driven to feed them exclusively upon the human character and as her science was but little obscured by personal prejudice, her results were generally trustworthy.

'He's very good,' she began; 'moral qualities excellent: brains fair: he'll do well of course: not a scrap of imagination or romance: he'd be very just to you.'

'In short we would be a worthy pair: something like our parents!'

'The question is,' went on Rosamond; 'is it worth while going through another year of slavery, till the next one comes along? And who is the next? Simpson, Rogers, [Leiscetter?].'

At each name her sister made a face.

'The conclusion seems to be: mark time and keep up apearances.'

'O let's enjoy ourselves while we may! If it weren't for you, Rosamond, I should have married a dozen times already.'

'You'd have been in the divorce court my dear.'

'I'm too respectable for that, really. I'm very weak without you. And now let's talk of your affairs.'

'My affairs can wait,' said Rosamond resolutely. And the two young women discussed their friends' characters, with some acuteness and not a little charity till it was time to change once more. But two features of their talk are worth remark. First, that they held intellect in great reverence and made that a cardinal point in their enquiry; secondly that whenever they suspected an unhappy home life, or a disappointed attachment, even in the case of the least attractive, their judgments were invariably gentle and sympathetic.

At four they drove out with Lady Hibbert to pay calls. This performance consisted in driving solemnly to one house after another where they had dined or hoped to dine, and depositing two or three cards in the servant's hand. At one place they entered and drank a cup of tea, and talked of the weather for precisely fifteen minutes. They wound up with a slow passage through the Park, making one of the procession of gay carriages which travel at a foot's pace at that hour round the statue of Achilles. Lady Hibbert wore a permanent and immutable smile.

By six o'clock they were home again and found Sir William entertaining an elderly cousin and his wife at tea. These people could be treated without ceremony, and Lady Hibbert went off to lie down; and left her daughters to ask how John was, and whether Milly had got over the measles. 'Remember; we dine out at eight, William,' she said, as she left the room.

Phyllis went with them; the party was given by a distinguished judge, and she had to entertain a respectable K.C.; her efforts in one direction at least might be relaxed; and her mother's eye regarded her with indifference. It was like a draught of clear cold water, Phyllis reflected, to talk with an intelligent elderly man upon impersonal subjects. They did not theorise, but he told her facts and she was glad to realise that the world was full of solid things, which were independent of her life.

When they left she told her mother that she was going on to the

Tristrams, to meet Rosamond there. Lady Hibbert pursed up her mouth, shrugged her shoulders and said 'very well,' as though she would have objected if she could have laid her hands on a sufficiently good reason. But Sir William was waiting, and a frown was the only argument.

So Phyllis went separately to the distant and unfashionable quarter of London where the Tristrams lived. That was one of the many enviable parts of their lot. The stucco fronts, the irreproachable rows of Belgravia and South Kensington seemed to Phyllis the type of her lot; of a life trained to grow in an ugly pattern to match the staid ugliness of its fellows. But if one lived here in Bloomsbury, she began to theorise waving with her hand as her cab passed through the great tranquil squares, beneath the pale green of umbrageous trees, one might grow up as one liked. There was room, and freedom, and in the roar and splendour of the Strand she read the live realities of the world from which her stucco and her pillars protected her so completely.

Her cab stopped before some lighted windows which, open in the summer night, let some of the talk and life within spill out upon the pavement. She was impatient for the door to open which was to let her enter, and partake. When she stood, however, within the room, she became conscious of her own appearance which, as she knew by heart, was on these occasions, like that of ladies whom Romney painted.[3] She saw herself enter into the smokey room where people sat on the floor, and the host wore a shooting jacket, with her arch little head held high, and her mouth pursed as though for an epigram. Her white silk and her cherry ribbons made her conspicuous. It was with some feeling of the difference between her and the rest that she sat very silent scarcely taking advantage of the openings that were made for her in the talk. She kept looking round at the dozen people who were sitting there, with a sense of bewilderment. The talk was of certain pictures then being shown, and their merits were discussed from a somewhat technical standpoint. Where was Phyllis to begin? She had seen them; but she knew that her platitudes would never stand the test of question and criticism to which they would be exposed. Nor, she knew, was there any scope here for those feminine graces which could veil so much. The time was passed; for the discussion was hot and serious, and no one of the combatants wished to be tripped by illogical devices. So she sat and watched, feeling like a bird with wings pinioned; and more acutely, because more genuinely, uncomfortable than she had ever been at ball or play. She repeated to herself the little bitter axiom that she had fallen between two stools; and tried meanwhile to use her brains soberly upon what was being said. Rosamond hinted from across the room that she was in the same predicament.

At last the disputants dissolved, and talk became general once more; but no one apologised for the concentrated character it had borne, and general conversation, the Miss Hibberts found, if it did occupy itself with more trivial subjects, tended to be scornful of the commonplace, and knew no hesitation in saying so. But it was amusing; and Rosamond acquitted herself creditably in discussing a certain character which came into question; although she was surprised to find that her most profound discoveries were taken as the starting point of further investigations, and represented no conclusions.

Moreover, the Miss Hibberts were surprised and a little dismayed to discover how much of their education had stuck to them. Phyllis could have beaten herself the next moment for her instinctive disapproval of some jest against Christianity which the Tristrams uttered and applauded as lightly as though religion was a small matter.

Even more amazing to the Miss Hibberts however was the manner in which their own department of business was transacted; for they supposed that even in this odd atmosphere 'the facts of life' were important. Miss Tristram, a young woman of great beauty, and an artist of real promise, was discussing marriage with a gentleman who might easily as far as one could judge, have a personal interest in the question. But the freedom and frankness with which they both explained their views and theorised upon the whole question of love and matrimony, seemed to put the whole thing in a new and sufficiently startling light. It fascinated the young ladies more than anything they had yet seen or heard. They had flattered themselves that every side and view of the subject was known to them; but this was something not only new, but unquestionably genuine.

'I have never yet had a proposal; I wonder what it feels like,' said the candid considering voice of the younger Miss Tristram; and Phyllis and Rosamond felt that they ought to produce their experiences for the instruction of the company. But then they could not adopt this strange new point of view, and their experiences after all were of a different quality entirely. Love to them was something induced by certain calculated actions; and it was cherished in ball rooms, in scented conservatories, by glances of the eyes, flashes of the fan, and faltering suggestive accents. Love here was a robust, ingenuous thing which stood out in the daylight, naked and solid, to be tapped and scrutinised as you thought best. Even were they free to love as they chose, Phyllis and Rosamond felt very doubtful that they could love in this way. With the rapid impulse of youth they condemned themselves utterly, and determined that all efforts at freedom were in vain: long captivity had corrupted them both within and without.

They sat thus, unconscious of their own silence, like people shut out from some merrymaking in the cold and the wind; invisible to the feasters within. But in reality the presence of these two silent and hungry eyed young women was felt to be oppressive by all the people there; although they did not exactly know why; perhaps they were bored. The Miss Tristrams, however, felt themselves responsible; and Miss Sylvia Tristram, the younger, as the result of a whisper, undertook a private conversation with Phyllis. Phyllis snatched at it like a dog at a bone; indeed her face wore a gaunt ravenous expression, as she saw the moments fly, and the substance of this strange evening remained beyond her grasp. At least, if she could not share, she might explain what forbade her. She was longing to prove to herself that there were good reasons for her impotence; and if she felt that Miss Sylvia was a solid woman in spite of her impersonal generalisations, there was hope that they might meet some day on common ground. Phyllis had an odd feeling, when she leant forward to speak, of searching feverishly through a mass of artificial frivolities to lay hands on the solid grain of pure self which, she supposed lay hid somewhere.

'O Miss Tristram,' she began, 'you are all so brilliant. I do feel frightened.'

'Are you laughing at us,' asked Sylvia.

'Why should I laugh? Don't you see what a fool I feel?'

Sylvia began to see, and the sight interested her.

'Yours is such a wonderful life; it is so strange to us.'

Sylvia who wrote and had a literary delight in seeing herself reflected in strange looking-glasses, and of holding up her own mirror to the lives of others, settled herself to the task with gusto. She had never considered the Hibberts as human beings before; but had called them 'young ladies'. She was all the more ready now therefore to revise her mistake; both from vanity and from real curiosity.

'What do you do?' she demanded suddenly, in order to get to business at once.

'What do I do?' echoed Phyllis. 'O order dinner and arrange the flowers!'

'Yes, but what's your trade,' pursued Sylvia, who was determined not to be put off with phrases.

'*That's* my trade; I wish it wasn't! Really Miss Tristram, you must remember that most young ladies are slaves; and you mustn't insult me because you happen to be free.'

'O do tell me,' broke forth Sylvia, 'exactly what you mean. I want to know. I like to know about people. After all you know, the human soul is the thing.'

'Yes,' said Phyllis, anxious to keep from theories. 'But our life's so simple and so ordinary. You must know dozens like us.'

'I know your evening dresses,' said Sylvia; 'I see you pass before me in beautiful processions, but I have never yet heard you speak. Are you solid all through?' It struck her that this tone jarred upon Phyllis: so she changed.

'I daresay we are sisters. But why are we so different outside?'

'O no, we're not sisters,' said Phyllis bitterly; 'at least I pity you if we are. You see, we are brought up just to come out in the evening and make pretty speeches, and well, marry I suppose, and of course we might have gone to college if we'd wanted to; but as we didn't we're just accomplished.'

'We never went to college,' said Sylvia.

'And you're not accomplished? Of course you and your sister are the real thing, and Rosamond and I are frauds: at least I am. But don't you see it all now and don't you see what an ideal life yours is?'

'I can't see why you shouldn't do what you like, as we do,' said Sylvia, looking round the room.

'Do you think we could have people like this? Why, we can never ask a friend, except when our parents are away.'

'Why not?'

'We haven't a room, for one thing: and then we should never be allowed to do it. We are daughters, until we become married women.'

Sylvia considered her a little grimly. Phyllis understood that she had spoken with the wrong kind of frankness about love.

'Do you want to marry?' asked Syvlia.

'Can you ask? You are an innocent young thing! – but of course you're quite right. It should be for love, and all the rest of it. But,' continued Phyllis, desperately speaking the truth, 'we can't think of it in that way. We want so many things, that we can never see marriage alone as it really is or ought to be. It is always mixed up with so much else. It means freedom and friends and a house of our own, and oh all the things you have already! Does that seem to you very dreadful and very mercenary?'

'It does seem rather dreadful; but not mercenary I think. I should write if I were you.'

'O there you go again, Miss Tristram!' exclaimed Phyllis in comic despair. 'I cannot make you understand that for one thing we haven't the brains; and for another, if we had them we couldn't use them. Mercifully the Good Lord made us fitted for our station. Rosamond might have done something; she's too old now.'

'My God,' exclaimed Sylvia. 'What a Black Hole! I should burn, shoot, jump out of the window; at least do something!'

'What?' asked Phyllis sardonically. 'If you were in our place you might; but I don't think you could be. O no,' she went on in a lighter and more cynical tone, 'this is our life, and we have to make the best of it. Only I want you to understand why it is that we come here and sit silent. You see, this is the life we should like to lead; and now I rather doubt that we can. You,' she indicated all the room, 'think us merely fashionable minxes; so we are, almost. But we might have been something better. Isn't it pathetic?' She laughed her dry little laugh.

'But promise me one thing, Miss Tristram: that you will come and see us, and that you will let us come here sometimes. Now Rosamond, we must really go.'

They left, and in the cab Phyllis wondered a little at her outburst; but felt that she had enjoyed it. They were both somewhat excited; and anxious to analyse their discomfort, and find out what it meant. Last night they had driven home at this hour in a more sullen but at the same time in a more self-satisfied temper; they were bored by what they had done, but they knew they had done it well. And they had the satisfaction of feeling that they were fit for far better things. Tonight they were not bored; but they did not feel that they had acquitted themselves well when they had the chance. The bedroom conference was a little dejected; in penetrating to her real self Phyllis had let in some chill gust of air to that closely guarded place; what did she really want, she asked herself? What was she fit for? to criticise both worlds and feel that neither gave her what she needed. She was too genuinely depressed to state the case to her sister; and her fit of honesty left her with the convinction that talking did no good; and if she could do anything, it must be done by herself. Her last thoughts that night were that it was rather a relief that Lady Hibbert had arranged a full day for them tomorrow: at any rate she need not think; and river parties were amusing.

The Mysterious Case of Miss V.

It is a commonplace that there is no loneliness like that of one who finds himself alone in a crowd; novelists repeat it; the pathos is undeniable; and now, since the case of Miss V., I at least have come to believe it. Such a story as hers and her sister's – but it is characteristic that in writing of them one name seems instinctively to do for both – indeed one might mention a dozen such sisters in one breath. Such a story is scarcely possible except in London. In the country there would have been the butcher or the postman or the parson's wife; but in a highly civilised town the civilities of human life are narrowed to the least possible space. The butcher drops his meat down the area; the postman shoves his letter into the box, and the parson's wife has been known to hurl the pastoral missives through the same convenient breach: no time, they all repeat, must be wasted. So, though the meat remain uneaten, the letters unread, and the pastoral comments disobeyed, no one is any the wiser; until there comes a day when these functionaries tacitly conclude that no. 16 or 23 need be attended to no longer. They skip it, on their rounds, and poor Miss J. or Miss V. drops out of the closeknit chain of human life; and is skipped by everyone and for ever.

The ease with which such a fate befalls you suggests that it is really necessary to assert yourself in order to prevent yourself from being skipped; how could you ever come to life again if the butcher[,] the postman and the policeman made up their minds to ignore you? It is a terrible fate; I think I will knock over a chair at this moment; now the lodger beneath knows that I am alive at any rate.

But to return to the mysterious case of Miss V., in which initial, be it understood is concealed the person also of Miss Janet V.: it is hardly necessary to split one letter into two parts.

They have been gliding about London for some fifteen years; you were to find them in certain drawing-rooms or picture galleries, and when you said, 'Oh how d'you do Miss V.' as though you have been in the habit of meeting her every day of your life, she would answer, 'Isn't it a pleasant day,' or 'What bad weather we are having' and then you moved on and she seemed to melt into some armchair or chest of drawers. At any rate you thought no more of her until she detached herself from the furniture in a year's time perhaps, and the same things were said over again.

A tie of blood – or whatever the fluid was that ran in Miss V.'s veins – made it my particular fate to run against her – or pass through her or dissipate her, whatever the phrase may be – more constantly perhaps than any other person, until this little performance became almost a habit. No party or concert or gallery seemed quite complete unless the familiar grey shadow was part of it; and when, some time ago, she ceased to haunt my path, I knew vaguely that something was missing. I will not exaggerate and say that I knew that *she* was missing; but there is no insincerity in using the neuter term.

Thus in a crowded room I began to find myself gazing round in nameless dissatisfaction; no, everyone seemed to be there – but surely there was something lacking in furniture or curtains – or was it that a print was moved from the wall?

Then one morning early, wakening at dawn indeed, I cried aloud, Mary V. Mary V!! It was the first time, I am sure that anyone had ever cried her name with such conviction; generally it seemed a colourless epithet, used merely to round a period. But my voice did not as I half expected, summon the person or semblance of Miss V. before me: the room remained vague. All day long my own cry echoed in my brain; till I made certain that at some street corner or another I should come across her as usual, and see her fade away, and be satisfied. Still, she came not; and I think I was discontented. At any rate the strange fantastic plan came into my head as I lay awake at night, a mere whim at first, which grew serious and exciting by degrees, that I would go and call on Mary V. in person.

O how mad and odd and amusing it seemed, now that I thought of it! – to track down the shadow, to see where she lived and if she lived, and talk to her as though she were a person like the rest of us!

Consider how it would seem to set out in an omnibus to visit the shadow of a blue bell in Kew Gardens, when the sun stands halfway down the sky! or to catch the down from a dandelion! at midnight in a Surrey meadow. Yet it was a much more fantastic expedition than any of these that I proposed; and as I put on my clothes to start I laughed and laughed to think that such substantial preparation was needed for my task. Boots and hat for Mary V.! It seemed incredibly incongruous.

At length I reached the flat where she lived, and on [looking at] the signboard I found it stated ambiguously – like the rest of us – that she was both out and in. At her door, high up in the topmost storey of the building, I knocked and rang, and waited and scrutinised; no one came; and I began to wonder if shadows could die, and how one buried them; when the door was gently opened by a maid. Mary V. had been ill for two months; she had died yesterday morning, at the very hour when I called her name. So I shall never meet her shadow any more.

The Journal of Mistress Joan Martyn

My readers may not know, perhaps, who I am. Therefore, although such a practice is unusual and unnatural – for we know how modest writers are – I will not hesitate to explain that I am Miss Rosamond Merridew, aged forty-five – my frankness is consistent! – and that I have won considerable fame among my profession for the researches I have made into the system of land tenure in mediaeval England. Berlin has heard my name; Frankfurt would give a soirée in my honour; and I am not absolutely unknown in one or two secluded rooms in Oxford and in Cambridge. Perhaps I shall put my case more cogently, human nature being what it is, if I state that I have exchanged a husband and a family and a house in which I may grow old for certain fragments of yellow parchment; which only a few people can read and still fewer would care to read if they could. But as a mother, so I read sometimes not without curiosity in the literature of my sex, cherishes most the ugliest and stupidest of her offspring, so a kind of maternal passion has sprung up in my breast for these shrivelled and colourless little gnomes; in real life I see them as cripples with fretful faces, but all the same, with the fire of genius in their eyes. I will not expound that sentence; it would be no more likely to succeed than if that same mother to whom I compare myself took pains to explain that her cripple was really a beautiful boy, more fair than all his brothers.

At any rate, my investigations have made a travelling pedlar of me; save that it is my habit to buy and not to sell. I present myself at old farm houses, decayed halls, parsonages, church vestries always with the same demand. Have you any old papers to show me? As you may imagine the palmy days for this kind of sport are over; age has become the most merchantable of qualities; and the state moreover with its Commissions has put an end for the most part to the enterprise of individuals. Some official, I am often told, has promised to come down and inspect their documents; and the favour of the 'State' which such a promise carries with it, robs my poor private voice of all its persuasion.

Still it is not for me to complain, looking back as I can look back, upon some very fine prizes that will have been of real interest to the historian, and upon others that because they are so fitful and so minute in their illumination please me even better. A sudden light upon the legs of Dame Elizabeth Partridge sends its beams over the whole state of England, to the King upon his throne; she wanted stockings! and no other need impresses you in quite the same way with the reality of mediaeval legs; and therefore with the reality of mediaeval bodies, and so, proceeding upward step by step, with the reality of mediaeval brains; and there you stand at the centre of all ages: middle beginning or end. And this brings me to a further confession of my own virtues. My researches into the system of land tenure in the 13th[,] 14th and 15th Centuries have been made doubly valuable, I am assured, by the remarkable gift I have for presenting them in relation to the life of the time. I have borne in mind that the intricacies of the land tenure were not always the most important facts in the lives of men and women and children; I have often made so bold as to hint that the subtleties which delight us so keenly were more a proof of our ancestors' negligence than a proof of their astonishing painstaking. For what sane man, I have had the audacity to remark, could have spent his time in complicating his laws for the benefit of half a dozen antiquaries who were to be born five centuries after he was in the grave?

We will not here discuss this argument on whose behalf I have given and taken many shrewd blows; I introduce the question merely to explain why it is that I have made all these enquiries subsidiary to certain pictures of the family life which I have introduced into my text; as the flower of all these intricate roots; the flash of all this scraping of flint.

If you read my work called 'The Manor Rolls' you will be pleased or disgusted according to your temperament by certain digressions which you will find there.

I have not scrupled to devote several pages of large print to an attempt to show, vividly as in a picture, some scene from the life of the time; here I knock at the serf's door, and find him roasting rabbits he has poached; I show you the Lord of the Manor setting out on some journey, or calling his dogs to him for a walk in the fields, or sitting in the high backed chair inscribing laborious figures upon a glossy sheet of parchment. In another room I show you Dame Elinor, at work with her needle; and by her on a lower stool sits her daughter stitching too, but less assiduously. 'Child, thy husband will be here before thy house linen is ready,' reproves the mother.

Ah, but to read this at large you must study my book! The critics have always threatened me with two rods; first, they say, such digressions are all very well in a history of the time, but they have nothing to do with the system [of] mediaeval land tenure; secondly, they complain that I have no materials at my side to stiffen these words into any semblance of the truth. It is well known that the period I have chosen is more bare than any other of private records; unless you choose to draw all your inspiration from the *Paston Letters*[1] you must be content to imagine merely, like any other story teller. And that, I am told, is a useful art in its place; but it should be allowed to claim no relationship with the sterner art of the Historian. But here, again, I verge upon that famous argument which I carried on once with so much zeal in the *Historian's Quarterly*. We must make way with our introduction, or some wilful reader may throw down the book and profess to have mastered its contents already: O the old story! Antiquaries' Quarrels! Let me draw a line here then so——and put the whole of this question of right and wrong, truth and fiction behind me.

On a June morning two years ago, it chanced that I was driving along the Thetford road from Norwich to East Harling. I had been on some expedition, a wild goose chase it was, to recover some documents which I believed to lie buried in the ruins of Caister Abbey. If we were to spend a tithe of the sums that we spend yearly upon excavating Greek cities in excavating our own ruins what a different tale the Historian would have to tell!

Such was the theme of my meditations; but nevertheless one eye, my archaeological eye, kept itself awake to the landscape through which we passed. And it was in obedience to a telegram from this that I leapt up in the carriage, at a certain point and directed the driver to turn sharply to the left. We passed down a regular avenue of ancient elm trees; but the bait which drew me was a little square picture, framed delicately between green boughs at the far end, in which an ancient doorway was drawn distinctly in lines of carved white stone.

As we approached[,] the doorway proved to be encircled by long low walls of buff coloured plaster; and on top of them, at no great distance was the roof of ruddy tiles, and finally I beheld in front of me the whole of the dignified little house, built like the letter E with the middle notch smoothed out of it.

Here was one of those humble little old Halls, then, which survive almost untouched, and practically unknown for centuries and centuries, because they are too insignificant to be pulled down or rebuilt; and their owners are too poor to be ambitious. And the descendants of the builder go on living here, with that curious unconsciousness that the house is in any way remarkable which serves to make them as much a part of it, as the tall chimney which has grown black with generations of kitchen smoke. Of course a larger house might be preferable, and I doubt not that they would hesitate to sell this old one, if a good offer were to be made for it. But that is the natural, and unself-conscious spirit which proves somehow how genuine the whole thing is. You can not be sentimental about a house you have lived in for five hundred years. This is the kind of place, I thought, as I stood with my hand on the bell, where the owners are likely to possess exquisite manuscripts, and sell them as easily [to] the first rag man who comes along, as they would sell their pig wash, or the timber from the park. My point of view is that of a morbid eccentric, after all, and these are the people of truly healthy nature. Can't they write? they will tell me; and what is the worth of old letters? I always burn mine – or use them to tie over jampots.

A maid came, at last, staring meditatively at me, as though she ought to have remembered my face and my business. 'Who lives here?' I asked her. 'Mr Martyn,' she gaped, as if I had asked the name of the reigning King of England. 'Is there a Mrs Martyn, and is she at home, and might I see her?' The girl waved to me to follow, and led me in silence to a person who could, presumably, undertake the responsibility of answering my strange questions.

I was shown across a large hall, panelled with oak, to a smaller room in which a rosy woman of my own age was using a machine upon a pair of trousers. She looked like a housekeeper; but she was, the maid whispered, Mrs Martyn.

She rose with a gesture that indicated that she was not precisely a lady to receive morning calls, but was nevertheless the person of authority, the mistress of the house; who had a right to know my business in coming there.

There are certain rules in the game of the antiquary, of which the first and simplest is that you must not state your object at the first encounter. 'I was passing by your door; and I took the liberty – I must tell you I am a great lover of the picturesque, to call, on the chance that I might be allowed to look over the house. It seems to me a particularly fine specimen.'

'Do you want to rent it, may I ask,' said Mrs Martyn, who spoke with a pleasant tinge of dialect.

'Do you let rooms then?' I questioned.

'O no,' rejoined Mrs Martyn, decisively: 'We never let rooms; I thought perhaps you wished to rent the whole house.'

'It's a little big for me; but still, I have friends.'

'As well, then,' broke in Mrs Martyn, cheerfully, setting aside the notion of profit, and looking merely to do a charitable act; 'I'm sure I should be very pleased to show you over the house – I don't know much about old things myself; and I never heard as the house was particular in any way. Still it's a pleasant kind of place – if you come from London.' She looked curiously at my dress and figure, which I confess felt more than usually bent beneath her fresh, and somewhat compassionate gaze; and I gave her the information she wanted. Indeed as we strolled through the long passages, pleasantly striped with bars of oak across the white wash, and looked into spotless little rooms with square green windows opening on the garden, and where I saw furniture that was spare but decent, we exchanged a considerable number of questions and answers. Her husband was a farmer on rather a large scale; but land had sunk terribly in value; and they were forced to live in the Hall now, which would not let; although it was far too large for them, and the rats were a nuisance. The Hall had been in her husband's family for many a year, she remarked with some slight pride; she did not know how long, but people said the Martyns had once been great people in the neighbourhood. She drew my attention to the 'y' in their name. Still she spoke with the very chastened and clear sighted pride of one who knows by hard personal experience how little nobility of birth avails, against certain material drawbacks, the poverty of the land, for instance, the holes in the roof, and the rapacity of rats.

Now although the place was scrupulously clean, and well kept there was a certain bareness in all the rooms, a prominence of huge oak tables, and an absence of other decorations than bright pewter cups and china plates which looked ominous to my inquisitive gaze. It seemed as though a great deal must have been sold, of those small portable things that make a room look furnished. But my hostess' dignity forbade me to suggest that her house had ever been other than it was at present. And yet I could not help fancying a kind of wistfulness in the way she showed me into rooms that were almost empty, compared the present poverty to days of greater affluence, and had it on the tip of her tongue to tell me that 'Things had once been better.' She seemed half apologetic, too, as she led me through a succession of bedrooms, and one or two rooms that might have served for sitting rooms if people had had leisure to sit there, as though she wished to show me that she was quite aware of the discrepancy between such a house and her own sturdy figure. All this being as it was, I did not like to ask the question that interested me most – whether they had any books? and I was beginning to feel that I had kept the good woman from her sewing machine long enough, when she suddenly looked out of the window, hearing a whistle below, and shouted something about coming in to dinner. Then she turned to me with some shyness, but an expression of hospitality, and begged me to 'Sit down to dinner' with them. 'John, my husband, knows a sight more than I do of these old things of his, and I know he's glad enough to find some one to talk to. It's in his blood, I tell him,' she laughed, and I saw no good reason why I should not accept the invitation. Now John did not fall so easily beneath any recognized heading as his wife did. He was a man of middle age and middle size, dark of hair and complexion, with a pallor of skin that did not seem natural to a farmer; and a drooping moustache which he smoothed slowly with one well shaped hand as he spoke. His eye was hazel and bright, but I fancied a hint of suspicion when its glance rested upon me. He began to speak however, with even more of a Norfolk accent than his wife; and his voice, and dress asserted that he was, in truth if not altogether in appearance, a solid Norfolk farmer.

He nodded merely when I told him that his wife had had the kindness to show me his house. And then, looking at her with a twinkle in his eye he remarked, 'If she had her way the old place would be left to the rats. The house is too big, and there are too many ghosts. Eh Betty.' She merely smiled, as though her share of the argument had been done long ago.

I thought to please him by dwelling upon its beauties, and its age; but he seemed little interested by my praises, munched largely of cold beef, and added 'ayes' and 'noes' indifferently.

A picture, painted perhaps in the time of Charles the First, which hung above his head, had so much the look of him had his collar and tweed been exchanged for a ruff and a silk doublet, that I made the obvious comparison.

'O aye,' he said, with no great show of interest, 'that's my grandfather; or my grandfather's grandfather. We deal in grandfathers here.'

'Was that the Martyn who fought at the Boyne,' asked Betty negligently while she pressed me to take another slice of beef.

'At the Boyne,' exclaimed her husband, with query and even irritation – 'Why, my good woman, you're thinking of Uncle Jasper. This fellow was in his grave long before the Boyne. His name's Willoughby,' he went on speaking to me, as though he wished me to understand the matter thoroughly; because a blunder about such a simple fact was unpardonable, even though the fact itself might not be of great interest.

'Willoughby Martyn: born 1625 died 1685: he fought at Marston Moor as Captain of a Troop of Norfolk men. We were always royalists. He was exiled in the Protectorate, went to Amsterdam; bought a bay horse off the Duke of Newcastle there; we have the breed still; he came back here at the Restoration, married Sally Hampton – of the Manor, but they died out last generation, and had six children, four sons and two daughters. He bought the Lower Meadow you know Betty,' he jerked at his wife, to goad her unaccountably sluggish memory.

'I call him to mind well enough now,' she answered, placidly.

'He lived here all the last part of his life; died of small pox, or what they called small pox then; and his daughter Joan caught it from him. They're buried in the same grave in the church yonder.' He pointed his thumb, and went on with his dinner. All this was volunteered as shortly and even curtly as though he were performing some necessary task, which from long familiarity had become quite uninteresting to him; though for some reason he had still to repeat it.

I could not help showing my interest in the story, although I was conscious that my questions did not entertain my host.

'You seem to have a queer liking for these old fathers of mine,' he commented, at last, with an odd little scowl of humorous irritation. 'You must show her the pictures after dinner, John,' put in his wife; 'and all the old things.'

'I should be immensely interested,' I said, 'but I must not take up your time.'

'O John knows a quantity about them; he's wonderful learned about pictures.'

'Any fool knows his own ancestors, Betty;' growled her husband; 'still, if you wish to see what we have, Madam, I shall be proud to show you.' The courtesy of the phrase, and the air with which he held the door open for me, made me remember the 'y' in his name.

He showed me round the Hall, pointing with a riding crop to one dark canvas after another; and rapping out two or three unhesitating words of description at each; they were hung apparently in chronological order, and it was clear in spite of the dirt and the dark that the later portraits were feebler examples of the art, and represented less distinguished looking heads. Military coats became less and less frequent, and in the 18th century the male Martyns were represented [in] snuff coloured garments of a homely cut, and were briefly described as 'Farmers' or 'him who sold the Fen Farm' by their descendant. Their wives and daughters at length dropped out altogether, as though in time a portrait had come to be looked upon more as the necessary appendage of the head of the house, rather than as the right which beauty by itself could claim.

Still, I could trace no sign in the man's voice that he was following the decline of his family with his riding crop, for there was neither pride nor regret in his tone; indeed it kept its level note, as of one who tells a tale so well known that the words have been rubbed smooth of meaning.

'There's the last of them – my father,' he said at length, when he had slowly traversed the four sides of the Hall; I looked upon a crude canvas, painted in the early sixties I gathered, by some travelling painter with a literal brush. Perhaps the unskilful hand had brought out the roughness of the features and the harshness of the complexion; had found it easier to paint the farmer than to produce the subtle balance which, one might gather, blent in the father as in the son. The artist had stuffed his sitter into a black coat, and wound a stiff white tie round his neck; the poor gentleman had never felt at ease in them, yet.

'And now, Mr Martyn,' I felt bound to say, 'I can only thank you, and your wife for . . .'

'Stop a moment,' he interrupted, 'we're not done yet. There are the books.'

His voice had a half comic doggedness about it; like one who is determined, in spite of his own indifference to the undertaking, to make a thorough job of it.

He opened a door and bade me enter a small room, or rather office; for the table heaped with papers, and the walls lined with ledgers, suggested the room where business is transacted by the master of an estate. There were pads and brushes for ornament; and there were mostly dead animals, raising lifeless paws, and grinning, with plaster tongues, from various brackets and cases.

'These go back beyond the pictures;' he said, as he stooped and lifted a great parcel of yellow papers with an effort. They were not bound, or kept together in any way, save by a thick cord of green silk, with bars at either end; such as you use to transfix bundles of greasy documents – butcher's bills, and the year's receipts. 'That's the first lot,' he said ruffling the leaves with his fingers, like a pack of cards; 'that's no. 1: 1480 to 1500.' I gasped, as anyone may judge: but the temperate voice of Martyn reminded me that enthusiasm was out of place, here; indeed enthusiasm began to look like a very cheap article when contrasted with the genuine thing.

'Ah indeed; that's very interesting; may I look?' was all I said, though my undisciplined hand shook a little when the bundle was carelessly dropped into it. Mr Martyn indeed offered to fetch a duster before desecrating my white skin; but I assured him it was of no consequence, too eagerly perhaps, because I had feared that there might be some more substantial reason why I should not hold these precious papers.

While he bent down before a book case, I hastily looked at the first inscription on the parchment. 'The Journal of Mistress Joan Martyn,' I spelt out, 'kept by her at Martyn's Hall, in the county of Norfolk the year of our Lord 1480.'

'My grandmother Joan's diary,' interrupted Martyn, turning round with his arm full of books. 'Queer old lady she must have been. I could never keep a diary myself. Never kept one beyond the 10th of February, though I tried often. But here you see,' he leant over me, turning the pages, and pointing with his finger, 'here is January, February, March, April – so on – a whole twelve months.'

'Have you read it, then?' I asked, expecting, nay, hoping that he would say no.

'O yes, I've read it;' he remarked casually, as though that were but a simple undertaking. 'It took me some time to get used to the writing, and the old girl's spelling is odd. But there are some queer things in it. I learnt a deal about the land from her, one way and another.' He tapped it meditatively.

'Do you know her history too?' I asked.

'Joan Martyn,' he began in the voice of a showman, 'was born 1495.

She was the daughter of Giles Martyn. She was his only daughter. He had three sons though; we always have sons. She wrote this diary when she was twenty-five. She lived here all her life – never married. Indeed she died at the age of thirty. I daresay you might see her tomb down there with the rest of them.'[2]

'Now this,' he said touching a thick book bound in parchment, 'is more interesting to my mind. This is the household book of Jasper for the year 1583. See how the old gentleman kept his accounts; what they eat and drank; how much meat and bread and wine cost; how many servants he kept – his horses, carriages, beds, furniture, everything. There's method for you. I have a set of ten of them.' He spoke of them with greater pride than I had heard him speak of any of his possessions yet.

'This one too makes good reading of a winter's night,' he went on, 'This is the Stud book of Willoughby; you remember Willoughby.'

'The one who bought the horse of the Duke, and died of small pox,' I repeated glibly.

'That's so,' he nodded. 'Now this is really fine stuff this one.' He went on, like a connoisseur, talking of some favourite brand of port. 'I wouldn't sell this for £20. Here are names, the pedigrees, the lives, values, descendants; all written out like a bible.' He rolled some of the strange old names of these dead horses upon his tongue, as though he relished the sound like wine. 'Ask my wife if I can't tell 'em all without the book,' he laughed, shutting it carefully and placing it on the shelf.

'These are the Estate books; they go down to this year; there's the last of 'em. Here's our family history.' He unrolled a long strip of parchment, upon which an elaborate genealogical tree had been inscribed, with many faded flourishes and extravagances of some mediaeval pen. The boughs spread so widely by degrees, that they were lopped unmercifully by the limits of the sheet – a husband depending, for instance, with a family of ten children and no wife. Fresh ink at the base of all recorded the names of Jasper Martyn, my host, and his wife Elizabeth Clay: they had three sons. His finger travelled sagaciously down the tree, as though it were so well used to this occupation that it could almost be trusted to perform it by itself. Martyn's voice murmured on as though it repeated a list of Saints or Virtues in some monotonous prayer.

'Yes,' he concluded, rolling up the sheet and laying it by, 'I think I like those two best. I could say them through with my eyes shut. Horses or Grandfathers!'

'Do you study here a great deal then?' I asked, somewhat puzzled by this strange man.

'I've no time for study,' he returned, rather roughly, as tho' the farmer cropped up in him at my question. 'I like to read something easy in the winter nights; and in the morning too, if I wake early. I keep them by my bed sometimes. I say them to send myself to sleep. It's easy to know the names of one's own family. They come natural. But I was never any good at book learning, more's the pity.'

Asking my permission, he lit a pipe and began puffing forth great curls of smoke, as he ranged the volumes in order before him. But I kept No. One, the bundle of parchment sheets, in my hand, nor did he seem to miss it from the rest.

'You would be sorry to part with any of these, I daresay?' I hazarded, at last, covering my real eagerness with an attempt at a laugh.

'Part with them?' he returned, 'what should I part with them for?' The idea was evidently so remote that my question had not, as I feared, irritated his suspicions.

'No, no,' he went on, 'I find them far too useful for that. Why, Madam, these old papers have stood out for my rights in a court of law before now; besides, a man likes to keep his family round him; I should feel – well kind of lonely if you take my meaning, without my Grandfathers and Grandmothers, and Uncles and Aunts.' He spoke as though he confessed a weakness.

'O,' I said, 'I quite understand –'

'I daresay you have the same feeling yourself Madam and down here, in a lonely place like this, company means more than you could well believe. I often think I shouldn't know how to pass the time, if it weren't for my relations.'

No words of mine, or attempts at a report of his words, can give the curious impression which he produced as he spoke, that all these 'relations' Grandfathers of the time of Elizabeth, nay Grandmothers of the time of Edward the Fourth, were just, so to speak, brooding round the corner; there was none of the pride of 'ancestry' in his voice but merely the personal affection of a son for his parents. All generations seemed bathed in his mind in the same clear and equable light: it was not precisely the light of the present day, but it certainly was not what we commonly call the light of the past. And it was not romantic, it was very sober, and very broad and the figures stood out in it, solid and capable, with a great resemblance, I suspect, to what they were in the flesh.

It really needed no stretch of the imagination to perceive that Jasper Martyn might come in from his farm and his fields, and sit down here alone to a comfortable gossip with his 'relations;' whenever he chose; and that their voices were very nearly as audible to him as those of the labourers in the field below, which came floating in, upon the level afternoon sunlight through the open window.

But my original intention of asking whether he would sell, almost made me blush when I remembered it now: so irrelevant and so impertinent. And also, strange though it may seem, I had lost for the time my proper antiquarian zeal; all my zest for old things, and the little distinguishing marks of age, left me, because they seemed the trivial and quite immaterial accidents of large substantial things. There was really no scope for antiquarian ingenuity in the case of Mr Martyn's ancestors, anymore than it needed an antiquary to expound the history of the man himself.

They are, he would have told me, all flesh and blood like I am; and the fact that they have been dead for four or five centuries makes no more diffence to them, than the glass you place over a canvas changes the picture beneath it.

But on the other hand, if it seemed impertinent to buy, it seemed natural, if perhaps a little simpleminded, to borrow.

'Well, Mr Martyn,' I said at length, with less eagerness and less trepidation than I could have thought possible under the circumstances, 'I am thinking of staying for a week or so in this neighbourhood – at the Swan at Gartham indeed – I should be much obliged to you if you would lend me these papers to look through during my stay. This is my card. Mr Lathom, (the great landowner of the place) will tell you all about me.' Instinct told me that Mr Martyn was not the man to trust the benevolent impulses of his heart.

'O Madam, there's no need to bother about that,' he said, carelessly, as though my request were not of sufficient importance to need his scrutiny. 'If these old papers please you, I'm sure you're welcome to 'em.' He seemed a little surprised, however, so that I added, 'I take a great interest in family histories, even when they're not my own.'

'It's amusing eno', I daresay, if you have the time,' he assented politely; but I think his opinion of my intelligence was lowered.

'Which would you like,' he asked, stretching his hand towards the Household Books of Jasper; and the Stud book of Willoughby.

'Well I think I'll begin with your grandmother Joan,' I said; 'I like beginning at the beginning.'

'O very well,' he smiled; 'though I don't think you'll find anything out of the way in her; she was very much the same as the rest of us – as far as I can see, not remarkable – '

But all the same, I walked off with Grandmother Joan beneath my arm; Betty insisted upon wrapping her in brown paper, to disguise the queer nature of the package, for I refused to let them send it over as they wished, by the boy who took the letters on his bicycle.

(1)

The state of the times, which my mother tells me, is less safe and less happy than when she was a girl, makes it necessary for us to keep much within our own lands. After dark indeed, and the sun sets terribly soon in January, we have to be safe behind the hall Gates; my mother goes out as soon as the dark makes her embroidery too dim to see, with the great keys on her arm. 'Is everybody within doors?' she cries, and swings the bells out upon the road, in case any of our men may still be working in the fields. Then she draws the Gates close, clamps them with the lock, and the whole world is barred away from us. I am very bold and impatient sometimes, when the moon rises, over a land gleaming with frost; and I think I feel the pressure of all this free and beautiful place – all England and the sea, and the lands beyond – rolling like sea waves, against our iron gates, breaking, and withdrawing – and breaking again – all through the long black night. Once I leapt from my bed, and ran to my mother's room, crying, 'Let them in. Let them in! We are starving!' 'Are the soldiers there, child,' she cried: 'or is it your father's voice?' She ran to the window, and together we gazed out upon the silver fields, and all was peaceful. But I could not explain what it was that I heard; and she bade me sleep, and be thankful that there were stout gates between me and the world.

But on other nights, when the wind is wild and the moon is sunk beneath hurrying clouds, I am glad to draw close to the fire, and to think that all those bad men who prowl in the lanes, and lie hidden in the woods at this hour cannot break through our great Gates, try as they will. Last night was such a night; they come often in Winter when my father is away in London, my brothers are with the army, save my little brother Jeremy, and my mother has to manage the farm, and order the people, and see that all our rights are looked to. We may not burn the tapers after the church bell has struck 8 times, and so we sit round the logs, with the priest, John Sandys, and one or two of the servants who sleep with us in the Hall. Then my mother, who cannot be idle even by fire light, winds her wool for her knitting, sitting in the great chair which stands by the cheek of the hearth. When her wool gets tangled she strikes a great blow with the iron rod, and sends the flames and the sparks spurting in showers; she stoops her head into the tawny light, and you see what a noble woman she is; in spite of age – she is more than forty – and the hard lines which much thought and watching have cut in her brow. She wears a fine linen cap, close fitting to the shape of her head, and her eyes are deep and stern, and her cheek is coloured like a healthy winter apple. It is a great thing to be the daughter of such a woman, and to hope that one day the same power may be mine. She rules us all.

Sir John Sandys, the priest, is, for all his sacred office, the servant of my mother; and does her will simply and querulously, and is never so happy as when she asks him for advice, and takes her own. But she would scold me well if I ever whispered such a thing: for she is the faithful daughter of the Church, and reverences her Priest. Again there are William and Anne, the servants who sit with us, because they are so old that my mother wishes them to share our fire. But William is so ancient, so curved with planting and digging, so bruised and battered by the sun and the wind that one might as well ask the pollard willow in the fen to share one's fire, or join one's talk. Still, his memory goes back a great way, and if he could tell us, as he sometimes tries to begin, of the things he has seen in his day, it would be curious to hear. Old Anne was my mother's nurse; she was mine; and still she mends our clothes, and knows more about household things than any, save my mother. She will tell you, too, the history of each chair and table or piece of tapestry in the house; but most of all she likes to discuss with mother and Sir John the men whom it would be most suitable for me to marry.

As long as the light serves it is my duty to read aloud – because I am the only one who can read though my mother can write, and spell words beyond the fashion of her time, and my father has sent me a manuscript from London; called The Palace of Glass, by Mr John Lydgate.[3] It is a poem, written about Helen and the Siege of Troy.

Last night I read of Helen, and her beauty and her suitors, and the fair town of Troy and they listened silently; for though we none of us know where those places are, we see very well what they must have been like; and we can weep for the sufferings of the soldiers, and picture to ourselves the stately woman herself, who must have been, I think, something like my mother. My mother beats with her foot and sees the whole processions pass I know, from the way her eyes gleam, and her head tosses. 'It must have been in Cornwall,' said Sir John, 'where King Arthur lived with his knights. I remember stories I could tell you of all their doings, but my memory is dim.'

'Ah but there are fine stories of the Northmen, too,' broke in Anne; whose mother was from those parts; 'but I have sung them often to my Mister, and to you too Miss Joan.'

'Read on Joan, while there is light,' commanded my mother. Indeed, of all I think she listened closest, and was most vexed when the Curfew tolled from the Church nearby. Yet she called herself an old fool for listening to stories, when the accounts had still to be made up for my father in London.

When the light is out and I can no longer see to read, they begin talking of the state of the country; and telling dreadful stories of the plots and the battles and the bloody deeds that are going on all round us. But for all I can see, we are not worse now than we have always been; and we in Norfolk today are much the same as we were in the days of Helen, wherever she may have lived. Was not Jane Moryson carried off on the eve of her wedding only last year?

But anyhow, the story of Helen is old; my mother says it happened long before her day; and these robbings and burnings are going on now. So the talk makes me, and Jeremy too, tremble and think that every rattle of the big door, is the battering ram of some wandering highwayman.

It is far worse tho', when the time for bed comes, and the fire sinks, and we have to feel our way up the great stairs, and along the passages, where the windows shine grey, and so into our cold bed rooms. The window in my room is broken, and stuffed with straw, but gusts come in and lift the tapestry on the wall, till I think that horses and men in armour are charging down upon me. My prayer last night was, that the great gates might hold fast, and all robbers and murderers might pass us by.

(2)

The dawn, even when it is cold and melancholy, never fails to shoot through my limbs as with arrows of sparkling piercing ice. I pull aside the thick curtains, and search for the first glow in the sky which shows that life is breaking through. And with my cheek leant upon the window pane I like to fancy that I am pressing as closely as can be upon the massy wall of time, which is for ever lifting and pulling and letting fresh spaces of life in upon us. May it be mine to taste the moment before it has spread itself over the rest of the world! Let me taste the newest and the freshest. From my window I look down upon the Church yard, where so many of my ancestors are buried, and in my prayer I pity those poor dead men who toss perpetually on the old recurring waters; for I see them, circling and eddying forever upon a pale tide. Let us, then, who have the gift of the present, use it and enjoy it: That I confess, is part of my morning prayer.

It rained steadily today, so that I had to spend the morning with my sewing. My mother was writing her letter to my father which John Ashe will take with him to London next week. My thoughts naturally dwelt upon this journey, and upon the great city which perhaps I may never see, though I am for ever dreaming of it. You start at dawn; for it is well to spend few nights on the road. John travels with three other men, bound to the same place; and I have often seen them set forth, and longed to ride with them. They gather in the courtyard, while the stars are still in the sky; and the people of the neighbourhood come out wrapped in cloaks and strange garments, and my mother carries out a tankard of strong Ale to each traveller; and gives it to him from her own hand. Their horses are laden with packs before and behind, but not so as to hinder them from starting out in a gallop if need be; and the men are well armed, and closely dressed in fur lined habits, for the winter days are short and cold, and maybe they will sleep beneath a hedge. It is a gallant sight in the dawn; for the horses champ and fret to be gone; the people cluster round. They wish their God speeds and their last messages to friends in London; and as the clock strikes four they wheel about, salute my mother and the rest, and turn sharply on their road. Many young men and women too, follow them some paces on the way till the mist comes between, for often men who set forth thus in the dawn, never ride home again.

I picture them riding all day along the white roads, and I see them dismount at the shrine of our Lady and do homage, pray [to] her for a safe journey. There is but one road, and it passes through vast lands, where no men live, but only those who have murdered or robbed; for they may not dwell with others in towns, but must pass their lives with the wild beasts, who murder also, and eat the clothes from your back. It is a fearful ride; but, truly, I think I should like to go that way once, and pass over the land, like a ship at sea.

At midday they reach an Inn – for there are Inns at all the stages upon the journey to London, where a traveller may rest in safety. The landlord will tell you the state of the road, and he will ask you of your adventures, so that he may give warning to others who travel the same way. But you must press on, to reach your sleeping place before the dark lets loose all those fierce creatures, who have lain hidden in the day. John has often told me how as the sun comes from the sky silence falls on the company, and each man has his gun swung beneath his hand, and even the horses prick their ears and need no urging. You reach the crest of the road, and look fearfully beneath you, lest something moves in the shade of the fir trees by the wayside. And then Robin, the cheerful Miller, shouts a snatch of a song, and they take heart, and step bravely down the hill, talking lest the deep breath of the wind, as of a woman who sighs deeply, may cast a panic into their hearts. Then some one rises in his stirrup and sees the spark of a lodging far off on the rim of the land. And if Our Lady is merciful to them they reach this in safety when we at home are on our knees in prayer for them.

(3)

My mother called me from my book this morning to talk with her in her room. I found her in the little chamber where my father is wont to sit, when he is at home, with the Manor Rolls and other legal papers before him. It is here that she sits when she has duty to do as the head of the household. I curtseyed deeply; thinking that I guessed already why she had sent for me.

She had a sheet spread before her, covered with close writing. She bade me read it; and then before I had taken the paper in my hand she cried, 'No – I will tell you myself.'

'Daughter,' she began, solemnly, 'it is high time that you were married. Indeed it is only the troubled state of the land' – she sighed – 'and our own perplexities, that have delayed the matter so long.'

'Do you think much of marriage?' she looked at me half smiling.

'I have no wish to leave you,' I said.

'Come, my child you speak like a Babe,' she laughed, though I think she was well pleased at my affection.

'And besides, if you married as I would have you marry' – she tapped the paper – 'you would not go far from me. You might for instance rule over the land of Kirflings – your land would touch ours – You would be our good neighbour. The Lord of Kirflings is Sir Amyas Bigod, a man of ancient name.'

'I think it is a suitable match; such as a mother might wish for her daughter,' she mused, always with the sheet before her.

As I have only seen Sir Amyas once, when he came home with my father from the sessions at Norwich, and as on that occasion my only speech with him was to invite him gravely to drink the sack which I proffered, curtseying, I could not pretend to add anything to what my mother said. All I knew was that he had a fair, straight face; and if his hair was gray, it was not so gray as my father's, and his land bordered ours so that we might well live happily together.

'Marriage, you must know my daughter,' went on my mother, 'is a great honour and a great burden. If you marry such a man as Sir Amyas you become not only the head of his household, and that is much, but the head of his race for ever and ever, and that is more. We will not talk of love – as that song writer of yours talks of love, as a passion and a fire and a madness.'

'O he is only a story teller, Mother,' I chimed in –

'And such things are not to be found in real life; at least I think not often.' My mother was used to consider gravely as she spoke.

'But that is beside the question. Here, my daughter,' and she spread the paper before her, 'is a writing from Sir Amyas, to your father; he asks for your hand, and wishes to know whether there are other treaties for you and what dowry we will give with you. He tells us what he will provide on his part. Now I give you this paper to read by yourself; that you may consider whether this exchange seems to you a fair one.'

I knew already what lands and monies I had as my portion; and I knew that as the only daughter of my father my dowry was no mean one.

So that I might continue in this country which I love, and might live on close to my mother, I would take less than my right both of wealth and of land. But the gravity of the compact is such that I felt as though several years were added to my age, when my mother handed me the roll of paper. Since I was a child, I have always heard my parents talk of my marriage; and during the last two or three years there have been several contracts almost made I know, that came to nothing in the end. I lose my youth however, and it is high time that a bargain were struck.

I thought, naturally, for a long time, until the dinner bell rung indeed at midday, of the general honour and burden, as my mother calls it, of marriage. No other event in the life of a woman can mean so great a change; for from flitting shadow like and unconsidered in her father's house, marriage suddenly forms her to a substantial body, with weight which people must see and make way for. That is of course, if her marriage is suitable. And so, every maiden waits this change with wonder and anxiety; for it will prove whether she is to be [an] honourable and authoritative woman for ever, like my mother; or it will show that she is of no weight or worth. Either in this world or in the next.

And if I marry well, the burden of a great name and of great lands will be on me; many servants will call me mistress; I shall be the mother of sons; in my husband's absence I shall rule his people, taking care for herds and crops and keeping watch on his enemies; within doors I shall store up fine linens and my chests shall be laden with spices and preserves; by the work of my needle all waste of time and use will be repaired and renewed so that at my death my daughter shall find her cupboards better lined with fine raiments than when I found them. And when I lie dead, the people from the countryside shall pass for three days before my body, praying and speaking good of me, and at the will of my children the priest shall say mass for my soul and candles shall burn in the church for ever and ever.

(4)

I was stopped in the midst of such reflections firstly by the dinner bell; and you must not be late, or you interfere with Sir John's grace and that means no pudding; and then, when I might have put myself more into the position of a married woman, Jeremy my brother, insisted that we should go for a walk with Anthony, my father's chief steward – after my mother that is.

He is a crass man, but I like him because he is a faithful servant, and knows as much about land and sheep as any man in Norfolk. It was he

also who broke Lancelot's head in last Michaelmas for using bad
language [to] my mother. He is for ever tramping our fields, and knows
them better and loves them more, so I tell him, than any human
creature. He is wedded to this clump of earth, and sees in it a thousand
beauties and gifts such as ordinary men see in their wives. And, as we
have trotted by his side since we could walk alone, some of his affection
has become ours too; Norfolk and the parish of Long Winton in
Norfolk is to me what my own grandmother is; a tender parent, dear
and familiar, and silent to whom I shall return in time. O how blessed it
would be never to marry, or grow old; but to spend one's life
innocently and indifferently among the trees and rivers which alone
can keep one cool and childlike in the midst of the troubles of the
world! Marriage or any other great joy would confuse the clear vision
which is still mine. And at the thought of losing that, I cried in my heart,
'No, I will never leave you – for a husband or a lover,' and straightway I
started chasing rabbits across the heath with Jeremy and the dogs.

   It was a cold afternoon, but a bright one; as though the sun were
made of gleaming ice and not of fire; and its rays were long icicles that
reached from sky to earth. They splintered on our cheeks, and went
glancing across the fen. And the whole country seemed empty, save of a
few swift rabbits, but very chaste and very glad in its solitude. We ran
to keep warm, and chattered when the blood raced sparkling through
our limbs. Anthony stalked straight on, as though his stride were the
best thing in the world against the cold. Certainly when we came to a
broken hedge, or a snare stretched for a rabbit, he took off his gloves
and leant on his knee and took note of it as though it were a
midsummer day. Once we came upon a strange man, slouching along
the road, in rusty green, with the look of one who knows not which
way to take. Anthony held my hand firmly; this was a Sanctuary man
he said, prowling out of bounds in search of food. He had robbed or
murdered, or perchance he was only a debtor. Jeremy swore he saw
blood on his hands: but Jeremy is a boy, and would like to defend us all
with his bow and arrows.

   Anthony had some business at one of the cottages, and we came in
with him out of the cold. But indeed, I could hardly stand the heat and
the smell. Beatrice Somers, and her husband Peter live here, and they
have children; but it was more like the burrow of some rabbit on the
heath than the house of a man. Their roof was of brush, and straw,
their floor was but the earth trodden bare of grass or flower; sticks

burnt in the corner, and sent the smoke stinging into our eyes. There was but a rotten log on which a woman sat, nursing a baby. She looked at us, not with fright, but with distrust and dislike written clear in her eyes; and she clasped her child more closely. Anthony spoke to her as he would have spoken to some animal who had strong claws and a wicked eye: he stood over her, and his great boot seemed ready to crush her. But she did not move or speak; and I doubt whether she could have spoken, or whether snarling and howling was her only language.

Outside we met Peter coming home from the fen, and tho' he touched his forehead to us, he seemed to have no more human sense in him than his wife. He looked at us, and seemed fascinated by a coloured cloak which I wore; and then he stumbled into his burrow, to lie on the ground I suppose, rolled in dried bracken till morning. These are the people we must rule; and tread under foot, and scourge them to do the only work they are fitted to do; as they will tear us to pieces with their fangs. Thus Anthony spoke as he took us away, and then clenched his fists and set his lips as though he were razing to the earth some such poor wretch already. Still the sight of that ugly face spoilt the rest of the walk; since it seemed that even my dear country bred pests like these. I saw such eyes staring at me from the furze bushes, and the tangles of the undergrowth.

It was like waking from a nightmare to enter our own clean hall, where the logs burnt tidily in the great chimney, and the oak shone bright; and my mother came down the staircase in her rich gown, with spotless linen on her head. But some of the lines on her face, and some of the sternness of her voice, had come there, I thought suddenly, because she always saw not far from her such sights as I had seen today.

(5)

May

The spring which has now reached us means more than the mere birth of green growing things; for once again the current of life which circles round England is melted from its winter frost, and in our little island we feel the tide chafing at our shores. For the last week or two strange wayfarers have been seen on the roads, who may be either pilgrims and pedlars, or gentlemen travelling in parties to London or the North. And at this season the mind becomes eager and hopeful even though the body must stay motionless. For as the evenings lengthen and new light seems to well up from the West so one may fancy that a new whiter light of another kind is spreading over the land; and you may feel it hitting your eyelids as you walk or sit over your embroidery.

In the midst of such a stir and tumult, one bright May morning, we saw the figure of a man striding along the road, walking fast and waving his arms as though he conversed with the air. He had a great wallet at his back and we saw that he held a stout book of parchment in one hand at which he glanced occasionally: and all the while he shouted words in a kind of measure with his feet, and his voice rose up and down, in [menace?] or in plaint till Jeremy and I shrank close against the hedge. But he saw us; and pulled off his cap and made a deep bow; to which I curtseyed as properly as I could.

'Madam,' he said, in a voice that rolled like summer thunder, 'may I ask if this is the road to Long Winton?'

'It is only a mile in front of you, Sir,' I said, and Jeremy waved down the road with his stick.

'Then Sir,' he went on, shutting his book, and looking at once more sober and more conscious of the time and place, 'may I ask further where is the house where I could sell my books most easily? I am come all the way from Cornwall, singing songs, and trying to sell the manuscripts I have with me. My wallet is still full. The times are not favourable to songs.'

Indeed the man, though ruddy of cheek, and lusty of frame, was as ill dressed as any hind; and his boots were so patched that walking must have been a penance. But he had a kind of gaiety and courtesy about him, as though the fine music of his own songs clung to him and set him above ordinary thoughts.

I pulled my brother's arm, and said, 'We belong to the Hall ourselves Sir, and we will gladly shew you the way. I should be very glad to see those books of yours.' His eye lost its merriment at once; and he asked me almost sternly, 'Can you read?'

'O Joan's always got her nose in a book,' called out Jeremy, starting to talk, and pulling me too.

'Tell us about your travels Sir. Have you been to London? What is your name?'

'I am called Richard Sir,' said the man smiling. 'Doubtless I have another name, but I never heard it. I come from Gwithian which is in Cornwall; and I can sing you more Cornish songs, Madam, than any man in the Duchy.' He turned to me, and wound up with a flourish of one hand with the book in it. 'Here for instance – in this little volume, are all the stories of the Knights of the round Table; written out by the hand of Master Anthony himself, and painted by the Monks of Cam Brea. I value this more than my wife or children; for I have none; it is meat and drink to me, because I am given supper and lodging for singing the tales in it; it is horse and staff to me, for it has lifted me over many miles of weary road; and it is the best of all companions on the way; for it has always something new to sing me; and it will be silent when I wish to sleep. There never was such a book!'

Such was the way he talked, as I have never heard any man talk. For in speaking he did not seem to speak his mind exactly, or to care whether we understood him. But words seemed dear to him, whether he spoke them in jest or earnest. We reached our courtyard, and he straightened himself, flicked his boots with a handkerchief; and tried with many swift touches of his fingers to set his dress somewhat more in order than it was. Also he cleared his throat, as one preparing to sing. I ran to fetch my mother, who came slowly, and looked at him from an upper window before she would promise to hear him.

'His bag is stuffed with books, mother,' I urged; 'he has all the Tales of Arthur and the Round Table; I daresay he can tell us what became of Helen when her husband took her. O Mother, do let us hear him!'

She laughed at my impatience; but bade me call Sir John, for after all it was a fine morning.

When we came down the man Richard was walking up and down, discoursing to my brother of his travels; how he had knocked one man on the head, cried to the other, '"Come on Rascal" and the whole lot had fled like,' here he saw my mother, and swept off his hat as was his way.

'My daughter tells me Sir that you come from foreign parts, and can sing. We are but country people; and therefore I fear very little acquainted with the tales of other parts. But we are ready to listen. Sing us something of your land; and then, if you will, you shall sit down to meat with us, and we will gladly hear news of the country.'

She sat down on a bench beneath the oak tree; and Sir John came puffing to stand by her side. She bade Jeremy open the Gates, and let any of our people in who cared to hear. They came in shyly and curiously, and stood gaping at Master Richard, who once again waved his cap at them.

He stood on a small mound of grass; and began in a high melodious voice, to tell the story of Sir Tristram and the Lady Iseult.

He dropped his gay manner, and looked past us all, with straight fixed eyes, as though he drew his words from some sight not far from him. And as the story grew passionate his voice rose, and his fists clenched, and he raised his foot and stretched forth his arms; and then, when the lovers part, he seemed to see the Lady sink away from him, and his eye sought farther and farther till the vision was faded away; and his arms were empty. And then he is wounded in Brittany; and he hears the Princess coming across the seas to him.

But I cannot tell how it seemed that the air was full of Knights and Ladies, who passed among us, hand in hand, murmuring, and seeing us not; and then the poplars and the beech trees sent grey figures, with silver gems, floating down the air; and the morning was full, suddenly, of whispers, and sighs, and lovers' laments.

But then the voice stopped; and all these figures withdrew, fading and trailing across the sky to the West where they live. And when I opened my eyes, the man, and the grey wall; the people by the Gate, slowly swam up, as from some depths, and settled on the surface, and stayed there clear and cold.

'Poor things!' spoke my mother.

Meanwhile Richard was like a man who lets something slip from his clasp; and beats thin air. He looked at us, and I had half a mind to stretch out a hand; and tell him he was safe. But then he recollected himself, and smiled as though he had reason to be pleased.

He saw the crowd at the Gate; and struck up a jolly tune, about a Nut Brown Maid and her lover, and they grinned and stamped with their feet. Then my mother bade us come into dinner; and she sat Master Richard at her right side.

He eat like a man who has fed upon hips and haws, and drunk water from the brook. And after the meat had been taken away, he solemnly swung round his wallet; and took from it various things; which he laid upon the table. There were clasps and brooches, and necklaces of beads: but there were also many sheets of parchment stiched together; though none of such a size as his book. And then seeing my desire he placed the precious volume in my hands and bade me look at its pictures. Indeed it was a beautiful work; for the capital letters framed bright blue skies, and golden robes; and in the midst of the writing there came broad spaces of colour, in which you might see princes and princesses walking in procession and towns with churches upon steep hills, and the sea breaking blue beneath them. They were like little mirrors, held up to those visions which I had seen passing in the air but here they were caught and stayed for ever.

'And have you ever seen such sights as these?' I asked him.

'They are to be seen by those who look,' he answered mysteriously. And he took his manuscript from me, and tied the covers safely across it. He placed it in his breast.

It was as yellow and gnarled outside as the missal of any pious priest; but inside the brilliant knights and ladies moved, undimmed, to the unceasing melody of beautiful words. It was a fairy world that he shut inside his coat.

We offered him a night's lodging, nay more, if he would but stay and sing to us again. But he listened to our prayers no more than the owl in the ivy: saying merely, 'I must go on my way.' By dawn he was out of the house, and we felt as though some strange bird had rested on our roof for a moment, and flown on.

(6)

Midsummer

There comes a week, or may be it is only a day, when the year seems poised consciously on its topmost peak; it stays there motionless for a long or a short time, as though in majestic contemplation, and then slowly sinks like a monarch descending from his throne, and wraps itself round in darkness.

But figures are slippery things!

At this moment I have the feeling of one swung high into tranquil regions; upon the great back of the world. The peace of the nation, and the prosperity of our own small corner of it – for my father and brothers are at home – make a complete circle of satisfaction; you may pass from the smooth dome of sky, to our own roof without crossing any gulf.

Thus it seemed a most suitable time for our midsummer pilgrimage to the shrine of Our Lady at Walsingham; more especially as I have this year to give thanks for much, and to pray for more. My marriage with Sir Amyas is settled for the 20th day of December; and we are busy making ready. So yesterday I started at dawn, and travelled on foot in order to show that I approached the shrine with a humble spirit. And a good walk is surely the best preparation for prayers!

Start with your spirit fresh like a corn fed horse; let her rear and race, and bucket you hither and thither. Nothing will keep her to the road;

and she will sport in dewy meadows, and crush a thousand delicate flowers beneath her feet.

But the day grows hot; and you may lead her, still with a springing step back to the straight way; and she will carry you lightly and swiftly, till the midday sun bids you rest. In sober truth, and without metaphor, the mind drives clearly through all the mazes of a stagnant spirit when a brisk pair of legs impells it; and the creature grows nimble, with its exercise. Thus I suppose I may have thought enough for a whole week lived indoors during those three hours that I spent striding along the road to Walsingham.

And my brain that was swift and merry at first, and leapt like a child at play, settled down in time to sober work upon the highway, though it was glad withal. For I thought of the serious things of life – such as age, and poverty and sickness and death, and considered that it would certainly be my lot to meet them; and I considered also those joys and sorrows that were for ever chasing themselves across my life. Small things would no longer please me or tease me as of old. But although this made me feel grave, I felt also that I had come to the time when such feelings are true; and further, as I walked, it seemed to me that one might enter within such feelings and study them, as, indeed, I had walked in a wide space within the covers of Master Richard's manuscript.

I saw them as solid globes of crystal; enclosing a round ball of coloured earth and air, in which tiny men and women laboured, as beneath the dome of the sky itself.

Walsingham, as all the world knows, is but a very small village on the top of a hill. But as you approach through a plain that is rich with green, you see this high ground rising above you for some time before you get there. The midday sun lit up all the soft greens and blues of the fen land; and made it seem as though one passed through a soft and luxurious land, glowing like a painted book; towards a stern summit, where the light struck upon something pointing upwards that was pale as bone.

At last I reached the top of the hill, joining with a stream of other pilgrims, and we clasped hands, to show that we came humbly as human beings and trod the last steps of the road together, singing our Miserere.

There were men and women, and lame people and blind people; and some were in rags, and some had ridden on horseback; I confess that my eyes sought their faces curiously, and I thought desperately for a moment that it was terrible that flesh and [fens?] should divide us. They would have strange, merry stories to tell.

But then the pale cross with the Image struck my eyes, and drew all my mind, in reverence towards it.

I will not pretend that I found that summons other than stern; for the sun and storm have made the figure harsh and white; but the endeavour to adore Her as others were doing round me filled my mind with an image that was so large and white that no other thought had room there. For one moment I submitted myself to her as I have never submitted to man or woman, and bruised my lips on the rough stone of her garment. White light and heat steamed on my bare head; and when the ecstasy passed the country beneath flew out like a sudden banner unfurled.

(7)

Autumn

The Autumn comes; and my marriage is not far off. Sir Amyas is a good gentleman, who treats me with great courtesy and hopes to make me happy. No poet could sing of our courtship; and, I must confess that since I have taken to reading of Princesses, I have sometimes grieved that my own lot was so little like theirs. But then they did not live in Norfolk, at the time of the Civil Wars; and my mother tells me that the truth is always finest.

To prepare me for my duties as a married woman, she has let me help her in the management of the house and lands; and I begin to understand how much of my time will be passed in thoughts which have nothing to do with men or with happiness. There are the sheep, the woods, the crops, the people, things all needing my care and judgment when my Lord is away as he will be so often; and if times are as troubled as they have been, I must also act as chief Lieutenant in the disposition of his forces against the enemy. And then there will be my proper work as a woman calling me within the house. Truly, as my mother says, there will be little time for Princes and Princesses! And she went on to expound to me what she calls her theory of ownership; how, in these times, one is as the Ruler of a small island set in the midst of turbulent waters; how one must plant it and cultivate it; and drive roads through it, and fence it securely from the tides; and one day perhaps the waters will abate and this plot of ground will be ready to make part of a new world. Such is her dream of what the future may bring to England; and it has been the hope of her life to order her own province in such a way that it may make one firm spot of ground to tread on at any rate. She bids me hope that I may live to see the whole of England thus solidly established; and if I do, I shall thank my mother, and other women like her.

But I confess that deeply though I honour my mother and respect her words, I cannot accept their wisdom without a sigh. She seems to look forward to nothing better than an earth rising solid out of the mists that now enwreathe it; and the fairest prospect in her mind is, I believe, a broad road running through the land, on which she sees long strings of horsemen, riding at their ease, pilgrims stepping cheerily unarmed, and waggons that pass each other going laden to the coast and returning as heavily laden with goods taken from ships. Then she would dream of certain great houses, lying open to the sight, with their moats filled up and their towers pulled down; and the gate would open freely to any passer by; and there would be cheer for guest or serving man at the same table with the Lord. And you would ride through fields brimming with corn, and there would be flocks and herds in all the pasture lands and cottages of stone for the poor. As I write this down, I see that it is good; and we should do right to wish it.

But at the same time, when I imagine such a picture, painted before me, I cannot think it pleasant to look upon; and I fancy that I should find it hard to draw my breath upon those smooth bright ways.

Yet what it is that I want, I cannot tell, although I crave for it, and in some secret way, expect it. For often, and oftener as time goes by, I find myself suddenly halting in my walk, as though I were stopped by a strange new look upon the surface of the land which I know so well. It hints at something; but it is gone before I know what it means. It is as though a new smile crept out of a well known face; it half frightens you, and yet it beckons.

Last Pages

My father came in yesterday when I was sitting before the desk at which I write these sheets. He is not a little proud of my skill in reading and writing; which indeed I have learnt mostly at his knee.

But confusion came over me when he asked me what I wrote; and stammering that it was a 'Diary' I covered the pages with my hands.

'Ah,' he cried, 'if my father had only kept a diary! But he, poor man, could not write his own name even. There's John and Pierce and Stephen all lying in the church yonder, and no word left to say whether they were good men or bad.' Thus he spoke till my cheeks were pale again.

'And so my grandson will say of me,' he went on. 'And if I could I should like to write a line myself: to say "I am Giles Martyn; I am a middle sized man, dark skinned, hazel eyed, with hair on my lip; I can read and write, but none too easy. I ride to London on as good a bay mare as is to be found in the County."'

'Well what more should I say? And would they care to hear it? And who will *they* be?' he laughed; for it was his temper to end his speech with a laugh, even though he began it soberly.

'You would like to hear of your father,' I said; 'why shouldn't they care to hear of you?'

'My fathers were much as I am;' he said; 'they lived here, all of 'em; they ploughed the same land that I plough; they married women from the countryside. Why they might walk in at the door this moment, and I should know 'em, and should think it nothing strange. But the future' – he spread out his hands – 'who can tell? We may be washed off the face of the earth, Joan.'

'Oh no,' I cried; 'I am certain we shall live here always.' This pleased my father secretly; for there is no man who cares more for his land and his name than he does; though he will always hold that had we been a prouder race, we should not have stayed so long in the same prosperity.

'Well then Joan, you must keep your writing,' he said; 'or rather, I must keep it for you. For you are going to leave us – not to go far though,' he added quickly; 'and names matter but little. Still, I should like to have some token of you when you are away; and our descendants shall have cause to respect one of us at least.' He looked with great admiration at the neat lines of my penmanship. 'Now my girl, come with me, to the Church, where I must see to the carving on my father's tomb.'

As I walked with him, I thought of his words and of the many sheets that lie written in my oaken desk. Winter had come round again since I made my first flourish so proudly. Thinking that there were few women in Norfolk who could do the like; and were it not that some such pride stayed with me I think that my writing would have ceased long before this. For, truly, there is nothing in the pale of my days that needs telling; and the record grows wearisome. And I thought as I went along in the sharp air of the winter morning, that if I ever write again it shall not be of Norfolk and myself, but of Knights and Ladies and of adventures in strange lands. The clouds even, which roll up from the west and advance across the sky take the likeness of Captains and of soldiery and I can scarcely cease from fashioning helmets and swords, as well as fair faces, and high headdresses from these waves of coloured mist.

But as my mother would say, the best of stories are those that are told over the fire side; and I shall be well content if I may end my days as one of those old women who can keep a household still on a winter's evening, with her tales of the strange sights that she saw and the deeds that were done in her youth. I have always thought that such stories came partly out of the clouds, or why should they stir us more than any thing we can see for ourselves? It is certain that no written book can stand beside them.

Such a woman was Dame Elsbeth Aske, who, when she grew too old to knit or stitch and too stiff to leave her chair, sat with clasped hands by the fire all day long, and you had only to pull her sleeve and her eyes grew bright, and she would tell you stories of fights and kings, and great nobles, and stories of the poor people too, till the air seemed to move and murmur. She could sing ballads also; which she made as she sat there. And men and women, old and young, came long distances to hear her; for all that she could neither write nor read. And they thought that she could tell the future too.

Thus we came to the church where my fathers lie buried. The famous stone Carver, Ralph of Norwich, has lately wrought a tomb for my grandfather, and it lies almost finished now, above his body; and the candles were flaring upright in the dim church when we entered. We knelt and whispered prayers for his soul; and then my father withdrew in talk with Sir John; and left me to my favourite task of spelling out the names and gazing down at the features of my dead kinsmen and ancestors. As a child I know the stark white figures used to frighten me; especially when I could read that they bore my name; but now that I know that they never move from their backs, and keep their hands crossed always, I pity them; and would fain do some small act that would give them pleasure. It must be something secret, and unthought of – a kiss or a stroke, such as you give a living person.

Memoirs of a Novelist

When Miss Willatt died, in October 1884, it was felt, as her biographer puts it, 'that the world had a right to know more of an admirable though retiring woman.' From the choice of adjectives it is clear that she would not have wished it herself unless one could have convinced her that the world would be the gainer. Perhaps, before she died, Miss Linsett did convince her, for the two volumes of life and letters which that lady issued were produced with the sanction of the family. If one chose to take the introductory phrase and moralise upon it one might ask a page full of interesting questions. What right has the world to know about men and women? What can a biographer tell it? and then, in what sense can it be said that the world profits? The objection to asking these questions is not only that they take so much room, but that they lead to an uncomfortable vagueness of mind. Our conception of the world is that it is a round ball, coloured green where there are fields and forests, wrinkled blue where there is sea, with little peaks pinched up upon it, where there are mountain ranges. When we are asked to imagine the effect of Miss Willatt or another upon this object, the enquiry is respectful but without animation. Yet, if it would be [a] waste of time to begin at the beginning and ask why lives are written, it may not be entirely without interest to ask why the life of Miss Willatt was written, and so to answer the question, who she was.

Miss Linsett, although she cloaked her motives under large phrases, had some stronger impulse at the back of her. When Miss Willatt died, 'after fourteen years of unbroken friendship,' Miss Linsett (if we may theorise) felt uneasy. It seemed to her that if she did not speak at once something would be lost. At the same time no doubt other thoughts pressed upon her; how pleasant mere writing is, how important and unreal people become in print so that it is a credit to have known them; how one's own figure can have justice done to it – but the first feeling was the most genuine. When she looked out of the window as she drove back from the funeral, she felt first that it was strange, and then that it was unseemly, that the people in the street should pass, whistling some of them, and all of them looking indifferent. Then, naturally, she had

63

letters from 'mutual friends'; the editor of a newspaper asked her to write an appreciation in a thousand words; and at last she suggested to Mr William Willatt that someone ought to write his sister's life. He was a solicitor, with no literary experience, but did not object to other people's writing so long as they did not 'break down the barriers'; in short Miss Linsett wrote the book which one may still buy with luck in the Charing Cross Road.

It does not seem, to judge by appearances, that the world has so far made use of its right to know about Miss Willatt. The volumes had got themselves wedged between Sturm 'On the Beauties of Nature'[1] and the 'Veterinary Surgeon's Manual' on the outside shelf, where the gas cracks and the dust grimes them, and people may read so long as the boy lets them. Almost unconsciously one begins to confuse Miss Willatt with her remains and to condescend a little to these shabby, slipshod volumes. One has to repeat that she did live once, and it would be more to the purpose could one see what she was like then than to say (although it is true) that she is slightly ridiculous now.

Who was Miss Willatt then? It is likely that her name is scarcely known to the present generation; it is a mere chance whether one has read any of her books. They lie with the three-volume novels of the sixties and the seventies upon the topmost shelves of little seaside libraries, so that one has to take a ladder to reach them, and a cloth to wipe off the dust.

She was born in 1823, and was the daughter of a solicitor in Wales. They lived for part of the year near Tenby, where her father had his office, and she 'came out' at a ball given by the officers of the local Masonic Guild in the Town Hall, at Pembroke. Although Miss Linsett takes thirty six pages to cover these seventeen years, she hardly mentions them. True, she tells us how the Willatts were descended from a merchant in the sixteenth century, who spelt his name with a V; and how Frances Ann, the novelist, had two uncles, one of whom invented a new way of washing sheep, and the other 'will long be remembered by his parishioners. It is said that even the very poorest wore some piece of mourning . . . in memory of "the good Parson."'' But these are merely biographer's tricks – a way of marking time, during those chill early pages when the hero will neither do nor say anything 'characteristic'. For some reason we are told little of Mrs Willatt, daughter of Mr Josiah Bond, a respected linendraper, who, at a later date seems to have bought 'a place'. She died when her only daughter was sixteen; there were two sons, Frederic, who died before his sister, and William, the solicitor, who survived her. It is perhaps worth while to say these things, although they are ugly and no one will remember them, because they help us somehow to believe in the otherwise visionary youth of our heroine. When Miss Linsett is forced to talk of her and not of her uncles, this is the result. 'Frances, thus, at the age of sixteen, was left without a mother's care. We can imagine how the lonely girl, for even the loving companionship of father and brothers could not fill *that* place [but we know nothing about Mrs Willatt][2] sought for consolation in solitude, and, wandering among the heaths and dunes where the castles of an earlier age are left to crumble into ruins, &c &c.' Mr William Willatt's contribution to his sister's biography is surely more to the purpose. 'My sister was a shy awkward girl, much given to "mooning." It was a standing joke in the family that she had once walked into the pigsty, mistaking it for the wash house, and had not discovered her whereabouts until Grunter (the old black sow) ate her book out of her hands. With reference to her studious habits, I should say that these were always very marked. . . . I may mention the fact that any act of disobedience was most effectually punished by the confiscation of her bedroom candle, by the light of which it was her habit to read in bed. I well remember, as a small boy, the look of my sister's figure as she leant out of bed, book in hand, so as to get the benefit of the chink of light which came through the door from the other room where our nurse was sewing. In this way she read the whole of Bright's history of the Church,[3] always a favourite book with her. I am afraid that we did not always treat her studies with respect. . . . She was not generally considered handsome, although she had (at the date of which I speak) a nearly perfect arm.' With respect to this last remark, an important one, we can consult the likeness which some local artist made of Miss Willatt at the age of seventeen. It needs no insight to affirm that it is not a face that would have found favour in the Pembroke Town Hall in 1840. A heavy plait of hair, (which the artist has made to shine) coils round the brow; she has large eyes, but they are slightly prominent; the lips are full, without being sensuous; the one feature which, when comparing her face with the faces of her friends, generally gave her courage, is the nose; perhaps someone had said in her hearing that it was a fine nose – a bold nose for a woman to have; at any rate her portraits, with one exception, are in profile.

We can imagine (to steal Miss Linsett's useful phrase) that this 'shy awkward girl much given to mooning' who walked in to pigsties, and read history instead of fiction, did not enjoy her first ball. Her brother's words evidently sum up what was in the air as they drove home. She found some angle in the great ball room where she could half hide her large figure, and there she waited to be asked to dance. She fixed her eyes upon the festoons which draped the city arms and tried to fancy that she sat on a rock with the bees humming round her; she bethought her how no one in that room perhaps knew as well as she did what was meant by the Oath of Uniformity; then she thought how in sixty years, or less perhaps, the worm would feed upon them all; then she wondered whether somehow before that day, every man now dancing there would not have reason to respect her. She wrote to Miss Ellen Buckle, to whom all her early letters are addressed, that 'disappointment is mixed with our pleasures, wisely enough, so that we may not forget &c &c.' And yet, it is likely that among all that company who danced in the Town Hall and are now fed on by the worm, Miss Willatt would have been the best to talk to, even if one did not wish to dance with her. Her face is heavy, but it is intelligent.

This impression is on the whole borne out by her letters. 'It is now ten o'clock, and I have come up to bed; but I shall write to you first. . . . It has been a heavy but I trust not an unprofitable day. . . . Ah, my dearest friend, for you *are* dearest, how should I bear the secrets of my soul and the weight of what the poet calls this "unintelligible world"[4] without you to impart them to?' One must brush aside a great deal of tarnished compliment, and then one gets a little further into Miss Willatt's mind. Until she was eighteen or so she had not realised that she had any relationship to the world; with self-consciousness came the need of settling the matter, and, consequently, a terrible depression. Without more knowledge than Miss Willatt gives us, we can only guess how she came by her conceptions of human nature and right and wrong. From histories she got a general notion of pride, avarice and bigotry; in the Waverley novels[5] she read about love. These ideas vaguely troubled her. Lent religious works by Miss Buckle, she learnt, with relief, how one may escape the world, and at the same time earn everlasting joy. There was never to be a greater saint than she was, by the simple device of saying, before she spoke or acted, is this right? The world then was very hideous, for the uglier she found it the more virtuous she became. 'Death was in that house, and Hell yawned before it,' she wrote, having passed, one evening, a room with crimson windows and heard the voices of dancers within; but the sensations with which she wrote were not entirely painful. Nevertheless her seriousness only half protected her, and left space for innumerable torments. 'Am I the only blot upon the face of nature?' she asked in May, 1841. 'The birds are carolling outside my windows, the very insects are putting off the winter's dross.' She alone was 'heavy as unleavened bread'. A terrible self-consciousness possessed her, and she writes to Miss Buckle as though she watched her shadow trembling over the entire world, beneath the critical eyes of the angels. It was humped and crooked and swollen with evil, and it taxed the powers of both the young women to put it straight. 'What would I not give to *help* you?' writes Miss Buckle. Our difficulty as we read now is to understand what their aim was; for it is clear that they imagined a state in which the soul lay tranquil and in bliss, and that if one could reach it one was perfect. Was it beauty that they were feeling for? As, at present, neither of them had any interest except in virtue, it is possible that aesthetic pleasure disguised had part in their religion. When they lay in these trances they were at any rate out of their surroundings. But the only pleasure that they allowed themselves to feel was the pleasure of submission.

Here, unfortunately, we come to an abyss. Ellen Buckle, as was likely, for she was less disgusted with the world than her friend and more capable of shifting her burdens on to human shoulders, married an engineer by whom her doubts were set at rest for ever. At the same time Frances had a strange experience of her own, which is concealed by Miss Linsett, in the most provoking manner conceivable, in the following passage. 'No one who has read the book (*Life's Crucifix*) can doubt that the heart which conceived the sorrows of Ethel Eden in her unhappy attachment had felt some of the pangs so feelingly described *itself*; so much we may say, more we may not.' The most interesting event in Miss Willatt's life, owing to the nervous prudery and the dreary literary conventions of her friend, is thus a blank. Naturally, one believes that she loved, hoped and saw her hopes extinguished, but what happened and what she felt we must guess. Her letters at this time are incurably dull, but that is partly because the word love and whole passages polluted by it, have shrunk into asterisks. There is no more talk of unworthiness and 'O might I find a retreat from the world I would then consider myself blessed'; death disappears altogether; she seems to have entered upon the second stage of her development, when, theories absorbed or brushed aside, she sought only to preserve herself. Her father's death, in 1855, is made to end a chapter, and her removal to London, where she kept house for her brothers in a Bloomsbury Square begins the next one.

At this point we can no longer disregard what has been hinted several times; it is clear that one must abandon Miss Linsett altogether, or take the greatest liberties with her text. What with 'a short sketch of the history of Bloomsbury may not be amiss,' accounts of charitable societies and their heroes, a chapter upon Royal visits to the hospital, praise of Florence Nightingale in the Crimea, we see only a wax work as it were of Miss Willatt preserved under glass. One is just on the point of shutting up the book for ever, when a reflection bids one pause; the whole affair is, after all, extraordinarily odd. It seems incredible that human beings should think that these things are true of each other, and if not[,] that they should take the trouble to say them. 'She was justly esteemed for her benevolence, and her strict uprightness of character, which however never brought upon her the reproach of hardness of heart. . . . She was fond of children animals and the spring, and Wordsworth was among her 'bedside poets' . . . Although she felt his (her father's) death with the tenderness of a devoted daughter, she did not give way to useless and therefore selfish repining. . . . The poor, it might be said, took the place to her of her own children.' To pick out such phrases is an easy way of satirising them, but the steady drone of the book in which they are imbedded makes satire an afterthought; it is the fact that Miss Linsett believed these things and not the absurdity of them that dismays one. She believed at any rate that one should admire such virtues and attribute them to one's friends both for their sake and for one's own; to read her therefore is to leave the world in daylight, and to enter a closed room, hung with claret coloured plush, and illustrated with texts. It would be interesting to discover what prompted this curious view of human life, but it is hard enough to rid Miss Willatt of her friend's disguises without enquiring where she found them. Happily there are signs that Miss Willatt was not what she seemed. They creep out in the notes, in her letters, and most clearly in her portraits. The sight of that large selfish face, with the capable forehead and the surly but intelligent eyes, discredits all the platitudes on the opposite page; she looks quite capable of having deceived Miss Linsett.

When her father died (she had always disliked him) her spirits rose, and she determined to find scope for the 'great powers of which I am conscious' in London. Living in a poor neighbourhood, the obvious profession for a woman in those days was to do good; and Miss Willatt devoted herself at first with exemplary vigour. Because she was unmarried she set herself to represent the unsentimental side of the community; if other women brought children into the world, she would do something for their health. She was in the habit of checking her spiritual progress, and casting up her accounts in the blank pages at the end of her diary, where one notes one's weight, and height and the number of one's watch; and she has often to rebuke her 'unstable spirit that is always seeking to distract me, and asking Whither?' Perhaps therefore she was not so well content with her philanthropy as Miss Linsett would have us believe. 'Do I know what happiness is?' she asks in 1859, with rare candour, and answers after thinking it over, 'No.' To imagine her then, as the sleek sober woman that her friend paints her, doing good wearily but with steadfast faith, is quite untrue; on the contrary she was a restless and discontented woman, who sought her own happiness rather than other people's. It was then that she bethought her of literature, taking the pen in hand, at the age of thirty-six, more to justify her complicated spiritual state than to say what must be said. It is clear that her state was complicated, even if we hesitate, remote as we are, to define it. She found at any rate that she had 'no vocation' for philanthropy, and told the Rev. R. S. Rogers so in an interview 'that was painful and agitating to us both' on February the 14th, 1856. But, in owning that, she admitted that she was without many virtues, and it was necessary to prove, to herself at least, that she had others. After all, merely to sit with your eyes open fills the brain, and perhaps in emptying it, one may come across something illuminating. George Eliot and Charlotte Brontë between them must share the parentage of many novels at this period, for they disclosed the secret that the precious stuff of which books are made lies all about one, in drawing-rooms and kitchens where women live, and accumulates with every tick of the clock.

Miss Willatt adopted the theory that no training is necessary, but thought it indecent to describe what she had seen, so that instead of a portrait of her brothers (and one had led a very queer life) or a memory of her father (for which we should have been grateful) she invented Arabian lovers and set them on the banks of the Orinoco. She made them live in an ideal community, for she enjoyed framing laws, and the scenery was tropical, because one gets one's effects quicker there than in England. She could write pages about 'mountains that looked like ramparts of cloud, save for the deep blue ravines that cleft their sides, and the diamond cascades that went leaping and flashing, now golden, now purple, as they entered the shade of the pine forests and passed out into the sun, to lose themselves in a myriad of streams upon the flower enamelled pasturage at their base.' But when she had to face her lovers, and the talk of the women in the tents at sundown when the goats came in to be milked, and the wisdom of 'that sage old man who had witnessed too many births and deaths to rejoice at the one or lament at the other' then she stammered and blushed perceptibly. She could not say 'I love you,' but used 'thee' and 'thou,' which, with their indirectness, seemed to hint that she was not committing herself. The same self-consciousness made it impossible for her to think herself the Arab or his bride, or any one indeed except the portentous voice that linked the dialogues, and explained how the same temptations assail us under the tropical stars and beneath the umbrageous elms of England.

For these reasons the book is now scarcely to be read through, and Miss Willatt also had scruples about writing well. There was something shifty, she thought, in choosing one's expressions; the straightforward way to write was the best, speaking out everything in one's mind, like a child at its mother's knee, and trusting that, as a reward, some meaning would be included. Nevertheless her book went into two editions, one critic likening it to the novels of George Eliot, save that the tone was 'more satisfactory', and another proclaiming that it was 'the work of Miss Martineau[6] or the Devil.'

If Miss Linsett were still alive (she died in Australia however, some years ago) one would like to ask her upon what system she cut her friend's life into chapters. They seem, when possible, to depend upon changes of address, and confirm us in our belief that Miss Linsett had no other guide to Miss Willatt's character. The great change came, surely, after the publication of *Lindamara: a Fantasy*. When Miss Willatt had her memorable 'scene' with Mr Rogers she was so much agitated that she walked twice round Bedford Square, with the tears sticking her veil to her face. It seemed to her that all this talk of philanthropy was great nonsense, and gave one no chance of 'an individual life' as she called it. She had thoughts of emigrating, and founding a society, in which she saw herself, by the time she had finished her second round, with white hair, reading wisdom from a book to a circle of industrious disciples, who were very like the people she knew, but called her by a word that is a euphemism for 'Mother.' There are passages in *Lindamara* which hint at it, and allude covertly to Mr Rogers – 'the man in whom wisdom was not.' But she was indolent, and praise made her plausible; it came from the wrong people. The best of her writing – for we have dipped into several books, and the results seem to square with our theory – was done to justify herself, but, having accomplished that, she went on to prophesy for others, dwelling in vague regions with great damage to her system. She grew enormously stout, 'a symptom of disease' says Miss Linsett, who loved that mournful subject – a symptom to us of tea parties in her hot little drawing-room with the spotted wall paper, and of intimate conversations about 'the Soul'. 'The Soul' became her province, and she deserted the Southern plains for a strange country draped in eternal twilight, where there are qualities without bodies. Thus, Miss Linsett being at the time in great despondency about life, 'the death of an adored parent having deprived me of all my earthly hope', she went to see Miss Willatt, and left her flushed and tremulous, but convinced that she knew a secret that explained everything. Miss Willatt was far too clever to believe that anyone could answer anything; but the sight of these queer little trembling women, who looked up at her, prepared for beating or caress, like spaniels, appealed to a mass of emotions, and they were not all of them bad. What such women wanted, she saw, was to be told that they were parts of a whole, as a fly in a milk jug seeks the support of a spoon. She knew further that one must have a motive in order to work; she was strong enough to convince; and power, which should have been hers as a mother, was dear to her even when it came by illegitimate means. Another gift was hers, without which the rest had been useless; she could take flights into obscurity. After telling people what to do, she gave them, in a whisper at first, later in a voice that lapsed and quavered, some mystic reasons why. She could only discover them by peeping, as it were, over the rim of the world; and to begin with she tried honestly to say no more than she saw there. The present state, where one is bound down, a target for pigmy arrows, seemed to her for the most part dull, and sometimes intolerable. Some draught, vague and sweet as chloroform, which confused outlines and made daily life dance before the eyes with hints of a vista beyond, was what they needed, and nature had fitted her to give it them. 'Life was a hard school,' she said, 'How could one bear it unless –' and then there came a rhapsody about trees and flowers and fishes in the deep, and an eternal harmony, with her head back, and her eyes half shut, to see better. 'We felt often that we had a Sibyl among us,' writes Miss Haig; and if Sibyls are only half inspired, conscious of the folly of their disciples, sorry for them, very vain of their applause and much muddled in their own brains all at once, then Miss Willatt was a Sibyl too. But the most striking part of the picture is the unhappy view that it gives of the spiritual state of Bloomsbury at this period – when Miss Willatt brooded in Woburn Square like some gorged spider at the centre of her web, and all along the filaments unhappy women came running, slight hen-like figures, frightened by the sun and the carts and the dreadful world, and longing to hide themselves from the entire panorama in the shade of Miss Willatt's skirts. The Andrews, the Spaldings, young Mr Charles Jenkinson 'who has since left us', old Lady Battersby, who suffered from the gout, Miss Cecily Haig, Ebenezer Umphelby who knew more about beetles than any one in Europe – all these people who dropped into tea and had Sunday supper and conversation afterwards, come to life again, and tempt us almost intolerably to know more about them. What did they look like, and do, what did they want from Miss Willatt and what did they think of her, in private? – but we shall never know, or hear of them again. They have been rolled into the earth irrecoverably.

Indeed there is only space left to give the pith of that last long chapter, which Miss Linsett called 'Fulfilment'. Certainly, it is one of the strangest. Miss Linsett who was powerfully fascinated by the idea of death, coos and preens herself in his presence and can hardly bring herself to make an end. It is easier to write about death, which is common, than about a single life; there are general statements which one likes to use once in a way for oneself, and there is something in saying good-bye to a person which leads to smooth manners and pleasant sensations. Moreover, Miss Linsett had a natural distrust of life, which was boisterous and commonplace, and had never treated her too well, and took every opportunity of proving that human beings die, as though she snubbed some ill-mannered schoolboy. If one wished it thus, one could give more details of those last months of Miss Willatt's life than of any that have gone before. We know precisely what she died of. The narrative slackens to a funeral pace and every word of it is relished; but in truth, it amounts to little more than this. Miss Willatt had suffered from an internal complaint for some years, but mentioned it only to her intimate friends. Then, in the autumn of 1884, she caught a chill. 'It was the beginning of the end, and from that date we had little hope.' They told her, once, that she was dying, but she 'seemed absorbed in a mat which she was working for her nephew.' When she took to her bed she did not ask to see any one, save her old servant Emma Grice who had been with her for thirty years. At length, on the night of the 18th of October, 'a stormy autumn night, with flying clouds and gusts of rain', Miss Linsett was summoned to say good-bye. Miss Willatt was lying on her back, with her eyes shut, and her head which was half in shadow looked 'very grand'. Miss Willatt lay thus all night long without speaking or turning or opening her eyes. Once she raised her left hand, 'upon which she wore her mother's wedding ring', and let it fall again; they expected something more, but not knowing what she wanted they did nothing, and half an hour later the counterpane lay still, and they crept from their corners, seeing that she was dead.

After reading this scene, with its accompaniment of inappropriate detail, its random flourishes whipping up a climax – how she changed colour, and they rubbed her forehead with eau-de-cologne, how Mr Sully called and went away again, how creepers tapped on the window, how the room grew pale as the dawn rose, how sparrows twittered and carts began to rattle through the square to market – one sees that Miss Linsett liked death because it gave her an emotion, and made her feel things for the time as though they meant something. For the moment she loved Miss Willatt; Miss Willatt's death the moment after made her even happy. It was an end undisturbed by the chance of a fresh beginning. But afterwards, when she went home and had her breakfast, she felt lonely, for they had been in the habit of going to Kew Gardens together on Sundays.

1917–1921

The Mark on the Wall

Perhaps it was the middle of January in the present year that I first looked up and saw the mark on the wall. In order to fix a date it is necessary to remember what one saw. So now I think of the fire; the steady film of yellow light upon the page of my book; the three chrysanthemums in the round glass bowl on the mantelpiece. Yes, it must have been the winter time, and we had just finished our tea, for I remember that I was smoking a cigarette when I looked up and saw the mark on the wall for the first time. I looked up through the smoke of my cigarette and my eye lodged for a moment upon the burning coals, and that old fancy of the crimson flag flapping from the castle tower came into my mind, and I thought of the cavalcade of red knights riding up the side of the black rock. Rather to my relief the sight of the mark interrupted the fancy, for it is an old fancy, an automatic fancy, made as a child perhaps. The mark was a small round mark, black upon the white wall, about six or seven inches above the mantelpiece.

How readily our thoughts swarm upon a new object, lifting it a little way, as ants carry a blade of straw so feverishly, and then leave it. . . . If that mark was made by a nail, it can't have been for a picture, it must have been for a miniature – the miniature of a lady with white powdered curls, powder-dusted cheeks, and lips like red carnations. A fraud of course, for the people who had this house before us would have chosen pictures in that way – an old picture for an old room. That is the sort of people they were – very interesting people, and I think of them so often, in such queer places, because one will never see them again, never know what happened next. They wanted to leave this house because they wanted to change their style of furniture, so he said, and he was in process of saying that in his opinion art should have ideas behind it when we were torn asunder, as one is torn from the old lady about to pour out tea and the young man about to hit the tennis ball in the back garden of the suburban villa as one rushes past in the train.

But as for that mark, I'm not sure about it; I don't believe it was made by a nail after all; it's too big, too round, for that. I might get up, but if I got up and looked at it, ten to one I shouldn't be able to say for certain; because once a thing's done, no one ever knows how it happened. Oh! dear me, the mystery of life! The inaccuracy of thought! The ignorance of humanity! To show how very little control of our possessions we have – what an accidental affair this living is after all our civilisation – let me just count over a few of the things lost in our lifetime, beginning, for that seems always the most mysterious of losses – what cat would gnaw, what rat would nibble – three pale blue canisters of book-binding tools? Then there were the bird cages, the iron hoops, the steel skates, the Queen Anne coal-scuttle, the bagatelle board, the hand organ – all gone, and jewels too. Opals and emeralds, they lie about the roots of turnips. What a scraping paring affair it is to be sure! The wonder is that I've any clothes on my back, that I sit surrounded by solid furniture at this moment. Why, if one wants to compare life to anything, one must liken it to being blown through the Tube at fifty miles an hour – landing at the other end without a single hairpin in one's hair! Shot out at the feet of God entirely naked! Tumbling head over heels in the asphodel meadows like brown paper parcels pitched down a shoot in the post office! With one's hair flying back like the tail of a racehorse. Yes, that seems to express the rapidity of life, the perpetual waste and repair; all so casual, all so haphazard. . . .

But after life. The slow pulling down of thick green stalks so that the cup of the flower, as it turns over, deluges one with purple and red light. Why, after all, should one not be born there as one is born here, helpless, speechless, unable to focus one's eyesight, groping at the roots of the grass, at the toes of the Giants? As for saying which are trees, and which are men and women, or whether there are such things, that one won't be in a condition to do for fifty years or so. There will be nothing but spaces of light and dark, intersected by thick stalks, and rather higher up perhaps, rose-shaped blots of an indistinct colour – dim pinks and blues – which will, as time goes on, become more definite, become – I don't know what. . . .

And yet the mark on the wall is not a hole at all. It may even be caused by some round black substance, such as a small rose leaf, left over from the summer, and I, not being a very vigilant housekeeper – look at the dust on the mantelpiece, for example, the dust which, so they say, buried Troy three times over, only fragments of pots utterly refusing annihilation, as one can believe.[1]

The tree outside the window taps very gently on the pane. . . . I want to think quietly, calmly, spaciously, never to be interrupted, never to have to rise from my chair, to slip easily from one thing to another, without any sense of hostility, or obstacle. I want to sink deeper and deeper, away from the surface, with its hard separate facts. To steady myself, let me catch hold of the first idea that passes. . . . Shakespeare. . . . Well, he will do as well as another. A man who sat himself solidly in an arm-chair, and looked into the fire, so – A shower of ideas fell perpetually from some very high Heaven down through his mind. He leant his forehead on his hand, and people, looking in through the open door – for this scene is supposed to take place on a summer's evening – But how dull this is, this historical fiction! It doesn't interest me at all. I wish I could hit upon a pleasant track of thought, a track indirectly reflecting credit upon myself, for those are the pleasantest thoughts, and very frequent even in the minds of modest mouse-coloured people, who believe genuinely that they dislike to hear their own praises. They are not thoughts directly praising oneself; that is the beauty of them; they are thoughts like this:

'And then I came into the room. They were discussing botany. I said how I'd seen a flower growing on a dust heap on the site of an old house in Kingsway. The seed, I said, must have been sown in the reign of Charles the First. What flowers grew in the reign of Charles the First?' I asked – (but I don't remember the answer). Tall flowers with purple tassels to them perhaps. And so it goes on. All the time I'm dressing up the figure of myself in my own mind, lovingly, stealthily, not openly adoring it, for if I did that, I should catch myself out, and stretch my hand at once for a book in self-protection. Indeed, it is curious how instinctively one protects the image of oneself from idolatry or any other handling that could make it ridiculous, or too unlike the original to be believed in any longer. Or is it not so very curious after all? It is a matter of great importance. Suppose the looking-glass smashes, the image disappears, and the romantic figure with the green of forest depths all about it is there no longer, but only that shell of a person which is seen by other people – what an airless, shallow, bald, prominent world it becomes! A world not to be lived in. As we face each other in omnibuses and underground railways we are looking into the mirror; that accounts for the vagueness, the gleam of glassiness, in our eyes. And the novelists in future will realise more and more the importance of these reflections, for of course there is not one reflection but an almost infinite number; those are the depths they will explore, those the phantoms they will pursue, leaving the description of reality more and more out of their stories, taking a knowledge of it for granted, as the Greeks did and Shakespeare perhaps – but these generalisations are very worthless. The military sound of the word is enough. It recalls leading articles, cabinet ministers – a whole class of things indeed which as a child one thought the thing itself, the standard thing, the real thing, from which one could not depart save at the risk of nameless damnation. Generalisations bring back somehow Sunday in London, Sunday afternoon walks, Sunday luncheons, and also ways of speaking of the dead, clothes, and habits – like the habit of sitting all together in one room until a certain hour, although nobody liked it. There was a rule for everything. The rule for tablecloths at that particular period was that they should be made of tapestry with little yellow compartments marked upon them, such as you may see in photographs of the carpets in the corridors of the royal palaces. Tablecloths of a different kind were not real tablecloths. How shocking, and yet how wonderful it was to discover that these real things, Sunday luncheons, Sunday walks, country houses, and tablecloths were not entirely real, were indeed half phantoms, and the damnation which visited the disbeliever in them was only a sense of illegitimate freedom. What now takes the place of those things I wonder, those real standard things? Men perhaps, should you be a woman; the masculine point of view which governs our lives, which sets the standard, which establishes Whitaker's Table of Precedency,[2] which has become, I suppose, since the war half a phantom to many men and women, which soon, one may hope, will be laughed into the dustbin where the phantoms go, the mahogany sideboards and the Landseer prints,[3] Gods and Devils, Hell and so forth, leaving us all with an intoxicating sense of illegitimate freedom – if freedom exists. . . .

In certain lights that mark on the wall seems actually to project from the wall. Nor is it entirely circular. I cannot be sure, but it seems to cast a perceptible shadow, suggesting that if I ran my finger down that strip of the wall it would, at a certain point, mount and descend a small tumulus, a smooth tumulus like those barrows on the South Downs which are, they say, either tombs or camps. Of the two I should prefer them to be tombs, desiring melancholy like most English people, and finding it natural at the end of a walk to think of the bones stretched beneath the turf. . . . There must be some book about it. Some antiquary must have dug up those bones and given them a name. . . . What sort of a man is an antiquary, I wonder? Retired Colonels for the most part, I daresay, leading parties of aged labourers to the top here, examining clods of earth and stone, and getting into correspondence with the neighbouring clergy, which, being opened at breakfast time, gives them a feeling of importance, and the comparison of arrowheads necessitates cross-country journeys to the country towns, an agreeable necessity both to them and to their elderly wives, who wish to make plum jam or to clean out the study, and have every reason for keeping that great question of the camp or the tomb in perpetual suspension, while the Colonel himself feels agreeably philosophic in accumulating evidence on both sides of the question. It is true that he does finally incline to believe in the camp; and, being opposed, indites a pamphlet which he is about to read at the quarterly meeting of the local society when a stroke lays him low, and his last conscious thoughts are not of wife or child, but of the camp and that arrowhead there, which is now in the case at the local museum, together with the foot of a Chinese murderess, a handful of Elizabethan nails, a great many Tudor clay pipes, a piece of Roman pottery, and the wine-glass that Nelson drank out of – proving I really don't know what.

No, no, nothing is proved, nothing is known. And if I were to get up at this very moment and ascertain that the mark on the wall is really – what shall I say? – the head of a gigantic old nail, driven in two hundred years ago, which has now, owing to the patient attrition of many generations of housemaids, revealed its head above the coat of paint, and is taking its first view of modern life in the sight of a white-walled fire-lit room, what should I gain? Knowledge? Matter for further speculation? I can think sitting still as well as standing up. And what is knowledge? What are our learned men save the descendants of witches and hermits who crouched in caves and in woods brewing herbs, interrogating shrew-mice and writing down the language of the stars? And the less we honour them as our superstitions dwindle and our respect for beauty and health of mind increases ... Yes, one could imagine a very pleasant world. A quiet spacious world, with the flowers so red and blue in the open fields. A world without professors or specialists or house-keepers with the profiles of policemen, a world which one could slice with one's thought as a fish slices the water with his fin, grazing the stems of the water-lilies, hanging suspended over nests of white sea eggs. . . . How peaceful it is down here, rooted in the centre of the world and gazing up through the grey waters, with their sudden gleams of light, and their reflections – if it were not for Whitaker's Almanack – if it were not for the Table of Precedency!

I must jump up and see for myself what that mark on the wall really is – a nail, a rose-leaf, a crack in the wood?

Here is Nature once more at her old game of self-preservation. This train of thought, she perceives, is threatening mere waste of energy, even some collision with reality, for who will ever be able to lift a finger against Whitaker's Table of Precedency? The Archbishop of Canterbury is followed by the Lord High Chancellor; the Lord High Chancellor is followed by the Archbishop of York. Everybody follows somebody, such is the philosophy of Whitaker; and the great thing is to know who follows whom. Whitaker knows, and let that, so Nature counsels, comfort you, instead of enraging you; and if you can't be comforted, if you must shatter this hour of peace, think of the mark on the wall.

I understand Nature's game – her prompting to take action as a way of ending any thought that threatens to excite or to pain. Hence, I suppose, comes our slight contempt for men of action – men, we assume, who don't think. Still, there's no harm in putting a full stop to one's disagreeable thoughts by looking at a mark on the wall.

Indeed, now that I have fixed my eyes upon it, I feel that I have grasped a plank in the sea; I feel a satisfying sense of reality which at once turns the two Archbishops and the Lord High Chancellor to the shadows of shades. Here is something definite, something real. Thus, waking from a midnight dream of horror, one hastily turns on the light and lies quiescent, worshipping the chest of drawers, worshipping solidity, worshipping reality, worshipping the impersonal world which is proof of some existence other than ours. That is what one wants to be sure of. . . . Wood is a pleasant thing to think about. It comes from a tree; and trees grow, and we don't know how they grow. For years and years they grow, without paying any attention to us, in meadows, in forests, and by the side of rivers – all things one likes to think about. The cows swish their tails beneath them on hot afternoons; they paint rivers so green that when a moorhen dives one expects to see its feathers all green when it comes up again. I like to think of the fish balanced against the stream like flags blown out; and of water-beetles slowly raising domes of mud upon the bed of the river. I like to think of the tree itself: first the close dry sensation of being wood; then the grinding of the storm; then the slow, delicious ooze of sap. I like to think of it, too, on winter's nights standing in the empty field with all leaves close-furled, nothing tender exposed to the iron bullets of the moon, a naked mast upon an earth that goes tumbling, tumbling all night long. The song of birds must sound very loud and strange in June; and how cold the feet of insects must feel upon it, as they make laborious progresses up the creases of the bark, or sun themselves upon the thin green awning of the leaves, and look straight in front of them with diamond-cut red eyes. . . . One by one the fibres snap beneath the immense cold pressure of the earth, then the last storm comes and, falling, the highest branches drive deep into the ground again. Even so, life isn't done with; there are a million patient, watchful lives still for a tree, all over the world, in bedrooms, in ships, on the pavement, lining rooms, where men and women sit after tea, smoking cigarettes. It is full of peaceful thoughts, happy thoughts, this tree. I should like to take each one separately – but something is getting in the way. . . . Where was I? What has it all been about? A tree? A river? The Downs? Whitaker's Almanack? The fields of asphodel? I can't remember a thing. Everything's moving, falling, slipping, vanishing. . . . There is a vast upheaval of matter. Someone is standing over me and saying –

'I'm going out to buy a newspaper.'

'Yes?'

'Though it's no good buying newspapers. . . . Nothing ever happens. Curse this war; God damn this war! . . . All the same, I don't see why we should have a snail on our wall.'

Ah, the mark on the wall! It was a snail.

Kew Gardens

From the oval-shaped flower-bed there rose perhaps a hundred stalks spreading into heart-shaped or tongue-shaped leaves half way up and unfurling at the tip red or blue or yellow petals marked with spots of colour raised upon the surface; and from the red, blue or yellow gloom of the throat emerged a straight bar, rough with gold dust and slightly clubbed at the end. The petals were voluminous enough to be stirred by the summer breeze, and when they moved, the red, blue and yellow lights passed one over the other, staining an inch of the brown earth beneath with a spot of the most intricate colour. The light fell either upon the smooth grey back of a pebble, or the shell of a snail with its brown circular veins, or, falling into a raindrop, it expanded with such intensity of red, blue and yellow the thin walls of water that one expected them to burst and disappear. Instead, the drop was left in a second silver grey once more, and the light now settled upon the flesh of a leaf, revealing the branching thread of fibre beneath the surface, and again it moved on and spread its illumination in the vast green spaces beneath the dome of the heart-shaped and tongue-shaped leaves. Then the breeze stirred rather more briskly overhead and the colour was flashed into the air above, into the eyes of the men and women who walk in Kew Gardens in July.

The figures of these men and women straggled past the flower-bed with a curiously irregular movement not unlike that of the white and blue butterflies who crossed the turf in zig-zag flights from bed to bed. The man was about six inches in front of the woman, strolling carelessly, while she bore on with greater purpose, only turning her head now and then to see that the children were not too far behind. The man kept this distance in front of the woman purposely, though perhaps unconsciously, for he wanted to go on with his thoughts.

'Fifteen years ago I came here with Lily,' he thought. 'We sat somewhere over there by a lake, and I begged her to marry me all through the hot afternoon. How the dragon-fly kept circling round us: how clearly I see the dragon-fly and her shoe with the square silver buckle at the toe. All the time I spoke I saw her shoe and when it moved impatiently I knew without looking up what she was going to say: the whole of her seemed to be in her shoe. And my love, my desire, were in the dragon-fly; for some reason I thought that if it settled there, on that leaf, the broad one with the red flower in the middle of it, if the dragon-fly settled on the leaf she would say "Yes" at once. But the dragon-fly went round and round: it never settled anywhere – of course not, happily not, or I shouldn't be walking here with Eleanor and the children – Tell me, Eleanor, d'you ever think of the past?'

'Why do you ask, Simon?'

'Because I've been thinking of the past. I've been thinking of Lily, the woman I might have married ... Well, why are you silent? Do you mind my thinking of the past?'

'Why should I mind, Simon? Doesn't one always think of the past, in a garden with men and women lying under the trees? Aren't they one's past, all that remains of it, those men and women, those ghosts lying under the trees, ... one's happiness, one's reality?'

'For me, a square silver shoe-buckle and a dragon-fly –'

'For me, a kiss. Imagine six little girls sitting before their easels twenty years ago, down by the side of a lake, painting the water-lilies, the first red water-lilies I'd ever seen. And suddenly a kiss, there on the back of my neck. And my hand shook all the afternoon so that I couldn't paint. I took out my watch and marked the hour when I would allow myself to think of the kiss for five minutes only – it was so precious – the kiss of an old grey-haired woman with a wart on her nose, the mother of all my kisses all my life. Come Caroline, come Hubert.'

They walked on past the flower-bed, now walking four abreast, and soon diminished in size among the trees and looked half transparent as the sunlight and shade swam over their backs in large trembling irregular patches.

In the oval flower-bed the snail, whose shell had been stained red, blue and yellow for the space of two minutes or so, now appeared to be moving very slightly in its shell, and next began to labour over the crumbs of loose earth which broke away and rolled down as it passed over them. It appeared to have a definite goal in front of it, differing in this respect from the singular high-stepping angular green insect who attempted to cross in front of it, and waited for a second with its antennae trembling as if in deliberation, and then stepped off as rapidly and strangely in the opposite direction. Brown cliffs with deep green lakes in the hollows, flat blade-like trees that waved from root to tip, round boulders of grey stone, vast crumpled surfaces of a thin crackling texture – all these objects lay across the snail's progress between one stalk and another to his goal. Before he had decided whether to circumvent the arched tent of a dead leaf or to breast it there came past the bed the feet of other human beings.

This time they were both men. The younger of the two wore an expression of perhaps unnatural calm; he raised his eyes and fixed them very steadily in front of him while his companion spoke, and directly his companion had done speaking he looked on the ground again and sometimes opened his lips only after a long pause and sometimes did not open them at all. The elder man had a curiously uneven and shaky method of walking, jerking his hand forward and throwing up his head abruptly, rather in the manner of an impatient carriage horse tired of waiting outside a house; but in the man these gestures were irresolute and pointless. He talked almost incessantly; he smiled to himself and again began to talk, as if the smile had been an answer. He was talking about spirits – the spirits of the dead, who, according to him, were even now telling him all sorts of odd things about their experiences in Heaven.

'Heaven was known to the ancients as Thessaly, William, and now, with this war, the spirit matter is rolling between the hills like thunder.' He paused, seemed to listen, smiled, jerked his head and continued: –

'You have a small electric battery and a piece of rubber to insulate the wire – isolate? – insulate? – well, we'll skip the details, no good going into details that wouldn't be understood – and in short the little machine stands in any convenient position by the head of the bed, we will say, on a neat mahogany stand. All arrangements being properly fixed by workmen under my direction, the widow applies her ear and summons the spirit by sign as agreed. Women! Widows! Women in black –'

Here he seemed to have caught sight of a woman's dress in the distance, which in the shade looked a purple black. He took off his hat, placed his hand upon his heart, and hurried towards her muttering and gesticulating feverishly. But William caught him by the sleeve and touched a flower with the tip of his walking-stick in order to divert the old man's attention. After looking at it for a moment in some confusion the old man bent his ear to it and seemed to answer a voice speaking from it, for he began talking about the forests of Uruguay which he had visited hundreds of years ago in company with the most beautiful young woman in Europe. He could be heard murmuring about forests of Uruguay blanketed with the wax petals of tropical roses, nightingales, sea beaches, mermaids and women drowned at sea, as he suffered himself to be moved on by William, upon whose face the look of stoical patience grew slowly deeper and deeper.

Following his steps so closely as to be slightly puzzled by his gestures came two elderly women of the lower middle class, one stout and ponderous, the other rosy-cheeked and nimble. Like most people of their station they were frankly fascinated by any signs of eccentricity betokening a disordered brain, especially in the well-to-do; but they were too far off to be certain whether the gestures were merely eccentric or genuinely mad. After they had scrutinised the old man's back in silence for a moment and given each other a queer, sly look, they went on energetically piecing together their very complicated dialogue:

'Nell, Bert, Lot, Cess, Phil, Pa, he says, I says, she says, I says, I says, I says –'

'My Bert, Sis, Bill, Grandad, the old man, sugar,
     Sugar, flour, kippers, greens
     Sugar, sugar, sugar.'[1]

The ponderous woman looked through the pattern of falling words at the flowers standing cool, firm and upright in the earth, with a curious expression. She saw them as a sleeper waking from a heavy sleep sees a brass candlestick reflecting the light in an unfamiliar way, and closes his eyes and opens them, and seeing the brass candlestick again, finally starts broad awake and stares at the candlestick with all his powers. So the heavy woman came to a standstill opposite the oval-shaped flower-bed, and ceased even to pretend to listen to what the other woman was saying. She stood there letting the words fall over her, swaying the top part of her body slowly backwards and forwards, looking at the flowers. Then she suggested that they should find a seat and have their tea.

The snail had now considered every possible method of reaching his goal without going round the dead leaf or climbing over it. Let alone the effort needed for climbing a leaf, he was doubtful whether the thin texture which vibrated with such an alarming crackle when touched even by the tip of his horns would bear his weight; and this determined him finally to creep beneath it, for there was a point where the leaf curved high enough from the ground to admit him. He had just inserted his head in the opening and was taking stock of the high brown roof and was getting used to the cool brown light when two other people came past outside on the turf. This time they were both young, a young man and a young woman. They were both in the prime of youth, or even in that season which precedes the prime of youth, the season before the smooth pink folds of the flower have burst their gummy case, when the wings of the butterfly, though fully grown, are motionless in the sun.

'Lucky it isn't Friday,' he observed.

'Why? D'you believe in luck?'

'They make you pay sixpence on Friday.'

'What's sixpence anyway? Isn't it worth sixpence?'

'What's "it" – what do you mean by "it"?'

'O anything – I mean – you know what I mean.'

Long pauses came between each of these remarks: they were uttered in toneless and monotonous voices. The couple stood still on the edge of the flower-bed, and together pressed the end of her parasol deep down into the soft earth. The action and the fact that his hand rested on the top of hers expressed their feelings in a strange way, as these short insignificant words also expressed something, words with short wings for their heavy body of meaning, inadequate to carry them far and thus alighting awkwardly upon the very common objects that surrounded them and were to their inexperienced touch so massive: but who knows (so they thought as they pressed the parasol into the earth) what precipices aren't concealed in them, or what slopes of ice don't shine in the sun on the other side? Who knows? Who has ever seen this before? Even when she wondered what sort of tea they gave you at Kew, he felt that something loomed up behind her words, and stood vast and solid behind them; and the mist very slowly rose and uncovered – O Heavens, – what were those shapes? – little white tables, and waitresses who looked first at her and then at him; and there was a bill that he would pay with a real two shilling piece, and it was real, all real, he assured himself, fingering the coin in his pocket, real to everyone except to him and to her; even to him it began to seem real; and then – but it was too exciting to stand and think any longer, and he pulled the parasol out of the earth with a jerk and was impatient to find the place where one had tea with other people, like other people.

'Come along, Trissie; it's time we had our tea.'

'Wherever *does* one have one's tea?' she asked with the oddest thrill of excitement in her voice, looking vaguely round and letting herself be drawn on down the grass path, trailing her parasol, turning her head this way and that way, forgetting her tea, wishing to go down there and then down there, remembering orchids and cranes among wild flowers, a Chinese pagoda and a crimson-crested bird; but he bore her on.

Thus one couple after another with much the same irregular and aimless movement passed the flower-bed and were enveloped in layer after layer of green-blue vapour, in which at first their bodies had substance and a dash of colour, but later both substance and colour dissolved in the green-blue atmosphere. How hot it was! So hot that even the thrush chose to hop, like a mechanical bird, in the shadow of the flowers, with long pauses between one movement and the next; instead of rambling vaguely the white butterflies danced once above another, making with their white shifting flakes the outline of a shattered marble column above the tallest flowers; the glass roofs of the palm house shone as if a whole market full of shiny green umbrellas had opened in the sun; and in the drone of the aeroplane the voice of the summer sky murmured its fierce soul. Yellow and black, pink and snow white, shapes of all these colours, men, women and children, were spotted for a second upon the horizon, and then, seeing the breadth of yellow that lay upon the grass, they wavered and sought shade beneath the trees, dissolving like drops of water in the yellow and green atmosphere, staining it faintly with red and blue. It seemed as if all gross and heavy bodies had sunk down in the heat motionless and lay huddled upon the ground, but their voices went wavering from them as if they were flames lolling from the thick waxen bodies of candles. Voices, yes, voices, wordless voices, breaking the silence suddenly with such depth of contentment, such passion of desire, or, in the voices of children, such freshness of surprise; breaking the silence? But there was no silence; all the time the motor omnibuses were turning their wheels and changing their gear; like a vast nest of Chinese boxes all of wrought steel turning ceaselessly one within another the city murmured; on the top of which the voices cried aloud and the petals of myriads of flowers flashed their colours into the air.

The Evening Party

Ah, but let us wait a little! – The moon is up; the sky open; and there, rising in a mound against the sky with trees upon it, is the earth. The flowing silvery clouds look down upon Atlantic waves. The wind blows soft round the corner of the street, lifting my cloak, holding it gently in the air and then letting it sink and droop as the sea now swells and brims over the rocks and again withdraws. – The street is almost empty; the blinds are drawn in the windows; the yellow and red panes of the ocean liners cast for a moment a spot upon the swimming blue. Sweet is the night air. The maids linger round the pillar box or dally in the shadow of the wall where the tree droops its dark shower of blossom. So on the bark of the apple tree the moths quiver drawing sugar through the long black thread of the proboscis. Where are we? Which house can be the house of the party? All these with their pink and yellow windows are uncommunicative. Ah, – round the corner, in the middle, there where the door stands open – wait a moment. Let us watch the people, one, two, three, precipitating themselves into the light, as the moths strike upon the pane of a lantern stood upon the ground in a forest. Here is a cab making swift for the same spot. A lady pale and voluminous descends and passes into the house; a gentleman in black and white evening dress pays the driver and follows her as if he too were in a hurry. Come, or we shall be late.

On every chair there is a little soft mound; pale whisps of gauze are curled upon bright silks; candles burn pear shaped flames upon either side of the oval looking-glass; there are brushes of thin tortoise-shell; cut bottles knobbed with silver. Can it always look like this – is this not the essence – the spirit? Something has dissolved my face. Through the mist of silver candle light it scarcely appears. People pass me without seeing me. They have faces. In their faces the stars seem to shine through rose coloured flesh. The room is full of vivid yet unsubstantial figures; they stand upright before shelves striped with innumerable little volumes; their heads and shoulders blot the corners of square golden picture frames; and the bulk of their bodies, smooth like stone statues, is massed against something grey, tumultuous, shining too as if with water beyond the uncurtained windows.

'Come into the corner and let us talk.'

'Wonderful! Wonderful human beings! Spiritual and wonderful!'

'But they don't exist. Don't you see the pond through the Professor's head? Don't you see the swan swimming through Mary's skirt?'

'I can fancy little burning roses dotted about them.'

'The little burning roses are only like the fireflies we've seen together in Florence, sprinkled in the wistaria, floating atoms of fire, burning as they float – burning, not thinking.'

'Burning not thinking. And so all the books at the back of us. Here's Shelley – here's Blake. Cast them up into the air and see their poems descend like golden parachutes twinkling and turning and letting fall their rain of star-shaped blossoms.

'Shall I quote you Shelley? "Away! the moor is dark beneath the moon –"'[1]

'Wait, wait! Don't condense our fine atmosphere into drops of rain spattering the pavement. Let us still breathe in the fire dust.'

'Fireflies among the wistaria.'

'Heartless, I grant you. But see how the great blossoms hang before us; vast chandeliers of gold and dim purple pendant from the skies. Don't you feel the fine gilt painting our thighs as we enter, and how the slate coloured walls flap clammily about us as we dart deeper and deeper into the petals, or grow taut like drums?'

'The professor looms upon us.'

'Tell us, Professor –'

'Madam?'

'Is it in your opinion necessary to write grammar? And punctuation. The question of Shelley's commas interests me profoundly.'

'Let us be seated. To tell the truth open windows after sunset – standing with my back – agreeable though conversation – You asked of Shelley's commas. A matter of some importance. There, a little to the right of you. The Oxford edition. My glasses! The penalty of evening dress! I dare not read – Moreover commas – The modern print is execrable. Designed to match the modern exiguity; for I confess I find little admirable among the moderns.'

'I am with you there entirely.'

'So? I feared opposition. At your age, in your – costume.'

'Sir, I find little admirable among the ancients. These classics –

Shelley, Keats; Browne; Gibbon; is there a page that you can quote entire, a paragraph perfect, a sentence even that one can't see amended by the pen of God or man?'

'S-s-s-sh, Madam. Your objection has weight but lacks sobriety. Moreover your choice of names – In what chamber of the spirit can you consort Shelley with Gibbon? Unless indeed their atheism – But to the point. The perfect paragraph, the perfect phrase; hum – my memory – and then my glasses left behind me on the mantelpiece. I declare. But your stricture applies to life itself.'

'Surely this evening –'

'The pen of man, I fancy, could have little trouble in re-writing that. The open window – standing in the draught – and, let me whisper it, the conversation of these ladies, earnest and benevolent, with exalted views upon the destiny of the negro who is at this moment toiling beneath the lash to procure rubber for some of our friends engaged in agreeable conversation here. To enjoy your perfection –'

'I take your point. One must exclude.'

'The greater part of everything.'

'But to argue that aright, we must strike down to the roots of things; for I fancy that your belief is only one of those fading pansies that one buys and plants for a night's festival to find withered in the morning. You maintain that Shakespeare excluded?'

'Madam, I maintain nothing. These ladies have put me out of temper.'

'They are benevolent. They have pitched their camp on the banks of one of the little tributary streams, whence picking reeds and dipping them in poison, with matted hair and yellow tinted skin, they issue forth now and then to plant them in the flanks of the comfortable; such are the benevolent.'

'Their darts tingle. That and the rheumatism –'

'The professor is already gone? Poor old man!'

'But at his age how could he still possess what we at ours are already losing. I mean —'

'Yes?'

'Don't you remember in early childhood, when, in play or talk, as one stepped across the puddle or reached the window on the landing, some imperceptible shock froze the universe to a solid ball of crystal which one held for a moment – I have some mystical belief that all time past and future too, the tears and powdered ashes of generations clotted to a ball; then we were absolute and entire; nothing then was excluded; that was certainty – happiness. But later these crystal globes dissolve as one holds them: some one talks of negroes. See what comes of trying to say what one means! Nonsense!'

'Precisely. Yet how sad a thing is sense! How vast a renunciation it represents! Listen for a moment. Distinguish one among the voices. Now. "So cold it must seem after India. Seven years too. But habit is everything." That's sense. That's agreement. They've fixed their eyes upon something visible to each of them. They attempt no more to look upon the little spark of light, the little purple shadow which may be fruitful land on the verge of the horizon, or only a flying gleam on the water. It's all compromise – all safety, the general intercourse of human beings. Therefore we discover nothing; we cease to explore; we cease to believe that there is anything to discover. "Nonsense" you say; meaning that I shan't see your crystal globe; and I'm half ashamed to try.'

'Speech is an old torn net, through which the fish escape as one casts it over them. Perhaps silence is better. Let us try it. Come to the window.'

'It's an odd thing, silence. The mind becomes like a starless night; and then a meteor slides, splendid, right across the dark and is extinct. We never give sufficient thanks for this entertainment.'

'Ah, we're an ungrateful race! When I look at my hand upon the window sill and think what pleasure I've had in it, how it's touched silk and pottery and hot walls, laid itself flat upon wet grass or sun-baked, let the Atlantic spurt through its fingers, snapped blue bells and daffodils, plucked ripe plums, never for a second since I was born ceased to tell me of hot and cold, damp or dryness, I'm amazed that I should use this wonderful composition of flesh and nerve to write the abuse of life. Yet that's what we do. Come to think of it, literature is the record of our discontent.'

'Our badge of superiority; our claim for preferment. Admit, you like the discontented people best.'

'I like the melancholy sound of the distant sea'

'What's this talk of melancholy at my party? Of course if you both stand whispering in a corner –. But come and let me introduce you. There's Mr Nevill, who likes your writing.'

'In that case – Good evening.'

'Somewhere, I forget the name of the paper – something or other of yours – I forget now the name of the article – or was it a story? You write stories? It's not poetry that you write? So many of one's friends – and then every day something new comes out which – which –'

'One does not read.'

'Well, ungracious as it seems, to be honest, occupied as I am all day with matters of an odious or rather fatiguing nature – what time I have for literature I spend with –'

'The dead.'

'I detect irony in your correction.'[2]

'Envy, not irony. Death is of the utmost importance. Like the French, the dead write so well, and, for some reason, one can respect them, and feel, while equal, that they're older, wiser, as our parents are; the relationship between living and dead is surely of the noblest.'

'Ah, if you feel that, let us talk of the dead. Lamb, Sophocles, de Quincey, Sir Thomas Browne.'

'Sir Walter Scott, Milton, Marlowe.'

'Pater, Tennyson.'

'Now, now, now.'

'Tennyson, Pater.'

'Lock the door; draw the curtains so that I see only your eyes. I fall on my knees. I cover my face with my hands. I adore Pater. I admire Tennyson.'

'Daughter, proceed.'

'It's an easy thing to confess one's faults. But what dusk is deep enough to hide one's virtues? I love, I adore – no, I can't tell you what a rose of worship my soul is – the name trembles on my lips – for Shakespeare.'

'I grant you absolution.'

'And yet how often does one read Shakespeare?'

'How often is the summer's night flawless, the moon up, the spaces between the stars deep as the Atlantic, through the dusk the roses showing white? The mind before reading Shakespeare –'

'The summer's night. O this is the way to read!'

'The roses nodding –'

'The waves breaking –'

'Over the fields coming those strange airs of dawn that try the doors of the house and fall flat –'

'Then, lying down to sleep, the bed's –'

'A boat! A boat! Over the sea all night long –'

'And sitting upright, the stars –'

'Out alone in mid-ocean our little boat floating isolated yet upheld, drawn on by the compulsion of the Northern lights, safe, surrounded, melts where the night rests upon the water; there diminishes and disappears, and we, submerged, sealed cold as smooth stones, widen our eyes again; dash, stroke, dot, splash, bedroom furniture, and the rattle of the curtain on the pole – I earn my living. – Introduce me! O he knew my brother at Oxford.'

'And you too. Come into the middle of the room. Here's someone who remembers you.'

'As a child, my dear. You wore a pink frock.'

'The dog bit me.'

'So dangerous, throwing sticks into the sea. But your mother –'

'On the beach, by the tent –'

'Sat smiling. She was fond of dogs. – You know my daughter? That's her husband. – Tray was he called? the big brown one, and there was another, smaller, who bit the postman. I can see it now. What one remembers! But I'm preventing –'

'O please (Yes, yes, I wrote, I'm coming) Please, please – Damn you, Helen, interrupting! There she goes, never again – pushing through the people, pinning on her shawl, slowly descending the steps: gone! The past! the past! –'

'Ah, but listen. Tell me; I'm afraid; so many strangers; some with beards; some so beautiful; she's touched the peony; all the petals fall. And fierce – the woman with the eyes. The Armenians die. And penal servitude. Why? Such a chatter too; except now – whisper – we all must whisper – are we listening – waiting – what for then? The lantern's caught! O take care of your gauze! A woman died once. They say it's waked the swan.'

'Helen's afraid. These paper lanterns catching, and the windows open letting the breeze lift our flounces. But I'm not afraid of the flame, you know. It's the garden – I mean the world. That frightens me. Those little lights out there each with a circle of earth beneath it – hills and towns; then the shadows; the lilac stirs. Don't stay talking. Let's be off. Through the garden; your hand in mine.'

'Away. The moon is dark upon the moor. Away, we'll breast them, those waves of darkness crested by the trees, rising for ever, lonely and dark. The lights rise and fall; the water's thin as air; the moon's behind it. D'you sink? D'you rise? D'you see the islands? Alone with me.'

Solid Objects

The only thing that moved upon the vast semicircle of the beach was one small black spot. As it came nearer to the ribs and spine of the stranded pilchard boat, it became apparent from a certain tenuity in its blackness that this spot possessed four legs; and moment by moment it became more unmistakable that it was composed of the persons of two young men. Even thus in outline against the sand there was an unmistakable vitality in them; an indescribable vigour in the approach and withdrawal of the bodies, slight though it was, which proclaimed some violent argument issuing from the tiny mouths of the little round heads. This was corroborated on closer view by the repeated lunging of a walking-stick on the right-hand side. 'You mean to tell me . . . You actually believe . . .' thus the walking-stick on the right-hand side next the waves seemed to be asserting as it cut long straight stripes on the sand.

'Politics be damned!' issued clearly from the body on the left-hand side, and, as these words were uttered, the mouths, noses, chins, little moustaches, tweed caps, rough boots, shooting coats, and check stockings of the two speakers became clearer and clearer; the smoke of their pipes went up into the air; nothing was so solid, so living, so hard, red, hirsute and virile as these two bodies for miles and miles of sea and sandhill.

They flung themselves down by the six ribs and spine of the black pilchard boat. You know how the body seems to shake itself free from an argument, and to apologise for a mood of exaltation; flinging itself down and expressing in the looseness of its attitude a readiness to take up with something new – whatever it may be that comes next to hand. So Charles, whose stick had been slashing the beach for half a mile or so, began skimming flat pieces of slate over the water; and John, who had exclaimed 'Politics be damned!' began burrowing his fingers down, down, into the sand. As his hand went further and further beyond the wrist, so that he had to hitch his sleeve a little higher, his eyes lost their intensity, or rather the background of thought and experience which gives an inscrutable depth to the eyes of grown people disappeared, leaving only the clear transparent surface, expressing nothing but wonder, which the eyes of young children display. No doubt the act of burrowing in the sand had something to do with it. He remembered that, after digging for a little, the water oozes round your finger-tips; the hole then becomes a moat; a well; a spring; a secret channel to the sea. As he was choosing which of these things to make it, still working his fingers in the water, they curled round something hard – a full drop of solid matter – and gradually dislodged a large irregular lump, and brought it to the surface. When the sand coating was wiped off, a green tint appeared. It was a lump of glass, so thick as to be almost opaque; the smoothing of the sea had completely worn off any edge or shape, so that it was impossible to say whether it had been bottle, tumbler or window-pane; it was nothing but glass; it was almost a precious stone. You had only to enclose it in a rim of gold, or pierce it with a wire, and it became a jewel; part of a necklace, or a dull, green light upon a finger. Perhaps after all it was really a gem; something worn by a dark Princess trailing her finger in the water as she sat in the stern of the boat and listened to the slaves singing as they rowed her across the Bay. Or the oak sides of a sunk Elizabethan treasure-chest had split apart, and, rolled over and over, over and over, its emeralds had come at last to shore. John turned it in his hands; he held it to the light; he held it so that its irregular mass blotted out the body and extended right arm of his friend. The green thinned and thickened slightly as it was held against the sky or against the body. It pleased him; it puzzled him; it was so hard, so concentrated, so definite an object compared with the vague sea and the hazy shore.

Now a sigh disturbed him – profound, final, making him aware that his friend Charles had thrown all the flat stones within reach, or had come to the conclusion that it was not worth while to throw them. They ate their sandwiches side by side. When they had done, and were shaking themselves and rising to their feet, John took the lump of glass and looked at it in silence. Charles looked at it too. But he saw immediately that it was not flat, and filling his pipe he said with the energy that dismisses a foolish strain of thought,

'To return to what I was saying –'

He did not see, or if he had seen would hardly have noticed, that John after looking at the lump for a moment, as if in hesitation, slipped it inside his pocket. That impulse, too, may have been the impulse which leads a child to pick up one pebble on a path strewn with them, promising it a life of warmth and security upon the nursery mantelpiece, delighting in the sense of power and benignity which such an action confers, and believing that the heart of the stone leaps with joy when it sees itself chosen from a million like it, to enjoy this bliss instead of a life of cold and wet upon the high road. 'It might so easily have been any other of the millions of stones, but it was I, I, I!'

Whether this thought or not was in John's mind, the lump of glass had its place upon the mantelpiece, where it stood heavy upon a little pile of bills and letters, and served not only as an excellent paper-weight, but also as a natural stopping place for the young man's eyes when they wandered from his book. Looked at again and again half consciously by a mind thinking of something else, any object mixes itself so profoundly with the stuff of thought that it loses its actual form and recomposes itself a little differently in an ideal shape which haunts the brain when we least expect it. So John found himself attracted to the windows of curiosity shops when he was out walking, merely because he saw something which reminded him of the lump of glass. Anything, so long as it was an object of some kind, more or less round, perhaps with a dying flame deep sunk in its mass, anything – china, glass, amber, rock, marble – even the smooth oval egg of a prehistoric bird would do. He took, also, to keeping his eyes upon the ground, especially in the neighbourhood of waste land where the household refuse is thrown away. Such objects often occurred there – thrown away, of no use to anybody, shapeless, discarded. In a few months he had collected four or five specimens that took their place upon the mantelpiece. They were useful, too, for a man who is standing for Parliament upon the brink of a brilliant career has any number of papers to keep in order – addresses to constituents, declarations of policy, appeals for subscriptions, invitations to dinner, and so on.

One day, starting from his rooms in the Temple to catch a train in order to address his constituents, his eyes rested upon a remarkable object lying half-hidden in one of those little borders of grass which edge the bases of vast legal buildings. He could only touch it with the point of his stick through the railings; but he could see that it was a piece of china of the most remarkable shape, as nearly resembling a starfish as anything – shaped, or broken accidentally, into five irregular but unmistakable points. The colouring was mainly blue, but green stripes or spots of some kind overlaid the blue, and lines of crimson gave it a richness and lustre of the most attractive kind. John was determined to possess it; but the more he pushed, the further it receded. At length he was forced to go back to his rooms and improvise a wire ring attached to the end of a stick, with which, by dint of great care and skill, he finally drew the piece of china within reach of his hands. As he seized hold of it he exclaimed in triumph. At that moment the clock struck. It was out of the question that he should keep his appointment. The meeting was held without him. But how had the piece of china been broken into this remarkable shape? A careful examination put it beyond doubt that the star shape was accidental, which made it all the more strange, and it seemed unlikely that there should be another such in existence. Set at the opposite end of the mantelpiece from the lump of glass that had been dug from the sand, it looked like a creature from another world – freakish and fantastic as a harlequin. It seemed to be pirouetting through space, winking light like a fitful star. The contrast between the china so vivid and alert, and the glass so mute and contemplative, fascinated him, and wondering and amazed he asked himself how the two came to exist in the same world, let alone to stand upon the same narrow strip of marble in the same room. The question remained unanswered.

He now began to haunt the places which are most prolific of broken china, such as pieces of waste land between railway lines, sites of demolished houses, and commons in the neighbourhood of London. But china is seldom thrown from a great height; it is one of the rarest of human actions. You have to find in conjunction a very high house, and a woman of such reckless impulse and passionate prejudice that she flings her jar or pot straight from the window without thought of who is below. Broken china was to be found in plenty, but broken in some trifling domestic accident, without purpose or character. Nevertheless, he was often astonished, as he came to go into the question more deeply, by the immense variety of shapes to be found in London alone, and there was still more cause for wonder and speculation in the differences of qualities and designs. The finest specimens he would bring home and place upon his mantelpiece, where, however, their duty was more and more of an ornamental nature, since papers needing a weight to keep them down became scarcer and scarcer.

He neglected his duties, perhaps, or discharged them absent-mindedly, or his constitutents when they visited him were unfavour-ably impressed by the appearance of his mantelpiece. At any rate he was not elected to represent them in Parliament, and his friend Charles, taking it much to heart and hurrying to condole with him, found him so little cast down by the disaster that he could only suppose that it was too serious a matter for him to realise all at once.

In truth, John had been that day to Barnes Common, and there under a furze bush had found a very remarkable piece of iron. It was almost identical with the glass in shape, massy and globular, but so cold and heavy, so black and metallic, that it was evidently alien to the earth and had its origin in one of the dead stars or was itself the cinder of a moon. It weighed his pocket down; it weighed the mantelpiece down; it radiated cold. And yet the meteorite stood upon the same ledge with the lump of glass and the star-shaped china.

As his eyes passed from one to another, the determination to possess objects that even surpassed these tormented the young man. He devoted himself more and more resolutely to the search. It he had not been consumed by ambition and convinced that one day some newly-discovered rubbish heap would reward him, the disappointments he had suffered, let alone the fatigue and derision, would have made him give up the pursuit. Provided with a bag and a long stick fitted with an adaptable hook, he ransacked all deposits of earth; raked beneath matted tangles of scrub; searched all alleys and spaces between walls where he had learned to expect to find objects of this kind thrown away. As his standard became higher and his taste more severe the disappointments were innumerable, but always some gleam of hope, some piece of china or glass curiously marked or broken, lured him on. Day after day passed. He was no longer young. His career – that is his political career – was a thing of the past. People gave up visiting him. He was too silent to be worth asking to dinner. He never talked to anyone about his serious ambitions; their lack of understanding was apparent in their behaviour.

He leaned back in his chair now and watched Charles lift the stones on the mantelpiece a dozen times and put them down emphatically to mark what he was saying about the conduct of the Government, without once noticing their existence.

'What was the truth of it, John?' asked Charles suddenly, turning and facing him. 'What made you give it up like that all in a second?'

'I've not given it up,' John replied.

'But you've not a ghost of a chance now,' said Charles roughly.

'I don't agree with you there,' said John with conviction. Charles looked at him and was profoundly uneasy; the most extraordinary doubts possessed him; he had a queer sense that they were talking about different things. He looked round to find some relief for his horrible depression, but the disorderly appearance of the room depressed him still further. What was that stick, and the old carpet bag hanging against the wall? And then those stones? Looking at John, something fixed and distant in his expression alarmed him. He knew only too well that his mere appearance upon the platform was out of the question.

'Pretty stones,' he said as cheerfully as he could; and saying that he had an appointment to keep, he left John – for ever.

Sympathy

Hammond, Humphry, on the 29th of April, at The Manor, High Wickham, Bucks. – Celia's husband! It must be Celia's husband. Dead! Good Heavens! Humphry Hammond dead! I meant to ask them – I forgot. Why didn't I go the day they wanted me to come? There was a concert where they played Mozart – I put them off for that. He scarcely spoke the night they dined here. He sat opposite in the yellow arm chair: he said that 'furniture' was what he liked. What did he mean? Why did I say nothing to make him explain? Why did I let him go with all that he might have said unsaid? Why did he sit there silent so long, and leave us, talking about motor omnibuses, in the hall? How plainly I see him now and fancy that shyness, or the feeling of meaning something that he could not say, determined him to stop when he had said that about 'liking furniture.' I shall never know now. Now the pink cheeks are pale and the eyes with the young man's look of resolution and defiance closed, defiant still beneath their lids. Male and unyielding stiff he lies upon his bed, so that I see it white and steep; the windows open, the birds singing, no concession to death; no tears no sentiment, a bunch of lilies scattered where the sheet folds perhaps – his mother's or Celia's. –

Celia. Yes . . . I see her, and then not. There is a moment I can't fancy: the moment in other people's lives that one always leaves out; the moment from which all that we know them by proceeds; I follow her to his door; I see her turn the handle; then comes the blind moment, and when my fancy opens its eyes again I find her equipped for the world – a widow; or is she not, in the early hours of the morning, veiled in white from head to foot as if the light cleft itself asunder on her brow? The outward sign I see and shall see for ever; but at the meaning of it I shall only guess. Enviously I shall mark her silences and her severities; I shall watch her moving among us with her secret unconfessed; I shall fancy her eager for the night to come with its lonely voyage; I shall picture her landing among us for the day's work, contemptuous and tolerant of our amusements. In the midst of clamour I shall think that she hears more; the emptiness has for her its ghost. For all this I shall envy her. I shall envy her the security – the knowledge. But the white veil, as the sun grows stronger, fades from her brow and she comes to the window. The carts rattle down the road, and the men standing upright to drive, whistle or sing or shout to one another.

Now I see her more distinctly. The colour has come back to her cheeks; but the bloom is gone; the film which made her glance gentle and vague has been rubbed from her eyes; the stir of life sounds harsh to her, and standing by the open window, she contracts and shrinks together. There I follow her; no longer with envy. Does she not shrink from the hand I stretch to her? [We are all robbers; all cruel; all drops in a stream which flows past her indifferently. I may cast myself out to her, but only to be drawn back again to flow swiftly on with the stream. The pity which bids me tender my hand to her to bite becomes, or will become, an impulse of compassion which in its generosity appears to her contemptuous.][1] Immediately she shouts to the woman shaking rugs next door, 'A fine morning!' The woman starts and looks at her, nods her head and hurries indoors. She stares at the fruit blossoms spread upon the ruddy wall, leaning her head on her hand. The tears slip down; but she rubs her knuckles in her eyes. Is she twenty-four? – at most twenty-five. Can one offer her – a day's walk in the hills? Striking our boots sturdily upon the high road we start out, jump the fence and so across the field and up into the wood. There she flings herself upon the anemones and picks them 'for Humphry'; and refrains, saying that they will be fresher in the evening. We sit down and look at the triangular space of yellow-green field beneath us through the arch of bramble twigs which divides them so queerly.

'What d'you believe?' she asks suddenly, (as I fancy) sucking at the stalk of a flower. 'Nothing – nothing,' I reply driven, against my intention[,] to speak abruptly. She frowns, throws away her flower, and jumps up. She strides ahead for a yard or two, and then swings herself impetuously by a low branch to look at a thrush's nest in the lap of a tree.

'Five eggs!' she cries. And abruptly again I call back, 'What fun!'

But it's all fancy. I'm not in the room with her, nor out in the wood. I'm here in London, standing by the window, holding *The Times*. But how death has changed everything! – as, in an eclipse of the sun, the colours go out, and the trees look thin as paper and livid while the shadow passes. The chill little breeze is perceptible and the roar of traffic sounds across a gulf. Then, a moment later, distances are bridged, sounds merged; and as I look the trees though still pale, become sentinel and guardian; the sky arranges its tender background; and all remote as if exalted to the summit of a mountain in the dawn. Death has done it; death lies behind leaves and houses and the smoke wavering up, composing them into something still in its tranquillity before it has taken on any of the disguises of life. So, from an express train, I have looked upon hills and fields and seen the man with the scythe look up from the hedge as we pass, and lovers lying in the long grass stare at me without disguise as I stared at them without disguise.[2] Some burden has fallen; some impediment has been removed. Freely in this fine air my friends pass dark across the horizon, all of them desiring goodness only, tenderly putting me by, and stepping off the rim of the world into the ship which waits to take them into storm or serenity. My eye cannot follow. But one after another with kisses of farewell and laughter sweeter than before they pass beyond me to set sail for ever; trooping orderly down to the water's edge as if this had always been their direction while we lived. Now all our tracks from the first become apparent, swerving and diverging to run together here under the solemn sycamore with the sky thus tender and the wheels and cries sounding now high, now low in harmony.

The simple young man whom I hardly knew had, then, concealed in him the immense power of death. He had removed the boundaries and fused the separate entities by ceasing – there in the room with the open windows and the bird's song outside. He silently withdrew, and though his voice was nothing his silence is profound. He has laid his life down like a cloak for us to tread over. Where does he lead us? We come to the edge and look out. But he has gone beyond us; he faints in the far sky; for us the tenderness of the green and the blue of the sky remain; but transparent as the world is he will have none of it; he has turned from us grouped on the very limit of the verge; he disappears cleaving the dawn asunder. He is gone. We must go back then.

The sycamore shakes its leaves stirring flakes of light in the deep pool of air in which it stands; the sun shoots straight between the leaves to the grass; the geraniums glow red in the earth. A cry starts to the left of me, and another, abrupt and dissevered, to the right. Wheels strike divergently; omnibuses conglomerate in conflict; the clock asseverates with twelve distinct strokes that it is midday.[3]

Must I then go back? Must I see the horizon shut in, the mountain sink and the coarse strong colours return? No, no, Humphry Hammond is dead. He is dead – the white sheets, the scent of flowers – the one bee humming through the room and out again. Where does it go next? There's one on the Canterbury Bell; but finds no honey there, and so tries the yellow wall flower, but in these ancient London gardens what hope of honey?[4] The earth must be dry as grains of salt scattered above great iron drain pipes, and the curves of tunnels. – But Humphry Hammond! Dead! Let me read the name in the paper again; let me come back to my friends; let me not desert them so soon; he died on Tuesday, three days ago, suddenly, two days illness; and then finished, the great operation of death. Finished; the earth is already over him perhaps; and people have set their courses a little differently; although some, not having heard, still address their letters to him; but the envelopes already look out of date upon the hall table. It seems to me that he has been dead for weeks, for years; when I think of him I see scarcely anything of him, and that saying of his about liking furniture means nothing at all. And yet he died; the utmost he could do gives me now scarcely any sensation at all. Terrible! Terrible! to be so callous! There is the yellow arm chair in which he sat, shabby but still solid enough, surviving us all; and the mantelpiece strewn with glass and silver, but he is ephemeral as the dusty light which stripes the wall and carpet. So will the sun shine on glass and silver the day I die. The sun stripes a million years into the future; a broad yellow path; passing an infinite distance beyond this house and town; passing so far that nothing but sea remains, stretching flat with its infinity of creases beneath the sunlight. Humphry Hammond – who was Humphry Hammond? – a curious sound, now crinkled now smooth as a sea shell.

The terrific battery! The post! These little white squares with black wriggling marks on them. 'My father-in-law . . . will you dine . . .' Is she mad, talking of her father-in-law? She wears the white veil still; the bed is white and steep; the lilies – the open window – the woman beating rugs outside. 'Humphry is managing the business' Humphry – who is dead? – 'we shall I suppose, move into the big house.' The house of death? 'where you must come and stay. I have to be in London, buying mourning.' O don't tell me he lives still! O why did you deceive me?[5]

An Unwritten Novel

Such an expression of unhappiness was enough by itself to make one's eyes slide above the paper's edge to the poor woman's face – insignificant without that look, almost a symbol of human destiny with it. Life's what you see in people's eyes; life's what they learn, and, having learnt it, never, though they seek to hide it, cease to be aware of – what? That life's like that, it seems. Five faces opposite – five mature faces – and the knowledge in each face. Strange though, how people want to conceal it! Marks of reticence are on all those faces: lips shut, eyes shaded, each one of the five doing something to hide or stultify his knowledge. One smokes; another reads; a third checks entries in a pocket-book; a fourth stares at the map of the line framed opposite; and the fifth – the terrible thing about the fifth is that she does nothing at all. She looks at life. Ah, but my poor, unfortunate woman, do play the game – do, for all our sakes, conceal it!

As if she heard me, she looked up, shifted slightly in her seat and sighed. She seemed to apologise and at the same time to say to me, 'If only you knew!' Then she looked at life again. 'But I do know,' I answered silently, glancing at *The Times* for manners' sake: 'I know the whole business. "Peace between Germany and the Allied Powers was yesterday officially ushered in at Paris[1] – Signor Nitti, the Italian Prime Minister – a passenger train at Doncaster was in collision with a goods train . . ." We all know – *The Times* knows – but we pretend we don't." My eyes had once more crept over the paper's rim. She shuddered, twitched her arm queerly to the middle of her back and shook her head. Again I dipped into my great reservoir of life. 'Take what you like,' I continued, 'births, deaths, marriages, Court Circular, the habits of birds, Leonardo da Vinci, the Sandhills murder, high wages and the cost of living – oh, take what you like,' I repeated, 'it's all in *The Times*!' Again with infinite weariness she moved her head from side to side until, like a top exhausted with spinning, it settled on her neck.

The Times was no protection against such sorrow as hers. But other human beings forbade intercourse. The best thing to do against life was to fold the paper so that it made a perfect square, crisp, thick, impervious even to life. This done, I glanced up quickly, armed with a shield of my own. She pierced through my shield; she gazed into my eyes as if searching any sediment of courage at the depths of them and damping it to clay. Her twitch alone denied all hope, discounted all illusion.

So we rattled through Surrey and across the border into Sussex. But with my eyes upon life I did not see that the other travellers had left, one by one, till, save for the man who read, we were alone together. Here was Three Bridges station. We drew slowly down the platform and stopped. Was he going to leave us? I prayed both ways – I prayed last that he might stay. At that instant he roused himself, crumpled his paper contemptuously, like a thing done with, burst open the door and left us alone.

The unhappy woman, leaning a little forward, palely and colourlessly addressed me – talked of stations and holidays, of brothers at Eastbourne, and the time of year, which was, I forget now, early or late. But at last looking from the window and seeing, I knew, only life, she breathed. 'Staying away – that's the drawback of it –' Ah, now we approached the catastrophe, 'My sister-in-law' – the bitterness of her tone was like lemon on cold steel, and speaking, not to me, but to herself, she muttered, 'Nonsense, she would say – that's what they all say,' and while she spoke she fidgeted as though the skin on her back were as a plucked fowl's in a poulterer's shop-window.

'Oh, that cow!' she broke off nervously, as though the great wooden cow in the meadow had shocked her and saved her from some indiscretion. Then she shuddered, and then she made the awkward angular movement that I had seen before, as if, after the spasm, some spot between the shoulders burnt or itched. Then again she looked the most unhappy woman in the world, and I once more reproached her, though not with the same conviction, for if there were a reason, and if I knew the reason, the stigma was removed from life.

'Sisters-in-law,' I said –

Her lips pursed as if to spit venom at the word; pursed they remained. All she did was to take her glove and rub hard at a spot on the window-pane. She rubbed as if she would rub something out for ever – some stain, some indelible contamination. Indeed, the spot remained for all her rubbing, and back she sank with the shudder and the clutch of the arm I had come to expect. Something impelled me to take my glove and rub my window. There, too, was a little speck on the glass. For all my rubbing it remained. And then the spasm went through me; I crooked my arm and plucked at the middle of my back. My skin, too, felt like the damp chicken's skin in the poulterer's shop-window; one spot between the shoulders itched and irritated, felt clammy, felt raw. Could I reach it? Surreptitiously I tried. She saw me. A smile of infinite irony, infinite sorrow, flitted and faded from her face. But she had communicated, shared her secret, passed her poison; she would speak no more. Leaning back in my corner, shielding my eyes from her eyes, seeing only the slopes and hollows, greys and purples, of the winter's landscape, I read her message, deciphered her secret, reading it beneath her gaze.

Hilda's the sister-in-law. Hilda? Hilda? Hilda Marsh – Hilda the blooming, the full bosomed, the matronly. Hilda stands at the door as the cab draws up, holding a coin. 'Poor Minnie, more of a grasshopper than ever – old cloak she had last year. Well, well, with two children these days one can't do more. No, Minnie. I've got it; here you are, cabby – none of your ways with me. Come in Minnie. Oh, I could carry *you*, let alone your basket!' So they go into the dining-room. 'Aunt Minnie, children.'

Slowly the knives and forks sink from the upright. Down they get (Bob and Barbara), hold out hands stiffly; back again to their chairs, staring between the resumed mouthfuls. [But this we'll skip; ornaments, curtains, trefoil china plate, yellow oblongs of cheese, white squares of biscuit – skip – oh, but wait! Half-way through luncheon one of those shivers; Bob stares at her, spoon in mouth. 'Get on with your pudding, Bob;' but Hilda disapproves. 'Why *should* she twitch?' Skip, skip, till we reach the landing on the upper floor; stairs brass-bound; linoleum worn; oh, yes! little bedroom looking out over the roofs of Eastbourne – zigzagging roofs like the spines of caterpillars, this way, that way, striped red and yellow, with blue-black slating.] Now, Minnie, the door's shut; Hilda heavily descends to the basement; you unstrap the straps of your basket, lay on the bed a meagre nightgown, stand side by side furred felt slippers. The looking-glass – no, you avoid the looking-glass. Some methodical disposition of hat-pins. Perhaps the shell box has something in it? You shake it; it's the pearly stud there was last year – that's all. And then the sniff, the sigh, the sitting by the window. Three o'clock on a December afternoon; the rain drizzling; one light low in the skylight of a drapery emporium;

another high in a servant's bedroom – this one goes out. That gives her nothing to look at. A moment's blankness – then, what are you thinking? (Let me peep across at her opposite; she's asleep or pretending it; so what would she think about sitting at the window at three o'clock in the afternoon? Health, money, bills, her God?) Yes, sitting on the very edge of the chair looking over the roofs of Eastbourne, Minnie Marsh prays to God. That's all very well; and she may rub the pane too, as though to see God better; but what God does she see? Who's the God of Minnie Marsh, the God of the back streets of Eastbourne, the God of three o'clock in the afternoon? I, too, see roofs, I see sky; but, oh, dear – this seeing of Gods! More like President Kruger than Prince Albert[2] – that's the best I can do for him; and I see him on a chair, in a black frock-coat, not so very high up either; I can manage a cloud or two for him to sit on; and then his hand trailing in the cloud holds a rod, a truncheon is it? – black, thick, thorned – a brutal old bully – Minnie's God! Did he send the itch and the patch and the twitch? Is that why she prays? What she rubs on the window is the stain of sin. Oh, she committed some crime!

I have my choice of crimes. The woods flit and fly – in summer there are bluebells; in the opening there, when Spring comes, primroses. A parting, was it, twenty years ago? Vows broken? Not Minnie's! . . . She was faithful. How she nursed her mother! All her savings on the tombstones – wreaths under glass – daffodils in jars. But I'm off the track. A crime . . . They would say she kept her sorrow, suppressed her secret – her sex, they'd say – the scientific people. But what flummery to saddle *her* with sex! No – more like this. Passing down the streets of Croydon twenty years ago, the violet loops of ribbon in the draper's window spangled in the electric light catch her eye. She lingers – past six. Still by running she can reach home. She pushes through the glass swing door. It's sale-time. Shallow trays brim with ribbons.[3] She pauses, pulls this, fingers that with the raised roses on it – no need to choose, no need to buy, and each tray with its surprises. 'We don't shut till seven', and then it *is* seven. She runs, she rushes, home she reaches, but too late. Neighbours – the doctor – baby brother – the kettle – scalded – hospital – dead – or only the shock of it, the blame? Ah, but the detail matters nothing! It's what she carries with her; the spot, the crime, the thing to expiate, always there between her shoulders. 'Yes,' she seems to nod to me, 'it's the thing I did.'

Whether you did, or what you did, I don't mind; it's not the thing I

want. The draper's window looped with violet – that'll do; a little
cheap perhaps, a little commonplace – since one has a choice of crimes,
but then so many (let me peep across again – still sleeping, or
pretending sleep! white, worn, the mouth closed – a touch of
obstinacy, more than one would think – no hint of sex) – so many
crimes aren't *your* crime; your crime was cheap; only the retribution
solemn; for now the church door opens, the hard wooden pew receives
her; on the brown tiles she kneels; every day, winter, summer, dusk,
dawn (here she's at it) prays. All her sins fall, fall, for ever fall. The spot
receives them. It's raised, it's red, it's burning. Next she twitches. Small
boys point. 'Bob at lunch today' – But elderly women are the worst.

Indeed now you can't sit praying any longer. Kruger's sunk beneath
the clouds – washed over as with a painter's brush of liquid grey, to
which he adds a tinge of black – even the tip of the truncheon gone
now. That's what always happens! Just as you've seen him, felt him,
someone interrupts. It's Hilda now.

How you hate her! She'll even lock the bathroom door overnight,
too, though it's only cold water you want, and sometimes when the
night's been bad it seems as if washing helped.[4] And John at breakfast –
the children – meals are worst, and sometimes there are friends – ferns
don't altogether hide 'em – they guess too; so out you go along the
front, where the waves are grey, and the papers blow, and the glass
shelters green and draughty, and the chairs cost tuppence – too much –
for there must be preachers along the sands. Ah, that's a nigger – that's
a funny man – that's a man with parakeets – poor little creatures! Is
there no one here who thinks of God? – just up there, over the pier,
with his rod – but no – there's nothing but grey in the sky or if it's blue
the white clouds hide him, and the music – it's military music – and
what are they fishing for? Do they catch them? How the children stare!
Well, then home a back way – 'Home a back way!' The words have
meaning; might have been spoken by the old man with whiskers – no,
no, he didn't really speak; but everything has meaning – placards
leaning against doorways – names above shop-windows – red fruit in
baskets – women's heads in the hairdresser's – all say 'Minnie Marsh!'
But here's a jerk. 'Eggs are cheaper!' That's what always happens! I
was heading her over the waterfall, straight for madness, when, like a
flock of dream sheep, she turns t'other way and runs between my
fingers. Eggs are cheaper. Tethered to the shores of the world, none of
the crimes, sorrows, rhapsodies, or insanities for poor Minnie Marsh;

never late for luncheon; never caught in a storm without a mackintosh; never utterly unconscious of the cheapness of eggs. So she reaches home – scrapes her boots.

Have I read you right? But the human face – the human face at the top of the fullest sheet of print holds more, withholds more. Now, eyes open, she looks out; and in the human eye – how d'you define it? – there's a break – a division – so that when you've grasped the stem the butterfly's off – the moth that hangs in the evening over the yellow flower – move, raise your hand, off, high, away. I won't raise my hand. Hang still, then, quiver, life, soul, spirit, whatever you are of Minnie Marsh – I, too, on my flower – the hawk over the down – alone, or what were the worth of life? To rise; hang still in the evening, in the midday; hang still over the down. The flicker of a hand – off, up! then poised again. Alone, unseen; seeing all so still down there, all so lovely. None seeing, none caring. The eyes of others our prisons; their thoughts our cages. Air above, air below. And the moon and immortality . . . Oh, but I drop to the turf! Are you down too, you in the corner, what's your name – woman – Minnie Marsh; some such name as that? There she is, tight to her blossom; opening her hand-bag, from which she takes a hollow shell – an egg – who was saying that eggs were cheaper? You or I? Oh, it was you who said it on the way home, you remember, when the old gentleman, suddenly opening his umbrella – or sneezing was it? Anyhow, Kruger went, and you came 'home a back way', and scraped your boots. Yes. And now you lay across your knees a pocket-handkerchief into which drop little angular fragments of eggshell – fragments of a map – a puzzle. I wish I could piece them together! If you would only sit still. She's moved her knees – the map's in bits again. Down the slopes of the Andes the white blocks of marble go bounding and hurtling, crushing to death a whole troop of Spanish muleteers, with their convoy – Drake's booty, gold and silver. But to return –

To what, to where? She opened the door, and, putting her umbrella in the stand – that goes without saying: so, too, the whiff of beef from the basement; dot, dot, dot. But what I cannot thus eliminate, what I must, head down, eyes shut, with the courage of a battalion and the blindness of a bull, charge and disperse are, indubitably, the figures behind the ferns, commercial travellers. There I've hidden them all this time in the hope that somehow they'd disappear, or better still emerge, as indeed they must, if the story's to go on gathering richness and rotundity, destiny and tragedy, as stories should, rolling along with it two, if not three, commercial travellers and a whole grove of aspidistra. 'The fronds of the aspidistra only partly concealed the commercial traveller –' Rhododendrons would conceal him utterly, and into the bargain give me my fling of red and white, for which I starve and strive; but rhododendrons in Eastbourne – in December – on the Marshes' table – no, no, I dare not; it's all a matter of crusts and cruets, frills and ferns. Perhaps there'll be a moment later by the sea. Moreover, I feel, pleasantly pricking through the green fretwork and over the glacis of cut glass, a desire to peer and peep at the man opposite – one's as much as I can manage. James Moggridge is it, whom the Marshes call Jimmy? [Minnie you must promise not to twitch till I've got this straight.] James Moggridge travels in – shall we say buttons? – but the time's not come for bringing *them* in – the big and the little on the long cards, some peacock-eyed, others dull gold; cairngorms some, and others coral sprays – but I say the time's not come. He travels, and on Thursday, his Eastbourne day, takes his meals with the Marshes. His red face, his little steady eyes – by no means altogether commonplace – his enormous appetite (that's safe; he won't look at Minnie till the bread's swamped the gravy dry), napkin tucked diamond-wise – but this is primitive, and whatever it may do the reader, don't take me in. Let's dodge to the Moggridge household, set that in motion. Well, the family boots are mended on Sundays by James himself. He reads *Truth*. But his passion? Roses – and his wife a retired hospital nurse – interesting – for God's sake let me have one woman with a name I like! But no; she's of the unborn children of the mind, illicit, none the less loved, like my rhododendrons. How many die in every novel that's written – the best, the dearest, while Moggridge lives. It's life's fault. Here's Minnie eating her egg at the moment opposite[5] and at t'other end of the line – are we past Lewes? – there must be Jimmy – or what's her twitch for?

There must be Moggridge – life's fault. Life imposes her laws; life blocks the way; life's behind the fern; life's the tyrant; oh, but not the bully! No, for I assure you I come willingly; I come wooed by Heaven knows what compulsion across ferns and cruets, table splashed and bottles smeared. I come irresistibly to lodge myself somewhere on the firm flesh, in the robust spine, wherever I can penetrate or find foothold on the person, in the soul, of Moggridge the man. The enormous stability of the fabric; the spine tough as whalebone, straight as oak-tree; the ribs radiating branches; the flesh taut tarpaulin; the red hollows; the suck and regurgitation of the heart; while from above meat falls in brown cubes and beer gushes to be churned to blood again – and so we reach the eyes. Behind the aspidistra they see something: black, white, dismal; now the plate again; behind the aspidistra they see an elderly woman; 'Marsh's sister. Hilda's more my sort'; the tablecloth now. 'Marsh would know what's wrong with Morrises . . .' talk that over; cheese has come; the plate again; turn it round – the enormous fingers; now the woman opposite. 'Marsh's sister – not a bit like Marsh; wretched, elderly female. . . You should feed your hens. . . . God's truth, what's set her twitching? Not what *I* said? Dear, dear, dear! these elderly women. Dear, dear!'

[Yes, Minnie; I know you've twitched, but one moment – James Moggridge.]

'Dear, dear, dear!' How beautiful the sound is! like the knock of a mallet on seasoned timber, like the throb of the heart of an ancient whaler when the seas press thick and the green is clouded. 'Dear, dear!' what a passing bell for the souls of the fretful to soothe them and solace them, lap them in linen, saying, 'So long. Good luck to you!' and then, 'What's your pleasure?' for though Moggridge would pluck his rose for her, that's done, that's over. Now what's the next thing? 'Madam, you'll miss your train,' for they don't linger.

That's the man's way; that's the sound that reverberates; that's St Paul's and the motor-omnibuses. But we're brushing the crumbs off. Oh, Moggridge, you won't stay? You must be off? Are you driving through Eastbourne this afternoon in one of those little carriages? Are you the man who's walled up in green cardboard boxes, and sometimes has the blinds down, and sometimes sits so solemn staring like a sphinx, and always there's a look of the sepulchral, something of the undertaker, the coffin, and the dusk about horse and driver? Do tell me – but the doors slammed. We shall never meet again. Moggridge, farewell!

Yes, yes, I'm coming. Right up to the top of the house. One moment I'll linger. How the mud goes round in the mind – what a swirl these monsters leave, the waters rocking, the weeds waving and green here, black there, striking to the sand, till by degrees the atoms reassemble, the deposit sifts itself, and again through the eyes one sees clear and still, and there comes to the lips some prayer for the departed, some obsequy for the souls of those one nods to, the people one never meets again.

James Moggridge is dead now, gone for ever. Well, Minnie – 'I can face it no longer.' If she said that – (Let me look at her. She is brushing the eggshell into deep declivities). She said it certainly, leaning against the wall of the bedroom, and plucking at the little balls which edge the claret-coloured curtain. But when the self speaks to the self, who is speaking? – the entombed soul, the spirit driven in, in, in to the central catacomb; the self that took the veil and left the world – a coward perhaps, yet somehow beautiful, as it flits with its lantern restlessly up and down the dark corridors. 'I can bear it no longer,' her spirit says. 'That man at lunch – Hilda – the children.' Oh, heavens, her sob! It's the spirit wailing its destiny, the spirit driven hither, thither, lodging on the diminishing carpets – meagre footholds – shrunken shreds of all the vanishing universe – love, life, faith, husband, children, I know not what splendours and pageantries glimpsed in girlhood. 'Not for me – not for me.'

But then – the muffins, the bald elderly dog? Bead mats I should fancy and the consolation of underlinen. If Minnie Marsh were run over and taken to hospital, nurses and doctors themselves would exclaim. . . . There's the vista and the vision – there's the distance – the blue blot at the end of the avenue, while, after all, the tea is rich, the muffin hot, and the dog – 'Benny, to your basket, sir, and see what mother's brought you!' So, taking the glove with the worn thumb, defying once more the encroaching demon of what's called going in holes, you renew the fortifications, threading the grey wool, running it in and out.

Running it in and out, across and over, spinning a web through which God himself – hush, don't think of God! How firm the stitches are! You must be proud of your darning. Let nothing disturb her. Let the light fall gently, and the clouds show an inner vest of the first green leaf. Let the sparrow perch on the twig and shake the raindrop hanging to the twig's elbow . . . Why look up? Was it a sound, a thought? Oh, heavens! Back again to the thing you did, the plate glass with the violet loops? But Hilda will come. Ignominies, humiliations, oh! Close the breach.

Having mended her glove, Minnie Marsh lays it in the drawer. She shuts the drawer with decision. I catch sight of her face in the glass. Lips are pursed. Chin held high. Next she laces her shoes. Then she touches her throat. What's your brooch? Mistletoe or merrythought? And what is happening? Unless I'm much mistaken, the pulse's quickened, the moment's coming, the threads are racing, Niagara's ahead. Here's the crisis! Heaven be with you! Down she goes. Courage, courage! Face it, be it! For God's sake don't wait on the mat now! There's the door! I'm on your side. Speak! Confront her, confound her soul!

'Oh, I beg your pardon! Yes, this is Eastbourne. I'll reach it down for you. Let me try the handle.' [But, Minnie, though we keep up pretences, I've read you right – I'm with you now.]

'That's all your luggage?'

'Much obliged, I'm sure.'

(But why do you look about you? Hilda won't come to the station, nor John; and Moggridge is driving at the far side of Eastbourne.)

'I'll wait by my bag, ma'am, that's safest. He said he'd meet me. . . . Oh, there he is! That's my son.'

So they walk off together.

Well, but I'm confounded. . . . Surely Minnie, you know better! A strange young man. . . . Stop! I'll tell him – Minnie! – Miss Marsh! – I don't know though. There's something queer in her cloak as it blows. Oh, but it's untrue, it's indecent. . . . Look how he bends as they reach the gateway. She finds her ticket. What's the joke? Off they go, down the road, side by side. . . . Well, my world's done for! What do I stand on? What do I know? That's not Minnie. There never was Moggridge. Who am I? Life's bare as bone.

And yet the last look of them – he stepping from the kerb and she following him round the edge of the big building brims me with wonder – floods me anew. Mysterious figures! Mother and son. Who are you? Why do you walk down the street? Where tonight will you sleep, and then, tomorrow? Oh, how it whirls and surges – floats me afresh! I start after them. People drive this way and that. The white light splutters and pours. Plate-glass windows. Carnations; chrysanthemums. Ivy in dark gardens. Milk carts at the door. Wherever I go, mysterious figures, I see you, turning the corner, mothers and sons; you, you, you. I hasten, I follow. This, I fancy, must be the sea. Grey is the landscape; dim as ashes; the water murmurs and moves. If I fall on my knees, if I go through the ritual, the ancient antics, it's you, unknown figures, you I adore; if I open my arms, it's you I embrace, you I draw to me – adorable world!

A Haunted House

Whatever hour you woke there was a door shutting. From room to room they went, hand in hand, lifting here, opening there, making sure – a ghostly couple.

'Here we left it,' she said. And he added, 'Oh, but here too!' 'It's upstairs,' she murmured, 'And in the garden,' he whispered. 'Quietly,' they said, 'or we shall wake them.'

But it wasn't that you woke us. Oh, no. 'They're looking for it; they're drawing the curtain,' one might say, and so read on a page or two. 'Now they've found it,' one would be certain, stopping the pencil on the margin. And then, tired of reading, one might rise and see for oneself, the house all empty, the doors standing open, only the wood pigeons bubbling with content and the hum of the threshing machine sounding from the farm. 'What did I come in here for? What did I want to find?' My hands were empty. 'Perhaps it's upstairs then?' The apples were in the loft. And so down again, the garden still as ever, only the book had slipped into the grass.

But they had found it in the drawing-room. Not that one could ever see them. The window-panes reflected apples, reflected roses; all the leaves were green in the glass. If they moved in the drawing-room, the apple only turned its yellow side. Yet, the moment after, if the door was opened, spread about the floor, hung upon the walls, pendant from ceiling – what? My hands were empty. The shadow of a thrush crossed the carpet; from the deepest wells of silence the wood pigeon drew its bubble of sound. 'Safe, safe, safe,' the pulse of the house beat softly. 'The treasure buried; the room . . .' the pulse stopped short. Oh, was that the buried treasure?

A moment later the light had faded. Out in the garden then? But the trees spun darkness for a wandering beam of sun. So fine, so rare, coolly sunk beneath the surface the beam I sought always burnt behind the glass. Death was the glass; death was between us; coming to the woman first, hundreds of years ago, leaving the house, sealing all the windows; the rooms were darkened. He left it, left her, went North, went East, saw the stars turned in the Southern sky; sought the house, found it dropped beneath the Downs. 'Safe, safe, safe,' the pulse of the house beat gladly, 'The treasure yours.'

The wind roars up the avenue. Trees stoop and bend this way and that. Moonbeams splash and spill wildly in the rain. But the beam of the lamp falls straight from the window. The candle burns stiff and still. Wandering through the house, opening the windows, whispering not to wake us, the ghostly couple seek their joy.

'Here we slept,' she says. And he adds, 'Kisses without number.' 'Waking in the morning –' 'Silver between the trees –' 'Upstairs –' 'In the garden –' 'When summer came –' 'In winter snowtime –' The doors go shutting far in the distance, gently knocking like the pulse of a heart.

Nearer they come; cease at the doorway. The wind falls, the rain slides silver down the glass. Our eyes darken; we hear no steps beside us; we see no lady spread her ghostly cloak. His hands shield the lantern. 'Look,' he breathes. 'Sound asleep. Love upon their lips.'

Stooping, holding their silver lamp above us, long they look and deeply. Long they pause. The wind drives straightly; the flame stoops slightly. Wild beams of moonlight cross both floor and wall, and, meeting, stain the faces bent; the faces pondering; the faces that search the sleepers and seek their hidden joy.

'Safe, safe, safe,' the heart of the house beats proudly. 'Long years –' he sighs. 'Again you found me.' 'Here,' she murmurs, 'sleeping; in the garden reading; laughing, rolling apples in the loft. Here we left our treasure –' Stooping, their light lifts the lids upon my eyes. 'Safe! safe! safe!' the pulse of the house beats wildly. Waking, I cry 'Oh, is this *your* – buried treasure? The light in the heart.'

A Society

This is how it all came about. Six or seven of us were sitting one day after tea. Some were gazing across the street into the windows of a milliner's shop where the light still shone brightly upon scarlet feathers and golden slippers. Others were idly occupied in building little towers of sugar upon the edge of the tea tray. After a time, so far as I can remember, we drew round the fire and began as usual to praise men – how strong, how noble, how brilliant, how courageous, how beautiful they were – how we envied those who by hook or by crook managed to get attached to one for life – when Poll, who had said nothing, burst into tears. Poll, I must tell you, has always been queer. For one thing her father was a strange man. He left her a fortune in his will, but on condition that she read all the books in the London Library. We comforted her as best we could; but we knew in our hearts how vain it was. For though we like her, Poll is no beauty; leaves her shoe laces untied; and must have been thinking, while we praised men, that not one of them would ever wish to marry her. At last she dried her tears. For some time we could make nothing of what she said. Strange enough it was in all conscience. She told us that, as we knew, she spent most of her time in the London Library, reading. She had begun, she said, with English literature on the top floor; and was steadily working her way down to *The Times* on the bottom. And now half, or perhaps only a quarter, way through a terrible thing had happened. She could read no more. Books were not what we thought them. 'Books,' she cried, rising to her feet and speaking with an intensity of desolation which I shall never forget, 'are for the most part unutterably bad!'

Of course we cried out that Shakespeare wrote books, and Milton and Shelley.

'Oh, yes,' she interrupted us. 'You've been well taught, I can see. But you are not members of the London Library.' Here her sobs broke forth anew. At length, recovering a little, she opened one of the pile of books which she always carried about with her – 'From a Window' or 'In a Garden' or some such name as that it was called, and it was written by a man called Benton or Henson or something of that kind.

She read the first few pages. We listened in silence. 'But that's not a book,' someone said. So she chose another. This time it was a history, but I have forgotten the writer's name. Our trepidation increased as she went on. Not a word of it seemed to be true, and the style in which it was written was execrable.

'Poetry! Poetry!' we cried, impatiently. 'Read us poetry!' I cannot describe the desolation which fell upon us as she opened a little volume and mouthed out the verbose, sentimental foolery which it contained.

'It must have been written by a woman,' one of us urged. But no. She told us that it was written by a young man, one of the most famous poets of the day. I leave you to imagine what the shock of the discovery was. Though we all cried and begged her to read no more she persisted and read us extracts from the Lives of the Lord Chancellors. When she had finished, Jane, the eldest and wisest of us, rose to her feet and said that she for one was not convinced.

'Why,' she asked 'if men write such rubbish as this, should our mothers have wasted their youth in bringing them into the world?'

We were all silent; and, in the silence, poor Poll could be heard sobbing out, 'Why, why did my father teach me to read?'

Clorinda was the first to come to her senses. 'It's all our fault,' she said. 'Every one of us knows how to read. But no one, save Poll, has ever taken the trouble to do it. I, for one, have taken it for granted that it was a woman's duty to spend her youth in bearing children. I venerated my mother for bearing ten; still more my grandmother for bearing fifteen; it was, I confess, my own ambition to bear twenty. We have gone on all these ages supposing that men were equally industrious, and that their works were of equal merit. While we have borne the children, they, we supposed, have borne the books and the pictures. We have populated the world. They have civilised it. But now that we can read, what prevents us from judging the results? Before we bring another child into the world we must swear that we will find out what the world is like.'

So we made ourselves into a society for asking questions. One of us was to visit a man-of-war; another was to hide herself in a scholar's study; another was to attend a meeting of business men; while all were to read books, look at pictures, go to concerts, keep our eyes open in the streets, and ask questions perpetually. We were very young. You can judge of our simplicity when I tell you that before parting that night we agreed that the objects of life were to produce good people and good books. Our questions were to be directed to find out how far these objects were now attained by men. We vowed solemnly that we would not bear a single child until we were satisfied.

Off we went then, some to the British Museum; others to the King's Navy; some to Oxford; others to Cambridge; we visited the Royal Academy and the Tate; heard modern music in concert rooms, went to the Law Courts, and saw new plays. No one dined out without asking her partner certain questions and carefully noting his replies. At intervals we met together and compared our observations. Oh, those were merry meetings! Never have I laughed so much as I did when Rose read her notes upon 'Honour' and described how she had dressed herself as an Aethiopian Prince and gone aboard one of His Majesty's ships.[1] Discovering the hoax, the Captain visited her (now disguised as a private gentleman) and demanded that honour should be satisfied. 'But how?' she asked. 'How?' he bellowed. 'With the cane of course!' Seeing that he was beside himself with rage and expecting that her last moment had come, she bent over and received, to her amazement, six light taps upon the behind. 'The honour of the British Navy is avenged!' he cried, and, raising herself, she saw him with the sweat pouring down his face holding out a trembling right hand. 'Away!' she exclaimed, striking an attitude and imitating the ferocity of his own expression, 'My honour has still to be satisfied!' 'Spoken like a gentleman!' he returned, and fell into profound thought. 'If six strokes avenge the honour of the King's Navy,' he mused, 'how many avenge the honour of a private gentleman?' He said he would prefer to lay the case before his brother officers. She replied haughtily that she could not wait. He praised her sensibility. 'Let me see,' he cried suddenly, 'did your father keep a carriage?' 'No,' she said. 'Or a riding horse?' 'We had a donkey,' she bethought her, 'which drew the mowing machine.' At this his face lightened. 'My mother's name –' she added. 'For God's sake, man, don't mention your mother's name!' he shrieked, trembling like an aspen and flushing to the roots of his hair, and it was ten minutes at least before she could induce him to proceed. At length he decreed that if she gave him four strokes and a half in the small of the back at a spot indicated by himself (the half conceded, he said, in recognition of the fact that her great grandmother's uncle was killed at Trafalgar) it was his opinion that her honour would be as good as new. This was done; they retired to a restaurant; drank two bottles of wine for which he insisted upon paying; and parted with protestations of eternal friendship.

Then we had Fanny's account of her visit to the Law Courts. At her first visit she had come to the conclusion that the Judges were either made of wood or were impersonated by large animals resembling man who had been trained to move with extreme dignity, mumble and nod their heads. To test her theory she had liberated a handkerchief of bluebottles at the critical moment of a trial, but was unable to judge whether the creatures gave signs of humanity for the buzzing of the flies induced so sound a sleep that she only woke in time to see the prisoners led into the cells below. But from the evidence she brought we voted that it is unfair to suppose that the Judges are men.

Helen went to the Royal Academy, but when asked to deliver her report upon the pictures she began to recite from a pale blue volume, 'O! for the touch of a vanished hand and the sound of a voice that is still.[2] Home is the hunter, home from the hill.[3] He gave his bridle reins a shake.[4] Love is sweet, love is brief.[5] Spring, the fair spring, is the year's pleasant King.[6] O! to be in England now that April's there.[7] Men must work and women must weep.[8] The path of duty is the way to glory –'[9] We could listen to no more of this gibberish.

'We want no more poetry!' we cried.

'Daughters of England!' she began, but here we pulled her down, a vase of water getting spilt over her in the scuffle.

'Thank God!' she exclaimed, shaking herself like a dog. 'Now I'll roll on the carpet and see if I can't brush off what remains of the Union Jack. Then perhaps –' here she rolled energetically. Getting up she began to explain to us what modern pictures are like when Castalia stopped her.

'What is the average size of a picture?' she asked. 'Perhaps two feet by two and a half,' she said. Castalia made notes while Helen spoke, and when she had done, and we were trying not to meet each other's eyes, rose and said, 'At your wish I spent last week at Oxbridge, disguised as a charwoman. I thus had access to the rooms of several Professors and will now attempt to give you some idea – only,' she broke off, 'I can't think how to do it. It's all so queer. These Professors,' she went on, 'live in large houses built round grass plots each in a kind of cell by himself. Yet they have every convenience and comfort. You have only to press a button or light a little lamp. Their papers are beautifully filed. Books abound. There are no children or animals, save half a dozen stray cats and one aged bullfinch – a cock. I remember,' she broke off, 'an Aunt of mine who lived at Dulwich and kept cactuses. You reached the conservatory through the double drawing-room, and there, on the hot pipes, were dozens of them, ugly, squat, bristly little plants each in a separate pot. Once in a hundred years the Aloe flowered, so my Aunt said. But she died before that happened –' We told her to keep to the point. 'Well,' she resumed, 'when Professor Hobkin was out I examined his life work, an edition of Sappho. It's a queer looking book, six or seven inches thick, not all by Sappho. Oh, no. Most of it is a defence of Sappho's chastity, which some German had denied, and I can assure you the passion with which these two gentlemen argued, the learning they displayed, the prodigious ingenuity with which they disputed the use of some implement which looked to me for all the world like a hairpin astounded me; especially when the door opened and Professor Hobkin himself appeared. A very nice, mild, old gentleman, but what could *he* know about chastity?' We misunderstood her.

'No, no,' she protested, 'he's the soul of honour I'm sure – not that he resembles Rose's sea captain in the least. I was thinking rather of my Aunt's cactuses. What could *they* know about chastity?'

Again we told her not to wander from the point, – did the Oxbridge professors help to produce good people and good books? – the objects of life.

'There!' she exclaimed. 'It never struck me to ask. It never occurred to me that they could possibly produce anything.'

'I believe,' said Sue, 'that you made some mistake. Probably Professor Hobkin was a gynaecologist. A scholar is a very different sort of man. A scholar is overflowing with humour and invention – perhaps addicted to wine, but what of that? – a delightful companion, generous, subtle, imaginative – as stands to reason. For he spends his life in company with the finest human beings that have ever existed.'

'Hum,' said Castalia. 'Perhaps I'd better go back and try again.'

Some three months later it happened that I was sitting alone when Castalia entered. I don't know what it was in the look of her that so moved me; but I could not restrain myself, and dashing across the room, I clasped her in my arms. Not only was she very beautiful; she seemed also in the highest spirits. 'How happy you look!' I exclaimed, as she sat down.

'I've been at Oxbridge,' she said.

'Asking questions?'

'Answering them,' she replied.

'You have not broken our vow?' I said anxiously, noticing something about her figure.

'Oh, the vow,' she said casually. 'I'm going to have a baby if that's what you mean. You can't imagine,' she burst out, 'how exciting, how beautiful, how satisfying –'

'What is?' I asked.

'To – to – answer questions,' she replied in some confusion. Whereupon she told me the whole of her story. But in the middle of an account which interested and excited me more than anything I had ever heard, she gave the strangest cry, half whoop, half holloa –

'Chastity! Chastity! Where's my chastity!' she cried. 'Help Ho! The scent bottle!'

There was nothing in the room but a cruet containing mustard, which I was about to administer when she recovered her composure.

'You should have thought of that three months ago,' I said severely.

'True,' she replied. 'There's not much good in thinking of it now. It was unfortunate, by the way, that my mother had me called Castalia.'

'Oh, Castalia, your mother –' I was beginning when she reached for the mustard pot.

'No, no, no,' she said shaking her head. 'If you'd been a chaste woman yourself you would have screamed at the sight of me – instead of which you rushed across the room and took me in your arms. No, Cassandra. We are neither of us chaste.' So we went on talking.

Meanwhile the room was filling up, for it was the day appointed to discuss the results of our observations. Everyone, I thought, felt as I did about Castalia. They kissed her and said how glad they were to see her again. At length, when we were all assembled, Jane rose and said that it was time to begin. She began by saying that we had now asked questions for over five years, and that though the results were bound to be inconclusive – here Castalia nudged me and whispered that she was not so sure about that. Then she got up, and, interrupting Jane in the middle of a sentence, said:

'Before you say any more, I want to know – am I to stay in the room? Because,' she added, 'I have to confess that I am an impure woman.'

Everyone looked at her in astonishment.

'You are going to have a baby?' asked Jane.

She nodded her head.

It was extraordinary to see the different expressions on their faces. A sort of hum went through the room, in which I could catch the words "impure", "baby", "Castalia", and so on. Jane who was herself considerably moved, put it to us:

'Shall she go? Is she impure?'

Such a roar filled the room as might have been heard in the street outside.

'No! No! No! Let her stay! Impure? Fiddlesticks!' Yet I fancied that some of the youngest, girls of nineteen or twenty, held back as if overcome with shyness. Then we all came about her and began asking questions, and at last I saw one of the youngest, who had kept in the background, approach shyly and say to her:

'What is chastity then? I mean is it good, or is it bad, or is it nothing at all?' She replied so low that I could not catch what she said.

'You know I was shocked,' said another, 'for at least ten minutes.'

'In my opinion,' said Poll, who was growing crusty from always reading in the London Library, 'chastity is nothing but ignorance – a most discreditable state of mind. We should admit only the unchaste to our society. I vote that Castalia shall be our President.'

This was violently disputed.

'It is as unfair to brand women with chastity as with unchastity,' said Poll. 'Some of us haven't the opportunity either. Moreover, I don't believe Cassy herself maintains that she acted as she did from a pure love of knowledge.'

'He is only twenty-one and divinely beautiful,' said Cassy, with a ravishing gesture.

'I move,' said Helen, 'that no one be allowed to talk of chastity or unchastity save those who are in love.'

'Oh, bother,' said Judith, who had been enquiring into scientific matters, 'I'm not in love and I'm longing to explain my measures for dispensing with prostitutes and fertilising virgins by Act of Parliament.'

She went on to tell us of an invention of hers to be erected at Tube stations and other public resorts, which, upon payment of a small fee, would safeguard the nation's health, accommodate its sons, and relieve its daughters. Then she had contrived a method of preserving in sealed tubes the germs of future Lord Chancellors 'or poets or painters or musicians,' she went on, 'supposing, that is to say, that these breeds are not extinct, and that women still wish to bear children –'

'Of course we wish to bear children!' cried Castalia impatiently. Jane rapped the table.

'That is the very point we are met to consider,' she said. 'For five years we have been trying to find out whether we are justified in continuing the human race. Castalia has anticipated our decision. But it remains for the rest of us to make up our minds.'

Here one after another of our messengers rose and delivered their reports. The marvels of civilisation far exceeded our expectations, and as we learnt for the first time how man flies in the air, talks across space, penetrates to the heart of an atom, and embraces the universe in his speculations a murmur of admiration burst from our lips.

'We are proud,' we cried, 'that our mothers sacrificed their youth in such a cause as this!' Castalia, who had been listening intently, looked prouder than all the rest. Then Jane reminded us that we had still much to learn, and Castalia begged us to make haste. On we went through a vast tangle of statistics. We learnt that England has a population of so many millions, and that such and such a proportion of them is constantly hungry and in prison; that the average size of a working man's family is such, and that so great a percentage of women die from maladies incident to childbirth. Reports were read of visits to factories, shops, slums, and dockyards. Descriptions were given of the Stock Exchange, of a gigantic house of business in the City, and of a Government Office. The British Colonies were now discussed, and some account was given of our rule in India, Africa and Ireland. I was sitting by Castalia and I noticed her uneasiness.

'We shall never come to any conclusion at all at this rate,' she said. 'As it appears that civilisation is so much more complex than we had any notion, would it not be better to confine ourselves to our original enquiry? We agreed that it was the object of life to produce good people and good books. All this time we have been talking of aeroplanes, factories, and money. Let us talk about men themselves and their arts, for that is the heart of the matter.'

So the diners out stepped forward with long slips of paper containing answers to their questions. These had been framed after much consideration. A good man, we had agreed, must at any rate be honest, passionate, and unworldly. But whether or not a particular man possessed those qualities could only be discovered by asking questions, often beginning at a remote distance from the centre. Is Kensington a nice place to live in? Where is your son being educated – and your daughter? Now please tell me, what do you pay for your cigars? By the way, is Sir Joseph a baronet or only a knight? Often it seemed that we learnt more from trivial questions of this kind than from more direct ones. 'I accepted my peerage,' said Lord Bunkum, 'because my wife wished it.' I forget how many titles were accepted for the same reason. 'Working fifteen hours out of the twenty-four, as I do –' ten thousand professional men began.

'No, no, of course you can neither read nor write. But why do you work so hard?' 'My dear lady, with a growing family –' 'But *why* does your family grow?' Their wives wished that too, or perhaps it was the British Empire. But more significant than the answers were the refusals to answer. Very few would reply at all to questions about morality and religion, and such answers as were given were not serious. Questions as to the value of money and power were almost invariably brushed aside, or pressed at extreme risk to the asker. 'I'm sure,' said Jill, 'that if Sir Harley Tightboots hadn't been carving the mutton when I asked him about the capitalist system he would have cut my throat. The only reason why we escaped with our lives over and over again is that men are at once so hungry and so chivalrous. They despise us too much to mind what we say.'

'Of course they despise us,' said Eleanor. 'At the same time how do you account for this – I made enquiries among the artists. Now no woman has ever been an artist, has she Poll?'

'Jane–Austen–Charlotte–Brontë–George–Eliot,' cried Poll, like a man crying muffins in a back street.

'Damn the woman!' someone exclaimed. 'What a bore she is!'

'Since Sappho there has been no female of first rate –' Eleanor began, quoting from a weekly newspaper.

'It's now well known that Sappho was the somewhat lewd invention of Professor Hobkin,' Ruth interrupted.

'Anyhow, there is no reason to suppose that any woman ever has been able to write or ever will be able to write,' Eleanor continued. 'And yet, whenever I go among authors they never cease to talk to me about their books. Masterly! I say, or Shakespeare himself! (for one must say something) and I assure you, they believe me.'

'That proves nothing,' said Jane. They all do it. 'Only,' she sighed, 'It doesn't seem to help *us* much. Perhaps we had better examine modern literature next. Liz, it's your turn.'

Elizabeth rose and said that in order to prosecute her enquiry she had dressed as a man and been taken for a reviewer.

'I have read new books pretty steadily for the past five years,' said she. 'Mr Wells is the most popular living writer; then comes Mr Arnold Bennett; then Mr Compton Mackenzie; Mr McKenna and Mr Walpole may be bracketed together.' She sat down.

'But you've told us nothing!' we expostulated. 'Or do you mean that these gentlemen have greatly surpassed Jane-Eliot and that English fiction is – where's that review of yours? Oh, yes, "safe in their hands."'

'Safe, quite safe,' she said, shifting uneasily from foot to foot. 'And I'm sure that they give away even more than they receive.'

We were all sure of that. 'But,' we pressed her, 'do they write good books?'

'Good books?' she said, looking at the ceiling. 'You must remember,' she began, speaking with extreme rapidity, 'that fiction is the mirror of life. And you can't deny that education is of the highest importance, and that it would be extremely annoying, if you found yourself alone at Brighton late at night, not to know which was the best boarding house to stay at, and suppose it was a dripping Sunday evening – wouldn't it be nice to go to the Movies?'

'But what has that got to do with it?' we asked.

'Nothing – nothing – nothing whatever,' she replied.

'Well, tell us the truth,' we bade her.

'The truth? But isn't it wonderful,' she broke off – 'Mr Chitter has written a weekly article for the past thirty years upon love or hot buttered toast and has sent all his sons to Eton –'

'The truth!' we demanded.

'Oh, the truth,' she stammered, 'the truth has nothing to do with literature,' and sitting down she refused to say another word.

It all seemed to us very inconclusive.

'Ladies, we must try to sum up the results,' Jane was beginning when a hum, which had been heard for some time through the open window, drowned her voice.

'War! War! War! Declaration of War!' men were shouting in the street below.

We looked at each other in horror.

'What war?' we cried. 'What war?' We remembered, too late, that we had never thought of sending anyone to the House of Commons.

We had forgotten all about it. We turned to Poll, who had reached the history shelves in the London Library, and asked her to enlighten us.

'Why,' we cried, 'do men go to war?'

'Sometimes for one reason, sometimes for another,' she replied calmly. 'In 1760, for example –' The shouts outside drowned her words. 'Again in 1797 – in 1804 – It was the Austrians in 1866 – 1870 was the Franco-Prussian – In 1900 on the other hand –'

'But it's now 1914!' we cut her short.

'Ah, I don't know what they're going to war for now,' she admitted.

*   *   *

The war was over and peace was in process of being signed, when I once more found myself with Castalia in the room where our meetings used to be held. We began idly turning over the pages of our old minute books. 'Queer,' I mused, 'to see what we were thinking five years ago.' 'We are agreed,' Castalia quoted, reading over my shoulder, 'that it is the object of life to produce good people and good books.' We made no comment upon *that*. 'A good man is at any rate honest, passionate and unworldly.' 'What a woman's language!' I observed. 'Oh, dear,' cried Castalia, pushing the book away from her, 'What fools we were! It was all Poll's father's fault,' she went on. 'I believe he did it on purpose – that ridiculous will, I mean, forcing Poll to read all the books in the London Library. If we hadn't learnt to read,' she said bitterly, 'we might still have been bearing children in ignorance and that I believe was the happiest life after all. I know what you're going to say about war,' she checked me, 'and the horror of bearing children to see them killed, but our mothers did it, and their mothers, and their mothers before them. And *they* didn't complain. They couldn't read. I've done my best,' she sighed, 'to prevent my little girl from learning to read, but what's the use? I caught Ann only yesterday with a newspaper in her hand and she was beginning to ask me if it was "true". Next she'll ask me whether Mr Lloyd George is a good man, then whether Mr Arnold Bennett is a good novelist, and finally whether I believe in God. How can I bring my daughter up to believe in nothing?' she demanded.

'Surely you could teach her to believe that a man's intellect is, and always will be, fundamentally superior to a woman's?' I suggested. She brightened at this and began to turn over our old minutes again. 'Yes,' she said, 'think of their discoveries, their mathematics, their science, their philosophy, their scholarship –' and then she began to laugh, 'I shall never forget old Hobkin and the hairpin,' she said, and went on reading and laughing and I thought she was quite happy, when suddenly she threw the book from her and burst out, 'Oh, Cassandra why do you torment me? Don't you know that our belief in man's intellect is the greatest fallacy of them all?' 'What?' I exclaimed. 'Ask any journalist, schoolmaster, politician or public house keeper in the land and they will all tell you that men are much cleverer than women.' 'As if I doubted it,' she said scornfully. 'How could they help it? Haven't we bred them and fed and kept them in comfort since the beginning of time so that they may be clever even if they're nothing else? It's all our doing!' she cried. 'We insisted upon having intellect and now we've got it. And it's intellect,' she continued, 'that's at the bottom of it. What could be more charming than a boy before he has begun to cultivate his intellect? He is beautiful to look at; he gives himself no airs; he understands the meaning of art and literature instinctively; he goes about enjoying his life and making other people enjoy theirs. Then they teach him to cultivate his intellect. He becomes a barrister, a civil servant, a general, an author, a professor. Every day he goes to an office. Every year he produces a book. He maintains a whole family by the products of his brain – poor devil! Soon he cannot come into a room without making us all feel uncomfortable; he condescends to every woman he meets, and dares not tell the truth even to his own wife; instead of rejoicing our eyes we have to shut them if we are to take him in our arms. True, they console themselves with stars of all shapes, ribbons of all shades, and incomes of all sizes – but what is to console us? That we shall be able in ten years time to spend a week-end at Lahore? Or that the least insect in Japan has a name twice the length of its body? Oh, Cassandra, for Heaven's sake let us devise a method by which men may bear children! It is our only chance. For unless we provide them with some innocent occupation we shall get neither good people nor good books; we shall perish beneath the fruits of their unbridled activity; and not a human being will survive to know that there once was Shakespeare!'

'It is too late,' I replied. 'We cannot provide even for the children that we have.'

'And then you ask me to believe in intellect,' she said.

While we spoke, men were crying hoarsely and wearily in the street, and, listening, we heard that the Treaty of Peace had just been signed.[10]

The voices died away. The rain was falling and interfered no doubt with the proper explosion of the fireworks.

'My cook will have bought the *Evening News*,' said Castalia, 'and Ann will be spelling it out over her tea. I must go home.'

'It's no good – not a bit of good,' I said. 'Once she knows how to read there's only one thing you can teach her to believe in – and that is herself.'

'Well, that would be a change,' said Castalia.

So we swept up the papers of our Society, and though Ann was playing with her doll very happily, we solemnly made her a present of the lot and told her we had chosen her to be President of the Society of the future – upon which she burst into tears, poor little girl.

Monday or Tuesday

Lazy and indifferent, shaking space easily from his wings, knowing his way, the heron passes over the church beneath the sky. White and distant, absorbed in itself, endlessly the sky covers and uncovers, moves and remains. A lake? Blot the shores of it out! A mountain? Oh, perfect – the sun gold on its slopes. Down that falls. Ferns then, or white feathers, for ever and ever –

Desiring truth, awaiting it, laboriously distilling a few words, for ever desiring – (a cry starts to the left, another to the right. Wheels strike divergently. Omnibuses conglomerate in conflict) – for ever desiring – (the clock asseverates with twelve distinct strokes that it is midday;[1] light sheds gold scales; children swarm) – for ever desiring truth. Red is the dome; coins hang on the trees; smoke trails from the chimneys; bark, shout, cry 'Iron for sale' – and truth?

Radiating to a point men's feet and women's feet, black or gold-encrusted – (This foggy weather – Sugar? No, thank you – The commonwealth of the future) – the firelight darting and making the room red, save for the black figures and their bright eyes, while outside a van discharges, Miss Thingummy drinks tea at her desk, and plate-glass preserves fur coats –

Flaunted, leaf-light, drifting at corners, blown across the wheels, silver-splashed, home or not home, gathered, scattered, squandered in separate scales, swept up, down, torn, sunk, assembled – and truth?

Now to recollect by the fireside on the white square of marble. From ivory depths words rising shed their blackness, blossom and penetrate. Fallen the book; in the flame, in the smoke, in the momentary sparks – or now voyaging, the marble square pendant, minarets beneath and the Indian seas, while space rushes blue and stars glint – truth? or now, content with closeness?

Lazy and indifferent the heron returns; the sky veils her stars; then bares them.

The String Quartet

Well, here we are, and if you cast your eye over the room you will see that Tubes and trams and omnibuses, private carriages not a few, even, I venture to believe, landaus with bays in them, have been busy at it, weaving threads from one end of London to the other. Yet I begin to have my doubts –

If indeed it's true, as they're saying, that Regent Street is up, and the Treaty signed,[1] and the weather not cold for the time of year, and even at that rent not a flat to be had, and the worst of influenza its after effects; if I bethink me of having forgotten to write about the leak in the larder, and left my glove in the train; if the ties of blood require me, leaning forward, to accept cordially the hand which is perhaps offered hesitatingly –

'Seven years since we met!'

'The last time in Venice.'

'And where are you living now?'

'Well, the late afternoon suits me the best, though, if it weren't asking too much –'

'But I knew you at once!'

'Still, the war made a break –'

If the mind's shot through by such little arrows, and – for human society compels it – no sooner is one launched than another presses forward; if this engenders heat and in addition they've turned on the electric light; if saying one thing does, in so many cases, leave behind it a need to improve and revise, stirring besides regrets, pleasures, vanities, and desires – if it's all the facts I mean, and the hats, the fur boas, the gentlemen's swallow-tail coats, and pearl tie-pins that come to the surface – what chance is there?

Of what? It becomes every minute more difficult to say why, in spite of everything, I sit here believing I can't now say what, or even remember the last time it happened.

'Did you see the procession?'

'The King looked cold.'

'No, no, no. But what was it?'

'She's bought a house at Malmesbury.'

'How lucky to find one!'

On the contrary, it seems to me pretty sure that she, whoever she may be, is damned, since it's all a matter of flats and hats and sea gulls, or so it seems to be for a hundred people sitting here well dressed, walled in, furred, replete. Not that I can boast, since I too sit passive on a gilt chair, only turning the earth above a buried memory, as we all do, for there are signs, if I'm not mistaken, that we're all recalling something, furtively seeking something. Why fidget? Why so anxious about the sit of cloaks; and gloves – whether to button or unbutton? Then watch that elderly face against the dark canvas, a moment ago urbane and flushed; now taciturn and sad, as if in shadow. Was it the sound of the second violin tuning in the ante-room? Here they come; four black figures, carrying instruments, and seat themselves facing the white squares under the downpour of light; rest the tips of their bows on the music stand; with a simultaneous movement lift them; lightly poise them, and, looking across at the player opposite, the first violin counts one, two, three –

Flourish, spring, burgeon, burst! The pear tree on the top of the mountain. Fountains jet; drops descend. But the waters of the Rhone flow swift and deep, race under the arches, and sweep the trailing water leaves, washing shadows over the silver fish, the spotted fish rushed down by the swift waters, now swept into an eddy where -- it's difficult this – conglomeration of fish all in a pool; leaping, splashing, scraping sharp fins; and such a boil of current that the yellow pebbles are churned round and round, round and round – free now, rushing downwards, or even somehow ascending in exquisite spirals into the air; curled like thin shavings from under a plane; up and up. . . . How lovely goodness is in those who, stepping lightly, go smiling through the world! Also in jolly old fishwives, squatted under arches, obscene old women, how deeply they laugh and shake and rollick, when they walk, from side to side, hum, hah!

'That's an early Mozart, of course –'

'But the tune, like all his tunes, makes one despair – I mean hope. What do I mean? That's the worst of music! I want to dance, laugh, eat pink cakes, yellow cakes, drink thin, sharp wine. Or an indecent story, now – I could relish that. The older one grows the more one likes indecency. Hah, hah! I'm laughing. What at? You said nothing, nor did the old gentleman opposite. . . . But suppose – suppose – Hush!'

The melancholy river bears us on. When the moon comes through the trailing willow boughs, I see your face, I hear your voice and the bird singing as we pass the osier bed. What are you whispering? Sorrow, sorrow. Joy, joy. Woven together, inextricably commingled, bound in pain and strewn in sorrow – crash!

The boat sinks. Rising, the figures ascend, but now leaf thin, tapering to a dusky wraith, which, fiery tipped, draws its twofold passion from my heart. For me it sings, unseals my sorrow, thaws compassion, floods with love the sunless world, nor, ceasing, abates its tenderness, but deftly, subtly, weaves in and out until in this pattern, this consummation, the cleft ones unify; soar, sob, sink to rest, sorrow and joy.

Why then grieve? Ask what? Remain unsatisfied? I say all's been settled; yes; laid to rest under a coverlet of rose leaves, falling. Falling. Ah, but they cease. One rose leaf, falling from an enormous height, like a little parachute dropped from an invisible balloon, turns, flutters waveringly. It won't reach us.[2]

'No, no. I noticed nothing. That's the worst of music – these silly dreams. The second violin was late, you say?'

'There's old Mrs Munro, feeling her way out – blinder each year, poor woman – on this slippery floor.'

Eyeless old age, grey-headed Sphinx. . . . There she stands on the pavement, beckoning, so sternly, to the red omnibus.

'How lovely! How well they play! How – how – how!'

The tongue is but a clapper. Simplicity itself. The feathers in the hat next me are bright and pleasing as a child's rattle. The leaf on the plane-tree flashes green through the chink in the curtain. Very strange, very exciting.

'How – how – how!' Hush!

These are the lovers on the grass.

'If, madam, you will take my hand –'

'Sir, I would trust you with my heart. Moreover, we have left our bodies in the banqueting hall. Those on the turf are the shadows of our souls.'

'Then these are the embraces of our souls.' The lemons nod assent. The swan pushes from the bank and floats dreaming into mid-stream.

'But to return. He followed me down the corridor, and, as we turned the corner, trod on the lace of my petticoat. What could I do but cry "Ah!" and stop to finger it? At which he drew his sword, made passes as if he were stabbing something to death, and cried, "Mad! Mad!

Mad!" Whereupon I screamed, and the Prince, who was writing in the large vellum book in the oriel window, came out in his velvet skull-cap and furred slippers, snatched a rapier from the wall – the King of Spain's gift, you know – on which I escaped, flinging on this cloak to hide the ravages to my skirt – to hide . . . But listen! the horns!'

The gentleman replies so fast to the lady, and she runs up the scale with such witty exchange of compliment now culminating in a sob of passion, that the words are indistinguishable though the meaning is plain enough – love, laughter, flight, pursuit, celestial bliss – all floated out on the gayest ripple of tender endearment – until the sound of the silver horns, at first far distant, gradually sounds more and more distinctly, as if seneschals were saluting the dawn or proclaiming ominously the escape of the lovers . . . The green garden, moonlit pool, lemons, lovers, and fish are all dissolved in the opal sky, across which, as the horns are joined by trumpets and supported by clarions there rise white arches firmly planted on marble pillars. . . . Tramp and trumpeting. Clang and clangour. Firm establishment. Fast foundations. March of myriads. Confusion and chaos trod to earth. But this city to which we travel has neither stone nor marble; hangs enduring; stands unshakable; nor does a face, nor does a flag greet or welcome. Leave then to perish your hope; droop in the desert my joy; naked advance. Bare are the pillars; auspicious to none; casting no shade; resplendent; severe. Back then I fall, eager no more, desiring only to go, find the street, mark the buildings, greet the applewoman, say to the maid who opens the door: A starry night.

'Good night, good night. You go this way?'
'Alas. I go that.'

Blue & Green

GREEN

The pointed fingers of glass hang downwards. The light slides down the glass, and drops a pool of green. All day long the ten fingers of the lustre drop green upon the marble. The feathers of parakeets – their harsh cries – sharp blades of palm trees – green, too; green needles glittering in the sun. But the hard glass drips on to the marble; the pools hover above the desert sand; the camels lurch through them; the pools settle on the marble; rushes edge them; weeds clog them; here and there a white blossom; the frog flops over; at night the stars are set there unbroken. Evening comes, and the shadow sweeps the green over the mantelpiece; the ruffled surface of ocean. No ships come; the aimless waves sway beneath the empty sky. It's night; the needles drip blots of blue. The green's out.

BLUE

The snub-nosed monster rises to the surface and spouts through his blunt nostrils two columns of water, which, fiery-white in the centre, spray off into a fringe of blue beads. Strokes of blue line the black tarpaulin of his hide. Slushing the water through mouth and nostrils he sinks, heavy with water, and the blue closes over him dowsing the polished pebbles of his eyes. Thrown upon the beach he lies, blunt, obtuse, shedding dry blue scales. Their metallic blue stains the rusty iron on the beach. Blue are the ribs of the wrecked rowing boat. A wave rolls beneath the blue bells. But the cathedral's different, cold, incense laden, faint blue with the veils of madonnas.

1922–1925

A Woman's College from Outside

The feathery-white moon never let the sky grow dark; all night the chestnut blossoms were white in the green, and dim was the cow-parsley in the meadows.[1] Neither to Tartary nor to Arabia went the wind of the Cambridge courts, but lapsed dreamily in the midst of grey-blue clouds over the roofs of Newnham. There, in the garden, if she needed space to wander, she might find it among the trees; and as none but women's faces could meet her face, she might unveil it blank, featureless, and gaze into rooms where at that hour, blank, featureless, eyelids white over eyes, ringless hands extended upon sheets, slept innumerable women. But here and there a light still burned.

A double light one might figure in Angela's room, seeing how bright Angela herself was, and how bright came back the reflection of herself from the square glass. The whole of her was perfectly delineated – perhaps the soul. For the glass held up an untrembling image – white and gold, red slippers, pale hair with blue stones in it, and never a ripple or shadow to break the smooth kiss of Angela and her reflection in the glass, as if she were glad to be Angela. Anyhow the moment was glad – the bright picture hung in the heart of night, the shrine hollowed in the nocturnal blackness. Strange indeed to have this visible proof of the rightness of things; this lily floating flawless upon Time's pool, fearless, as if this were sufficient – this reflection. Which meditation she betrayed by turning, and the mirror held nothing at all, or only the brass bedstead, and she, running here and there, patting, and darting, became like a woman in a house, and changed again, pursing her lips over a black book and marking with her finger what surely could not be a firm grasp of the science of economics. Only Angela Williams was at Newnham for the purpose of earning her living, and could not forget even in moments of impassioned adoration the cheques of her father at Swansea; her mother washing in the scullery: pink frocks out to dry on the line; tokens that even the lily no longer floats flawless upon the pool, but has a name on a card like another.

A. Williams – one may read it in the moonlight; and next to it some Mary or Eleanor, Mildred, Sarah, Phoebe upon square cards on their doors. All names, nothing but names. The cool white light withered them and starched them until it seemed as if the only purpose of all these names was to rise martially in order should there be a call on them to extinguish a fire, suppress an insurrection, or pass an examination. Such is the power of names written upon cards pinned upon doors. Such too the resemblance, what with tiles, corridors, and bedroom doors, to dairy or nunnery, a place of seclusion or discipline, where the bowl of milk stands cool and pure and there's a great washing of linen.

At that very moment soft laughter came from behind a door. A prim-voiced clock struck the hour – one, two. Now if the clock were issuing his commands, they were disregarded. Fire, insurrection, examination, were all snowed under by laughter, or softly uprooted, the sound seeming to bubble up from the depths and gently waft away the hour, rules, discipline. The bed was strewn with cards. Sally was on the floor. Helena in the chair. Good Bertha clasping her hands by the fire-place. A. Williams came in yawning.

'Because it's utterly and intolerably damnable,' said Helena.

'Damnable,' echoed Bertha. Then yawned.

'We're not eunuchs.'

'I saw her slipping in by the back gate with that old hat on. They don't want us to know.'

'They?' said Angela. 'She.'

Then the laughter.

The cards were spread, falling with their red and yellow faces on the table, and hands were dabbled in the cards. Good Bertha, leaning with her head against the chair, sighed profoundly. For she would willingly have slept, but since night is free pasturage, a limitless field, since night is unmoulded richness, one must tunnel into its darkness. One must hang it with jewels. Night was shared in secret, day browsed on by the whole flock. The blinds were up. A mist was on the garden. Sitting on the floor by the window (while the others played), body, mind, both together, seemed blown through the air, to trail across the bushes. Ah, but she desired to stretch out in bed and to sleep! She believed that no one felt her desire for sleep; she believed humbly – sleepily – with sudden nods and lurchings, that other people were wide awake. When they laughed all together a bird chirped in its sleep out in the garden, as if the laughter –

Yes, as if the laughter (for she dozed now) floated out much like mist and attached itself by soft elastic shreds to plants and bushes, so that the garden was vaporous and clouded. And then, swept by the wind, the bushes would bow themselves and the white vapour blow off across the world.

From all the rooms where women slept this vapour issued, attaching itself to shrubs, like mist, and then blew freely out into the open. Elderly women slept, who would on waking immediately clasp the ivory rod of office. Now smooth and colourless, reposing deeply, they lay surrounded, lay supported, by the bodies of youth recumbent or grouped at the window; pouring forth into the garden this bubbling laughter, this irresponsible laughter: this laughter of mind and body floating away rules, hours, discipline: immensely fertilising, yet formless, chaotic, trailing and straying and tufting the rose-bushes with shreds of vapour.

'Ah,' breathed Angela, standing at the window in her night-gown. Pain was in her voice. She leant her head out. The mist was cleft as if her voice parted it. She had been talking, while the others played, to Alice Avery, about Bamborough Castle; the colour of the sands at evening; upon which Alice said she would write and settle the day, in August, and stooping, kissed her, at least touched her head with her hand, and Angela, positively unable to sit still, like one possessed of a wind-lashed sea in her heart, roamed up and down the room (the witness of such a scene) throwing her arms out to relieve this excitement, this astonishment at the incredible stooping of the miraculous tree with the golden fruit at its summit – hadn't it dropped into her arms? She held it glowing to her breast, a thing not to be touched, thought of, or spoken about, but left to glow there. And then, slowly putting there her stockings, there her slippers, folding her petticoat neatly on top, Angela, her other name being Williams, realised – how could she express it? – that after the dark churning of myriad ages here was light at the end of the tunnel; life; the world. Beneath her it lay – all good; all lovable. Such was her discovery.

Indeed, how could one then feel surprise if, lying in bed, she could not close her eyes? – something irresistibly unclosed them – if in the shallow darkness chair and chest of drawers looked stately, and the looking-glass precious with its ashen hint of day? Sucking her thumb like a child (her age nineteen last November), she lay in this good world, this new world, this world at the end of the tunnel, until a desire to see it or forestall it drove her, tossing her blankets, to guide herself to the window, and there, looking out upon the garden, where the mist lay, all the windows open, one fiery-bluish, something murmuring in the distance, the world of course, and the morning coming, 'Oh,' she cried, as if in pain.

In the Orchard

Miranda slept in the orchard, lying in a long chair beneath the apple-tree. Her book had fallen into the grass, and her finger still seemed to point at the sentence 'Ce pays est vraiment un des coins du monde où le rire des filles éclate le mieux . . . ' as if she had fallen asleep just there. The opals on her finger flushed green, flushed rosy, and again flushed orange as the sun, oozing through the apple-trees, filled them. Then, when the breeze blew, her purple dress rippled like a flower attached to a stalk; the grasses nodded; and the white butterfly came blowing this way and that just above her face.

Four feet in the air over her head the apples hung. Suddenly there was a shrill clamour as if they were gongs of cracked brass beaten violently, irregularly, and brutally. It was only the school-children saying the multiplication table in unison, stopped by the teacher, scolded, and beginning to say the multiplication table over again. But this clamour passed four feet above Miranda's head, went through the apple boughs, and, striking against the cowman's little boy who was picking blackberries in the hedge when he should have been at school, made him tear his thumb on the thorns.

Next there was a solitary cry – sad, human, brutal. Old Parsley was, indeed, blind drunk.

Then the very topmost leaves of the apple-tree, flat like little fish against the blue, thirty feet above the earth, chimed with a pensive and lugubrious note. It was the organ in the church playing one of Hymns Ancient and Modern. The sound floated out and was cut into atoms by a flock of fieldfares flying at an enormous speed – somewhere or other. Miranda lay asleep thirty feet beneath.

Then above the apple-tree and the pear-tree two hundred feet above Miranda lying asleep in the orchard bells thudded, intermittent, sullen, didactic, for six poor women of the parish were being churched and the Rector was returning thanks to heaven.

And above that with a sharp squeak the golden feather of the church tower turned from south to east. The wind changed. Above everything else it droned, above the woods, the meadows, the hills, miles above

Miranda lying in the orchard asleep. It swept on, eyeless, brainless, meeting nothing that could stand against it, until, wheeling the other way, it turned south again. Miles below, in a space as big as the eye of a needle, Miranda stood upright and cried aloud: 'Oh, I shall be late for tea!'

Miranda slept in the orchard – or perhaps she was not asleep, for her lips moved very slightly as if they were saying, 'Ce pays est vraiment un des coins du monde . . . où le rire des filles . . . éclate . . . éclate . . . éclate . . .' and then she smiled and let her body sink all its weight on to the enormous earth which rises, she thought, to carry me on its back as if I were a leaf, or a queen (here the children said the multiplication table), or, Miranda went on, I might be lying on the top of a cliff with the gulls screaming above me. The higher they fly, she continued, as the teacher scolded the children and rapped Jimmy over the knuckles till they bled, the deeper they look into the sea – into the sea, she repeated, and her fingers relaxed and her lips closed gently as if she were floating on the sea, and then, when the shout of the drunken man sounded overhead, she drew breath with an extraordinary ecstasy, for she thought that she heard life itself crying out from a rough tongue in a scarlet mouth, from the wind, from the bells, from the curved green leaves of the cabbages.

Naturally she was being married when the organ played the tune from Hymns Ancient and Modern, and, when the bells rang after the six poor women had been churched, the sullen intermittent thud made her think that the very earth shook with the hoofs of the horse that was galloping towards her ('Ah, I have only to wait!' she sighed), and it seemed to her that everything had already begun moving, crying, riding, flying round her, across her, towards her in a pattern.

Mary is chopping the wood, she thought; Pearman is herding the cows; the carts are coming up from the meadows; the rider – and she traced out the lines that the men, the carts, the birds, and the rider made over the countryside until they all seemed driven out, round, and across by the beat of her own heart.

Miles up in the air the wind changed; the golden feather of the church tower squeaked; and Miranda jumped up and cried: 'Oh, I shall be late for tea!'

Miranda slept in the orchard, or was she asleep or was she not asleep?

Her purple dress stretched between the two apple-trees. There were twenty-four apple-trees in the orchard, some slanting slightly, others growing straight with a rush up the trunk which spread wide into branches and formed into round red or yellow drops. Each apple-tree had sufficient space. The sky exactly fitted the leaves. When the breeze blew, the line of the boughs against the wall slanted slightly and then returned. A wagtail flew diagonally from one corner to another. Cautiously hopping, a thrush advanced towards a fallen apple; from the other wall a sparrow fluttered just above the grass. The uprush of the trees was tied down by these movements; the whole was compacted by the orchard walls. For miles beneath the earth was clamped together; rippled on the surface with wavering air; and across the corner of the orchard the blue-green was slit by a purple streak. The wind changing, one bunch of apples was tossed so high that it blotted out two cows in the meadow ('Oh, I shall be late for tea!' cried Miranda), and the apples hung straight across the wall again.

Mrs Dalloway in Bond Street

Mrs Dalloway said she would buy the gloves herself.

Big Ben was striking as she stepped out into the street. It was eleven o'clock and the unused hour was fresh as if issued to children on a beach. But there was something solemn in the deliberate swing of the repeated strokes; something stirring in the murmur of wheels and the shuffle of footsteps.

No doubt they were not all bound on errands of happiness. There is much more to be said about us than that we walk the streets of Westminster. Big Ben too is nothing but steel rods consumed by rust were it not for the care of H.M.'s Office of Works. Only for Mrs Dalloway the moment was complete; for Mrs Dalloway June was fresh. A happy childhood – and it was not to his daughters only that Justin Parry had seemed a fine fellow (weak of course on the Bench); flowers at evening, smoke rising; the caw of rooks falling from ever so high, down down through the October air – there is nothing to take the place of childhood. A leaf of mint brings it back: or a cup with a blue ring.

Poor little wretches, she sighed, and pressed forward. Oh, right under the horses' noses, you little demon! and there she was left on the kerb stretching her hand out, while Jimmy Dawes grinned on the further side.

A charming woman, poised, eager, strangely white-haired for her pink cheeks, so Scope Purvis, C. B., saw her as he hurried to his office. She stiffened a little, waiting for Durtnall's van to pass. Big Ben struck the tenth; struck the eleventh stroke. The leaden circles dissolved in the air. Pride held her erect, inheriting, handing on, acquainted with discipline and with suffering. How people suffered, how they suffered, she thought, thinking of Mrs Foxcroft at the Embassy last night decked with jewels, eating her heart out, because that nice boy was dead, and now the old Manor House (Durtnall's van passed) must go to a cousin.

'Good morning to you!' said Hugh Whitbread raising his hat rather extravagantly by the china shop, for they had known each other as children. 'Where are you off to?'

'I love walking in London,' said Mrs Dalloway. 'Really it's better than walking in the country!'

'We've just come up,' said Hugh Whitbread. 'Unfortunately to see doctors.'

'Milly?' said Mrs Dalloway, instantly compassionate.

'Out of sorts,' said Hugh Whitbread. 'That sort of thing. Dick all right?'

'First rate!' said Clarissa.

Of course, she thought, walking on, Milly is about my age – fifty– fifty-two. So it is probably *that*, Hugh's manner had said so, said it perfectly – dear old Hugh, thought Mrs Dalloway, remembering with amusement, with gratitude, with emotion, how shy, like a brother – one would rather die than speak to one's brother – Hugh had always been, when he was at Oxford, and came over, and perhaps one of them (drat the thing!) couldn't ride. How then could women sit in Parliament? How could they do things with men? For there is this extra- ordinarily deep instinct, something inside one; you can't get over it; it's no use trying; and men like Hugh respect it without our saying it, which is what one loves, thought Clarissa, in dear old Hugh.

She had passed through the Admiralty Arch and saw at the end of the empty road with its thin trees Victoria's white mound, Victoria's billowing motherliness, amplitude and homeliness, always ridiculous, yet how sublime, thought Mrs Dalloway, remembering Kensington Gardens and the old lady in horn spectacles and being told by Nanny to stop dead still and bow to the Queen. The flag flew above the Palace. The King and Queen were back then. Dick had met her at lunch the other day – a thoroughly nice woman. It matters so much to the poor, thought Clarissa, and to the soldiers. A man in bronze stood heroically on a pedestal with a gun on her left hand side – the South African war. It matters, thought Mrs Dalloway walking towards Buckingham Palace. There it stood four-square, in the broad sunshine, uncom- promising, plain. But it was character, she thought; something inborn in the race; what Indians respected. The Queen went to hospitals, opened bazaars – the Queen of England, thought Clarissa, looking at the Palace. Already at this hour a motor car passed out at the gates; soldiers saluted; the gates were shut. And Clarissa, crossing the road, entered the Park, holding herself upright.

June had drawn out every leaf on the trees. The mothers of West- minster with mottled breasts gave suck to their young. Quite respectable girls lay stretched on the grass. An elderly man, stooping very stiffly, picked up a crumpled paper, spread it out flat and flung it away. How horrible! Last night at the Embassy Sir Dighton had said, 'If I want a fellow to hold my horse, I have only to put up my hand.' But the religious question is far more serious than the economic, Sir Dighton had said, which she thought extraordinarily interesting, from a man like Sir Dighton. 'Oh, the country will never know what it has lost,' he had said, talking of his own accord, about dear Jack Stewart.

She mounted the little hill lightly. The air stirred with energy. Messages were passing from the Fleet to the Admiralty. Piccadilly and Arlington Street and the Mall seemed to chafe the very air in the Park and lift its leaves hotly, brilliantly, upon waves of that divine vitality which Clarissa loved. To ride; to dance; she had adored all that. Or going long walks in the country, talking, about books, what to do with one's life, for young people were amazingly priggish – oh, the things one had said! But one had conviction. Middle age is the devil. People like Jack'll never know that, she thought; for he never once thought of death, never, they said, knew he was dying. And now can never mourn – how did it go? – a head grown grey . . . From the contagion of the world's slow stain[1] . . . have drunk their cup a round or two before.[2] . . . From the contagion of the world's slow stain! She held herself upright.

But how Jack would have shouted! Quoting Shelley, in Piccadilly! 'You want a pin,' he would have said. He hated frumps. 'My God Clarissa! My God Clarissa!" – she could hear him now at the Devonshire House party, about poor Sylvia Hunt in her amber necklace and that dowdy old silk. Clarissa held herself upright for she had spoken aloud and now she was in Piccadilly, passing the house with the slender green columns, and the balconies; passing club windows full of newspapers; passing old Lady Burdett-Coutts' house where the glazed white parrot used to hang; and Devonshire House, without its gilt leopards; and Claridge's, where she must remember Dick wanted her to leave a card on Mrs Jepson or she would be gone. Rich Americans can be very charming. There was St James's Palace; like a child's game with bricks; and now – she had passed Bond Street – she was by Hatchard's book shop. The stream was endless – endless – endless. Lords, Ascot, Hurlingham – what was it? What a duck, she thought, looking at the frontispiece of some book of memoirs spread wide in the bow window, Sir Joshua perhaps or Romney; arch, bright, demure; the sort of girl – like her own Elizabeth – the only *real* sort of girl. And there was that absurd book, Soapy Sponge,[3] which Jim used to quote by the yard; and Shakespeare's Sonnets. She knew them by heart. Phil and she had argued all day about the Dark Lady, and Dick had said straight out at dinner that night that he had never heard of her. Really, she had married him for that! He had never read Shakespeare! There must be some little cheap book she could buy for Milly – *Cranford*[4] of course! Was there ever anything so enchanting as the cow in petticoats? If only people had that sort of humour, that sort of self-respect now, thought Clarissa, for she remembered the broad pages; the sentences ending; the characters – how one talked about them as if they were real. For all the great things one must go to the past, she thought. From the contagion of the world's slow stain . . . Fear no more the heat o' the sun.[5] . . . And now can never mourn, can never mourn, she repeated, her eyes straying over the window; for it ran in her head; the test of great poetry; the moderns had never written anything one wanted to read about death, she thought; and turned.

Omnibuses joined motor cars; motor cars vans; vans taxicabs, taxicabs motor cars – here was an open motor car with a girl, alone. Up till four, her feet tingling, I know, thought Clarissa, for the girl looked washed out, half asleep, in the corner of the car after the dance. And another car came; and another. No! No! No! Clarissa smiled good-naturedly. The fat lady had taken every sort of trouble, but diamonds! orchids! at this hour of the morning! No! No! No! The excellent policeman would, when the time came, hold up his hand. Another motor car passed. How utterly unattractive! Why should a girl of that age paint black round her eyes? And a young man, with a girl, at this hour, when the country – The admirable policeman raised his hand and Clarissa acknowledging his sway, taking her time, crossed, walked towards Bond Street; saw the narrow crooked street, the yellow banners; the thick notched telegraph wires stretched across the sky.

A hundred years ago her great-great-grandfather, Seymour Parry, who ran away with Conway's daughter, had walked down Bond Street. Down Bond Street the Parrys had walked for a hundred years, and might have met the Dalloways (Leighs on the mother's side) going up. Her father got his clothes from Hill's. There was a roll of cloth in the window, and here just one jar on a black table, incredibly expensive; like the thick pink salmon on the ice block at the fish-monger's. The jewels were exquisite – pink and orange stars, paste,

Spanish, she thought, and chains of old gold; starry buckles, little brooches which had been worn on sea-green satin by ladies with high head-dresses. But no good looking! One must economise. She must go on past the picture dealer's where one of the odd French pictures hung, as if people had thrown confetti – pink and blue – for a joke. If you had lived with pictures (and it's the same with books and music) thought Clarissa, passing the Aeolian Hall, you can't be taken in by a joke.

The river of Bond Street was clogged. There, like a Queen at a tournament, raised, regal, was Lady Bexborough. She sat in her carriage, upright, alone, looking through her glasses. The white glove was loose at her wrist. She was in black, quite shabby, yet, thought Clarissa, how extraordinarily it tells, breeding, self-respect, never saying a word too much or letting people gossip; an astonishing friend; no one can pick a hole in her after all these years, and now, there she is, thought Clarissa, passing the Countess who waited powdered, per- fectly still, and Clarissa would have given anything to be like that, the mistress of Clarefield, talking politics, like a man. But she never goes anywhere, thought Clarissa, and it's quite useless to ask her, and the carriage went on and Lady Bexborough was borne past like a Queen at a tournament, though she had nothing to live for and the old man is failing and they say she is sick of it all, thought Clarissa and the tears actually rose to her eyes as she entered the shop.

'Good morning,' said Clarissa in her charming voice. 'Gloves,' she said with her exquisite friendliness and putting her bag on the counter began, very slowly, to undo the buttons. 'White gloves,' she said. 'Above the elbow,' and she looked straight into the shop-woman's face – but this was not the girl she remembered? She looked quite old. 'These really don't fit,' said Clarissa. The shop-girl looked at them. 'Madame wears bracelets?' Clarissa spread out her fingers. 'Perhaps it's my rings.' And the girl took the grey gloves with her to the end of the counter.

Yes, thought Clarissa, if it's the girl I remember, she's twenty years older. . . . There was only one other customer, sitting sideways at the counter, her elbow poised, her bare hand drooping, vacant; like a figure on a Japanese fan, thought Clarissa, too vacant perhaps, yet some men would adore her. The lady shook her head sadly. Again the gloves were too large. She turned round the glass. 'Above the wrist,' she reproached the grey-headed woman; who looked and agreed.

They waited; a clock ticked; Bond Street hummed, dulled, distant;

the woman went away holding gloves. 'Above the wrist,' said the lady, mournfully, raising her voice. And she would have to order chairs, ices, flowers, and cloak-room tickets, thought Clarissa. The people she didn't want would come; the others wouldn't. She would stand by the door. They sold stockings – silk stockings. A lady is known by her gloves and her shoes, old Uncle William used to say. And through the hanging silk stockings quivering silver she looked at the lady, sloping shouldered, her hand drooping, her bag slipping, her eyes vacantly on the floor. It would be intolerable if dowdy women came to her party! Would one have liked Keats if he had worn red socks? Oh, at last – she drew into the counter and it flashed into her mind:

'Do you remember before the war you had gloves with pearl buttons?'

'French gloves, Madame?'

'Yes, they were French,' said Clarissa. The other lady rose very sadly and took her bag, and looked at the gloves on the counter. But they were all too large – always too large at the wrist.

'With pearl buttons,' said the shop-girl, who looked ever so much older. She split the lengths of tissue paper apart on the counter. With pearl buttons, thought Clarissa, perfectly simple – how French!

'Madame's hands are so slender,' said the shop-girl, drawing the glove firmly, smoothly, down over her rings. And Clarissa looked at her arm in the looking-glass. The glove hardly came to the elbow. Were there others half an inch longer? Still it seemed tiresome to bother her – perhaps the one day in the month, thought Clarissa, when it's an agony to stand. 'Oh, don't bother,' she said. But the gloves were brought.

'Don't you get fearfully tired,' she said in her charming voice, 'standing? When d'you get your holiday?'

'In September, Madame, when we're not so busy.'

When we're in the country thought Clarissa. Or shooting. She has a fortnight at Brighton. In some stuffy lodging. The landlady takes the sugar. Nothing would be easier than to send her to Mrs Lumley's right in the country (and it was on the tip of her tongue). But then she remembered how on their honeymoon Dick had shown her the folly of giving impulsively. It was much more important, he said, to get trade with China. Of course he was right. And she could feel the girl wouldn't like to be given things. There she was in her place. So was Dick. Selling gloves was her job. She had her own sorrows quite separate, 'and now can never mourn, can never mourn,' the words ran in her head. 'From the contagion of the world's slow stain,' thought Clarissa holding her arm stiff, for there are moments when it seems utterly futile (the glove was drawn off leaving her arm flecked with powder) – simply one doesn't believe, thought Clarissa, any more in God.

The traffic suddenly roared; the silk stockings brightened. A customer came in.

'White gloves,' she said, with some ring in her voice that Clarissa remembered.

It used, thought Clarissa, to be so simple. Down down through the air came the caw of the rooks. When Sylvia died, hundreds of years ago, the yew hedges looked so lovely with the diamond webs in the mist before early church. But if Dick were to die tomorrow, as for believing in God – no, she would let the children choose, but for herself, like Lady Bexborough, who opened the bazaar, they say, with the telegram in her hand – Roden, her favourite, killed – she would go on. But why, if one doesn't believe? For the sake of others, she thought, taking the glove in her hand. The girl would be much more unhappy if she didn't believe.

'Thirty shillings,' said the shop-woman. 'No, pardon me Madame, thirty-five. The French gloves are more.'

For one doesn't live for oneself, thought Clarissa.

And then the other customer took a glove, tugged it, and it split.

'There!' she exclaimed.

'A fault of the skin,' said the grey-headed woman hurriedly. 'Sometimes a drop of acid in tanning. Try this pair, Madame.'

'But it's an awful swindle to ask two pound ten!'

Clarissa looked at the lady; the lady looked at Clarissa.

'Gloves have never been quite so reliable since the war,' said the shop-girl, apologising, to Clarissa.

But where had she seen the other lady? – elderly, with a frill under her chin; wearing a black ribbon for gold eyeglasses; sensual, clever, like a Sargent drawing.[6] How one can tell from a voice when people are in the habit, thought Clarissa, of making other people – 'It's a shade too tight,' she said – obey. The shop-woman went off again. Clarissa was left waiting. Fear no more she repeated, playing her finger on the counter. Fear no more the heat o' the sun. Fear no more she repeated. There were little brown spots on her arm. And the girl crawled like a snail. Thou thy worldly task hast done. Thousands of young men had died that things might go on. At last! Half an inch above the elbow; pearl buttons; five and a quarter. My dear slow coach, thought Clarissa, do you think I can sit here the whole morning? Now you'll take twenty-five minutes to bring me my change!

There was a violent explosion in the street outside. The shop-women cowered behind the counters. But Clarissa, sitting very upright, smiled at the other lady. 'Miss Anstruther!' she exclaimed.

Nurse Lugton's Curtain

Nurse Lugton was asleep. She had given one great snore. She had dropped her head; thrust her spectacles up her forehead; and there she sat by the fender with her finger sticking up and a thimble on it; and her needle full of cotton hanging down; and she was snoring, snoring; and on her knees, covering the whole of her apron, was a large piece of figured blue stuff.

The animals with which it was covered did not move till Nurse Lugton snored for the fifth time. One, two, three, four, five – ah, the old woman was at last asleep. The antelope nodded to the zebra; the giraffe bit through the leaf on the tree top; all the animals began to toss and prance. For the pattern on the blue stuff was made of troops of wild beasts and below them was a lake and a bridge and a town with round roofs and little men and women looking out of the windows and riding over the bridge on horseback. But directly the old nurse snored for the fifth time, the blue stuff turned to blue air; the trees waved; you could hear the water of the lake breaking; and see the people moving over the bridge and waving their hands out of the windows.

The animals now began to move. First went the elephant and the zebra; next the giraffe and the tiger; the ostrich, the mandrill, twelve marmots and a pack of mongeese followed; the penguins and the pelicans waddled and waded, often pecking at each other, alongside. Over them burnt Nurse Lugton's golden thimble like a sun; and as Nurse Lugton snored, the animals heard the wind roaring through the forest. Down they went to drink, and as they trod, the blue curtain (for Nurse Lugton was making a curtain for Mrs John Jasper Gingham's drawing-room window) became made of grass, and roses and daisies; strewn with white and black stones; with puddles on it, and cart tracks, and little frogs hopping quickly lest the elephants should tread on them. Down they went, down the hill to the lake to drink. And soon all were gathered on the edge of the lake, some stooping down, others throwing their heads up. Really, it was a beautiful sight – and to think of all this lying across old Nurse Lugton's knees while she slept, sitting on her Windsor chair in the lamplight – to think of her apron covered with roses and grass, and with all these wild beasts trampling on it, when Nurse Lugton was mortally afraid even of poking through the bars with her umbrella at the Zoo! Even a little black beetle made her jump. But Nurse Lugton slept; Nurse Lugton saw nothing at all.

The elephants drank; and the giraffes snipped off the leaves on the highest tulip trees; and the people who crossed the bridges threw bananas at them, and tossed pineapples up into the air, and beautiful golden rolls stuffed with quinces and rose leaves, for the monkeys loved them. The old Queen came by in her palanquin; the general of the army passed; so did the Prime Minister; the Admiral, the Executioner; and great dignitaries on business in the town, which was a very beautiful place called Millamarchmantopolis. Nobody harmed the lovely beasts; many pitied them; for it was well known that even the smallest monkey was enchanted. For a great ogress had them in her toils, the people knew; and the great ogress was called Lugton. They could see her, from their windows, towering over them. She had a face like the side of a mountain with great precipices and avalanches, and chasms for her eyes and hair and nose and teeth. And every animal which strayed into her territories she froze alive, so that all day they stood stock still on her knee, but when she fell asleep, then they were released, and down they came in the evening to Millamarchmantopolis to drink.

Suddenly old Nurse Lugton twitched the curtain all in crinkles.

For a big bluebottle was buzzing round the lamp, and woke her. Up she sat and stuck her needle in.

The animals flashed back in a second. The air became blue stuff. And the curtain lay quite still on her knee. Nurse Lugton took up her needle, and went on sewing Mrs Gingham's drawing-room curtain.

The Widow and the Parrot: A True Story

Some fifty years ago Mrs Gage, an elderly widow, was sitting in her cottage in a village called Spilsby in Yorkshire. Although lame, and rather short sighted she was doing her best to mend a pair of clogs, for she had only a few shillings a week to live on. As she hammered at the clog, the postman opened the door and threw a letter into her lap.

It bore the address 'Messrs Stagg and Beetle, 67 High Street, Lewes, Sussex.'

Mrs Gage opened it and read:

'Dear Madam; We have the honour to inform you of the death of your brother Mr Joseph Brand.'

'Lawk a mussy,' said Mrs Gage. 'Old brother Joseph gone at last!'

'He has left you his entire property,' the letter went on, 'which consists of a dwelling house, stable, cucumber frames, mangles, wheelbarrows &c &c. in the village of Rodmell, near Lewes. He also bequeaths to you his entire fortune; Viz: £3,000. (three thousand pounds) sterling.'

Mrs Gage almost fell into the fire with joy. She had not seen her brother for many years, and, as he did not even acknowledge the Christmas card which she sent him every year, she thought that his miserly habits, well known to her from childhood, made him grudge even a penny stamp for a reply. But now it had all turned out to her advantage. With three thousand pounds, to say nothing of house &c &c, she and her family could live in great luxury for ever.

She determined that she must visit Rodmell at once. The village clergyman, the Rev Samuel Tallboys, lent her two pound ten, to pay her fare, and by next day all preparations for her journey were complete. The most important of these was the care of her dog Shag during her absence, for in spite of her poverty she was devoted to animals, and often went short herself rather than stint her dog of his bone.

She reached Lewes late on Tuesday night. In those days, I must tell you, there was no bridge over the river at Southease, nor had the road to Newhaven yet been made. To reach Rodmell it was necessary to cross the river Ouse by a ford, traces of which still exist, but this could only be attempted at low tide, when the stones on the river bed appeared above the water. Mr Stacey, the farmer, was going to Rodmell in his cart, and he kindly offered to take Mrs Gage with him. They reached Rodmell about nine o'clock on a November night and Mr Stacey obligingly pointed out to Mrs Gage the house at the end of the village which had been left her by her brother. Mrs Gage knocked at the door. There was no answer. She knocked again. A very strange high voice shrieked out 'Not at home.' She was so much taken aback that if she had not heard footsteps coming she would have run away. However the door was opened by an old village woman, by name Mrs Ford.

'Who was that shrieking out "Not at home"?' said Mrs Gage.

'Drat the bird!' said Mrs Ford very peevishly, pointing to a large grey parrot. 'He almost screams my head off. There he sits all day humped up on his perch like a monument screeching "Not at home" if ever you go near his perch.' He was a very handsome bird, as Mrs Gage could see; but his feathers were sadly neglected. 'Perhaps he is unhappy, or he may be hungry,' she said. But Mrs Ford said it was temper merely; he was a seaman's parrot and had learnt his language in the east. However, she added, Mr Joseph was very fond of him, had called him James; and, it was said, talked to him as if he were a rational being. Mrs Ford soon left. Mrs Gage at once went to her box and fetched some sugar which she had with her and offered it to the parrot, saying in a very kind tone that she meant him no harm, but was his old master's sister, come to take possession of the house, and she would see to it that he was as happy as a bird could be. Taking a lantern she next went round the house to see what sort of property her brother had left her. It was a bitter disappointment. There were holes in all the carpets. The bottoms of the chairs had fallen out. Rats ran along the mantelpiece. There were large toadstools growing through the kitchen floor. There was not a stick of furniture worth seven pence halfpenny; and Mrs Gage only cheered herself by thinking of the three thousand pounds that lay safe and snug in Lewes Bank.

She determined to set off to Lewes next day in order to claim her money from Messrs Stagg and Beetle the solicitors, and then to return home as quick as she could. Mr Stacey, who was going to market with some fine Berkshire pigs, again offered to take her with him, and told her some terrible stories of young people who had been drowned through trying to cross the river at high tide, as they drove. A great disappointment was in store for the poor old woman directly she got in to Mr Stagg's office.

'Pray take a seat, Madam,' he said, looking very solemn and grunting slightly. 'The fact is,' he went on, 'that you must prepare to face some very disagreeable news. Since I wrote to you I have gone carefully through Mr Brand's papers. I regret to say that I can find no trace whatever of the three thousand pounds. Mr Beetle, my partner, went himself to Rodmell and searched the premises with the utmost care. He found absolutely nothing – no gold, silver, or valuables of any kind – except a fine grey parrot which I advise you to sell for whatever he will fetch. His language, Benjamin Beetle said, is very extreme. But that is neither here nor there. I much fear you have had your journey for nothing. The premises are dilapidated; and of course our expenses are considerable.' Here he stopped, and Mrs Gage well knew that he wished her to go. She was almost crazy with disappointment. Not only had she borrowed two pound ten from the Rev. Samuel Tallboys, but she would return home absolutely empty handed, for the parrot James would have to be sold to pay her fare. It was raining hard, but Mr Stagg did not press her to stay, and she was too beside herself with sorrow to care what she did. In spite of the rain she started to walk back to Rodmell across the meadows.

Mrs Gage, as I have already said, was lame in her right leg. At the best of times she walked slowly, and now, what with her disappointment and the mud on the bank her progress was very slow indeed. As she plodded along, the day grew darker and darker, until it was as much as she could do to keep on the raised path by the river side. You might have heard her grumbling as she walked, and complaining of her crafty brother Joseph, who had put her to all this trouble 'Express,' she said, 'to plague me. He was always a cruel little boy when we were children,' she went on. 'He liked worrying the poor insects, and I've known him trim a hairy caterpillar with a pair of scissors before my very eyes. He was such a miserly varmint too. He used to hide his pocket money in a tree, and if anyone gave him a piece of iced cake for tea, he cut the sugar off and kept it for his supper. I make no doubt he's all aflame at this very moment in Hell fire, but what's the comfort of that to me?' she asked, and indeed it was very little comfort, for she ran slap into a great cow which was coming along the bank, and rolled over and over in the mud.

She picked herself up as best she could and trudged on again. It seemed to her that she had been walking for hours. It was now pitch dark and she could scarcely see her own hand before her nose. Suddenly she bethought her of Farmer Stacey's words about the ford. 'Lawk a mussy,' she said, 'however shall I find my way across? If the tide's in, I shall step into deep water and be swept out to sea in a jiffy! Many's the couple that been drowned here; to say nothing of horses, carts, herds of cattle, and stacks of hay.'

Indeed what with the dark and the mud she had got herself into a pretty pickle. She could hardly see the river itself, let alone tell whether she had reached the ford or not. No lights were visible anywhere, for, as you may be aware, there is no cottage or house on that side of the river nearer than Asheham House, lately the seat of Mr Leonard Woolf. It seemed that there was nothing for it but to sit down and wait for the morning. But at her age, with the rheumatics in her system, she might well die of cold. On the other hand, if she tried to cross the river it was almost certain that she would be drowned. So miserable was her state that she would gladly have changed places with one of the cows in the field. No more wretched old woman could have been found in the whole county of Sussex; standing on the river bank, not knowing whether to sit or to swim, or merely to roll over in the grass, wet though it was, and sleep or freeze to death, as her fate decided.

At that moment a wonderful thing happened. An enormous light shot up into the sky, like a gigantic torch, lighting up every blade of grass, and showing her the ford not twenty yards away. It was low tide, and the crossing would be an easy matter if only the light did not go out before she had got over.

'It must be a Comet or some such wonderful monstrosity,' she said as she hobbled across. She could see the village of Rodmell brilliantly up in front of her.

'Bless us and save us!' she cried out. 'There's a house on fire – thanks be to the Lord' – for she reckoned that it would take some minutes at least to burn a house down, and in that time she would be well on her way to the village.

'It's an ill wind that blows nobody any good,' she said as she hobbled along the Roman road. Sure enough, she could see every inch of the way, and was almost in the village street when for the first time it struck her, 'Perhaps it's my own house that's blazing to cinders before my eyes!'

She was perfectly right.

A small boy in his nightgown came capering up to her and cried out, 'Come and see old Joseph Brand's house ablaze!'

All the villagers were standing in a ring round the house handing buckets of water which were filled from the well in Monks House kitchen, and throwing them on the flames. But the fire had got a strong hold, and just as Mrs Gage arrived, the roof fell in.

'Has anybody saved the parrot?' she cried.

'Be thankful you're not inside yourself, Madam,' said the Rev James Hawkesford, the clergyman. 'Do not worry for the dumb creatures. I make no doubt the parrot was mercifully suffocated on his perch.'

But Mrs Gage was determined to see for herself. She had to be held back by the village people, who remarked that she must be crazy to hazard her life for a bird.

'Poor old woman,' said Mrs Ford, 'she has lost all her property, save one old wooden box, with her night things in it. No doubt we should be crazed in her place too.'

So saying, Mrs Ford took Mrs Gage by the hand and led her off to her own cottage, where she was to sleep the night. The fire was now extinguished, and everybody went home to bed.

But poor Mrs Gage could not sleep. She tossed and tumbled thinking of her miserable state, and wondering how she could get back to Yorkshire and pay the Rev Samuel Tallboys the money she owed him. At the same time she was even more grieved to think of the fate of the poor parrot James. She had taken a liking to the bird, and thought that he must have an affectionate heart to mourn so deeply for the death of old Joseph Brand, who had never done a kindness to any human creature. It was a terrible death for an innocent bird, she thought; and if only she had been in time, she would have risked her own life to save his.

She was lying in bed thinking these thoughts when a slight tap at the window made her start. The tap was repeated three times over. Mrs Gage got out of bed as quickly as she could and went to the window. There, to her utmost surprise, sitting on the window ledge was an enormous parrot. The rain had stopped and it was a fine moonlight night. She was greatly alarmed at first, but soon recognised the grey parrot, James, and was overcome with joy at his escape. She opened the window, stroked his head several times, and told him to come in. The parrot replied by gently shaking his head from side to side, then flew to the ground, walked away a few steps, looked back as if to see whether Mrs Gage were coming, and then returned to the window sill, where she stood in amazement.

'The creature has more meaning in its acts than we humans know,' she said to herself. 'Very well, James,' she said aloud, talking to him as though he were a human being, 'I'll take your word for it. Only wait a moment while I make myself decent.'

So saying she pinned on a large apron, crept as lightly as possible downstairs, and let herself out without rousing Mrs Ford.

The parrot James was evidently satisfied. He now hopped briskly a few yards ahead of her in the direction of the burnt house. Mrs Gage followed as fast as she could. The parrot hopped, as if he knew his way perfectly, round to the back of the house, where the kitchen had originally been. Nothing now remained of it except the brick floor, which was still dripping with the water which had been thrown to put out the fire. Mrs Gage stood still in amazement while James hopped about, pecking here and there, as if he were testing the bricks with his beak. It was a very uncanny sight, and had not Mrs Gage been in the habit of living with animals, she would have lost her head, very likely, and hobbled back home. But stranger things yet were to happen. All this time the parrot had not said a word. He suddenly got into a state of the greatest excitement, fluttering his wings, tapping the floor repeatedly with his beak, and crying so shrilly, 'Not at home! Not at home!' that Mrs Gage feared that the whole village would be roused.

'Don't take on so James; you'll hurt yourself,' she said soothingly. But he repeated his attack on the bricks more violently than ever.

'Whatever can be the meaning of it?' said Mrs Gage, looking carefully at the kitchen floor. The moonlight was bright enough to show her a slight unevenness in the laying of the bricks, as if they had been taken up and then relaid not quite flat with the others. She had fastened her apron with a large safety pin, and she now prised this pin between the bricks and found that they were only loosely laid together. Very soon she had taken one up in her hands. No sooner had she done this than the parrot hopped onto the brick next to it, and, tapping it smartly with his beak, cried, 'Not at home!' which Mrs Gage understood to mean that she was to move it. So they went on taking up the bricks in the moonlight until they had laid bare a space some six feet by four and a half. This the parrot seemed to think was enough. But what was to be done next?

Mrs Gage now rested, and determined to be guided entirely by the behaviour of the parrot James. She was not allowed to rest for long. After scratching about in the sandy foundations for a few minutes, as you may have seen a hen scratch in the sand with her claws, he unearthed what at first looked like a round lump of yellowish stone. His excitement became so intense, that Mrs Gage now went to his help. To her amazement she found that the whole space which they had uncovered was packed with long rolls of these round yellow stones, so neatly laid together that it was quite a job to move them. But what could they be? And for what purpose had they been hidden here? It was not until they had removed the entire layer on the top, and next a piece of oil cloth which lay beneath them, that a most miraculous sight was displayed before their eyes – there, in row after row, beautifully polished, and shining brightly in the moonlight, were thousands of brand new sovereigns!!!!

This, then, was the miser's hiding place; and he had made sure that no one would detect it by taking two extraordinary precautions. In the first place, as was proved later, he had built a kitchen range over the spot where his treasure lay hid, so that unless the fire had destroyed it, no one could have guessed its existence; and secondly he had coated the top layer of sovereigns with some sticky substance, then rolled them in the earth, so that if by chance one had been laid bare no one would have suspected that it was anything but a pebble such as you may see for yourself any day in the garden. Thus, it was only by the extraordinary coincidence of the fire and the parrot's sagacity that old Joseph's craft was defeated.

Mrs Gage and the parrot now worked hard and removed the whole hoard – which numbered three thousand pieces, neither more nor less – placing them in her apron which was spread upon the ground. As the three thousandth coin was placed on the top of the pile, the parrot flew up into the air in triumph and alighted very gently on the top of Mrs Gage's head. It was in this fashion that they returned to Mrs Ford's cottage, at a very slow pace, for Mrs Gage was lame, as I have said, and now she was almost weighted to the ground by the contents of her apron. But she reached her room without any one knowing of her visit to the ruined house.

Next day she returned to Yorkshire. Mr Stacey once more drove her into Lewes and was rather surprised to find how heavy Mrs Gage's wooden box had become. But he was a quiet sort of man, and merely concluded that the kind people at Rodmell had given her a few odds and ends to console her for the dreadful loss of all her property in the fire. Out of sheer goodness of heart Mr Stacey offered to buy the parrot off her for half a crown; but Mrs Gage refused his offer with such indignation, saying that she would not sell the bird for all the wealth of the Indies, that he concluded that the old woman had been crazed by her troubles.

It now only remains to be said that Mrs Gage got back to Spilsby in safety; took her black box to the Bank; and lived with James the parrot and her dog Shag in great comfort and happiness to a very great age.

It was not till she lay on her death bed that she told the clergyman (the son of the Rev Samuel Tallboys) the whole story, adding that she was quite sure that the house had been burnt on purpose by the parrot James, who, being aware of her danger on the river bank, flew into the scullery, and upset the oil stove which was keeping some scraps warm for her dinner. By this act, he not only saved her from drowning, but brought to light the three thousand pounds, which could have been found in no other manner. Such, she said, is the reward of kindness to animals.

The clergyman thought that she was wandering in her mind. But it is certain that the very moment the breath was out of her body, James the parrot shrieked out, 'Not at home! Not at home!' and fell off his perch stone dead. The dog Shag had died some years previously.

Visitors to Rodmell may still see the ruins of the house, which was burnt down fifty years ago, and it is commonly said that if you visit it in the moonlight you may hear a parrot tapping with his beak upon the brick floor, while others have seen an old woman sitting there in a white apron.

The New Dress

Mabel had her first serious suspicion that something was wrong as she took her cloak off and Mrs Barnet, while handing her the mirror and touching the brushes and thus drawing her attention, perhaps rather markedly, to all the appliances for tidying and improving hair, complexion, clothes, which existed on the dressing-table, confirmed the suspicion – that it was not right, not quite right, which growing stronger as she went upstairs and springing at her with conviction as she greeted Clarissa Dalloway, she went straight to the far end of the room, to a shaded corner where a looking-glass hung and looked. No! It was not *right*. And at once the misery which she always tried to hide, the profound dissatisfaction – the sense she had had, ever since she was a child, of being inferior to other people – set upon her, relentlessly, remorselessly, with an intensity which she could not beat off, as she would when she woke at night at home, by reading Borrow or Scott; for oh these men, oh these women, all were thinking – 'What's Mabel wearing? What a fright she looks! What a hideous new dress!' – their eyelids flickering as they came up and then their lids shutting rather tight. It was her own appalling inadequacy; her cowardice; her mean, water-sprinkled blood that depressed her. And at once the whole of the room where, for ever so many hours, she had planned with the little dressmaker how it was to go, seemed sordid, repulsive; and her own drawing-room so shabby, and herself, going out, puffed up with vanity as she touched the letters on the hall table and said: 'How dull!' to show off – all this now seemed unutterably silly, paltry, and provincial. All this had been absolutely destroyed, shown up, exploded, the moment she came into Mrs Dalloway's drawing-room.

What she had thought that evening when, sitting over the teacups, Mrs Dalloway's invitation came, was that, of course, she could not be fashionable. It was absurd to pretend it even – fashion meant cut, meant style, meant thirty guineas at least – but why not be original? Why not be herself, anyhow? And, getting up, she had taken that old fashion book of her mother's, a Paris fashion book of the time of the Empire, and had thought how much prettier, more dignified, and more womanly they were then, and so set herself – oh, it was foolish – trying to be like them, pluming herself in fact, upon being modest and old-fashioned, and very charming, giving herself up, no doubt about it, to an orgy of self-love, which deserved to be chastised, and so rigged herself out like this.

But she dared not look in the glass. She could not face the whole horror – the pale yellow, idiotically old-fashioned silk dress with its long skirt and its high sleeves and its waist and all the things that looked so charming in the fashion book, but not on her, not among all these ordinary people. She felt like a dressmaker's dummy standing there, for young people to stick pins into.

'But, my dear, it's perfectly charming!' Rose Shaw said, looking her up and down with that little satirical pucker of the lips which she expected – Rose herself being dressed in the height of fashion, precisely like everybody else, always.

We are all like flies trying to crawl over the edge of the saucer, Mabel thought, and repeated the phrase as if she were crossing herself, as if she were trying to find some spell to annul this pain, to make this agony endurable. Tags of Shakespeare, lines from books she had read ages ago, suddenly came to her when she was in agony, and she repeated them over and over again. 'Flies trying to crawl,' she repeated.[1] If she could say that over often enough and make herself see the flies, she would become numb, chill, frozen, dumb. Now she could see flies crawling slowly out of a saucer of milk with their wings stuck together; and she strained and strained (standing in front of the looking-glass, listening to Rose Shaw) to make herself see Rose Shaw and all the other people there as flies, trying to hoist themselves out of something, or into something, meagre, insignificant, toiling flies. But she could not see them like that, not other people. She saw herself like that – she was a fly, but the others were dragon-flies, butterflies, beautiful insects, dancing, fluttering, skimming, while she alone dragged herself up out of the saucer. (Envy and spite, the most detestable of the vices, were her chief faults.)

'I feel like some dowdy, decrepit, horribly dingy old fly,' she said, making Robert Haydon stop just to hear her say that, just to reassure herself by furbishing up a poor weak-kneed phrase and so showing how detached she was, how witty, that she did not feel in the least out of anything. And, of course, Robert Haydon answered something quite polite, quite insincere, which she saw through instantly, and said to herself, directly he went (again from some book), 'Lies, lies, lies!'[2] For a party makes things either much more real, or much less real, she thought; she saw in a flash to the bottom of Robert Haydon's heart; she saw through everything. She saw the truth. *This* was true, this drawing-room, this self, the other false. Miss Milan's little workroom was really terribly hot, stuffy, sordid. It smelt of clothes and cabbage cooking; and yet when Miss Milan put the glass in her hand, and she looked at herself with the dress on, finished, an extraordinary bliss shot through her heart. Suffused with light, she sprang into existence. Rid of cares and wrinkles, what she had dreamed of herself was there – a beautiful woman. Just for a second (she had not dared look longer, Miss Milan wanted to know about the length of the skirt), there looked at her, framed in the scrolloping mahogany, a grey-white, mysteriously smil-ing, charming girl, the core of herself, the soul of herself; and it was not vanity only, not only self-love that made her think it good, tender, and true. Miss Milan said the skirt could not well be longer; if anything the skirt, said Miss Milan, puckering her forehead, considering with all her wits about her, must be shorter; and she felt, suddenly, honestly, full of love for Miss Milan, much, much fonder of Miss Milan than of anyone in the whole world, and could have cried for pity that she should be crawling on the floor with her mouth full of pins, and her face red and her eyes bulging – that one human being should be doing this for another, and she saw them all as human beings merely, and herself going off to her party, and Miss Milan pulling the cover over the canary's cage, or letting him pick a hemp-seed from between her lips, and the thought of it, of this side of human nature and its patience and its endurance and its being content with such miserable, scanty, sordid, little pleasures filled her eyes with tears.

And now the whole thing had vanished. The dress, the room, the love, the pity, the scrolloping looking-glass, and the canary's cage – all had vanished, and here she was in a corner of Mrs Dalloway's drawing-room, suffering tortures, woken wide awake to reality.

But it was all so paltry, weak-blooded, and petty-minded to care so much at her age with two children, to be still so utterly dependent on people's opinions and not have principles or convictions, not to be able to say as other people did, 'There's Shakespeare! There's death! We're all weevils in a captain's biscuit' – or whatever it was that people did say.

She faced herself straight in the glass; she pecked at her left shoulder;

she issued out into the room, as if spears were thrown at her yellow dress from all sides. But instead of looking fierce or tragic, as Rose Shaw would have done – Rose would have looked like Boadicea[3] – she looked foolish and self-conscious, and simpered like a schoolgirl and slouched across the room, positively slinking, as if she were a beaten mongrel, and looked at a picture, an engraving. As if one went to a party to look at a picture! Everybody knew why she did it – it was from shame, from humiliation.

'Now the fly's in the saucer,' she said to herself, 'right in the middle, and can't get out, and the milk,' she thought, rigidly staring at the picture, 'is sticking its wings together.'

'It's so old-fashioned,' she said to Charles Burt, making him stop (which by itself he hated) on his way to talk to someone else.

She meant, or she tried to make herself think that she meant, that it was the picture and nòt her dress, that was old-fashioned. And one word of praise, one word of affection from Charles would have made all the difference to her at the moment. If he had only said, 'Mabel, you're looking charming tonight!' it would have changed her life. But then she ought to have been truthful and direct. Charles said nothing of the kind, of course. He was malice itself. He always saw through one, especially if one were feeling particularly mean, paltry, or feeble-minded.

'Mabel's got a new dress!' he said, and the poor fly was absolutely shoved into the middle of the saucer. Really, he would like her to drown, she believed. He had no heart, no fundamental kindness, only a veneer of friendliness. Miss Milan was much more real, much kinder. If only one could feel that and stick to it, always. 'Why,' she asked herself – replying to Charles much too pertly, letting him see that she was out of temper, or 'ruffled' as he called it ('Rather ruffled?' he said and went on to laugh at her with some woman over there) – 'Why,' she asked herself, 'can't I feel one thing always, feel quite sure that Miss Milan is right, and Charles wrong and stick to it, feel sure about the canary and pity and love and not be whipped all round in a second by coming into a room full of people?' It was her odious, weak, vacillating character again, always giving at the critical moment and not being seriously interested in conchology, etymology, botany, archaeology, cutting up potatoes and watching them fructify like Mary Dennis, like Violet Searle.

Then Mrs Holman, seeing her standing there, bore down upon her.

Of course a thing like a dress was beneath Mrs Holman's notice, with her family always tumbling downstairs or having the scarlet fever. Could Mabel tell her if Elmthorpe was ever let for August and September? Oh, it was a conversation that bored her unutterably! – it made her furious to be treated like a house agent or a messenger boy, to be made use of. Not to have value, that was it, she thought, trying to grasp something hard, something real, while she tried to answer sensibly about the bathroom and the south aspect and the hot water to the top of the house; and all the time she could see little bits of her yellow dress in the round looking-glass which made them all the size of boot-buttons or tadpoles; and it was amazing to think how much humiliation and agony and self-loathing and effort and passionate ups and downs of feeling were contained in a thing the size of a three penny bit. And what was still odder, this thing, this Mabel Waring, was separate, quite disconnected; and though Mrs Holman (the black button) was leaning forward and telling her how her eldest boy had strained his heart running, she could see her, too, quite detached in the looking-glass, and it was impossible that the black dot, leaning forward, gesticulating, should make the yellow dot, sitting solitary, self-centred, feel what the black dot was feeling, yet they pretended.

'So impossible to keep boys quiet' – that was the kind of thing one said.

And Mrs Holman, who could never get enough sympathy and snatched what little there was greedily, as if it were her right (but she deserved much more for there was her little girl who had come down this morning with a swollen knee-joint), took this miserable offering and looked at it suspiciously, grudgingly, as if it were a halfpenny when it ought to have been a pound and put it away in her purse, must put up with it, mean and miserly though it was, times being hard, so very hard; and on she went, creaking, injured Mrs Holman, about the girl with the swollen joints. Ah, it was tragic, this greed, this clamour of human beings, like a row of cormorants, barking and flapping their wings for sympathy – it was tragic, could one have felt it and not merely pretended to feel it!

But in her yellow dress tonight she could not wring out one drop more; she wanted it all, all for herself. She knew (she kept on looking into the glass, dipping into that dreadfully showing-up blue pool) that she was condemned, despised, left like this in a backwater, because of her being like this a feeble, vacillating creature; and it seemed to her that the yellow dress was a penance which she had deserved, and if she had been dressed like Rose Shaw, in lovely, clinging green with a ruffle of swansdown, she would have deserved that; and she thought that there was no escape for her – none whatever. But it was not her fault altogether, after all. It was being one of a family of ten; never having money enough, always skimping and paring; and her mother carrying great cans, and the linoleum worn on the stair edges, and one sordid little domestic tragedy after another – nothing catastrophic, the sheep farm failing, but not utterly; her eldest brother marrying beneath him but not very much – there was no romance, nothing extreme about them all. They petered out respectably in seaside resorts; every watering-place had one of her aunts even now asleep in some lodging with the front windows not quite facing the sea. That was so like them – they had to squint at things always. And she had done the same – she was just like her aunts. For all her dreams of living in India, married to some hero like Sir Henry Lawrence, some empire builder (still the sight of a native in a turban filled her with romance), she had failed utterly. She had married Hubert, with his safe, permanent underling's job in the Law Courts, and they managed tolerably in a smallish house, without proper maids, and hash when she was alone or just bread and butter, but now and then – Mrs Holman was off, thinking her the most dried-up, unsympathetic twig she had ever met, absurdly dressed, too, and would tell everyone about Mabel's fantastic appearance – now and then, thought Mabel Waring, left alone on the blue sofa, punching the cushion in order to look occupied, for she would not join Charles Burt and Rose Shaw, chattering like magpies and perhaps laughing at her by the fireplace – now and then, there did come to her delicious moments, reading the other night in bed, for instance, or down by the sea on the sand in the sun, at Easter – let her recall it – a great tuft of pale sand-grass standing all twisted like a shock of spears against the sky, which was blue like a smooth china egg, so firm, so hard, and then the melody of the waves – 'Hush, hush,' they said, and the children's shouts paddling – yes, it was a divine moment, and there she lay, she felt, in the hand of the Goddess who was the world; rather a hard-hearted, but very beautiful Goddess, a little lamb laid on the altar (one did think these silly things and it didn't matter so long as one never said them). And also with Hubert sometimes she had quite unexpectedly – carving the mutton for Sunday lunch, for no reason, opening a letter, coming into a room – divine moments, when she said to herself (for she would never say this to anybody else), 'This is it. This has happened. This is it!' And the other way about it was equally surprising – that is, when everything was arranged – music, weather, holidays, every reason for happiness was there – then nothing happened at all. One wasn't happy. It was flat, just flat, that was all.

Her wretched self again, no doubt! She had always been a fretful, weak, unsatisfactory mother, a wobbly wife, lolling about in a kind of twilight existence with nothing very clear or very bold or more one thing than another, like all her brothers and sisters, except perhaps Herbert – they were all the same poor water-veined creatures who did nothing. Then in the midst of this creeping, crawling life, suddenly she was on the crest of a wave. That wretched fly – where had she read the story that kept coming into her mind about the fly and the saucer? – struggled out. Yes, she had those moments. But now that she was forty, they might come more and more seldom. By degrees she would cease to struggle any more. But that was deplorable! That was not to be endured! That made her feel ashamed of herself!

She would go to the London Library tomorrow. She would find some wonderful, helpful, astonishing book, quite by chance, a book by a clergyman, by an American no one had ever heard of; or she would walk down the Strand and drop, accidentally, into a hall where a miner was telling about the life in the pit and suddenly she would become a new person. She would be absolutely transformed. She would wear a uniform; she would be called Sister Somebody; she would never give a thought to clothes again. And for ever after she would be perfectly clear about Charles Burt and Miss Milan and this room and that room; and it would be always, day after day, as if she were lying in the sun or carving the mutton. It would be it!

So she got up from the blue sofa, and the yellow button in the looking-glass got up too, and she waved her hand to Charles and Rose to show them she did not depend on them one scrap, and the yellow button moved out of the looking-glass, and all the spears were gathered into her breast as she walked towards Mrs Dalloway and said, 'Good night.'

'But it's too early to go,' said Mrs Dalloway, who was always so charming.

'I'm afraid I must,' said Mabel Waring. 'But,' she added in her weak, wobbly voice which only sounded ridiculous when she tried to strengthen it, 'I have enjoyed myself enormously.'

'I have enjoyed myself,' she said to Mr Dalloway, whom she met on the stairs.

'Lies, lies, lies!' she said to herself, going downstairs, and 'Right in the saucer!' she said to herself as she thanked Mrs Barnet for helping her and wrapped herself, round and round and round, in the Chinese cloak she had worn these twenty years.

Happiness

As Stuart Elton stooped and flicked off his trousers a white thread, the trivial act accompanied as it was by a slide and avalanche of sensation, seemed like a petal falling from a rose, and Stuart Elton straightening himself to resume his conversation with Mrs Sutton felt that he was compact of many petals laid firmly and closely on top of each other all reddened, all warmed through, all tinged with this inexplicable glow. So that when he stooped a petal fell. When he was young he had not felt it – no – now aged forty-five, he had only to stoop, to flick a thread off his trousers, and it rushed down all through him, this beautiful orderly sense of life, this slide, this avalanche of sensation, to be at one, when he stood up again adjusted – but what was she saying?

Mrs Sutton (still being dragged by the hair over the stubble and up and down the ploughed land of early middle age) was saying that managers wrote to her, even made appointments to see her, but nothing came of it. What made it so difficult for her was that she had naturally no connections with the stage, her father, all her people, being just country people. (It was then that Stuart Elton flicked the thread off.) She stopped; she felt rebuked. Yes, Stuart Elton had what she wanted, she felt, as he stooped. And when he stood up again, she apologised – she talked too much about herself she said – and added,

'You seem to me far the happiest person I know.'

It chimed oddly with what he had been thinking and that sense of the soft downward rush of life and its orderly readjustment, that sense of the falling petal and the complete rose. But was it 'happiness'? No. The big word did not seem to fit it, did not seem to refer to this state of being curled in rosy flakes round a bright light. Anyhow said Mrs Sutton, he was of all her friends the one she envied most. He seemed to have everything; she nothing. They counted – each had money enough; she a husband and children; he was a bachelor; she was thirty-five; he forty-five; she had never been ill in her life and he was a positive martyr, he said, to some internal complaint – longed to eat lobster all day long and could not touch it. There she exclaimed! as if she had her fingers on it. Even his illness was a joke to him. Was it balancing one thing against another, she asked? Was it a sense of proportion, was it? Was what, he asked, knowing quite well what she meant, but warding off this harum scarum ravaging woman with her hasty ways[,] with her grievances and her vigour, skirmishing and scrimmaging[,] who might knock over and destroy this very valuable possession, this sense of being – two figures flashed into his mind simultaneously – a flag in a breeze, a trout in a stream – poised, balanced, in a current of clean fresh clear bright lucid tingling impinging sensation which like the air or the stream held him upright so that if he moved a hand, stooped or said anything he dislodged the pressure of the innumerable atoms of happiness which closed and held him up again.

'Nothing matters to you,' said Mrs Sutton. 'Nothing changes you,' she said awkwardly making dashes and splashes about him like a man dabbing putty here there trying to cement bricks together while he stood there very silent, very cryptic, very demure; trying to get something from him, a clue, a key, a guide, envying him, resenting him, and feeling that if she with her emotional range, her passion, her capacity, her gifts had that added, she could straight off be the rival of Mrs Siddons herself.[1] He would not tell her; he must tell her.

'I went to Kew this afternoon,' he said, bending his knee and flicking it again not that there was a white thread there, but to make sure, by repeating the act, that his machine was in order, as it was.

So if one were being pursued through a forest by wolves one would tear off little bits of clothing and break off biscuits and throw them to the unhappy wolves, feeling almost, but not quite secure oneself, on one's high swift safe sledge.

With this whole pack of famished wolves in pursuit, now worrying the little bit of biscuit he had thrown them, – those words, 'I went to Kew this afternoon' – Stuart Elton raced swiftly ahead of them back to Kew, to the magnolia tree, to the lake, to the river, holding up his hand, to keep them off. Among them (for now the world seemed full of howling wolves) he remembered people asking him to dinner and lunch, now accepted now not, and his sense there on the sunny stretch of grass at Kew of mastery, even as he could swing his stick so he could choose, this that, go here, there, break off bits of biscuit and toss them to the wolves, read this, look at that, meet him or her, alight at some good fellow's rooms – 'To Kew alone?' Mrs Sutton repeated. 'By yourself?'

Ah! the wolf yapped in his ear. Ah! he sighed, as he had for one instant thinking of the past sighed ah by the lake that afternoon, by some woman stitching white stuff under a tree with geese waddling past, he had sighed, seeing the usual sight, lovers, arm in arm, where there was now this peace, this health once there had been ruin storm despair; so again this wolf Mrs Sutton reminded him; alone; yes quite alone; but he recovered, as he had recovered then, as the young people passed, grasping this, this, whatever it was and held it tight and walked on, pitying them.

'Quite alone,' Mrs Sutton repeated. That was what she could not conceive she said, with a despairing swoop of her dark bright haired head – being happy, quite alone.

'Yes,' he said.

In happiness there is always this terrific exaltation. It is not high spirits; nor rapture; nor praise, fame or health (he could not walk two miles without feeling done up) it is a mystic state, a trance, an ecstasy which, for all that he was atheistical, sceptical, unbaptised and all the rest of it, had[,] he suspected[,] some affinity with the ecstasy that turned men priests, sent women in the prime of life trudging the streets with starched cyclamen-like frills about their faces, and set lips and stony eyes; but with this difference; them it prisoned; him it set free. It freed him from all dependence upon anyone upon anything.

Mrs Sutton felt that too, as she waited for him to speak.

Yes he would stop his sledge, get out, let the wolves crowd all about him, he would pat their poor rapacious muzzles.

'Kew was lovely – full of flowers – magnolias azaleas,' he could never remember names he told her.

It was nothing that they could destroy. No; but if it came so inexplicably, so it might go, he had felt, leaving Kew, walking on the river bank up to Richmond. Why, some branch might fall; the colour might change; green turn blue; or a leaf shake; and that would be enough; yes; that would be enough to shiver, shatter, utterly destroy this amazing thing this miracle, this treasure which was his had been his was his must always be his, he thought getting restive and anxious and without thinking about Mrs Sutton he left her instantly and walked across the room and picked up a paper knife. Yes; it was all right. He had it still.

Ancestors

Mrs Vallance, as Jack Renshaw made that silly, rather conceited remark of his about not liking to watch cricket matches, felt that she must draw his attention somehow, must make him understand, yes, and all the other young people whom she saw, what her father would have said; how different her father and mother, yes and she too were from all this; and how compared to really dignified simple men and women like her father, like her dear mother, all *this* seemed to her so trivial.

'Here we all are,' she said suddenly, 'cooped up in this stuffy room while in the country at home – in Scotland' (she owed it to these foolish young men who were after all quite nice, though a little under-sized[,] to make them understand what her father, what her mother and she herself too, for she was like them at heart, felt).

'Are you Scotch?' he asked.

He did not know then, he did not know who her father was; that he was John Ellis Rattray; and her mother was Catherine Macdonald.

He had stopped in Edinburgh for a night once, Mr Renshaw said.

One night in Edinburgh! And she had spent all those wonderful years there – there and at Elliottshaw, on the Northumbrian border. There she had run wild among the currant bushes; there her father's friends had come, and [she] only a girl as she was, had heard the most wonderful talk of her time. She could see them still, her father, Sir Duncan Clements, Mr Rogers (old Mr Rogers was her ideal of a Greek sage), sitting under the cedar tree; after dinner in the starlight. They talked [about] everything in the whole world, it seemed to her now; they [were too] large minded ever to laugh at other people. They had taught her to revere beauty. What was there beautiful in this stuffy London room?

'Those poor flowers,' she exclaimed, for petals of flowers all crumpled and crushed, a carnation or two, were actually trodden under foot; but, she felt, she cared almost too much for flowers. Her mother had loved flowers: ever since she was a child she had been brought up to feel that to hurt a flower was to hurt the most exquisite thing in nature. Nature had always been a passion with her; the mountains, the sea. Here in London, one looked out of the window and saw more houses – human beings packed on top of each other in little boxes. It was an atmosphere in which she could not possibly live; herself. She could not bear to walk in London and see the children playing in the streets. She was perhaps too sensitive; life would be impossible if everyone was like her, but when she remembered her own childhood, and her father and mother, and the beauty and care that were lavished on them –

'What a lovely frock!' said Jack Renshaw; and *that* seemed to her altogether wrong – for a young man to be noticing women's clothes at all.

Her father was full of reverence for women but he never thought of noticing what they wore. And of all these girls, there was not a single one of them one could call beautiful – as she remembered her mother, – her dear stately mother, who never seemed to dress differently summer or winter, whether they had people or were alone, but always looked *herself* in lace, and as she grew older, a little cap. When she was a widow, [she] would sit among her flowers by the hour, and she seemed to be more with ghosts than with them all, dreaming of the past, which is, Mrs Vallance thought, somehow so much more real than the present. But why. It is in the past, with those wonderful men and women, she thought, that I really live: it is they who know me; it is those people only (and she thought of the starlit garden and the trees and old Mr Rogers, and her father, in his white linen coat smoking) who understood me. She felt her eyes soften and deepen as at the approach of tears, standing there in Mrs Dalloway's drawing-room, looking not at these people, these flowers, this chattering crowd, but at herself, that little girl who was to travel so far, picking Sweet Alice, and then sitting up in bed in the attic which smelt of pine wood reading stories, poetry. She had read all Shelley between the ages of twelve and fifteen, and used to say it to her father, holding her hands behind her back, while he shaved. The tears began, down in the back of her head to rise, as she looked at this picture of herself, and added the suffering of a lifetime (she had suffered abominably) – life had passed over her like a wheel – life was not what it had seemed then – it was like this party) to the child standing there, reciting Shelley; with her dark wild eyes. But what had they not seen later. And it was only those people, dead now, laid away in quiet Scotland, who had known her, who knew what she had it in her to be – and now the tears came closer, as she thought of the little girl in the cotton frock; how large and dark her eyes were; how beautiful she looked repeating the 'Ode to the West Wind'; how proud her father was of her, and how great he was, and how great her mother was, and how when she was with them she was so pure so good so gifted that she had it in her to be anything. That if they had lived, and she had always been with them in that garden (which now appeared to her the place where she had spent her whole childhood, and it was always starlit, and always summer, and they were always sitting out under the cedar tree smoking, except that somehow her mother was dreaming alone, in her widow's cap among her flowers – and how good and kind and respectful the old servants were, Andrewes the gardener, Jersy the cook; and old Sultan, the Newfoundland dog; and the vine, and the pond, and the pump – and Mrs Vallance looking very fierce and proud and satirical, compared her life with other peoples' lives) and if that life could have gone on for ever, then Mrs Vallance felt none of this – and she looked at Jack Renshaw and the girl whose clothes he admired – could have had any existence, and she would have been oh perfectly happy, perfectly good, instead of which here she was forced to listen to a young man saying – and she laughed almost scornfully and yet tears were in her eyes – that he could not bear to watch cricket matches!

The Introduction

Lily Everit saw Mrs Dalloway bearing down on her from the other side
of the room, and could have prayed her not to come and disturb her;
and yet, as Mrs Dalloway approached with her right hand raised and a
smile which Lily knew (though this was her first party) meant: 'But
you've got to come out of your corner and talk,' a smile at once
benevolent and drastic, commanding, she felt the strangest mixture of
excitement and fear, of desire to be left alone and of longing to be taken
out and thrown down, down into the boiling depths. But Mrs Dalloway was intercepted; caught by an old gentleman with white
moustaches, and thus Lily Everit had two minutes respite in which to
hug to herself, like a spar in the sea, to sip, like a glass of wine, the
thought of her essay upon the character of Dean Swift which Professor
Miller had marked that morning with three red stars; First rate. First
rate; she repeated that to herself, but the cordial was ever so much
weaker now than it had been when she stood before the long glass
being finished off (a pat here, a dab there) by her sister and Mildred, the
housemaid. For as their hands moved about her, she felt that they were
fidgeting agreeably on the surface but beneath lay untouched like a
lump of glowing metal her essay on the character of Dean Swift, and all
their praises when she came downstairs and stood in the hall waiting
for a cab – Rupert had come out of his room and said what a swell she
looked – ruffled the surface, went like a breeze among ribbons, but no
more. One divided life (she felt sure of it) into fact, this essay, and into
fiction, this going out, into rock and into wave, she thought, driving
along and seeing things with such intensity that for ever she would see
the truth and herself, a white reflection in the driver's dark back
inextricably mixed: the moment of vision. Then as she came into the
house, at the very first sight of people moving up stairs, down stairs,
this hard lump (her essay on the character of Swift) wobbled, began
melting, she could not keep hold of it, and all her being (no longer
sharp as a diamond cleaving the heart of life asunder) turned to a mist
of alarm, apprehension, and defence as she stood at bay in her corner.
This was the famous place: the world.

Looking out, Lily Everit instinctively hid that essay of hers, so ashamed was she now, so bewildered too, and on tiptoe nevertheless to adjust her focus and get into right proportions (the old having been shamefully wrong) these diminishing and expanding things (what could one call them? people – impressions of people's lives?) which seemed to menace her and mount over her, to turn everything to water, leaving her only – for that she would not resign – the power to stand at bay.

Now Mrs Dalloway, who had never quite dropped her arm, had shown by the way she moved it while she stood talking that she remembered, was only interrupted by the old soldier with the white moustaches, raised it again definitely and came straight down on her, and said to the shy charming girl, with her pale skin, her bright eyes, the dark hair which clustered poetically round her head and the thin body in a dress which seemed slipping off,

'Come and let me introduce you,' and there Mrs Dalloway hesitated, and then remembering that Lily was the clever one, who read poetry, looked about for some young man, some young man just down from Oxford, who would have read everything and could talk about Shelley. And holding Lily Everit's hand [she] led her towards a group where there were young people talking, and Bob Brinsley.

Lily Everit hung back a little, might have been the wayward sailing boat curtseying in the wake of a steamer, and felt as Mrs Dalloway led her on, that it was now going to happen; that nothing could prevent it now; or save her (and she only wanted it to be over now) from being flung into a whirlpool where either she would perish or be saved. But what was the whirlpool?

Oh it was made of a million things and each was distinct to her; Westminster Abbey; the sense of enormously high solemn buildings surrounding them; being a woman. Perhaps that was the thing that came out, that remained, it was partly the dress, but all the little chivalries and respects of the drawing-room – all made her feel that she had come out of her chrysalis and was being proclaimed what in the comfortable darkness of childhood she had never been – this frail and beautiful creature, before whom men bowed, this limited and circum-scribed creature who could not do what she liked, this butterfly with a thousand facets to its eyes and delicate fine plumage, and difficulties and sensibilities and sadnesses innumerable; a woman.

As she walked with Mrs Dalloway across the room she accepted the part which was now laid on her and, naturally, overdid it a little as a soldier, proud of the traditions of an old and famous uniform might overdo it, feeling conscious as she walked, of her finery; of her tight shoes; of her coiled and twisted hair; and how if she dropped a handkerchief (this had happened) a man would stoop precipitately and give it her; thus accentuating the delicacy, the artificiality of her bearing unnaturally, for they were not hers after all.

Hers it was, rather, to run and hurry and ponder on long solitary walks, climbing gates, stepping through the mud, and through the blur, the dream, the ecstasy of loneliness, to see the plover's wheel and surprise the rabbits, and come in the hearts of woods or wide lonely moors upon little ceremonies which had no audience, private rites, pure beauty offered by beetles and lilies of the valley and dead leaves and still pools, without any care whatever what human beings thought of them, which filled her mind with rapture and wonder and held her there till she must touch the gate post to recollect herself – all this was, until tonight her ordinary being, by which she knew and liked herself and crept into the heart of mother and father and brothers and sisters; and this other was a flower which had opened in ten minutes. As the flower opened so too [came], incontrovertibly, the flower's world, so different, so strange; the towers of Westminster; the high and formal buildings; talk; this civilisation, she felt, hanging back, as Mrs Dalloway led her on, this regulated way of life, which fell like a yoke about her neck, softly, indomitably, from the skies, a statement which there was no gainsaying. Glancing at her essay, the three red stars dulled to obscurity, but peacefully, pensively, as if yielding to the pressure of unquestionable might, that is the conviction that it was not hers to dominate, or to assert; rather to air and embellish this orderly life where all was done already; high towers, solemn bells, flats built every brick of them by men's toil, churches built by men's toil, parliaments too; and even the criss-cross of telegraph wires she thought looking at the window as she walked. What had she to oppose to this massive masculine achievement? An essay on the character of Dean Swift! And as she came up to the group, which Bob Brinsley dominated, (with his heel on the fender, and his head back), with his great honest forehead, and his self-assurance, and his delicacy, and honour and robust physical well being, and sunburn, and airiness and direct descent from Shakespeare, what could she do but lay her essay, oh and the whole of her being, on the floor as a cloak for him to trample on, as a rose for him to rifle. Which she did, emphatically, when Mrs Dalloway said, still holding her hand as if she would run away from this supreme trial, this introduction, 'Mr Brinsley – Miss Everit. Both of you love Shelley.' But hers was not love compared with his.

Saying this, Mrs Dalloway felt, as she always felt remembering her youth, absurdly moved; youth meeting youth at her hands, and there flashing, as at the concussion of steel upon flint (both stiffened to her feeling perceptibly) the loveliest and most ancient of all fires as she saw in Bob Brinsley's change of expression from carelessness to conformity, to formality, as he shook hands, which foreboded Clarissa thought, the tenderness, the goodness, the carefulness of women latent in all men, to her a sight to bring tears to the eyes, as it moved her even more intimately, to see in Lily herself the shy look, the startled look, surely the loveliest of all looks on a girl's face; and man feeling this for woman, and woman that for man, and there flowing from that contact all those homes, trials, sorrows, profound joy and ultimate staunchness in the face of catastrophe, humanity was sweet at its heart, thought Clarissa, and her own life (to introduce a couple made her think of meeting Richard for the first time!) infinitely blessed. And on she went.

But, thought Lily Everit. But – but – but what?

Oh nothing, she thought hastily smothering down softly her sharp instinct.[1] Yes, she said. She did like reading.

'And I suppose you write?'' he said, 'poems presumably?'

'Essays,' she said. And she would not let this horror get possession of her. Churches and parliaments, flats, even the telegraph wires – all, she told herself, made by men's toil, and this young man, she told herself, is in direct descent from Shakespeare, so she would not let this terror, this suspicion of something different, get hold of her and shrivel up her wings and drive her out into loneliness. But as she said this, she saw him – how else could she describe it – kill a fly. He tore the wings off a fly, standing with his foot on the fender his head thrown back, talking insolently about himself, arrogantly, but she didn't mind how insolent and arrogant he was to her, if only he had not been brutal to flies.

But she said, fidgeting as she smothered down that idea, why not, since he is the greatest of all worldly objects? And to worship, to adorn, to embellish was her task, and to be worshipped, her wings were for that. But he talked; but he looked; but he laughed; he tore the wings off a fly. He pulled the wings off its back with his clever strong hands, and she saw him do it; and she could not hide the knowledge from herself. But it is necessary that it should be so, she argued, thinking of the churches, of the parliaments and the blocks of flats, and so tried to crouch and cower and fold the wings down flat on her back. But – but, what was it why was it? In spite of all she could do her essay upon the character of Swift became more and more obtrusive and the three stars burnt quite bright again, only no longer clear and brilliant, but troubled and bloodstained as if this man, this great Mr Brinsley, had just by pulling the wings off a fly as he talked (about his essay, about himself and once laughing, about a girl there) charged her light being with cloud, and confused her for ever and ever and shrivelled her wings on her back, and, as he turned away from her, he made her think of the towers and civilisation with horror, and the yoke that had fallen from the skies onto her neck crushed her, and she felt like a naked wretch who having sought shelter in some shady garden is turned out and told – no, that there are no sanctuaries, or butterflies, in this world, and this civilisation, churches, parliaments and flats – this civilisation, said Lily Everit to herself, as she accepted the kind compliments of old Mrs Bromley on her appearance[, depends upon me,] and Mrs Bromley said later that like all the Everits Lily looked 'as if she had the weight of the world upon her shoulders'.

Together and Apart

Mrs Dalloway introduced them, saying you will like him. The conversation began some minutes before anything was said, for both Mr Serle and Miss Anning looked at the sky and in both of their minds the sky went on pouring its meaning[,] though very differently[,] until the presence of Mr Serle by her side became so distinct to Miss Anning that she could not see the sky, simply, itself, any more, but the sky shored up by the tall body, dark eyes, grey hair, clasped hands, the stern melancholy (but she had been told 'falsely melancholy') face of Roderick Serle, and, knowing how foolish it was, she yet felt impelled to say:

'What a beautiful night!'

Foolish! Idiotically foolish! But if one mayn't be foolish at the age of forty in the presence of the sky, which makes the wisest imbecile – mere wisps of straw – she and Mr Serle atoms, motes, standing there at Mrs Dalloway's window, and their lives, seen by moonlight, as long as an insect's and no more important.

'Well!' said Miss Anning, patting the sofa cushion emphatically. And down he sat beside her. Was he 'falsely melancholy,' as they said? Prompted by the sky, which seemed to make it all a little futile – what they said, what they did – she said something perfectly commonplace again:

'There was a Miss Serle who lived at Canterbury when I was a girl there.'

With the sky in his mind, all the tombs of his ancestors immediately appeared to Mr Serle in a blue romantic light, and his eyes expanding and darkening, he said: 'Yes.'

'We are originally a Norman family, who came over with the Conqueror. There is a Richard Serle buried in the cathedral. He was a Knight of the Garter.'

Miss Anning felt that she had struck accidentally the true man, upon whom the false man was built. Under the influence of the moon (the moon which symbolised man to her, she could see it through a chink of the curtain, and she took dips of the moon, sips of the moon) she was capable of saying almost anything and she settled in to disinter the true man who was buried under the false, saying to herself: 'On, Stanley, on'[1] – which was a watchword of hers, a secret spur, or scourge such as middle-aged people often have to flagellate some inveterate vice, hers being a deplorable timidity, or rather indolence, for it was not so much that she lacked courage, but lacked energy, especially in talking to men, who frightened her rather, and so often her talks petered out into dull commonplaces, and she had very few men friends – very few intimate friends at all, she thought, but after all, did she want them? No. She had Sarah, Arthur, the cottage, the chow and, of course *that*, she thought dipping herself, sousing herself, even as she sat on the sofa beside Mr Serle, in *that*, in the sense she had coming home of something collected there, a cluster of miracles, which she could not believe other people had (since it was she only who had Arthur, Sarah, the cottage, and the chow), and she soused herself again in the deep satisfactory possession, feeling that what with this and the moon (music that was, the moon), she could afford to leave this man and that pride of his in the Serles buried. No! That was the danger – she must not sink into torpidity – not at her age. 'On, Stanley, on,' she said to herself, and asked him:

'Do you know Canterbury yourself?'

Did he know Canterbury! Mr Serle smiled, thinking how absurd a question it was – how little she knew, this nice quiet woman who played some instrument and seemed intelligent and had good eyes, and was wearing a nice old necklace – knew what it meant. To be asked if he knew Canterbury – when the best years of his life, all his memories, things he had never been able to tell anybody, but had tried to write – ah, had tried to write (and he sighed) all had centred in Canterbury: it made him laugh.

His sigh and then his laugh, his melancholy and his humour, made people like him and he knew it, and yet being liked had not made up for the disappointment, and if he sponged on the liking people had for him (paying long calls on sympathetic ladies, long, long calls), it was half bitterly, for he had never done a tenth part of what he could have done, and had dreamed of doing as a boy in Canterbury. With a stranger he felt a renewal of hope because they could not say that he had not done what he had promised, and yielding to his charm would give him a fresh start – at fifty! She had touched the spring. Fields and flowers and grey buildings formed silver drops on the gaunt, dark walls of his mind and dripped down. With such an image his poems often began. He felt the desire to make images now, sitting by this quiet woman.

'Yes, I know Canterbury,' he said reminiscently, sentimentally, inviting, Miss Anning felt, discreet questions, and that was what made him interesting to so many people, and it was this extraordinary facility and responsiveness to talk on his part that had been his undoing, so he thought, often, taking his studs out and putting his keys and small change on the dressing-table after one of these parties (and he went out sometimes almost every night in the season), and, going down to breakfast, becoming quite different, grumpy, unpleasant at breakfast to his wife, who was an invalid, and never went out, but had old friends to see her sometimes, women friends for the most part, interested in Indian philosophy and different cures and different doctors, which Roderick Serle snubbed off by some caustic remark too clever for her to meet, except by gentle expostulations and a tear or two – he had failed, he often thought, because he could not cut himself off utterly from society and the company of women, which was so necessary to him, and write. He had involved himself too deep in life – and here he would cross his knees (all his movements were a little unconventional and distinguished) and not blame himself, but put the blame off upon the richness of his nature, which he compared favourably with Words-worth's, for example, and, since he had given so much to people, he felt, resting his head on his hands, they in their turn should help him, and this was the prelude, tremulous, fascinating, exciting, to talk; and images bubbled up in his mind.

'She's like a fruit tree – like a flowering cherry tree,' he said, looking at a youngish woman with fine white hair. It was a nice sort of image, Ruth Anning thought – rather nice, yet she did not feel sure that she liked this distinguished, melancholy man with his gestures; and it's odd, she thought, how one's feelings are influenced. She did not like *him*, though she rather liked that comparison of his of a woman to a cherry tree. Fibres of her were floated capriciously this way and that, like the tentacles of a sea anemone, now thrilled, now snubbed, and her brain, miles away, cool and distant, up in the air, received messages which it would sum up in time so that when people talked about Roderick Serle (and he was a bit of a figure) she would say unhesitatingly: 'I like him', or 'I don't like him', and her opinion would be made up for ever. An odd thought; a solemn thought; throwing a queer light on what human fellowship consisted of.

'It's odd that you should know Canterbury,' said Mr Serle. 'It's always a shock,' he went on (the white haired lady having passed), 'when one meets someone' (they had never met before), 'by chance, as it were, who touches the fringe of what has meant a great deal to oneself, touches accidentally, for I suppose Canterbury was nothing but a nice old town to you. So you stayed there one summer with an aunt?' (That was all Ruth Anning was going to tell him about her visit to Canterbury.) 'And you saw the sights and went away and never thought of it again.'

Let him think so; not liking him, she wanted him to run away with an absurd idea of her. For really, her three months in Canterbury had been amazing. She remembered to the last detail, though it was merely a chance visit, going to see Miss Charlotte Serle, an acquaintance of her aunt's. Even now she could repeat Miss Serle's very words about the thunder. 'Whenever I wake and hear thunder in the night, I think "Someone has been killed".' And she could see the hard hairy, diamond-patterned carpet, and the twinkling suffused, brown eyes of the elderly lady, holding the teacup out unfilled, while she said that about the thunder. And always she saw Canterbury, all thundercloud and livid apple blossom, and the long grey backs of the buildings.

The thunder roused her from her plethoric middle-aged swoon of indifference; 'On, Stanley, on,' she said to herself; that is, this man shall not glide away from me, like everybody else, on this false assumption; I will tell him the truth.

'I loved Canterbury,' she said.

He kindled instantly. It was his gift, his fault, his destiny.

'Loved it,' he repeated. 'I can see that you did.'

Their eyes met; collided rather, for each felt that behind the eyes the secluded being, who sits in darkness while his shallow agile companion does all the tumbling and beckoning, and keeps the show going, suddenly stood erect; flung off his cloak; confronted the other. It was alarming; it was terrific. They were elderly and burnished into a glowing smoothness, so that Roderick Serle would go, perhaps to a dozen parties in a season, and feel nothing out of the common, or only sentimental regrets, and the desire for pretty images – like this of the flowering cherry tree – and all the time there stagnated in him unstirred a sort of superiority to his company, a sense of untapped resources, which sent him back home dissatisfied with his life, with himself, yawning, empty, capricious. But now, quite suddenly, like a white bolt in a mist (but this image forged itself with the inevitability of lightning and loomed up), there it had happened; the old ecstasy of life; its invincible assault; for it was unpleasant, at the same time that it rejoiced and rejuvenated and filled the veins and nerves with threads of ice and fire; it was terrifying.

'Canterbury twenty years ago,' said Miss Anning, as one lays a shade over an intense light, or covers some burning peach with a green leaf, for it is too strong, too ripe, too full.

Sometimes she wished she had married. Sometimes the cool peace of middle life, with its automatic devices for shielding mind and body from bruises, seemed to her, compared with the thunder and the livid apple blossom of Canterbury, base. She could imagine something different, more like lightning, more intense. She could imagine some physical sensation. She could imagine –

And, strangely enough, for she had never seen him before, her senses, those tentacles which were thrilled and snubbed, now sent no more messages, now lay quiescent, as if she and Mr Serle knew each other so perfectly, were in fact, so closely united that they had only to float side by side down this stream.

Of all things, nothing is so strange as human intercourse, she thought, because of its changes, its extraordinary irrationality, her dislike being now nothing short of the most intense and rapturous love, but directly the word 'love' occurred to her, she rejected it, thinking again how obscure the mind was, with its very few words for all these astonishing perceptions, these alternations of pain and pleasure. For how did one name this. That is what she felt now, the withdrawal of human affection, Serle's disappearance, and the instant need they were both under to cover up what was so desolating and degrading to human nature that everyone tried to bury it decently from sight – this withdrawal, this violation of trust, and, seeking some decent acknowledged and accepted burial form, she said:

'Of course, whatever they may do, they can't spoil Canterbury.'

He smiled; he accepted it; he crossed his knees the other way about. She did her part; he his. So things came to an end. And over them both came instantly that paralysing blankness of feeling, when nothing bursts from the mind, when its walls appear like slate; when vacancy almost hurts, and the eyes petrified and fixed see the same spot – a pattern, a coal scuttle – with an exactness which is terrifying, since no emotion, no idea, no impression of any kind comes to change it, to modify it, to embellish it, since the fountains of feeling seem sealed and as the mind turns rigid, so does the body; stark, statuesque, so that neither Mr Serle nor Miss Anning could move or speak, and they felt as if an enchanter had freed them, and spring flushed every vein with streams of life, when Mira Cartwright, tapping Mr Serle archly on the shoulder, said:

'I saw you at the *Meistersinger*, and you cut me. Villain,' said Miss Cartwright, 'you don't deserve that I should ever speak to you again.'

And they could separate.

The Man Who Loved His Kind

Trotting through Deans Yard that afternoon, Prickett Ellis ran straight into Richard Dalloway, or rather, just as they were passing the covert side glance which each was casting on the other, under his hat, over his shoulder, broadened and burst into recognition; they had not met for twenty years. They had been at school together. And what was Ellis doing? The Bar? Of course, of course – he had followed the case in the papers. But it was impossible to talk here. Wouldn't he drop in that evening. (They lived in the same old place – just round the corner.) One or two people were coming. Joynson perhaps. 'An awful swell now,' said Richard.

'Good – till this evening then,' said Richard, and went his way, 'jolly glad' (that was quite true) to have met that queer chap, who hadn't changed one bit since he had been at school – just the same knobbly, chubby little boy then, with prejudices sticking out all over him, but uncommonly brilliant – won the Newcastle. Well – off he went.

Prickett Ellis, however, as he turned and looked at Dalloway disappearing, wished now he had not met him or, at least, for he had always liked him personally, hadn't promised to come to this party. Dalloway was married, gave parties; wasn't his sort at all. He would have to dress. However, as the evening drew on, he supposed, as he had said that, and didn't want to be rude, he must go there.

But what an appalling entertainment! There was Joynson; they had nothing to say to each other. He had been a pompous little boy; he had grown rather more self-important – that was all; there wasn't a single other soul in the room that Prickett Ellis knew. Not one. So, as he could not go at once, without saying a word to Dalloway, who seemed altogether taken up with his duties, bustling about in a white waist-coat, there he had to stand. It was the sort of thing that made his gorge rise. Think of grown up, responsible men and women doing this every night of their lives! The lines deepened on his blue and red shaven cheeks, as he leant against the wall, in complete silence; for though he worked like a horse, he kept himself fit by exercise; and he looked hard and fierce, as if his moustaches were dipped in frost. He bristled; he

grated. His meagre dress clothes made him look unkempt, insignificant, angular.

Idle, chattering, overdressed, without an idea in their heads, these
fine ladies and gentlemen went on talking and laughing; and Prickett
Ellis watched them and compared them with the Brunners who, when
they won their case against Fenners' Brewery and got two hundred
pounds compensation (it was not half what they should have got) went
and spent five of it on a clock for him. That was a decent sort of thing to
do; that was the sort of thing that moved one, and he glared more
severely than ever at these people, overdressed, cynical, prosperous,
and compared what he felt now with what he felt at eleven o'clock that
morning when old Brunner and Mrs Brunner in their best clothes,
awfully respectable and clean looking old people, had called in to give
him that small token, as the old man put it, standing perfectly upright
to make his speech of gratitude and respect for the very able way in
which you conducted our case, and Mrs Brunner piped up, how it was
all due to him they felt. And they deeply appreciated his generosity –
because of course he hadn't taken a fee.

And as he took the clock and put it on the middle of his mantelpiece,
he had felt that he wished nobody to see his face. That was what he
worked for – that was his reward; and he looked at the people who
were actually before his eyes as if they danced over that scene in his
chambers and were exposed by it, and as it faded – the Brunners faded
– there remained as if left of that scene, himself, confronting this hostile
population, a perfectly plain unsophisticated man, a man of the people
(he straightened himself), very badly dressed, glaring, with not an air
or a grace about him, a man who was an ill hand at concealing his
feelings, a plain man, an ordinary human being, pitted against the evil,
the corruption, the heartlessness of society. But he would not go on
staring. Now he put on his spectacles and examined the pictures. He
read the titles on a line of books; for the most part poetry. He would
have liked well enough to read some of his old favourites again –
Shakespeare, Dickens – he wished he ever had time to turn into the
National Gallery, but he couldn't – no, one could not. Really one could
not – with the world in the state it was in. Not when people all day long
wanted your help, fairly clamoured for help. This wasn't an age for
luxuries. And he looked at the arm chairs and the paper knives and the
well bound books, and shook his head, knowing that he would never
have the time, never he was glad to think have the heart, to afford

himself such luxuries. The people here would be shocked if they knew what he paid for his tobacco; how he had borrowed his clothes. His one and only extravagance was his little yacht on the Norfolk Broads. And that he did allow himself. He did like once a year to get right away from everybody and lie on his back in a field. He thought how shocked they would be – these fine folk – if they realised the amount of pleasure he got from what he was old fashioned enough to call a love of nature; trees and fields he had known ever since he was a boy.

These fine people would be shocked. Indeed, standing there, putting his spectacles away in his pocket, he felt himself grow more and more shocking every instant. And it was a very disagreeable feeling. He did not feel this – that he loved humanity, that he paid only five pence an ounce for tobacco and loved nature – naturally and quietly. Each of these pleasures had been turned into a protest. He felt that these people whom he despised made him stand and deliver and justify himself. 'I am an ordinary man,' he kept saying. And what he said next he was really ashamed of saying, but he said it. 'I have done more for my kind in one day than the rest of you in all your lives.' Indeed, he could not help himself; he kept recalling scene after scene, like that when the Brunners gave him the clock – he kept reminding himself of the nice things people had said of his humanity, of his generosity, how he had helped them. He kept seeing himself as the wise and tolerant servant of humanity. And he wished he could repeat his praises aloud. It was unpleasant that the sense of his goodness should boil within him. It was still more unpleasant that he could tell no one what people had said about him. Thank the Lord, he kept saying, I shall be back at work tomorrow; and yet he was no longer satisfied simply to slip through the door and go home. He must stay, he must stay until he had justified himself. But how could he? In all that room full of people, he did not know a soul to speak to.

At last Richard Dalloway came up.

'I want to introduce Miss O'Keefe,' he said. Miss O'Keefe looked him full in the eyes. She was a rather arrogant, abrupt mannered woman in the thirties.

Miss O'Keefe wanted an ice or something to drink. And the reason why she asked Prickett Ellis to give it her in what he felt a haughty, unjustifiable manner, was that she had seen a woman and two children, very poor, very tired, pressing against the railings of a square, peering in, that hot afternoon. Can't they be let in? she had thought, her pity rising like a wave; her indignation boiling. No; she rebuked herself the next moment, roughly, as if she boxed her own ears. The whole force of the world can't do it. So she picked up the tennis ball and hurled it back. The whole force of the world can't do it, she said in a fury, and that was why she said so commandingly, to the unknown man:

'Give me an ice.'

Long before she had eaten it, Prickett Ellis, standing beside her without taking anything, told her that he had not been to a party for fifteen years; told her that his dress suit was lent him by his brother-in-law; told her that he did not like this sort of thing, and it would have eased him greatly to go on to say that he was a plain man, who happened to have a liking for ordinary people, and then would have told her (and been ashamed of it afterwards) about the Brunners and the clock, but she said:

'Have you seen the *Tempest*?'

Then, (for he had not seen the *Tempest*) had he read some book? Again no, and then, putting her ice down, did he ever read poetry?

And Prickett Ellis feeling something rise within him which would decapitate this young woman, make a victim of her, massacre her, made her sit down there, where they would not be interrupted, on two chairs, in the empty garden, for everyone was upstairs, only you could hear a buzz and a hum and a chatter and a jingle, like the mad accompaniment of some phantom orchestra to a cat or two slinking across the grass, and the wavering of leaves, and the yellow and red fruit like Chinese lanterns wobbling this way and that – the talk seemed like a frantic skeleton dance music set to something very real, and full of suffering.

'How beautiful!' said Miss O'Keefe.

Oh, it was beautiful, this little patch of grass, with the towers of Westminster massed round it black high in the air, after the drawing-room; it was silent, after that noise. After all, they had that – the tired woman, the children.

Prickett Ellis lit a pipe. That would shock her; he filled it with shag tobacco – five pence halfpenny an ounce. He thought how he would lie in his boat smoking, he could see himself, alone, at night, smoking under the stars. For always tonight he kept thinking how he would look if these people here were to see him. He said to Miss O'Keefe, striking a match on the sole of his boot, that he couldn't see anything particularly beautiful out here.

'Perhaps,' said Miss O'Keefe, 'you don't care for beauty.' (He had told her that he had not seen the *Tempest*; that he had not read a book; he looked ill kempt, all moustache, chin, and silver watch chain.) She thought nobody need pay a penny for this; the Museums are free and the National Gallery; and the country. Of course she knew the objections – the washing, cooking, children; but the root of things, what they were all afraid of saying, was that happiness is dirt cheap. You can have it for nothing. Beauty.

Then Prickett Ellis let her have it – this pale, abrupt, arrogant woman. He told her, puffing his shag tobacco, what he had done that day. Up at six; interviews; smelling a drain in a filthy slum; then to court.

Here he hesitated, wishing to tell her something of his own doings. Suppressing that, he was all the more caustic. He said it made him sick to hear well fed, well dressed women (she twitched her lips, for she was thin, and her dress not up to standard) talk of beauty.

'Beauty!' he said. He was afraid he did not understand beauty apart from human beings.

So they glared into the empty garden where the lights were swaying, and one cat hesitating in the middle, its paw lifted.

Beauty apart from human beings? What did he mean by that? she demanded suddenly.

Well this: getting more and more wrought up, he told her the story of the Brunners and the clock, not concealing his pride in it. That was beautiful, he said.

She had no words to specify the horror his story roused in her. First his conceit; then his indecency in talking about human feelings; it was a blasphemy; no one in the whole world ought to tell a story to prove that they had loved their kind. Yet as he told it – how the old man had stood up and made his speech – tears came into her eyes; ah, if any one had ever said that to her! but then again, she felt how it was just this that condemned humanity for ever; never would they reach beyond affecting scenes with clocks; Brunners making speeches to Prickett Ellises, and the Prickett Ellises would always say how they had loved their kind; they would always be lazy, compromising, and afraid of beauty. Hence sprung revolutions; from laziness and fear and this love of affecting scenes. Still this man got pleasure from his Brunners; and she was condemned to suffer for ever and ever from her poor women shut out from squares. So they sat silent. Both were very unhappy. For

Prickett Ellis was not in the least solaced by what he had said; instead of picking her thorn out he had rubbed it in; his happiness of the morning had been ruined. Miss O'Keefe was muddled and annoyed; she was muddy instead of clear.

'I'm afraid I am one of those very ordinary people,' he said, getting up, 'who love their kind.'

Upon which Miss O'Keefe almost shouted, 'So do I.'

Hating each other, hating the whole houseful of people who had given them this painful, this disillusioning evening, these two lovers of their kind got up, and without a word parted for ever.

A Simple Melody

As for the picture itself it was one of those landscapes which the unlearned suppose to have been painted when Queen Victoria was very young, and it was the fashion for young ladies to wear straw hats shaped like coal scuttles. Time had smoothed away all the joins and irregularities of the paint and the canvas seemed spread with a fine layer, here the palest blue, here the brownest shadow, of smooth lacquer-like glaze. It was a picture of a heath; and a very beautiful picture.

Mr Carslake, at least, thought it very beautiful because, as he stood in the corner where he could see it, it had the power to compose and tranquillize his mind. It seemed to him to bring the rest of his emotions – and how scattered and jumbled they were at a party like this! – into proportion. It was as if a fiddler were playing a perfectly quiet old English song while people gambled and tumbled and swore, picked pockets, rescued the drowning, and did astonishing – but quite unnecessary – feats of skill. He was unable to perform himself. All he could do was say that Wembley was very tiring; and that he believed it was not being a success; and things like that.[1] Miss Merewether did not listen; after all, why should she? She played her part; she did one or two rather clumsy somersaults; skipping that is to say from Wembley to the character of Queen Mary,[2] which she thought sublime. Of course, she thought nothing of the sort really. Mr Carslake assured himself of this by looking at the picture of the heath. All human beings were very simple underneath, he felt. Put Queen Mary, Miss Merewether and himself on that heath; it was late in the evening; after sunset; and they had to find their way back to Norwich. Soon they would all be talking quite naturally. He made not a doubt of it.

As for nature herself, few people loved her better than he did. If he had been walking with Queen Mary and Miss Merewether he would have been often silent; and they too, he was sure; calmly floating off; and he looked at the picture again; into that happy and far more severe and exalted world, which, was also so much simpler than this.

Just as he was thinking this, he saw Mabel Waring[3] going away, in her pretty yellow dress. She looked agitated, with a strained expression and fixed unhappy eyes for all she tried to look animated.

What was the cause of her unhappiness? He looked again at the picture. The sun had set, but every colour was still bright, so that it was not long set, only just gone beyond the brown mound of the heath. The light was very becoming: and he supposed that Mabel Waring was with him and the Queen and Miss Merewether, walking back to Norwich. They would be talking about the way; how far it was; and whether this was the sort of country they liked; also, if they were hungry; and what they would have for dinner. That was natural talk. Stuart Elton[4] himself – Mr Carslake saw him standing alone lifting a paper knife up in his hands and looking at it in a very strange way – Stuart himself, if he were on the heath, would just drop it, just toss it away. For underneath, though people seeing him casually would never believe it, Stuart was the gentlest, simplest of creatures, content to ramble all day with quite undistinguished people, like himself, and this oddity – it looked like affectation to stand in the middle of a drawing-room holding a tortoise-shell paper knife in his hand – was only manner. When they once got out on the heath and started to walk to Norwich this was what they would say: I find rubber soles make all the difference. But don't they draw the feet? Yes – no. On grass like this they're perfect. But on the pavement? And then socks and sock suspenders; men's clothes, women's clothes. Why, very likely they would talk about their own habits for a whole hour; and all in the freest, easiest way, so that suppose he, or Mabel Waring, or Stuart, or that angry looking chap with the tooth brush moustache who seemed to know nobody[5] – wanted to explain Einstein, or make a statement – something quite private perhaps – (he had known it happen) – it would come quite natural.

It was a very beautiful picture. Like all landscapes it made one sad, because that heath would so long outlast all people; but the sadness was so elevated – turning away from Miss Merewether, George Carslake gazed at the picture – arose so plainly from the thought that it was calm, it was beautiful, that it should endure. But I cannot quite explain it, he thought. He did not like churches at all; indeed, if he said what he felt about the heath remaining and them all perishing and yet that this was right and there was nothing sad about it – he would laugh; he would dispose of that silly sentimental twaddle in a moment. For such it would be, spoken: but not, he felt, thought. No, he would not give up his belief that to walk over a heath in the evening was perhaps the best way of passing one's time.

One did come across tramps and queer people of course. Now a little deserted farm; now a man and a cart; sometimes – but this was perhaps a little too romantic – a man on a horse. There would be shepherds very likely: a windmill: or if these failed, some bush against the sky, or cart track which had this power – again he trembled on the silly words, – 'to reconcile differences – to make one believe in God'. It almost stung him that last! To believe in God indeed! When every rational power protested against the crazy and craven idiocy of such a saying! It seemed to him as if he had been trapped into the words. 'To believe in God'. What he believed in was a little simple talk with people like Mabel Waring, Stuart Elton, the Queen of England for the matter of that – on a heath. At least he had found great comfort in their having much in common – boots, hunger, fatigue. But then he could figure Stuart Elton, for example stopping, or falling silent. If you asked him What are you thinking about? perhaps he would say nothing at all, or something not true. Perhaps he would not be able to speak the truth.

Mr Carslake again looked at the picture. He was troubled by the sense of something remote. Indeed people did think about things, did paint things. Indeed, these parties on the heath do not annihilate differences, he thought; but he maintained, he did believe this – that the only differences remaining (out there, with that line of heath in the distance, and never a house to break the view) are fundamental differences – like this, what the man thought who painted the picture, what Stuart Elton thought about – about what? It was probably a belief of some kind.

Anyhow, on they went; for the great point of walking is that nobody can stand still very long; they have to rouse themselves up, and on a long walk fatigue, and the desire to end the fatigue, give the most philosophic, or those even distracted by love and its torments, an overpowering reason for setting their minds upon getting home.

Every phrase he used, alas, tinkled in his ears with a sham religious flavour. 'Getting home' – the religious had appropriated that. It meant going to Heaven. His thoughts could not find any pure new words which had never been ruffled and creased and had the starch taken out of them by others' use.

Only when he was walking, with Mabel Waring[,] Stuart Elton[,] the Queen of England and that fierce bolteyed looking uncompromising man there, this old melodious singsong stopped. Perhaps one was a little brutalised by the open air. Thirst brutalised; a blister on the heel. When he was walking there was a hardness and a freshness about things: no confusion; no wobbling; the division at least between the known and the unknown was as distinct as the rim of a pond – here was dry land, here water. Now a curious thought struck him – that the waters possessed an attraction for the people on earth. When Stuart Elton took his paper knife or Mabel Waring looked about to burst into tears, and that man with the tooth brush moustache glared, it was because they all wished to take to the water. But what was the water? Understanding perhaps. There must be someone who was so miraculously endowed, so fitted with all the parts of human nature, that these silences and unhappinesses, which were the result of being unable to fit one's mind to other people's, were all rightly understood. Stuart Elton dived in: Mabel dived. Some went under and were satisfied; others came gasping to the top. He was relieved to find himself thinking of death as a plunge into a pond; for he was alarmed at his mind's instinct, when unguarded, to rise into clouds and Heaven, and rig up the old comfortable figure, the old flowing garments and mild eyes and cloud-like mantle.

In the pond, on the other hand, were newts, and fish and mud. The point about the pond was that one had to create it for oneself; new, brand new. No longer did one want to be rapt off to Heaven, there to sing and meet the dead. One wanted something here and now. Understanding meant an increase of life; a power to say what one could not say; to make such vain attempts as Mabel Waring's – he knew her way of doing something suddenly quite out of her character, rather startling and dashing, [would] succeed – instead of failing and plunging her deeper into gloom.

So the old fiddler played his tune, as George Carslake looked from the picture at the people, and back again. His round face, his rather squarely built body expressed a philosophic calm which gave him, even among all these people, a look of detachment, of calm, of restfulness, which was not sluggish, but alert. He had sat down, and Miss Merewether who might easily have drifted off sat beside him. People said that he made very brilliant after-dinner speeches. They said he never married because his mother needed him. No one thought of him, however, as an heroic character – there was nothing tragic about him. He was a barrister. Hobbies, [tastes?], gifts over and above his able mind, he had none in particular – except that he walked. People tolerated him, liked him, sneered at him slightly, for he had done nothing that you could lay your hands on, and he had a butler who was like an elder brother.

But Mr Carslake did not bother his head. People were very simple – men and women much alike; it was a great pity to quarrel with anyone; and indeed he never did. That is not to say that his feelings were not sometimes hurt; unexpectedly. Living near Gloucester, he had an absurd touchiness about the Cathedral; he fought its battles, he resented its criticism as if the Cathedral were his blood relation. But he would let anyone say what they liked about his own brother. Also, anybody might laugh at him for walking. His was a nature smooth all over but not soft; and suddenly little spikes jutted out – about the Cathedral, or some glaring injustice.

The old fiddler fiddled his simple melody to this effect: We are not here, but on a heath, walking back to Norwich. Sharp, self-assertive Miss Merewether who said that the Queen was 'sublime' had joined the party on condition that she talked no more silly nonsense that she did not believe. 'The school of Crome?' she said, looking at the picture.[6]

Very well. This being settled, they went on, it might be a matter of six or seven miles. It often happened to George Carslake; there was nothing strange about it – this sense of being in two places at once, with one body here in a London drawing-room, but so severed, that the peace of the country, its uncompromising bareness and hardness and [spirit?], affected that body. He stretched his legs. He felt the breeze on his cheek. Above all he felt, we are all of us, very different superficially, but now united; we may stray; we may seek the water; but it is perfectly true that we are all cool, friendly, physically easy.

Rip off all those clothes my dear, he thought looking at Mabel Waring. Make a bundle of them. Then he thought, don't worry, my dear Stuart, about your soul, its extreme unlikeness to anyone else's. The glaring man seemed to him positively amazing.

It was impossible to put this into words, and it was unnecessary. Beneath the fidgety flicker of these little creatures was always a deep reservoir: and the simple melody without expressing it, did something queer to it – rippled it, liquefied it, made it start and turn and quiver in the depths of one's being, so that all the time ideas were rising from this pool and bubbling up into one's brain. Ideas that were half feelings. They had that kind of emotional quality. It was impossible to analyse them – to say whether they were on the whole happy or unhappy, gay or sad.

His desire was to be sure that all people were the same. He felt that if he could prove it, he would have solved a great problem. But was it true? He kept looking at the picture. Was he not trying to impose on human beings who are by their very nature opposed, different, at war, a claim which is perhaps incongruous – a simplicity that does not belong to their natures? Art has it; a picture has it; but men do not feel it. These states of mind when one is walking, in company, on a heath, produce a sense of similarity. On the other hand, social converse, when everyone wants to shine, and to enforce his own point of view, produces dissimilarity; and which is the more profound?

He tried to analyse this favourite theme of his – walking, different people walking to Norwich. He thought at once of the lark, of the sky, of the view. The walker's thoughts and emotions were largely made up of these outside influences. Walking thoughts were half sky; if you could submit them to chemical analysis you would find that they had some grains of colour in them, some gallons or quarts or pints of air attached to them. This at once made them airier, more impersonal. But in this room, thoughts were jostled together like fish in a net, struggling, scraping each other's scales off, and becoming, in the effort to escape, – for all thinking was an effort to make thought escape from the thinker's mind past all obstacles as completely as possible: all society is an attempt to seize and influence and coerce each thought as it appears and force it to yield to another.

So he could see everyone now engaged. But it was not, strictly, thought; it was being, oneself, that was here in conflict with other beings and selves. Here there was no impersonal colouring mixture: here walls, lights, the houses outside, all reenforced humanity, being themselves the expression of humanity. People pressed upon each other; rubbed each other's bloom off; or, for it told both ways, stimulated and called out an astonishing animation, made each other glow.

Whether pleasure or pain predominated, he could not say. On the heath, there would be no doubt about it. As they walked – Merewether, the Queen, Elton, Mabel Waring and himself – the fiddler played; far from rubbing each other's scales off, they swam side by side in the greatest comfort.

It was a beautiful picture, a very beautiful picture.

He felt a stronger and stronger wish to be there, on the Norfolk heath, indeed.

He then told Miss Merewether a story about his small nephew at Wembley; and as he told it she felt, as his friends always felt, that though he was one of the nicest people she had ever met, George Carslake was a dark horse, a queer fish. There was no saying what he was after. Had he any affections, she wondered? She smiled[,] remembering his butler. And then he made off, [that was all?] he said – went back to [Dittering?] tomorrow.

A Summing Up

Since it had grown hot and crowded indoors, since there could be no danger on a night like this of damp, since the Chinese lanterns seemed hung like red and green fruit in the depths of an enchanted forest, Mr Bertram Pritchard led Mrs Latham into the garden.

The open air and the sense of being out of doors bewildered Sasha Latham, the tall, handsome, rather indolent looking lady whose majesty of presence was so great that people never credited her with feeling perfectly inadequate and gauche when she had to say something at a party. But so it was; and she was glad that she was with Bertram, who could be trusted, even out of doors, to talk without stopping. Written down what he said would be incredible – not only was each thing he said in itself insignificant, but there was no connection between the different remarks. Indeed if one had taken a pencil and written down his very words – and one night of his talk would have filled a whole book – no one could doubt, reading them, that the poor man was intellectually deficient. This was far from the case, for Mr Pritchard was an esteemed civil servant and a Companion of the Bath, but what was even stranger was that he was almost invariably liked. There was a sound in his voice, some accent or emphasis, some lustre in the incongruity of his ideas, some emanation from his round chubby brown face and robin redbreast's figure, something immaterial, unseizable, which existed and flourished and made itself felt independently of his words, indeed, often in opposition to them. Thus Sasha Latham would be thinking while he chattered on about his tour in Devonshire, about inns and landladies, about Eddie and Freddie, about cows and night travelling, about cream and stars, about continental railways and Bradshaw, catching cod, catching cold, influenza, rheumatism and Keats – she was thinking of him in the abstract as a person whose existence was good, creating him as he spoke in a guise that was different from what he said, and was certainly the true Bertram Pritchard, even though one could not prove it. How could one prove that he was a loyal friend and very sympathetic and – but here, as so often happened talking to Bertram Pritchard, she forgot his existence, and began to think of something else.

It was the night she thought of, hitching herself together in some way, taking a look up into the sky. It was the country she smelt suddenly, the sombre stillness of fields under the stars, but here, in Mrs Dalloway's back garden, in Westminster, the beauty, country born and bred as she was, thrilled her because of the contrast presumably; there the smell of hay in the air and behind her the rooms full of people. She walked with Bertram; she walked rather like a stag, with a little give of the ankles, fanning herself, majestic, silent, with all her senses roused, her ears pricked, snuffing the air, as if she had been some wild, but perfectly controlled creature taking its pleasure by night.

This, she thought, is the greatest of marvels; the supreme achievement of the human race. Where there were osier beds and coracles paddling through a swamp, there is this; and she thought of the dry thick well built house, stored with valuables, humming with people coming close to each other, going away from each other, exchanging their views, stimulating each other. And Clarissa Dalloway had made it open in the wastes of the night, had laid paving stones over the bog, and, when they came to the end of the garden (it was in fact extremely small) and she and Bertram sat down on deck chairs, she looked at the house veneratingly, enthusiastically, as if a golden shaft ran through her and tears formed on it and fell, in profound thanksgiving. Shy though she was and almost incapable when suddenly presented to someone of saying anything, fundamentally humble, she cherished a profound admiration for other people. To be them would be marvellous, but she was condemned to be herself and could only in this silent enthusiastic way, sitting outside in a garden, applaud the society of humanity from which she was excluded. Tags of poetry in praise of them rose to her lips; they were adorable and good, above all courageous, triumphers over night and fens, the survivors, the company of adventurers who, set about with dangers, sail on.

By some malice of fate she was unable to join, but she could sit and praise while Bertram chattered on, he being among the voyagers, as cabin boy or common seaman – someone who ran up masts, gaily whistling. Thinking thus, the branch of some tree in front of her became soaked and steeped in her admiration for the people of the house; dripped gold; or stood sentinel erect. It was part of the gallant and carousing company – a mast from which the flag streamed. There was a barrel of some kind against the wall, and this too she endowed.

Suddenly Bertram, who was restless physically, wanted to explore the grounds, and, jumping on to a heap of bricks, he peered over the garden wall. Sasha peered over too. She saw a bucket or perhaps a boot. In a second the illusion vanished. There was London again; the vast inattentive impersonal world; motor omnibuses; affairs; lights before public houses; and yawning policemen.

Having satisfied his curiosity, and replenished, by a moment's silence, his bubbling fountains of talk, Bertram invited Mr and Mrs Somebody to sit with them, pulling up two more chairs. There they sat again, looking at the same house, the same tree, the same barrel; only having looked over the wall and had a glimpse of the bucket, or rather of London going its ways unconcernedly, Sasha could no longer spray over the world that cloud of gold. Bertram talked and the somebodies – for the life of her she could not remember if they were called Wallace or Freeman – answered, and all their words passed through a thin haze of gold and fell into prosaic daylight. She looked at the dry thick Queen Anne House; she did her best to remember what she had read at school about the Isle of Thorney and men in coracles, oysters, and wild duck and mists, but it seemed to her a logical affair of drains and carpenters, and this party – nothing but people, in evening dress.

Then she asked herself, which view is the true one? She could see the bucket and the house half lit up, half unlit.

She asked this question of that somebody whom in her humble way, she had composed out of the wisdom and power of other people. The answer came often by accident – she had known her old spaniel answer her by wagging his tail.

Now the tree, denuded of its gilt and majesty, seemed to supply her with an answer; became a field tree – the only one in a marsh. She had often seen it; seen the red-flushed clouds between its branches or the moon split up, darting irregular flashes of silver. But what answer? Well that the soul – for she was conscious of a movement in her of some creature beating its way about her and trying to escape which momentarily she called the soul – is by nature unmated, a widow bird; a bird perched aloof on that tree.

But then Bertram, putting his arm through hers in his familiar way, for he had known her all her life, remarked that they were not doing their duty and must go in.

At that moment, in some back street or public house, the usual terrible sexless inarticulate voice rang out; a shriek, a cry. And the widow bird startled flew away, descrying wider and wider circles until it became (what she called her soul) remote as a crow which has been startled up into the air by a stone thrown at it.

It now appeared that during the conversation to which Sasha had scarcely listened, Bertram had come to the conclusion that he liked Mr Wallace, but disliked his wife – who was 'very clever, no doubt'.

1926–1941

Moments of Being:
'Slater's Pins Have No Points'

'Slater's pins have no points – don't you always find that?' said Miss
Craye, turning round as the rose fell out of Fanny Wilmot's dress, and
Fanny stooped with her ears full of the music, to look for the pin on the
floor.

The words gave her an extraordinary shock, as Miss Craye struck
the last chord of the Bach fugue. Did Miss Craye actually go to Slater's
and buy pins then, Fanny Wilmot asked herself, transfixed for a
moment? Did she stand at the counter waiting like anybody else, and
was she given a bill with coppers wrapped in it, and did she slip them
into her purse and then, an hour later, stand by her dressing table and
take out the pins? What need had she of pins? For she was not so much
dressed as cased, like a beetle compactly in its sheath, blue in winter,
green in summer. What need had she of pins – Julia Craye – who lived,
it seemed, in the cool, glassy world of Bach fugues, playing to herself
what she liked and only consenting to take one or two pupils at the
Archer Street College of Music (so the Principal, Miss Kingston said) as
a special favour to herself, who had 'the greatest admiration for her in
every way'. Miss Craye was left badly off, Miss Kingston was afraid, at
her brother's death. Oh, they used to have such lovely things, when
they lived at Salisbury and her brother Julius was, of course, a very
well-known man: a famous archaeologist. It was a great privilege to
stay with them, Miss Kingston said ('My family had always known
them – they were regular Salisbury people,' Miss Kingston said), but a
little frightening for a child; one had to be careful not to slam the door
or bounce into the room unexpectedly. Miss Kingston, who gave little
character sketches like this on the first day of term while she received
cheques and wrote out receipts for them, smiled here. Yes, she had been
rather a tomboy; she had bounced in and set all those green Roman
glasses and things jumping in their case. The Crayes were none of them
married. The Crayes were not used to children. They kept cats. The
cats, one used to feel, knew as much about the Roman urns and things
as anybody.

'Far more than I did!' said Miss Kingston brightly, writing her name across the stamp, in her dashing, cheerful, full-bodied hand, for she had always been practical.

Perhaps then, Fanny Wilmot thought, looking for the pin, Miss Craye said that about 'Slater's pins having no points', at a venture. None of the Crayes had ever married. She knew nothing about pins – nothing whatever. But she wanted to break the spell that had fallen on the house; to break the pane of glass which separated them from other people. When Polly Kingston, that merry little girl, had slammed the door and made the Roman vases jump, Julius, seeing that no harm was done (that would be his first instinct) looked, for the case was stood in the window, at Polly skipping home across the fields; looked with the look his sister often had, that lingering, desiring look.

'Stars, sun, moon,' it seemed to say, 'the daisy in the grass, fires, frost on the window pane, my heart goes out to you. But,' it always seemed to add, 'you break, you pass, you go.' And simultaneously it covered the intensity of both these states of mind with 'I can't reach you – I can't get at you,' spoken wistfully, frustratedly. And the stars faded, and the child went.

That was the kind of spell, that was the glassy surface that Miss Craye wanted·to break by showing, when she had played Bach beautifully as a reward to a favourite pupil (Fanny Wilmot knew that she was Miss Craye's favourite pupil) that she too felt as other people felt about pins. Slater's pins had no points.

Yes, the 'famous archaeologist' had looked like that, too. 'The famous archaeologist' – as she said that endorsing cheques, ascertaining the day of the month, speaking so brightly and frankly, there was in Miss Kingston's voice an indescribable tone which hinted at something odd, something queer, in Julius Craye. It was the very same thing that was odd perhaps in Julia too. One could have sworn, thought Fanny Wilmot, as she looked for the pin, that at parties, meetings (Miss Kingston's father was a clergyman) she had picked up some piece of gossip, or it might only have been a smile, or a tone when his name was mentioned, which had given her 'a feeling' about Julius Craye. Needless to say, she had never spoken about it to anybody. Probably she scarcely knew what she meant by it. But whenever she spoke of Julius, or heard him mentioned, that was the first thought that came to mind: there was something odd about Julius Craye.

It was so that Julia looked too, as she sat half turned on the music stool, smiling. It's on the field, it's on the pane, it's in the sky – beauty; and I can't get at it; I can't have it – I, she seemed to add, with that little clutch of the hand which was so characteristic, who adore it so passionately, would give the whole world to possess it! And she picked up the carnation which had fallen on the floor, while Fanny searched for the pin. She crushed it, Fanny felt, voluptuously in her smooth, veined hands stuck about with water-coloured rings set in pearls. The pressure of her fingers seemed to increase all that was most brilliant in the flower; to set it off; to make it more frilled, fresh, immaculate. What was odd in her, and perhaps in her brother too, was that this crush and grasp of the fingers was combined with a perpetual frustration. So it was even now with the carnation. She had her hands on it; she pressed it; but she did not possess it, enjoy it, not altogether.

None of the Crayes had married, Fanny Wilmot remembered. She had in mind how one evening when the lesson had lasted longer than usual and it was dark, Julia Craye had said, 'It's the use of men, surely, to protect us,' smiling at her that same odd smile, as she stood fastening her cloak, which made her, like the flower, conscious to her finger tips of youth and brilliance, but, like the flower too, Fanny suspected, inhibited.

'Oh, but I don't want protection,' Fanny had laughed, and when Julia Craye, fixing on her that extraordinary look, had said she was not so sure of that, Fanny positively blushed under the admiration in her eyes.

It was the only use of men, she had said. Was it for that reason then, Fanny wondered, with her eyes on the floor, that she had never married? After all, she had not lived all her life in Salisbury. 'Much the nicest part of London,' she had said once, '(but I'm speaking of fifteen or twenty years ago) is Kensington. One was in the Gardens in ten minutes – it was like the heart of the country. One could dine out in one's slippers without catching cold. Kensington – it was like a village then, you know,' she had said.

Here she had broken off, to denounce acridly, the draughts in the Tubes.

'It was the use of men,' she had said, with a queer, wry acerbity. Did that throw any light on the problem why she had not married? One could imagine every sort of scene in her youth, when with her good, blue eyes, her straight, firm nose, her piano playing, her rose flowering with chaste passion in the bosom of her muslin dress, she had attracted first the young men to whom such things, and the china tea-cups and the silver candlesticks, and the inlaid tables (for the Crayes had such nice things) were wonderful; young men not sufficiently distinguished; young men of the Cathedral town with ambitions. She had attracted them first, and then her brother's friends from Oxford or Cambridge. They would come down in the summer, row her up the river, continue the argument about Browning by letter, and arrange perhaps on the rare occasions when she stayed in London to show her – Kensington Gardens?

'Much the nicest part of London – Kensington. I'm speaking of fifteen or twenty years ago,' she had said once. 'One was in the Gardens in ten minutes – in the heart of the country.' One could make that yield what one liked, Fanny Wilmot thought, single out for instance, Mr Sherman, the painter, an old friend of hers; make him call for her by appointment one sunny day in June; take her to have tea under the trees. (They had met, too, at those parties to which one tripped in slippers without fear of catching cold.) The aunt or other elderly relative was to wait there while they looked at the Serpentine. They looked at the Serpentine. He may have rowed her across. They compared it with the Avon. She would have considered the comparison very seriously, for views of rivers were important to her. She sat hunched a little, a little angular, though she was graceful then, steering. At the critical moment, for he had determined that he must speak now – it was his only chance of getting her alone – he was speaking with his head turned at an absurd angle, in his great nervousness, over his shoulder – at that very moment she interrupted fiercely. He would have them into the Bridge, she cried. It was a moment of horror, of disillusionment, of revelation for both of them. I can't have it, I can't possess it, she thought. He could not see why she had come then. With a great splash of his oar he pulled the boat round. Merely to snub him? He rowed her back and said good-bye to her.

The setting of that scene could be varied as one chose, Fanny Wilmot reflected. (Where had that pin fallen?) It might be Ravenna – or Edinburgh, where she had kept house for her brother. The scene could be changed and the young man and the exact manner of it all; but one thing was constant – her refusal and her frown and her anger with herself afterwards and her argument, and her relief – yes, certainly her immense relief. The very next day perhaps she would get up at six, put on her cloak, and walk all the way from Kensington to the river. She was so thankful that she had not sacrificed her right to go and look at things when they are at their best – before people are up, that is to say. She could have her breakfast in bed if she liked. She had not sacrificed her independence.

Yes, Fanny Wilmot smiled, Julia had not endangered her habits. They remained safe, and her habits would have suffered if she had married. 'They're ogres,' she had said one evening, half laughing, when another pupil, a girl lately married, suddenly bethinking her that she would miss her husband, had rushed off in haste.

'They're ogres,' she had said, laughing grimly. An ogre would have interfered perhaps with breakfast in bed; with walks at dawn down to the river. What would have happened (but one could hardly conceive this) had she had children? She took astonishing precautions against chills, fatigue, rich food, the wrong food, draughts, heated rooms, journeys in the Tube, for she could never determine which of these it was exactly that brought on those terrible headaches that gave her life the semblance of a battlefield. She was always engaged in outwitting the enemy, until it seemed as if the pursuit had its interest; could she have beaten the enemy finally she would have found life a little dull. As it was, the tug-of-war was perpetual – on one side the nightingale or the view which she loved with passion – yes, for views and birds she felt nothing less than passion; on the other, the damp path or the horrid long drag up a steep hill which would certainly make her good for nothing next day and bring on one of her headaches. When, therefore, from time to time, she managed her forces adroitly and brought off a visit to Hampton Court the week the crocuses (those glossy bright flowers were her favourites) were at their best, it was a victory. It was something that lasted; something that mattered for ever. She strung the afternoon on the necklace of memorable days, which was not too long for her to be able to recall this one or that one; this view, that city; to finger it, to feel it, to savour, sighing, the quality that made it unique.

'It was so beautiful last Friday,' she said, 'that I determined I must go there.' So she had gone off to Waterloo on her great undertaking – to visit Hampton Court – alone. Naturally, but perhaps foolishly, one pitied her for the thing she never asked pity for (indeed she was reticent habitually, speaking of her health only as a warrior might speak of his foe) – one pitied her for always doing everything alone. Her brother was dead. Her sister was asthmatic. She found the climate of Edinburgh good for her. It was too bleak for Julia. Perhaps too she found the associations painful, for her brother, the famous archaeologist, had died there; and she had loved her brother. She lived in a little house off the Brompton Road entirely alone.

Fanny Wilmot saw the pin on the carpet; she picked it up. She looked at Miss Craye. Was Miss Craye so lonely? No, Miss Craye was steadily, blissfully, if only for a moment, a happy woman. Fanny had surprised her in a moment of ecstasy. She sat there, half turned away from the piano, with her hands clasped in her lap holding the carnation upright, while behind her was the sharp square of the window, uncurtained, purple in the evening, intensely purple after the brilliant electric lights which burnt unshaded in the bare music room. Julia Craye sitting hunched and compact holding her flower seemed to emerge out of the London night, seemed to fling it like a cloak behind her. It seemed in its bareness and intensity the effluence of her spirit, something she had made which surrounded her, which was her. Fanny stared.

All seemed transparent for a moment to the gaze of Fanny Wilmot, as if looking through Miss Craye, she saw the very fountain of her being spurt up in pure, silver drops. She saw back and back into the past behind her. She saw the green Roman vases stood in their case; heard the choristers playing cricket; saw Julia quietly descend the curving steps on to the lawn; saw her pour out tea beneath the cedar tree; softly enclose the old man's hand in hers; saw her going round and about the corridors of that ancient Cathedral dwelling place with towels in her hand to mark them; lamenting as she went the pettiness of daily life; and slowly ageing, and putting away clothes when summer came, because at her age they were too bright to wear; and tending her father's sickness; and cleaving her way ever more definitely as her will stiffened towards her solitary goal; travelling frugally; counting the cost and measuring out of her tight shut purse the sum needed for this journey, or for that old mirror; obstinately adhering whatever people might say in choosing her pleasures for herself. She saw Julia –

She saw Julia open her arms; saw her blaze; saw her kindle. Out of the night she burnt like a dead white star. Julia kissed her. Julia possessed her.

'Slater's pins have no points,' Miss Craye said, laughing queerly and relaxing her arms, as Fanny Wilmot pinned the flower to her breast with trembling fingers.

The Lady in the Looking-Glass: A Reflection

People should not leave looking-glasses hanging in their rooms any more than they should leave open cheque books or letters confessing some hideous crime. One could not help looking, that summer afternoon, in the long glass that hung outside in the hall. Chance had so arranged it. From the depths of the sofa in the drawing-room one could see reflected in the Italian glass not only the marble-topped table opposite, but a stretch of the garden beyond. One could see a long grass path leading between banks of tall flowers until, slicing off an angle, the gold rim cut it off.

The house was empty, and one felt, since one was the only person in the drawing-room, like one of those naturalists who, covered with grass and leaves, lie watching the shyest animals – badgers, otters, kingfishers – moving about freely, themselves unseen. The room that afternoon was full of such shy creatures, lights and shadows, curtains blowing, petals falling – things that never happen, so it seems, if someone is looking. The quiet old country room with its rugs and stone chimney pieces, its sunken book-cases and red and gold lacquer cabinets, was full of such nocturnal creatures. They came pirouetting across the floor, stepping delicately with high-lifted feet and spread tails and pecking allusive beaks as if they had been cranes or flocks of elegant flamingoes whose pink was faded, or peacocks whose trains were veined with silver. And there were obscure flushes and darkenings too, as if a cuttlefish had suddenly suffused the air with purple; and the room had its passions and rages and envies and sorrows coming over it and clouding it, like a human being. Nothing stayed the same for two seconds together.

But, outside, the looking-glass reflected the hall table, the sun-flowers, the garden path so accurately and so fixedly that they seemed held there in their reality unescapably. It was a strange contrast – all changing here, all stillness there. One could not help looking from one to the other. Meanwhile, since all the doors and windows were open in the heat, there was a perpetual sighing and ceasing sound, the voice of the transient and the perishing, it seemed, coming and going like human breath, while in the looking-glass things had ceased to breathe and lay still in the trance of immortality.

Half an hour ago the mistress of the house, Isabella Tyson, had gone down the grass path in her thin summer dress, carrying a basket, and had vanished, sliced off by the gilt rim of the looking-glass. She had gone presumably into the lower garden to pick flowers; or as it seemed more natural to suppose, to pick something light and fantastic and leafy and trailing, traveller's joy, or one of those elegant sprays of convolvulus that twine round ugly walls and burst here and there into white and violet blossoms. She suggested the fantastic and the tremulous convolvulus rather than the upright aster, the starched zinnia, or her own burning roses alight like lamps on the straight posts of their rose trees. The comparison showed how very little, after all these years, one knew about her; for it is impossible that any woman of flesh and blood of fifty-five or sixty should be really a wreath or a tendril. Such comparisons are worse than idle and superficial – they are cruel even, for they come like the convolvulus itself trembling between one's eyes and the truth. There must be truth; there must be a wall. Yet it was strange that after knowing her all these years one could not say what the truth about Isabella was; one still made up phrases like this about convolvulus and traveller's joy. As for facts, it was a fact that she was a spinster; that she was rich; that she had bought this house and collected with her own hands – often in the most obscure corners of the world and at great risk from poisonous stings and Oriental diseases – the rugs, the chairs, the cabinets which now lived their nocturnal life before one's eyes. Sometimes it seemed as if they knew more about her than we, who sat on them, wrote at them, and trod on them so carefully, were allowed to know. In each of these cabinets were many little drawers, and each almost certainly held letters, tied with bows of ribbon, sprinkled with sticks of lavender or rose leaves. For it was another fact – if facts were what one wanted – that Isabella had known many people, had had many friends; and thus if one had the audacity to open a drawer and read her letters, one would find the traces of many agitations, of appointments to meet, of upbraidings for not having met, long letters of intimacy and affection, violent letters of jealousy and reproach, terrible final words of parting – for all those interviews and assignations had led to nothing – that is, she had never married, and yet, judging from the mask-like indifference of her face, she had gone through twenty times more of passion and experience than those whose loves are trumpeted forth for all the world to hear. Under the stress of thinking about Isabella, her room became more shadowy and symbolic; the corners seemed darker, the legs of chairs and tables more spindly and hieroglyphic.

Suddenly these reflections were ended violently and yet without a sound. A large black form loomed into the looking-glass; blotted out everything, strewed the table with a packet of marble tablets veined with pink and grey, and was gone. But the picture was entirely altered. For the moment it was unrecognisable and irrational and entirely out of focus. One could not relate these tablets to any human purpose. And then by degrees some logical process set to work on them and began ordering and arranging them and bringing them into the fold of common experience. One realised at last that they were merely letters. The man had brought the post.

There they lay on the marble-topped table, all dripping with light and colour at first and crude and unabsorbed. And then it was strange to see how they were drawn in and arranged and composed and made part of the picture and granted that stillness and immortality which the looking-glass conferred. They lay there invested with a new reality and significance and with a greater heaviness, too, as if it would have needed a chisel to dislodge them from the table. And, whether it was fancy or not, they seemed to have become not merely a handful of casual letters but to be tablets graven with eternal truth – if one could read them, one would know everything there was to be known about Isabella, yes, and about life, too. The pages inside those marble-looking envelopes must be cut deep and scored thick with meaning. Isabella would come in, and take them, one by one, very slowly, and open them, and read them carefully word by word, and then with a profound sigh of comprehension, as if she had seen to the bottom of everything, she would tear the envelopes to little bits and tie the letters together and lock the cabinet drawer in her determination to conceal what she did not wish to be known.

The thought served as a challenge. Isabella did not wish to be known – but she should no longer escape. It was absurd, it was monstrous. If she concealed so much and knew so much one must prize her open with the first tool that came to hand – the imagination. One must fix one's mind upon her at that very moment. One must fasten her down there.

One must refuse to be put off any longer with sayings and doings such as the moment brought forth – with dinners and visits and polite conversations. One must put oneself in her shoes. If one took the phrase literally, it was easy to see the shoes in which she stood, down in the lower garden, at this moment. They were very narrow and long and fashionable – they were made of the softest and most flexible leather. Like everything she wore, they were exquisite. And she would be standing under the high hedge in the lower part of the garden, raising the scissors that were tied to her waist to cut some dead flower, some overgrown branch. The sun would beat down on her face, into her eyes; but no, at the critical moment a veil of cloud covered the sun, making the expression of her eyes doubtful – was it mocking or tender, brilliant or dull? One could only see the indeterminate outline of her rather faded, fine face looking at the sky. She was thinking, perhaps, that she must order a new net for the strawberries; that she must send flowers to Johnson's widow; that it was time she drove over to see the Hippesleys in their new house. Those were the things she talked about at dinner certainly. But one was tired of the things that she talked about at dinner. It was her profounder state of being that one wanted to catch and turn to words, the state that is to the mind what breathing is to the body, what one calls happiness or unhappiness. At the mention of those words it became obvious, surely, that she must be happy. She was rich; she was distinguished; she had many friends; she travelled – she bought rugs in Turkey and blue pots in Persia. Avenues of pleasure radiated this way and that from where she stood with her scissors raised to cut the trembling branches while the lacy clouds veiled her face.

Here with a quick movement of her scissors she snipped the spray of traveller's joy and it fell to the ground. As it fell, surely some light came in too, surely one could penetrate a little farther into her being. Her mind then was filled with tenderness and regret. . . . To cut an overgrown branch saddened her because it had once lived, and life was dear to her. Yes, and at the same time the fall of the branch would suggest to her how she must die herself and all the futility and evanescence of things. And then again quickly catching this thought up, with her instant good sense, she thought life had treated her well; even if fall she must, it was to lie on the earth and moulder sweetly into the roots of violets. So she stood thinking. Without making any thought precise – for she was one of those reticent people whose minds hold their thoughts enmeshed in clouds of silence – she was filled with thoughts. Her mind was like her room, in which lights advanced and retreated, came pirouetting and stepping delicately, spread their tails, pecked their way; and then her whole being was suffused, like the room again, with a cloud of some profound knowledge, some unspoken regret, and then she was full of locked drawers, stuffed with letters, like her cabinets. To talk of 'prizing her open' as if she were an oyster, to use any but the finest and subtlest and most pliable tools upon her was impious and absurd. One must imagine — here was she in the looking-glass. It made one start.

She was so far off at first that one could not see her clearly. She came lingering and pausing, here straightening a rose, there lifting a pink to smell it, but she never stopped; and all the time she became larger and larger in the looking-glass, more and more completely the person into whose mind one had been trying to penetrate. One verified her by degrees — fitted the qualities one had discovered into this visible body. There were her grey-green dress, and her long shoes, her basket, and something sparkling at her throat. She came so gradually that she did not seem to derange the pattern in the glass, but only to bring in some new element which gently moved and altered the other objects as if asking them, courteously, to make room for her. And the letters and the table and the grass walk and the sunflowers which had been waiting in the looking-glass separated and opened out so that she might be received among them. At last there she was, in the hall. She stopped dead. She stood by the table. She stood perfectly still. At once the looking-glass began to pour over her a light that seemed to fix her; that seemed like some acid to bite off the unessential and superficial and to leave only the truth. It was an enthralling spectacle. Everything dropped from her — clouds, dress, basket, diamond — all that one had called the creeper and convolvulus. Here was the hard wall beneath. Here was the woman herself. She stood naked in that pitiless light. And there was nothing. Isabella was perfectly empty. She had no thoughts. She had no friends. She cared for nobody. As for her letters, they were all bills. Look, as she stood there, old and angular, veined and lined, with her high nose and her wrinkled neck, she did not even trouble to open them.

People should not leave looking-glasses hanging in their rooms.

The Fascination of the Pool

It may have been very deep – certainly one could not see to the bottom of it. Round the edge was so thick a fringe of rushes that their reflections made a darkness like the darkness of very deep water. However in the middle was something white. The big farm a mile off was to be sold and some zealous person, or it may have been a joke on the part of a boy, had stuck one of the posters advertising the sale, with farm horses, agricultural implements, and young heifers, on a tree stump by the side of the pool. The centre of the water reflected the white placard and when the wind blew the centre of the pool seemed to flow and ripple like a piece of washing. One could trace the big red letters in which Romford Mill was printed in the water. A tinge of red was in the green that rippled from bank to bank.

But if one sat down among the rushes and watched the pool – pools have some curious fascination, one knows not what – the red and black letters and the white paper seemed to lie very thinly on the surface, while beneath went on some profound under-water life like the brooding, the ruminating of a mind. Many, many people must have come there alone, from time to time, from age to age, dropping their thoughts into the water, asking it some question, as one did oneself this summer evening. Perhaps that was the reason of its fascination – that it held in its waters all kinds of fancies, complaints, confidences, not printed or spoken aloud, but in a liquid state, floating one on top of another, almost disembodied. A fish would swim through them, be cut in two by the blade of a reed; or the moon would annihilate them with its great white plate. The charm of the pool was that thoughts had been left there by people who had gone away and without their bodies their thoughts wandered in and out freely, friendly and communicative, in the common pool.

Among all these liquid thoughts some seemed to stick together and to form recognisable people – just for a moment. And one saw a whiskered red face formed in the pool leaning low over it, drinking it. I came here in 1851 after the heat of the Great Exhibition. I saw the Queen open it.[1] And the voice chuckled liquidly, easily, as if he had thrown off his elastic side boots and put his top hat on the edge of the pool. Lord, how hot it was! and now all gone, all crumbled, of course, the thoughts seemed to say, swaying among the reeds. But I was a lover, another thought began, sliding over the other silently and orderly as fish not impeding each other. A girl; we used to come down from the farm (the placard of its sale was reflected on the top of the water) that summer, 1662. The soldiers never saw us from the road. It was very hot. We lay here. She was lying hidden in the rushes with her lover, laughing into the pool and slipping into it, thoughts of eternal love, of fiery kisses and despair. And I was very happy, said another thought glancing briskly over the girl's despair (for she had drowned herself). I used to fish here. We never caught the giant carp but we saw him once – the day Nelson fought at Trafalgar.[2] We saw him under the willow – my word! what a great brute he was! They say he was never caught. Alas, alas sighed a voice, slipping over the boy's voice. So sad a voice must come from the very bottom of the pool. It raised itself under the others as a spoon lifts all the things in a bowl of water. This was the voice we all wished to listen to. All the voices slipped gently away to the side of the pool to listen to the voice[3] which so sad it seemed – it must surely know the reason of all this. For they all wished to know.

One drew closer to the pool and parted the reeds so that one could see deeper, through the reflections, through the faces, through the voices to the bottom. But there under the man who had been to the Exhibition; and the girl who had drowned herself and the boy who had seen the fish; and the voice which cried alas alas! yet there was always something else. There was always another face, another voice. One thought came and covered another. For though there are moments when a spoon seems about to lift all of us, and our thoughts and longings and questions and confessions and disillusions into the light of day, somehow the spoon always slips beneath and we flow back again over the edge into the pool. And once more the whole of its centre is covered over with the reflection of the placard which advertises the sale of Romford Mill Farm. That perhaps is why one loves to sit and look into pools.

Three Pictures

The First Picture

It is impossible that one should not see pictures; because if my father was a blacksmith and yours was a peer of the realm, we must needs be pictures to each other. We cannot possibly break out of the frame of the picture by speaking natural words. You see me leaning against the door of the smithy with a horseshoe in my hand and you think as you go by: 'How picturesque!' I, seeing you sitting so much at your ease in the car, almost as if you were going to bow to the populace, think what a picture of old luxurious aristocratical England! We both are quite wrong in our judgments no doubt, but that is inevitable.

So now at the turn of the road I saw one of these pictures. It might have been called 'The Sailor's Homecoming' or some such title. A fine young sailor carrying a bundle; a girl with her hand on his arm; neighbours gathering round; a cottage garden ablaze with flowers; as one passed one read at the bottom of that picture that the sailor was back from China, and there was a fine spread waiting for him in the parlor; and he had a present for his young wife in his bundle; and she was soon going to bear him their first child. Everything was right and good and as it should be, one felt about that picture. There was something wholesome and satisfactory in the sight of such happiness; life seemed sweeter and more enviable than before.

So thinking I passed them, filling in the picture as fully, as completely as I could, noticing the colour of her dress, of his eyes, seeing the sandy cat slinking round the cottage door.

For some time the picture floated in my eyes, making most things appear much brighter, warmer, and simpler than usual; and making some things appear foolish; and some things wrong and some things right, and more full of meaning than before. At odd moments during that day and the next the picture returned to one's mind, and one thought with envy, but with kindness, of the happy sailor and his wife; one wondered what they were doing, what they were saying now. The imagination supplied other pictures springing from that first one, a picture of the sailor cutting firewood, drawing water; and they talked about China; and the girl set his present on the chimneypiece where everyone who came could see it; and she sewed at her baby clothes, and all the doors and windows were open into the garden so that the birds were flittering and the bees humming, and Rogers – that was his name – could not say how much to his liking all this was after the China seas. As he smoked his pipe, with his foot in the garden.

The Second Picture

In the middle of the night a loud cry rang through the village. Then there was a sound of something scuffling; and then dead silence. All that could be seen out of the window was the branch of lilac tree hanging motionless and ponderous across the road. It was a hot still night. There was no moon. The cry made everything seem ominous. Who had cried? Why had she cried? It was a woman's voice, made by some extremity of feeling almost sexless, almost expressionless. It was as if human nature had cried out against some iniquity, some inexpressible horror. There was dead silence. The stars shone perfectly steadily. The fields lay still. The trees were motionless. Yet all seemed guilty, convicted, ominous. One felt that something ought to be done. Some light ought to appear tossing, moving agitatedly. Someone ought to come running down the road. There should be lights in the cottage windows. And then perhaps another cry, but less sexless, less wordless, comforted, appeased. But no light came. No feet were heard. There was no second cry. The first had been swallowed up, and there was dead silence.

One lay in the dark listening intently. It had been merely a voice. There was nothing to connect it with. No picture of any sort came to interpret it, to make it intelligible to the mind. But as the dark arose at last all one saw was an obscure human form, almost without shape, raising a gigantic arm in vain against some overwhelming iniquity.

The Third Picture

The fine weather remained unbroken. Had it not been for that single cry in the night one would have felt that the earth had put into harbour; that life had ceased to drive before the wind; that it had reached some quiet cove and there lay anchored, hardly moving, on the quiet waters. But the sound persisted. Wherever one went, it might be for a long walk up into the hills, something seemed to turn uneasily beneath the surface, making the peace, the stability all round one seem a little unreal. There were the sheep clustered on the side of the hill; the valley broke in long tapering waves like the fall of smooth waters. One came on solitary farmhouses. The puppy rolled in the yard. The butterflies gambolled over the gorse. All was as quiet, as safe [as] could be. Yet, one kept thinking, a cry had rent it; all this beauty had been an accomplice that night; had consented to remain calm, to be still beautiful; at any moment it might be sundered again. This goodness, this safety were only on the surface.

And then to cheer oneself out of this apprehensive mood one turned to the picture of the sailor's homecoming. One saw it all over again producing various little details – the blue colour of her dress, the shadow that fell from the yellow flowering tree – that one had not used before. So they had stood at the cottage door, he with his bundle on his back, she just lightly touching his sleeve with her hand. And a sandy cat had slunk round the door. Thus gradually going over the picture in every detail, one persuaded oneself by degrees that it was far more likely that this calm and content and goodwill lay beneath the surface than anything treacherous, sinister. The sheep grazing, the waves of the valley, the farmhouse, the puppy, the dancing butterflies were in fact like that all through. And so one turned back home, with one's mind fixed on the sailor and his wife, making up picture after picture of them so that one picture after another of happiness and satisfaction might be laid over that unrest, that hideous cry, until it was crushed and silenced by their pressure out of existence.

Here at last was the village, and the churchyard through which one must pass; and the usual thought came, as one entered it, of the peacefulness of the place, with its shady yews, its rubbed tombstones, its nameless graves. Death is cheerful here, one felt. Indeed, look at that picture! A man was digging a grave, and children were picnicking at the side of it while he worked. As the shovels of yellow earth were thrown up, the children were sprawling about eating bread and jam and drinking milk out of large mugs. The gravedigger's wife, a fat fair woman, had propped herself against a tombstone and spread her apron on the grass by the open grave to serve as a tea-table. Some lumps of clay had fallen among the tea things. Who was going to be buried, I asked. Had old Mr Dodson died at last? 'Oh! no. It's for young Rogers, the sailor,' the woman answered, staring at me. 'He died two nights ago, of some foreign fever. Didn't you hear his wife? She rushed into the road and cried out . . . Here, Tommy, you're all covered with earth!'

What a picture it made!

Scenes from the Life of a British Naval Officer

The rushed waters of the Red Sea dashed past the porthole; occasion-ally a dolphin leapt high into the air, or a flying fish exploded an arch of fire in mid air. Captain Brace sat in his cabin with a map spread on the vast equality of the table in front of him. His face had a carved look as if it had been cut by a negro from a well seasoned log, had been polished for fifty years, had been dried in a tropical sun; had stood out in the freezing cold; had been sluiced by tropical rains; had then been erected before grovelling multitudes as their idol. It had acquired the inscrut-able expression of the idol to whom questions have been put for many centuries without eliciting an answer.

The cabin held no furniture save the vast table and the swivel chair. But on the wall behind the Captain's back hung seven or eight white faced instruments whose dials were inscribed with figures and symbols to which very fine hands were moving, sometimes with so slow an advance as to be imperceptible, sometimes with a sudden decisive spring. Some invisible substance was being divided[,] measured, weighed and counted in seven or eight different ways simultaneously. And as the substance itself was invisible, so was the measuring, dividing[,] weighing and counting carried on inaudibly. Not a sound broke the silence. In the centre of the instruments hung the photograph of a lady's head surmounted by three ostrich feathers.

Suddenly Captain Brace swung round in his chair so that he faced all the dials and the photograph. The idol had suddenly turned its back upon the suppliants. The back of Captain Brace was cased in a suit that fitted his bulk as tightly as a snake skin. [His back] was as inscrutable as his face. The suppliants might well address their prayers to back or front indifferently. Suddenly, after a long scrutiny of the wall, Captain Brace swung back. He took a pair of compasses, and began to draw on a large sheet neatly divided into squares a design of such immense elaboration and exactness that each stroke seemed to create an immortal object that would endure precisely so for ever. The silence was unbroken, since the rush of the sea and the throb of the engines was so regular and so much in the same key that they too seemed to be silence expressed in a different medium.

Suddenly – every movement, every sound was sudden in an atmosphere of such tension – a gong blared out. Tremors sharp as muscular contractions, twitched the air. Three times sound blared. Three times the atmosphere thus twitched was crisped into sharp muscular contractions. The last had lapsed for three seconds precisely when the Captain rose. With the sweep of an automatic action, he pressed a blotting paper over his design with one hand; with the other he placed his cap on his head. Then he marched to the door; then he marched down the three steps that led to the deck. Each distance seemed already cut up into so many stages; and his last step brought him exactly to a particular plank[,] to his station in front of five hundred blue jackets. Five hundred right hands flew exactly to their heads. Five seconds later the Captain's right hand flew to his head. After waiting precisely two seconds it fell as the signal falls when an express train has passed. Captain Brace passed with the same measured stride through the ranks of the blue jackets and behind him at their proper distance marched a group of officers in their order too. But at the door of his dining room the Captain faced them, received their salute[,] acknowledged it by his own and withdrew to dine alone.

He sat alone at his dinner table as he had sat alone at his desk. Of the servants who put plates before him he had never seen more than the white hands, putting down plates, taking plates away. When the hands were not white, they were dismissed. His eyes never raised themselves above the hands and the plates. In orderly procession meat, bread[,] pastry[,] fruit were placed before the idol. The red fluid in the wine glass slowly sank, rose, sank[,] rose and sank again. All the meat disappeared, all the pastry, all the fruit. At last, taking a piece of crumb about the size of a billiard ball the Captain swept this round the plate[,] devoured it and rose. Now his eyes were raised until they looked at their own level straight ahead. Whatever came before them – wall, mirror, brass rod – they passed through as if nothing had any solidity to intercept them. So he marched as if he followed in the wake of the beam cast by his eyes up an iron ladder onto a platform[,] higher and higher up beyond these impediments until he had mounted onto an iron platform upon which stood a telescope. When he put his eye to the telescope the telescope became immediately an extension of his eyes as if it were a horn casing that had formed itself to enclose the penetration of his sight. When he moved the telescope up and down it seemed as if his own long horn covered eye were moving.

Miss Pryme

It was the determination to leave the world better than she found it –
and she had found it, in Wimbledon very dull, very prosperous, very
fond of tennis, very inconsiderate, inattentive, and disinclined to pay
any sort of attention to what she said or wished – that made Miss
Pryme[,] the third daughter of one of Wimbledon's doctors[,] to settle
at the age of thirty-five at Rusham.

It was a corrupt village – partly, it was said because there were no
omnibuses; and the road to the town was impassable in winter; hence
Rusham felt no pressure of opinion; Mr Pember, the Rector[,] never
wore a clean collar; never took a bath; and had it not been for Mabel
his old servant, would have been often too unpresentable to appear in
church.[1] Naturally there were no candles on the altar; the font was
cracked; and Miss Pryme had caught him slipping out in the middle of
the service and smoking a cigarette in the graveyard. She spent the first
three years of her residence catching people doing what they should not
do. The tips of Mr Bent's elm tree's branches swept the coffins as they
passed up the lane; it should be trimmed; Mr Carr's wall bulged; it
must be rebuilt. Mrs Pye drank; Mrs Cole lived notoriously with the
policeman. As Miss Pryme caught out all these people doing wrong she
acquired a sour expression; she stooped; and she scowled askance at
people she met; and she determined to buy the cottage which she
rented; for she could certainly do good here.

First she took up the matter of the candles. She went without a
servant; thus she saved enough to buy tall thick sacerdotal candles
from an ecclesiastical shop in London. She earned the right to instal
them on the altar by scrubbing the church floor; by working a mat for
the altar; and by getting a scene from *Twelfth Night* so as to pay for
mending the font. Then she faced old Mr Pember with her candles. He
lit another cigarette holding it between fingers that looked jaundiced
with nicotine. His face, his body was like a bramble spray straying,
bristling, red, unkempt. And he mumbled that he wanted no candle.
Didn't hold with popish ways – never had. And off he shambled to
swing, smoking, on the farm yard gate, talking about Cropper's pigs.

Miss Pryme waited. She held a bazaar to get up funds for reshingling the church. The Bishop was present. Once more she asked Mr Pember about the candles. She mentioned the Bishop[,] it is said[,] in her support – it is said; for there were now two parties in the village, both gave versions of what happened when Miss Pryme countered the Rector; some sided with Miss Pryme; others with Mr Pember. Some sided with candles; and strictness; others with the dear old man and ease[;] and Mr Pember said quite testily that he was Rector of the parish; he didn't hold with candles; there was an end on't. Miss Pryme retired to her cottage and wrapped the candles carefully in the long drawer. She never went to the rectory again.

But the Rector was a very old man; she had only to wait. Meanwhile Miss Pryme went on improving the world. For nothing gave her a quicker sense of the passage of time. At Wimbledon it flagged; here it raced. She washed up her breakfast and then filled up forms. Then she drew up reports. Then she nailed a notice to a board in her garden. Then she visited the cottages. She sat with old Malthouse night after night when he was dying and saved his relations a lot of trouble.[2] By degrees a new and most delicious sensation began to prick and stir in her veins. It was better than married love; better than children; it was power to improve the world; power over the infirm; the illiterate; the drunken. By degrees as she tripped up the village street with her basket, or went to church with her broom she was attended by a second Miss Pryme, who was larger, fairer, more radiant and remarkable than the first; indeed she was rather like Florence Nightingale to look at; and before five years were out these two ladies were one and identical.[3]

Ode Written Partly in Prose on Seeing the Name of Cutbush Above a Butcher's Shop in Pentonville

Oh Cutbush, little John, standing glum between
your father and mother, the day they decided what
to make of you, should you be florist or butcher,
hearing them decide your fate; shall you be florist
or butcher; while the long wave lies iridescent
on the shores of California; and the elephant in
Abyssinia and the humming bird in
Aethiopeia and the King in Buckingham Palace
go their ways:
Shall John be florist or butcher?

  Coming down the asphalt path,
with her velvet beret on her head, saucily
askew,
Comes Louie, betweenmaid to Mrs Mump at the
Rectory, infant still innocent still; but
avid for love; sixteen years old; glancing
saucily; past the pond where the dogs bark; and the
ducks quack;
Lovely are the willows
and lilies sliding and twitching; and
behold the old gentleman trying to disentangle the
child's boat with his stick from the willows; and John says to Louie,
In summer I swim here; Sure? Yes I swim here.
making believe he is among the great athletes;
like Byron he could swim the Hellespont;[1] John
Cutbush of Pentonville. And the dusk falls;
dusk gilt with lights from the upper windows;
one reads Herodotus in the original at his upper
window; and another cuts waistcoats in the basement;

and another makes coins; and another turns pieces
of wood that shall be chairlegs; lights fall
on the dusk; on the pond; lights are
zigzagged in the water. Cheek and shoulder together
cuddling kissing; pressing; there they
stand while the gentleman disentangles the boat
with his stick; and the church tolls.
From the harsh steeple fall the iron notes;
warning Louie Louie of time and tea;
how Cook will say, If you're out larking with the
boys again I'll tell Her meaning Mumps, Adela,
wife of Cuthbert the clergyman.
Up she starts from her couch on Primrose Hill;
from her couch on the sweet cold bed of earth;
earth laid over buds and bulbs; over pipes and
wires; taking to its cold sweet breast now the
water pipe; now the wire; which flashes messages
to China where the mandarins go, mute, cruel; delicate;
past the gold pagodas; and the houses have paper
walls; and the people smile wise inscrutable smiles.
Up she gets and he follows her, down the Avenue
as far as the corner, by the paper shop; Man
murdered in Pimlico is on the placard; where they
kiss by the paper shop; and so part, and dark
night enfolds them; and she hurries down the area
to the lit kitchen with the saucepans steaming
for master's dinner.

And he hires a barrow and goes to Smithfield
at dawn; at chill dawn sees the cold meat,
shrouded in white nets borne on men's shoulders;
meat from the Argentines; from haired and red pelted
hogs and bullocks.

All in white like surgeons go the butchers of
Smithfield, handling the shrouded cadavers;
the stark and frozen corpses that shall lie like
mummies in the ice house till the Sunday fire revives
them and they drip juice into the big plate to
revive church goers.

But I swam the Hellespont – he dreams; he had read
Byron in the Charing Cross Road he had sipped and
tasted *Don Juan* where it stood dust parched wind
blown exposed to the lights of the pavement.
Shall I serve for ever Massey and Hodge meat
merchants of Smithfield? He stands cap in hand
but upright in front of his master, having served
his apprenticeship. A young chap must fend for
himself.

And he sees the violets and the asphodel and the
naked swimmers on the bank in robes like
those worn by the Leighton pictures at Leighton
house.[2] Louie of the Avenue kitchenmaid to the
clergyman, watches and waves her bare arm as he
dives.

  So he sets up shop on his own.
To the passer by it is another of those shops
that stay open till one on Saturdays. Although the
west end is curtained and shuttered, here, in the
purlieus of London, the residue of London,
the night is the time
of gala. The flares are lit over barrows. The
feathers and blouses blow like flowers. The
meat blazes. The sides of oxen are patterned with
flower leaves in the pink flesh. Knives slice.
The lumps are tossed and wrapped. Bags bulge on
women's arms. They stand first on this foot then on
that. The children gaze up at the flares and the
coarse light and the red and white faces burn them
selves for ever on the pure eyeballs. The barrel organ
plays and the dogs snuffle in the dust for scraps
of meat. And all over Pentonville and Islington
floats a coarse balloon of yellow colour and far
away in the city there is a white faced church and
steeple.

John Cutbush butcher of Pentonville stands at the
door of his shop.

He stands at the door of his shop.
Still he stands at the door of his shop.
But time has run its wheels over him. So many million miles
have the trams passed; so many million hogs and
bullocks have been sliced and tossed; so many bags
bulged. His face is red; his eyes bleared;
staring at the flares so many nights. And sometimes
he stares past the faces, past the new shop opposite
where the young man inveigles; into the gloomy
hollow. And he wakes and says And for you, Maam?
and for you?
But some note the new butcher opposite; and shuffle
past Cutbush to try Ainslies.
And Louie in the room behind the shop is broad
thighed, sullen eyed; and the little boy died;
and the girl is a worry, always after the boys;
and there framed on the wall is Mrs Mump in the dress
she wore to be presented; and meat smells everywhere
and the day's takings diminish.
These are semblances of human faces seen in passing
translated from a foreign language.
And the language always makes up new words.
For next door are urns and slabs of marble in an
undertaker's window; next door are musical instruments
next a home for cats and dogs; and then the Convent
and there on that eminence stands
sublime the tower of the Prison; and there is the
waterworks; and here is a whole dark private street
like those lines of burrows where nocturnal animals
dwell in deserts; but here not marmots and sand
martins; but borough inspectors; rate collectors;
officials of the gas company, the
waterworks; with their wives and children;
also some clerks fresh from Somerset and Suffolk;
also a maiden lady who does her own house work.

And so home along the High Street past the churchyard
where the cats celebrate their rites and butchers
promise eternal faith to kitchenmaids;

The flower of life ever shakes free from the
bud; the flower of life flaunts on placards
in our faces; and we give thanks to the armies
and navies and flying men and actresses
who provide our nightly entertainment and as we
hold the *Evening Standard* under the lamp how little
we think of the wealth we can gather between the
palms of two hands; how little we can grasp;
how little we can interpret and read aright
the name John Cutbush but only as we pass his
shop on Saturday night, cry out Hail Cutbush,
of Pentonville, I salute thee; passing.

Portraits

WAITING FOR DÉJEUNER

When the humming birds quivered in the flower's trumpet; when the vast slab-footed elephants squelched through the mud; when the animal-eyed savage pushed off from the reeds in his canoe; when the Persian woman picked a louse from the hair of the child; when the zebras galloped across the horizon in wild arabesques of mating; when the blue-black hollow of the sky resounded with the tap tap tap of the vulture's beak on skeleton that had a little flesh and only a half tail: – Monsieur and Madame Louvois neither saw nor heard.

When the waiter in his creased shirt, shiny coat, apron tied in the middle and sleeked back hair spat on his hands then wiped the plate to save the trouble of rinsing it; when the sparrows in the road collected over a spot of dung; when the iron gates of the level crossing swung to; and the traffic coagulated; one lorry with iron rails; one with crates of oranges; several cars; a barrow drawn by a donkey; when the old man impaled a paper bag in the public gardens; when the lights flickered over the Cinema announcing the new Jungle Film; when the grey-blue clouds of the northern hemisphere let a grey-blue patch shine for a moment on the waters of the Seine: – Monsieur and Madame Louvois stared at the mustard pot and the cruet; at the yellow crack on the marble topped table.

The humming bird quivered; the gates opened; the lorries jerked on; and the eyes on Monsieur and Madame Louvois lit with lustre; for down on the marble topped table in front of them the sleek haired waiter slapped a plate of tripe.

THE FRENCHWOMAN IN THE TRAIN

Most garrulous, pendulous, snuffing like a tapir the succulent lower leaves of the cabbages; rootling among the herbage; even in the third class railway carriage avid for some titbit of gossip ... Madame Alphonse said to her cook ... the earrings swinging as in the large lobed ears of some pachydermatous monster. A hiss with a little saliva comes from the front teeth which have been yellowed and blunted, biting at cabbage stalks. And all the time behind her pendulous nid-nodding head and the drip of saliva the grey olives of Provence ray out, come to a point; make a wrinkled background with wry angular branches and peasants stooping.

In London in a third class carriage against black walls pasted with shiny advertisements she would be running through Clapham on her way to Highgate to renew the circle of china flowers on the grave of her husband. There at the Junction she sits in her corner[,] on her knee a black bag; in the bag a copy of the *Mail*; a picture of the Princesses – in her bag redolent of cold beef, of pickles, of tented curtains, of church bells on Sunday and the Vicar calling.

Here she bears on her immense and undulating shoulder the tradition; even when her mouth dribbles, when her wild pig eyes glitter one hears the croak of the frog in the wild tulip field; the hush of the Mediterranean lipping the sand; and the language of Molière. Here the bull neck bears baskets of grapes; through the train rattle comes the din of the market; a butting ram, men astride it; ducks in wicker cages; ice cream in cornets; rushes laid over cheese; over butter; men playing boules by a plane tree; a fountain; the acrid smell at the corner where peasants openly obey the dictates of nature.

PORTRAIT 3

And it seemed to me sitting in the courtyard of the French Inn, that the secret of existence was nothing but a bat's skeleton in a cupboard; and the riddle nothing but a criss-cross of spider's web; so very solid she looked. She was sitting in the sun. She had no hat. The light fixed her. There was no shadow. Her face was yellow and red; round too; a fruit on a body; another apple, only not on a plate. Breasts had formed apple-hard under the blouse on her body.

I watched her. She flicked her skin as if a fly had walked over it. Some one passed; I saw the narrow leaves of the apple trees that her eyes were flicker. And her coarseness, her cruelty, was like bark rough with lichen and she was everlasting and entirely solved the problem of life.

PORTRAIT 4

She had taken him to Harrods and to the National Gallery since he had to buy shirts before he went back to Rugby and acquired culture. He did not brush his teeth. And now she must really think, as they sat in the restaurant which Uncle Hal had recommended if they wanted something not cheap, not dear either, what she ought to say to him before he went back to Rugby. . . . They were a long time bringing the hors d'oeuvres. . . . She could remember dining here with a sandy haired boy before the War. He had admired her, without actually asking her to marry him. . . . Yet how could she put it, about being more like his father; she was a widow; the one she did marry had been killed; and brushing his teeth? She would have Minestrone? Yes. And after that? Wiener Schnitzel? Poulet Marengo? That's with mushrooms? Are they fresh? . . . But I must say something he can keep by him, to help him, in moments you know, of temptation. 'My mother . . . ' What a time they take! That's the hors d'oeuvres at the next table, but all the sardines are gone already. . . .

And George sat silent; looking with the eyes of a carp which after a winter's immersion comes flush with the surface, and sees over the rim of the Soho carafe flies dancing, girls' legs.

PORTRAIT 5

'I am one of those people,' she said looking down with secret satisfaction at the still substantial crescent of white sugared pastry in which she had as yet made one bite only, 'who feel everything dreadfully.'

And here with her three-pronged fork half way to her mouth she yet contrived to brush her hand over her fur as if to indicate the motherly sisterly wifely tenderness with which, even if there were only a cat in the room to stroke, she stroked it. Then she let fall one more drop from the scent bottle which she carried in a gland in her cheek with which to sweeten the sometimes malodorous emanations of her own not sufficiently appreciated character, and added:

'At the Hospital the men used to call me Little Mother,' and looked at her friend opposite as if waiting for her to confirm or deny the portrait she had drawn, but since there was silence she pronged the last inch of sugared pastry and swallowed it, as if only from inanimate things did she get that tribute which the selfishness of humanity denied her.

PORTRAIT 6

It's very hard on me – I who should have been born in the eighties find myself something of an outcast here. Can't even wear a rose suitably in my button hole. Should have carried a cane, like my father; must wear a felt hat with a dent in it, even walking up Bond Street, not a topper. I still love though, if the word's proper now, society, graded like one of those ices wrapped in frilled paper – it's true they said the Italians kept them under their beds in Bethnal Green. And Oscar being witty;[1] and the lady with the red lips standing on a tiger skin on a slippery floor – the tiger's mouth wide open. 'But she paints!' (so my mother said) which meant of course the women in Piccadilly. That was my world. Now every one paints. Everything's sugar white, even the houses, in Bond Street, made of concrete, with bits of steel filing.

Whereas I like cool things; pictures of Venice; girls on a bridge; a man fishing; Sunday calm; perhaps a punt. I'm off now in the next motor omnibus to tea with Aunt Mabel in the Addison Road. Her house now keeps something of what I mean; the goat, I mean, lying in the sun on the pavement; the distinguished aristocratic old goat; and the bus drivers wearing the Rothschild pheasants slung on their whips;[2] and a young man like myself sitting on the box by the driver.

But here they come brandishing ash plants even in Piccadilly; some hatless; all rouged. And virtuous; serious; so desperate the young are nowadays, driving in their racing cars to revolution. I can assure you the Traveller's Joy in Surrey smells of petrol. And look there at the corner; rose red brick giving up its soul in a puff of powder. Nobody but myself minds a scrap – and Uncle Edwin and Aunt Mabel. They hold up against these horrors their little candle; as we can't do it, who lapse and crash and bring the old chandelier down on top of us. I always say anyone can smash a plate; but what I admire is old china, riveted.

PORTRAIT 7

Yes, I knew Vernon Lee.[3] That is to say we had a villa. I used to get up before breakfast. I used to go to the Galleries before they were crowded. I'm devoted to beauty. . . . No, I don't paint myself; but then one appreciates art all the better perhaps. They're so narrow, artists; nowadays too they live so wildly. Fra Angelico, you remember, painted on his knees.[4] But I was saying, I knew Vernon Lee. She had a villa. We had a villa. One of those villas hung with wistaria – something like our lilac, but better – and Judas trees. Oh why does one live in Kensington? Why not in Italy? But I always feel, still, I do live in Florence – in the spirit. And don't you think we do live in the spirit – our real life? But then I'm one of those people who want beauty, if it's only a stone, or a pot – I can't explain. Anyhow in Florence one meets people who love beauty. We met a Russian Prince there; also at a party a very well known man whose name I forget. And one day as I was standing in the road, outside my villa, a little old woman came along leading a dog on a chain. It might have been Ouida.⁵ Or Vernon Lee? I never spoke to her. But in a sense, the true sense, I who love beauty always feel, I knew Vernon Lee.

PORTRAIT 8

'I'm one of those simple folk, who may be old fashioned, but I do believe in the lasting things – love, honour, patriotism. I really believe, and I don't mind confessing it, in loving one's wife.'

Yes, the tag *Nihil humanum* often falls from your lips. But you take care not to talk Latin too often. For you have to make money – first to live on; then to sit on: Queen Anne furniture; mostly fakes.

'I'm not one of the clever ones. But I will say this for myself – I've blood in my veins. I'm at home with the parson; with the publican. I go to the pub, and play darts with the men.'

Yes you're the middle man; the go between; a dress suit for London; tweeds for the country. Shakespeare and Wordsworth you can equally 'Bill'.

'What I must say I loathe are those poor bloodless creatures who live in . . .'

The high ground or the low ground. You're all for betwixt and between.

'And I have my family . . .'

Yes you're highly prolific. You're everywhere. When one walks in the garden, what's that on the cabbage? Middle brow. Middle brow infecting the sheep. The moon too is under your sway. Misted. You dull tarnish and make respectable even the silver edge (excuse the expression) of heaven's own scythe. And I ask of the gulls who are crying on desolate sea sands and of the farm hands who are coming home to their wives, what will become of us, birds, men and women, if middle brow has his way, and there's only a middle sex, but no lovers or friends?

'Yes, I'm one of the simple folk, who may be old fashioned, but I do believe, I don't mind admitting it, in loving one's kind.'

Uncle Vanya

'Don't they see through everything – the Russians? all the little disguises we've put up? Flowers against decay; gold and velvet against poverty; the cherry trees, the apple trees – they see through them too,' she was thinking at the play. Then a shot rang out.

'There! now he's shot him. That's a mercy. Oh but the shots missed! The old villain with the dyed whiskers in the check ulster isn't hurt a bit. . . . Still he tried to shoot him; he suddenly rose erect, reeled up the stairs and got his pistol. He pressed the trigger. The ball lodged in the wall; perhaps in the table leg. It came to nothing anyhow. "Let it all be forgotten, dear Vanya. Let us be friends as of old," he's saying. . . . Now they've gone. Now we hear the bells of the horses tinkling away in the distance. And is that also true of us?' she said, leaning her chin on her hand and looking at the girl on the stage. 'Do we hear the bells tinkling away down the road?' she asked, and thought of the taxis and omnibuses in Sloane Street, for they lived in one of the big houses in Cadogan Square.

'We shall rest,' the girl was saying now, as she clasped Uncle Vanya in her arms. 'We shall rest,' she said. Her words were like drops falling – one drop, then another drop. 'We shall rest,' she said again. 'We shall rest, Uncle Vanya.' And the curtain fell.

'As for us,' she said, as her husband helped her on with her cloak, 'We've not even loaded the pistol. We're not even tired.'

And they stood still for a moment in the gangway, while they played 'God Save the King'.

'Aren't the Russians morbid?' she said, taking his arm.

The Duchess and the Jeweller

Oliver Bacon lived at the top of a house overlooking the Green Park. He had a flat; chairs jutted out at the right angles – chairs covered in hide. Sofas filled the bays of the windows – sofas covered in tapestry. The windows, the three long windows, had the proper allowance of discreet net and figured satin. The mahogany sideboard bulged discreetly with the right brandies, whiskeys and liqueurs. And from the middle window he looked down upon the glossy roofs of fashionable cars packed in the narrow straits of Piccadilly. A more central position could not be imagined. And at eight in the morning he would have his breakfast brought in on a tray by a manservant; the manservant would unfold his crimson dressing-gown; he would rip his letters open with his long pointed nails and would extract thick white cards of invitation upon which the engraving stood up roughly from duchesses, countesses, viscountesses and Honourable Ladies. Then he would wash; then he would eat his toast; then he would read his paper by the bright burning fire of electric coals.

'Behold Oliver,' he would say, addressing himself. 'You who began life in a filthy little alley, you who . . .' and he would look down at his legs, so shapely in their perfect trousers; at his boots; at his spats. They were all shapely, shining; cut from the best cloth by the best scissors in Savile Row. But he dismantled himself often and became again a little boy in a dark alley. He had once thought that the height of his ambition – selling stolen dogs to fashionable women in Whitechapel. And once he had been done. 'Oh, Oliver,' his mother had wailed. 'Oh, Oliver! When will you have sense, my son?' . . . Then he had gone behind a counter; had sold cheap watches; then he had taken a wallet to Amsterdam. . . . At that memory he would chuckle – the old Oliver remembering the young. Yes, he had done well with the three diamonds; also there was the commission on the emerald. After that he went into the private room behind the shop in Hatton Garden; the room with the scales, the safe, the thick magnifying glasses. And then . . . and then . . . He chuckled. When he passed through the knots of jewellers in the hot evening who were discussing prices, gold mines, diamonds, reports from South Africa, one of them would lay a finger to the side of his nose and murmur, 'Hum–m–m,' as he passed. It was no more than a murmur; no more than a nudge on the shoulder, a finger on the nose, a buzz that ran through the cluster of jewellers in Hatton Garden on a hot afternoon – oh, many years ago now! But still Oliver felt it purring down his spine, the nudge, the murmur that meant, 'Look at him – young Oliver, the young jeweller – there he goes.' Young he was then. And he dressed better and better; and had, first a hansom cab; then a car; and first he went up to the dress circle, then down into the stalls. And he had a villa at Richmond, overlooking the river, with trellises of red roses; and Mademoiselle used to pick one every morning and stick it in his buttonhole.

'So,' said Oliver Bacon, rising and stretching his legs. 'So . . . '

And he stood beneath the picture of an old lady on the mantelpiece and raised his hands. 'I have kept my word,' he said, laying his hands together, palm to palm, as if he were doing homage to her. 'I have won my bet.' That was so; he was the richest jeweller in England; but his nose, which was long and flexible, like an elephant's trunk, seemed to say by its curious quiver at the nostrils (but it seemed as if the whole nose quivered, not only the nostrils) that he was not satisfied yet; still smelt something under the ground a little further off. Imagine a giant hog in a pasture rich with truffles; after unearthing this truffle and that, still it smells a bigger, a blacker truffle under the ground further off. So Oliver snuffed always in the rich earth of Mayfair another truffle, a blacker, a bigger further off.

Now then he straightened the pearl in his tie, cased himself in his smart blue overcoat; took his yellow gloves and his cane; and swayed as he descended the stairs and half snuffed, half sighed through his long sharp nose as he passed out into Piccadilly. For was he not still a sad man, a dissatisfied man, a man who seeks something that is hidden, though he had won his bet?

He swayed slightly as he walked, as the camel at the zoo sways from side to side when it walks along the asphalt paths laden with grocers and their wives eating from paper bags and throwing little bits of silver paper crumpled up on to the path. The camel despises the grocers; the camel is dissatisfied with its lot; the camel sees the blue lake and the fringe of palm trees in front of it. So the great jeweller, the greatest jeweller in the whole world, swung down Piccadilly, perfectly dressed, with his gloves, with his cane; but dissatisfied still, till he reached the dark little shop, that was famous in France, in Germany, in Austria, in Italy, and all over America – the dark little shop in the street off Bond Street.

As usual he strode through the shop without speaking, though the four men, the two old men, Marshall and Spencer, and the two young men, Hammond and Wicks, stood straight behind the counter as he passed and looked at him, envying him. It was only with one finger of the amber-coloured glove, waggling, that he acknowledged their presence. And he went in and shut the door of his private room behind him.

Then he unlocked the grating that barred the window. The cries of Bond Street came in; the purr of the distant traffic. The light from reflectors at the back of the shop struck upwards. One tree waved six green leaves, for it was June. But Mademoiselle had married Mr Pedder of the local brewery – no one stuck roses in his buttonhole now.

'So,' he half sighed, half snorted, 'so . . . '

Then he touched a spring in the wall and slowly the panelling slid open, and behind it were the steel safes, five, no, six of them, all of burnished steel. He twisted a key; unlocked one; then another. Each was lined with a pad of deep crimson velvet; in each lay jewels – bracelets, necklaces, rings, tiaras, ducal coronets; loose stones in glass shells; rubies, emeralds, pearls, diamonds. All safe, shining, cool, yet burning, eternally, with their own compressed light.

'Tears!' said Oliver, looking at the pearls.

'Heart's blood!' he said, looking at the rubies.

'Gunpowder!' he continued, rattling the diamonds so that they flashed and blazed.

'Gunpowder enough to blow up Mayfair – sky high, high, high!' He threw his head back and made a sound like a horse neighing as he said it.

The telephone buzzed obsequiously in a low muted voice on his table. He shut the safe.

'In ten minutes,' he said. 'Not before.' And he sat down at his desk and looked at the heads of the Roman emperors that were graved on his sleeve links. And again he dismantled himself and became once more the little boy playing marbles in the alley where they sell stolen dogs on Sunday. He became that wily astute little boy, with lips like wet cherries. He dabbled his fingers in ropes of tripe; he dipped them in pans of frying fish; he dodged in and out among the crowds. He was slim, lissome, with eyes like licked stones. And now – now – the hands of the clock ticked on. One, two, three, four ... The Duchess of Lambourne waited his pleasure; the Duchess of Lambourne, daughter of a hundred Earls. She would wait for ten minutes on a chair at the counter. She would wait his pleasure. She would wait till he was ready to see her. He watched the clock in its shagreen case. The hand moved on. With each tick the clock handed him – so it seemed – pâté de foie gras; a glass of champagne; another of fine brandy; a cigar costing one guinea. The clock laid them on the table beside him, as the ten minutes passed. Then he heard soft slow footsteps approaching; a rustle in the corridor. The door opened. Mr Hammond flattened himself against the wall.

'Her Grace!' he announced.

And he waited there, flattened against the wall.

And Oliver, rising, could hear the rustle of the dress of the Duchess as she came down the passage. Then she loomed up, filling the door, filling the room with the aroma, the prestige, the arrogance, the pomp, the pride of all the Dukes and Duchesses swollen in one wave. And as a wave breaks, she broke, as she sat down, spreading and splashing and falling over Oliver Bacon the great jeweller, covering him with sparkling bright colours, green, rose, violet; and odours; and iridescences; and rays shooting from fingers, nodding from plumes, flashing from silk; for she was very large, very fat, tightly girt in pink taffeta, and past her prime. As a parasol with many flounces, as a peacock with many feathers, shuts its flounces, folds its feathers, so she subsided and shut herself as she sank down in the leather armchair.

'Good morning, Mr Bacon,' said the Duchess. And she held out her hand which came through the slit of her white glove. And Oliver bent low as he shook it. And as their hands touched the link was forged between them once more. They were friends, yet enemies; he was master, she was mistress; each cheated the other, each needed the other, each feared the other, each felt this and knew this every time they touched hands thus in the little back room with the white light outside, and the tree with its six leaves, and the sound of the street in the distance and behind them the safes.

'And today, Duchess – what can I do for you today?' said Oliver, very softly.

The Duchess opened; her heart, her private heart, gaped wide. And with a sigh, but no words, she took from her bag a long wash-leather pouch – it looked like a lean yellow ferret. And from a slit in the ferret's belly she dropped pearls – ten pearls. They rolled from the slit in the ferret's belly – one, two, three, four – like the eggs of some heavenly bird.

'All that's left me, dear Mr Bacon,' she moaned. Five, six, seven – down they rolled, down the slopes of the vast mountain sides that fell between her knees into one narrow valley – the eighth, the ninth, and the tenth. There they lay in the glow of the peach-blossom taffeta. Ten pearls.

'From the Appleby cincture,' she mourned. 'The last . . . the last of them all.'

Oliver stretched out and took one of the pearls between finger and thumb. It was round, it was lustrous. But real was it, or false? Was she lying again? Did she dare?

She laid her plump padded finger across her lips. 'If the Duke knew . . . ' she whispered. 'Dear Mr Bacon, a bit of bad luck . . .'

Been gambling again, had she?

'That villain! That sharper!' she hissed.

The man with the chipped cheek bone? A bad 'un. And the Duke was straight as a poker; with side whiskers; would cut her off, shut her up down there if he knew – what I know, thought Oliver, and glanced at the safe.

'Araminta, Daphne, Diana,' she moaned. 'It's for *them*.'

The Ladies Araminta, Daphne, Diana – her daughters. He knew them; adored them. But it was Diana he loved.

'You have all my secrets,' she leered. Tears slid; tears fell; tears, like diamonds, collecting powder in the ruts of her cherry-blossom cheeks.

'Old friend,' she murmured, 'old friend.'

'Old friend,' he repeated, 'old friend,' as if he licked the words.

'How much?' he queried.

She covered the pearls with her hand.

'Twenty thousand,' she whispered.

But was it real or false, the one he held in his hand? The Appleby cincture – hadn't she sold it already? He would ring for Spencer or Hammond. 'Take it and test it,' he would say. He stretched to the bell.

'You will come down tomorrow?' she urged, she interrupted. 'The Prime Minister – His Royal Highness . . .' She stopped. 'And Diana,' she added.

Oliver took his hand off the bell.

He looked past her, at the backs of the houses in Bond Street. But he saw, not the houses in Bond Street, but a dimpling river; and trout rising and salmon; and the Prime Minister; and himself too; in white waistcoats; and then, Diana. He looked down at the pearl in his hand. But how could he test it, in the light of the river, in the light of the eyes of Diana? But the eyes of the Duchess were on him.

'Twenty thousand,' she moaned. 'My honour!'

The honour of the mother of Diana! He drew his cheque book towards him; he took out his pen.

'Twenty,' he wrote. Then he stopped writing. The eyes of the old woman in the picture were on him – of the old woman, his mother.

'Oliver!' she warned him. 'Have sense? Don't be a fool!'

'Oliver!' the Duchess entreated – it was 'Oliver' now, not 'Mr Bacon'. 'You'll come for a long week-end?'

Alone in the woods with Diana! Riding alone in the woods with Diana!

'Thousand,' he wrote, and signed it.

'Here you are,' he said.

And there opened all the flounces of the parasol, all the plumes of the peacock, the radiance of the wave, the swords and spears of Agincourt, as she rose from her chair. And the two old men and the two young men, Spencer and Marshall, Wicks and Hammond, flattened themselves behind the counter envying him as he led her through the shop to the door. And he waggled his yellow glove in their faces, and she held her honour – a cheque for twenty thousand pounds with his signature – quite firmly in her hands.

'Are they false or are they real?' asked Oliver, shutting his private door. There they were, ten pearls on the blotting paper on the table. He took them to the window. He held them under his lens to the light. . . . This, then, was the truffle he had routed out of the earth! Rotten at the centre – rotten at the core!

'Forgive me, oh my mother!' he sighed, raising his hands as if he asked pardon of the old woman in the picture. And again he was a little boy in the alley where they sold dogs on Sunday.

'For,' he murmured, laying the palms of his hands together, 'it is to be a long week-end.'

The Shooting Party

She got in and put her suit case in the rack, and the brace of pheasants on top of it. Then she sat down in the corner. The train was rattling through the midlands, and the fog, which came in when she opened the door, seemed to enlarge the carriage and set the four travellers apart. Obviously M. M. – those were the initials on the suit case – had been staying the week-end with a shooting party, obviously, for she was telling over the story now, lying back in her corner. She did not shut her eyes. But clearly she did not see the man opposite, nor the coloured photograph of York Minster. She must have heard, too, what they had been saying. For as she gazed, her lips moved; now and then she smiled. And she was handsome; a cabbage rose; a russet apple; tawny; but scarred on the jaw – the scar lengthened when she smiled. Since she was telling over the story she must have been a guest there, and yet, dressed as she was, out of fashion as women dressed, years ago, in pictures in fashion plates of sporting newspapers, she did not seem exactly a guest, nor yet a maid. Had she had a basket with her she would have been the woman who breeds fox terriers; the owner of the Siamese cat; some one connected with hounds and horses. But she had only a suit case and the pheasants. Somehow therefore she must have wormed her way into the room that she was seeing through the stuffing of the carriage, and the man's bald head, and the picture of York Minster. And she must have listened to what they were saying, for now, like somebody imitating the noise that someone else makes, she made a little click at the back of her throat: 'Chk. Chk.' Then she smiled.

'Chk,' said Miss Antonia, pinching her glasses on her nose. The damp leaves fell across the long windows of the gallery; one or two stuck, fish-shaped, and lay like inlaid brown wood upon the window-panes. Then the trees in the Park shivered, and the leaves, flaunting down, seemed to make the shiver visible – the damp brown shiver.

'Chk,' Miss Antonia sniffed again, and pecked at the flimsy white stuff that she held in her hands, as a hen pecks nervously rapidly at a piece of white bread.

The wind sighed. The room was draughty. The doors did not fit, nor the windows. Now and then a ripple, like a reptile, ran under the carpet. On the carpet lay panels of green and yellow, where the sun rested, and then the sun moved and pointed a finger as if in mockery at a hole in the carpet and stopped. And then on it went, the sun's feeble but impartial finger, and lay upon the coat of arms over the fireplace – gently illumined the shield; the pendant grapes; the mermaid; and the spears. Miss Antonia looked up as the light strengthened. Vast lands, so they said, the old people had owned – her forefathers – the Rashleighs. Over there. Up the Amazons. Freebooter. Voyagers. Sacks of emeralds. Nosing round the islands. Taking captives. Maidens. There she was, all scales from the tail to the waist. Miss Antonia grinned. Down struck the finger of the sun and her eye went with it. Now it rested on a silver frame; on a photograph; on an egg-shaped baldish head; on a lip that stuck out under the moustache; and the name 'Edward' written with a flourish beneath.

'The King . . .' Miss Antonia muttered, turning the film of white upon her knee, 'had the Blue Room,' she added with a toss of her head. The light faded.

Out in the King's Ride the pheasants were being driven across the noses of the guns. Up they spurted from the underwood like heavy rockets, reddish purple rockets, and as they rose the guns cracked in order, eagerly, sharply, as if a line of dogs had suddenly barked. Tufts of white smoke held together for a moment; then gently solved themselves, faded, and dispersed.

In the deep cut road beneath the hanger a cart stood, laid already with soft warm bodies, with limp claws, and still lustrous eyes. The birds seemed alive still, but swooning under their rich damp feathers. They looked relaxed and comfortable, stirring slightly, as if they slept upon a warm bank of soft feathers on the floor of the cart.

Then the Squire, with the hang-dog, purple-stained face, in the shabby gaiters, cursed and raised his gun.

Miss Antonia stitched on. Now and then a tongue of flame reached round the grey log that stretched from one bar to another across the grate; ate it greedily, then died out, leaving a white bracelet where the bark had been eaten off. Miss Antonia looked up for a moment, stared wide-eyed, instinctively, as a dog stares at a flame. Then the flame sank and she stitched again.

Then, silently, the enormously high door opened. Two lean men came in, and drew a table over the hole in the carpet. They went out; they came in. They laid a cloth upon the table. They went out; they came in. They brought a green baize basket of knives and forks; and glasses; and sugar casters; and salt-cellars; and bread; and a silver vase with three chrysanthemums in it. And the table was laid. Miss Antonia stitched on.

Again the door opened, pushed feebly this time. A little dog trotted in, a spaniel, nosing nimbly; it paused. The door stood open. And then, leaning on her stick, heavily, old Miss Rashleigh entered. A white shawl, diamond-fastened, clouded her baldness. She hobbled; crossed the room; hunched herself in the high-backed chair by the fireside. Miss Antonia went on stitching.

'Shooting,' she said at last.

Old Miss Rashleigh nodded. 'In the King's Ride,' she said. She gripped her stick. They sat waiting.

The shooters had moved now from the King's Ride to the Home Woods. They stood in the purple ploughed field outside. Now and then a twig snapped; leaves came whirling. But above the mist and the smoke was an island of blue – faint blue, pure blue – alone in the sky. And in the innocent air, as if straying alone like a cherub, a bell from a far hidden steeple frolicked, gambolled, then faded. Then again up shot the rockets, the reddish purple pheasants. Up and up they went. Again the guns barked; the smoke balls formed; loosened, dispersed. And the busy little dogs ran nosing nimbly over the fields; and the warm damp bodies, still languid and soft, as if in a swoon, were bunched together by the men in gaiters and flung into the cart.

'There!' grunted Milly Masters, the house-keeper, throwing down her glasses. She was stitching too in the small dark room that overlooked the stable-yard. The jersey, the rough woollen jersey for her son, the boy who cleaned the church, was finished. 'The end o' that!' she muttered. Then she heard the cart. Wheels ground on the cobbles. Up she got. With her hands to her hair, her chestnut-coloured hair, she stood in the yard, in the wind.

'Coming!' she laughed, and the scar on her cheek lengthened. She unbolted the door of the game room as Wing, the keeper, drove the cart over the cobbles. The birds were dead now, their claws gripped tight, though they gripped nothing. The leathery eyelids were creased greyly over their eyes. Mrs Masters the housekeeper, Wing the gamekeeper, took bunches of dead birds by the neck and flung them down on the slate floor of the game larder. The slate floor became smeared and spotted with blood. The pheasants looked smaller now, as if their bodies had shrunk together. Then Wing lifted the tail of the cart and drove in the pins which secured it. The sides of the cart were stuck about with little grey-blue feathers, and the floor was smeared and stained with blood. But it was empty.

'The last of the lot!' Milly Masters grinned as the cart drove off.

'Luncheon is served, ma'am,' said the butler. He pointed at the table; he directed the footman. The dish with the silver cover was placed precisely there where he pointed. They waited, the butler and the footman.

Miss Antonia laid her white film upon the basket; put away her silk; her thimble; stuck her needle through a piece of flannel; and hung her glasses on a hook upon her breast. Then she rose.

'Luncheon!' she barked in old Miss Rashleigh's ear. One second later old Miss Rashleigh stretched her leg out; gripped her stick; and rose too. Both old women advanced slowly to the table; and were tucked in by the butler and the footman, one at this end, one at that. Off came the silver cover. And there was the pheasant, featherless, gleaming; the thighs tightly pressed to its side; and little mounds of breadcrumbs were heaped at either end.

Miss Antonia drew the carving knife across the pheasant's breast firmly. She cut two slices and laid them on a plate. Deftly the footman whipped it from her, and old Miss Rashleigh raised her knife. Shots rang out in the wood under the window.

'Coming?' said old Miss Rashleigh, suspending her fork.

The branches flung and flaunted on the trees in the Park.

She took a mouthful of pheasant. Falling leaves flicked the window-pane; one or two stuck to the glass.

'In the Home Woods, now,' said Miss Antonia. 'Hugh's last shoot.' She drew her knife down the other side of the breast. She added potatoes and gravy, Brussels sprouts and bread sauce methodically in a circle round the slices on her plate. The butler and the footman stood watching, like servers at a feast. The old ladies ate quietly; silently; nor did they hurry themselves; methodically they cleaned the bird. Bones only were left on their plates. Then the butler drew the decanter towards Miss Antonia, and paused for a moment with his head bent.

'Give it here, Griffiths,' said Miss Antonia, and took the carcass in her fingers and tossed it to the spaniel beneath the table. The butler and the footman bowed and went out.

'Coming closer,' said Miss Rashleigh, listening. The wind was rising. A brown shudder shook the air; leaves flew too fast to stick. The glass rattled in the windows.

'Birds wild,' Miss Antonia nodded, watching the helter-skelter.

Old Miss Rashleigh filled her glass. As they sipped their eyes became lustrous like half-precious stones held to the light. Slate blue were Miss Rashleigh's; Miss Antonia's red, like port. And their laces and their flounces seemed to quiver, as if their bodies were warm and languid underneath their feathers as they drank.

'It was a day like this, d'you remember?' said old Miss Rashleigh, fingering her glass. 'They brought him home . . . a bullet through his heart. A bramble, so they said. Tripped. Caught his foot. . . .' She chuckled as she sipped her wine.

'And John . . .' said Miss Antonia. 'The mare, they said, put her foot in a hole. Died in the field. The hunt rode over him. He came home, too, on a shutter. . . .' They sipped again.

'Remember Lily?' said old Miss Rashleigh. 'A bad 'un.' She shook her head. 'Riding with a scarlet tassel on her cane. . . .'

'Rotten at the heart!' cried Miss Antonia. 'Remember the Colonel's letter? "Your son rode as if he had twenty devils in him – charged at the head of his men." . . . Then one white devil – ah hah!' She sipped again.

'The men of our house . . .' began Miss Rashleigh. She raised her glass. She held it high, as if she toasted the mermaid carved in plaster on the fireplace. She paused. The guns were barking. Something cracked in the woodwork. Or was it a rat running behind the plaster?

'Always women . . .' Miss Antonia nodded. 'The men of our house. Pink and white Lucy at the Mill – d'you remember?'

'Ellen's daughter at the Goat and Sickle,' Miss Rashleigh added.

'And the girl at the tailor's,' Miss Antonia murmured, 'where Hugh bought his riding-breeches, the little dark shop on the right . . .'

'. . . that used to be flooded every winter. It's *his* boy,' Miss Antonia chuckled, leaning towards her sister, 'that cleans the church.'

There was a crash. A slate had fallen down the chimney. The great log had snapped in two. Flakes of plaster fell from the shield above the fireplace.

'Falling,' old Miss Rashleigh chuckled, 'falling.'

'And who,' said Miss Antonia, looking at the flakes on the carpet, 'who's to pay?'

Crowing like old babies, indifferent, reckless, they laughed; crossed to the fireplace, and sipped their sherry by the wood ashes and the plaster until each glass held only one drop of wine, reddish purple, at the bottom. And this the old women did not wish to part with so it seemed; for they fingered their glasses, as they sat side by side by the ashes; but they never raised them to their lips.

'Milly Masters in the still room,' began old Miss Rashleigh. 'She's our brother's . . .'

A shot barked beneath the window. It cut the string that held the rain. Down it poured, down, down, down, in straight rods whipping the windows. Light faded from the carpet. Light faded in their eyes too, as they sat by the white ashes listening. Their eyes became like pebbles, taken from water; grey stones dulled and dried. And their hands gripped their hands like the claws of dead birds gripping nothing. And they shrivelled as if the bodies inside the clothes had shrunk. Then Miss Antonia raised her glass to the mermaid. It was the last toast, the last drop; she drank it off. 'Coming!' she croaked, and slapped the glass down. A door banged below. Then another. Then another. Feet could be heard trampling, yet shuffling, along the corridor towards the gallery.

'Closer! Closer!' grinned Miss Rashleigh, baring her three yellow teeth.

The immensely high door burst open. In rushed three great hounds and stood panting. Then there entered, slouching, the Squire himself in shabby gaiters. The dogs pressed round him, tossing their heads, snuffling at his pockets. Then they bounded forward. They smelt the meat. The floor of the gallery waved like a wind-lashed forest with the tails and backs of the great questing hounds. They snuffed the table. They pawed the cloth. Then with a wild neighing whimper they flung themselves upon the little yellow spaniel who was gnawing the carcass under the table.

'Curse you, curse you!' howled the Squire. But his voice was weak, as if he shouted against a wind. 'Curse you, curse you!' he shouted, now cursing his sisters.

Miss Antonia and Miss Rashleigh rose to their feet. The great dogs had seized the spaniel. They worried him, they mauled him with their great yellow teeth. The Squire swung a leather knotted tawse this way, that way, cursing the dogs, cursing his sisters, in the voice that sounded so loud yet so weak. With one lash he curled to the ground the vase of chrysanthemums. Another caught old Miss Rashleigh on the cheek. The old woman staggered backwards. She fell against the mantelpiece. Her stick striking wildly, struck the shield above the fireplace. She fell with a thud upon the ashes. The shield of the Rashleighs crashed from the wall. Under the mermaid, under the spears, she lay buried.

The wind lashed the panes of glass; shots volleyed in the Park and a tree fell. And then King Edward in the silver frame slid, toppled and fell too.

The grey mist had thickened in the carriage. It hung down like a veil; it seemed to put the four travellers in the corners at a great distance from each other, though in fact they were as close as a third-class railway carriage could bring them. The effect was strange. The handsome, if elderly, the well-dressed, if rather shabby woman who had got into the train at some station in the midlands seemed to have lost her shape. Her body had become all mist. Only her eyes gleamed, changed, lived all by themselves it seemed; eyes without a body; blue-grey eyes seeing something invisible. In the misty air they shone out, they moved, so that in the sepulchral atmosphere – the windows were blurred, the lamps haloed with fog – they were like lights dancing, will-o'-the-wisps that move, people say, over the graves of unquiet sleepers in churchyards. An absurd idea? Mere fancy! Yet after all since there is nothing that does not leave some residue, and memory is a light that dances in the mind when the reality is buried, why should not the eyes there, gleaming, moving, be the ghost of a family, of an age, of a civilisation dancing over the grave?

The train slowed down. One after another lamps stood up; held their yellow heads erect for a second; then were felled. Up they stood again as the train slid into the station. The lights massed and blazed. And the eyes in the corner? They were shut; the lids were closed. They saw nothing. Perhaps the light was too strong. And of course in the full blaze of the station lamps it was plain – she was quite an ordinary rather elderly woman, travelling to London on some quite ordinary piece of business – something connected with a cat or a horse or a dog. She reached for her suit case, rose, and took the pheasants from the rack. But did she, all the same, as she opened the carriage door and stepped out, murmur, 'Chk. Chk.' as she passed?

Lappin and Lapinova

They were married. The wedding march pealed out. The pigeons fluttered. Small boys in Eton jackets threw rice; a fox terrier sauntered across the path; and Ernest Thorburn led his bride to the car through the small inquisitive crowd of complete strangers which always collects in London to enjoy other people's happiness or unhappiness. Certainly he looked handsome and she looked shy. More rice was thrown, and the car moved off.

That was on Tuesday. Now it was Saturday. Rosalind had still to get used to the fact that she was Mrs Ernest Thorburn. Perhaps she never would get used to the fact that she was Mrs Ernest Anybody, she thought, as she sat in the bow window of the hotel looking over the lake to the mountains, and waited for her husband to come down to breakfast. Ernest was a difficult name to get used to. It was not the name she would have chosen. She would have preferred Timothy, Antony, or Peter. He did not look like Ernest either. The name suggested the Albert Memorial, mahogany sideboards, steel engravings of the Prince Consort with his family – her mother-in-law's dining-room in Porchester Terrace in short.

But here he was. Thank goodness he did not look like Ernest – no. But what did he look like? She glanced at him sideways. Well, when he was eating toast he looked like a rabbit. Not that anyone else would have seen a likeness to a creature so diminutive and timid in this spruce, muscular young man with the straight nose, the blue eyes, and the very firm mouth. But that made it all the more amusing. His nose twitched very slightly when he ate. So did her pet rabbit's. She kept watching his nose twitch; and then she had to explain, when he caught her looking at him, why she laughed.

'It's because you're like a rabbit, Ernest,' she said. 'Like a wild rabbit,' she added, looking at him. 'A hunting rabbit; a King Rabbit; a rabbit that makes laws for all the other rabbits.'

Ernest had no objection to being that kind of rabbit, and since it amused her to see him twitch his nose – he had never known that his nose twitched – he twitched it on purpose. And she laughed and laughed; and he laughed too, so that the maiden ladies and the fishing man and the Swiss waiter in his greasy black jacket all guessed right; they were very happy. But how long does such happiness last? they asked themselves; and each answered according to his own circumstances.

At lunch time, seated on a clump of heather beside the lake, 'Lettuce, rabbit?' said Rosalind, holding out the lettuce that had been provided to eat with the hard-boiled eggs. 'Come and take it out of my hand,' she added, and he stretched out and nibbled the lettuce and twitched his nose.

'Good rabbit, nice rabbit,' she said, patting him, as she used to pat her tame rabbit at home. But that was absurd. He was not a tame rabbit, whatever he was. She turned it into French. 'Lapin,' she called him. But whatever he was, he was not a French rabbit. He was simply and solely English – born at Porchester Terrace, educated at Rugby; now a clerk in His Majesty's Civil Service. So she tried 'Bunny' next; but that was worse. 'Bunny' was someone plump and soft and comic; he was thin and hard and serious. Still, his nose twitched. 'Lappin,' she exclaimed suddenly; and gave a little cry as if she had found the very word she looked for.

'Lappin, Lappin, King Lappin,' she repeated. It seemed to suit him exactly; he was not Ernest, he was King Lappin. Why? She did not know.

When there was nothing new to talk about on their long solitary walks – and it rained, as everyone had warned them that it would rain; or when they were sitting over the fire in the evening, for it was cold, and the maiden ladies had gone and the fishing man, and the waiter only came if you rang the bell for him, she let her fancy play with the story of the Lappin tribe. Under her hands – she was sewing; he was reading – they became very real, very vivid, very amusing. Ernest put down the paper and helped her. There were the black rabbits and the red; there were the enemy rabbits and the friendly. There were the wood in which they lived and the outlying prairies and the swamp. Above all there was King Lappin, who, far from having only the one trick – that he twitched his nose – became as the days passed an animal of the greatest character; Rosalind was always finding new qualities in him. But above all he was a great hunter.

'And what,' said Rosalind, on the last day of the honeymoon, 'did the King do today?'

In fact they had been climbing all day; and she had worn a blister on her heel; but she did not mean that.

'Today,' said Ernest, twitching his nose as he bit the end off his cigar, 'he chased a hare.' He paused; struck a match, and twitched again.

'A woman hare,' he added.

'A white hare!' Rosalind exclaimed, as if she had been expecting this. 'Rather a small hare; silver grey; with a big bright eyes?'

'Yes,' said Ernest, looking at her as she had looked at him, 'a smallish animal; with eyes popping out of her head, and two little front paws dangling.' It was exactly how she sat, with her sewing dangling in her hands; and her eyes, that were so big and bright, were certainly a little prominent.

'Ah, Lapinova,' Rosalind murmured.

'Is that what she's called?' said Ernest – 'the real Rosalind?' He looked at her. He felt very much in love with her.

'Yes; that's what she's called,' said Rosalind. 'Lapinova.' And before they went to bed that night it was all settled. He was King Lappin; she was Queen Lapinova. They were the very opposite of each other; he was bold and determined; she wary and undependable. He ruled over the busy world of rabbits; her world was a desolate, mysterious place, which she ranged mostly by moonlight. All the same, their territories touched; they were King and Queen.

Thus when they came back from their honeymoon they possessed a private world, inhabited, save for the one white hare, entirely by rabbits. No one guessed that there was such a place, and that of course made it all the more amusing. It made them feel, more even than most young married couples, in league together against the rest of the world. Often they looked slyly at each other when people talked about rabbits and woods and traps and shooting. Or they winked furtively across the table when Aunt Mary said that she could never bear to see a hare in a dish – it looked so like a baby: or when John, Ernest's sporting brother, told them what price rabbits were fetching that autumn in Wiltshire, skins and all. Sometimes when they wanted a gamekeeper, or a poacher or a Lord of the Manor, they amused themselves by distributing the parts among their friends. Ernest's mother, Mrs Reginald Thorburn, for example, fitted the part of the Squire to perfection. But it was all secret – that was the point of it; nobody save themselves knew that such a world existed.

Without that world, how, Rosalind wondered, that winter could she have lived at all? For instance, there was the golden-wedding party, when all the Thorburns assembled at Porchester Terrace to celebrate the fiftieth anniversary of that union which had been so blessed – had it not produced Ernest Thorburn? and so fruitful – had it not produced nine other sons and daughters into the bargain, many themselves married and also fruitful? She dreaded that party. But it was inevitable. As she walked upstairs she felt bitterly that she was an only child and an orphan at that; a mere drop among all those Thorburns assembled in the great drawing-room with the shiny satin wallpaper and the lustrous family portraits. The living Thorburns much resembled the painted; save that instead of painted lips they had real lips; out of which came jokes; jokes about schoolrooms, and how they had pulled the chair from under the governess; jokes about frogs and how they had put them between the virgin sheets of maiden ladies. As for herself, she had never even made an apple-pie bed. Holding her present in her hand she advanced toward her mother-in-law sumptuous in yellow satin; and toward her father-in-law decorated with a rich yellow carnation. All round them on tables and chairs there were golden tributes; some nestling in cotton wool; others branching resplendent – candlesticks; cigar boxes; chains; each stamped with the goldsmith's proof that it was solid gold, hall-marked, authentic. But her present was only a little pinchbeck box pierced with holes; an old sand caster, an eighteenth-century relic, once used to sprinkle sand over wet ink. Rather a senseless present she felt – in an age of blotting paper; and as she proffered it, she saw in front of her the stubby black handwriting in which her mother-in-law when they were engaged had expressed the hope that 'My son will make you happy'. No, she was not happy. Not at all happy. She looked at Ernest, straight as a ramrod with a nose like all the noses in the family portraits; a nose that never twitched at all.

Then they went down to dinner. She was half hidden by the great chrysanthemums that curled their red and gold petals into large tight balls. Everything was gold. A gold-edged card with gold initials intertwined recited the list of all the dishes that would be set one after another before them. She dipped her spoon in a plate of clear golden fluid. The raw white fog outside had been turned by the lamps into a golden mesh that blurred the edges of the plates and gave the pine-apples a rough golden skin. Only she herself in her white wedding dress peering ahead of her with her prominent eyes seemed insoluble as an icicle.

As the dinner wore on, however, the room grew steamy with heat. Beads of perspiration stood out on the men's foreheads. She felt that her icicle was being turned to water. She was being melted; dispersed; dissolved into nothingness; and would soon faint. Then through the surge in her head and the din in her ears she heard a woman's voice exclaim, 'But they breed so!'

The Thorburns – yes; they breed so, she echoed; looking at all the round red faces that seemed doubled in the giddiness that overcame her; and magnified in the gold mist that enhaloed them. 'They breed so.' Then John bawled:

'Little devils! . . . Shoot 'em! Jump on 'em with big boots! That's the only way to deal with 'em . . . rabbits!'

At that word, that magic word, she revived. Peeping between the chrysanthemums she saw Ernest's nose twitch. It rippled, it ran with successive twitches. And at that a mysterious catastrophe befell the Thorburns. The golden table became a moor with the gorse in full bloom; the din of voices turned to one peal of lark's laughter ringing down from the sky. It was a blue sky – clouds passed slowly. And they had all been changed – the Thorburns. She looked at her father-in-law, a furtive little man with dyed moustaches. His foible was collecting things – seals, enamel boxes, trifles from eighteenth-century dressing tables which he hid in the drawers of his study from his wife. Now she saw him as he was – a poacher, stealing off with his coat bulging with pheasants and partridges to drop them stealthily into a three-legged pot in his smoky little cottage. That was her real father-in-law – a poacher. And Celia, the unmarried daughter, who always nosed out other people's secrets, the little things they wished to hide – she was a white ferret with pink eyes, and a nose clotted with earth from her horrid underground nosings and pokings. Slung round men's shoulders, in a net, and thrust down a hole – it was a pitiable life – Celia's; it was none of her fault. So she saw Celia. And then she looked at her mother-in-law – whom they dubbed The Squire. Flushed, coarse, a bully – she was all that, as she stood returning thanks, but now that Rosalind – that is Lapinova – saw her, she saw behind her the decayed family mansion, the plaster peeling off the walls, and heard her, with a sob in her voice, giving thanks to her children (who hated her) for a world that had ceased to exist. There was a sudden silence. They all stood with their glasses raised; they all drank; then it was over.

'Oh, King Lappin!' she cried as they went home together in the fog, 'if your nose hadn't twitched just at the moment, I should have been trapped!'

'But you're safe,' said King Lappin, pressing her paw.

'Quite safe,' she answered.

And they drove back through the Park, King and Queen of the marsh, of the mist, and of the gorse-scented moor.

Thus time passed; one year; two years of time. And on a winter's night, which happened by a coincidence to be the anniversary of the golden-wedding party – but Mrs Reginald Thorburn was dead; the house was to let; and there was only a caretaker in residence – Ernest came home from the office. They had a nice little home; half a house above a saddler's shop in South Kensington, not far from the tube station. It was cold, with fog in the air, and Rosalind was sitting over the fire, sewing.

'What d'you think happened to me today?' she began as soon as he had settled himself down with his legs stretched to the blaze. 'I was crossing the stream when –'

'What stream?' Ernest interrupted her.

'The stream at the bottom, where our wood meets the black wood,' she explained.

Ernest looked completely blank for a moment.

'What the deuce are you talking about?' he asked.

'My dear Ernest!' she cried in dismay. 'King Lappin,' she added, dangling her little front paws in the firelight. But his nose did not twitch. Her hands – they turned to hands – clutched the stuff she was holding; her eyes popped half out of her head. It took him five minutes at least to change from Ernest Thorburn to King Lappin; and while she waited she felt a load on the back of her neck, as if somebody were about to wring it. At last he changed to King Lappin; his nose twitched; and they spent the evening roaming the woods much as usual.

But she slept badly. In the middle of the night she woke, feeling as if something strange had happened to her. She was stiff and cold. At last she turned on the light and looked at Ernest lying beside her. He was sound asleep. He snored. But even though he snored, his nose remained perfectly still. It looked as if it had never twitched at all. Was it possible that he was really Ernest; and that she was really married to Ernest? A vision of her mother-in-law's dining-room came before her; and there they sat, she and Ernest, grown old, under the engravings, in front of the sideboard. . . . It was their golden-wedding day. She could not bear it.

'Lappin, King Lappin!' she whispered, and for a moment his nose seemed to twitch of its own accord. But he still slept. 'Wake up, Lappin, wake up!' she cried.

Ernest woke; and seeing her sitting bolt upright beside him he asked: 'What's the matter?'

'I thought my rabbit was dead!' she whimpered. Ernest was angry.

'Don't talk such rubbish, Rosalind,' he said. 'Lie down and go to sleep.'

He turned over. In another moment he was sound asleep and snoring.

But she could not sleep. She lay curled up on her side of the bed, like a hare in its form. She had turned out the light, but the street lamp lit the ceiling faintly, and the trees outside made a lacy network over it as if there were a shadowy grove on the ceiling in which she wandered, turning, twisting, in and out, round and round, hunting, being hunted, hearing the bay of hounds and horns; flying, escaping . . . until the maid drew the blinds and brought their early tea.

Next day she could settle to nothing. She seemed to have lost something. She felt as if her body had shrunk; it had grown small, and black and hard. Her joints seemed stiff too, and when she looked in the glass, which she did several times as she wandered about the flat, her eyes seemed to burst out of her head, like currants in a bun. The rooms also seemed to have shrunk. Large pieces of furniture jutted out at odd angles and she found herself knocking against them. At last she put on her hat and went out. She walked along the Cromwell Road; and every room she passed and peered into seemed to be a dining-room where people sat eating under steel engravings, with thick yellow lace curtains, and mahogany sideboards. At last she reached the Natural History Museum; she used to like it when she was a child. But the first thing she saw when she went in was a stuffed hare standing on sham snow with pink glass eyes. Somehow it made her shiver all over. Perhaps it would be better when dusk fell. She went home and sat over the fire, without a light, and tried to imagine that she was out alone on a moor; and there was a stream rushing; and beyond the stream a dark wood. But she could get no further than the stream. At last she squatted down on the bank on the wet grass, and sat crouched in her chair, with her hands dangling empty, and her eyes glazed, like glass eyes, in the firelight. Then there was the crack of a gun. . . . She started as if she had been shot. It was only Ernest, turning his key in the door. She waited, trembling. He came in and switched on the light. There he stood tall, handsome, rubbing his hands that were red with cold.

'Sitting in the dark?' he said.

'Oh, Ernest, Ernest!' she cried, starting up in her chair.

'Well, what's up now?' he asked briskly, warming his hands at the fire.

'It's Lapinova . . . ' she faltered, glancing wildly at him out of her great startled eyes. 'She's gone, Ernest. I've lost her!'

Ernest frowned. He pressed his lips tight together. 'Oh, that's what's up, is it?' he said, smiling rather grimly at his wife. For ten seconds he stood there, silent; and she waited, feeling hands tightening at the back of her neck.

'Yes,' he said at length. 'Poor Lapinova . . .' He straightened his tie at the looking-glass over the mantelpiece.

'Caught in a trap,' he said, 'killed', and sat down and read the newspaper.

So that was the end of that marriage.

The Searchlight

The mansion of the eighteenth century Earl had been changed in the twentieth century into a Club. And it was pleasant, after dining in the great room with the pillars and the chandeliers under a glare of light to go out on to the balcony overlooking the Park. The trees were in full leaf, and had there been a moon, one could have seen the pink and cream coloured cockades on the chestnut trees. But it was a moonless night; very warm, after a fine summer's day.

Mr and Mrs Ivimey's party were drinking coffee and smoking on the balcony. As if to relieve them from the need of talking, to entertain them without any effort on their part, rods of light wheeled across the sky. It was peace then; the air force was practising; searching for enemy aircraft in the sky. After pausing to prod some suspected spot, the light wheeled, like the wings of a windmill, or again like the antennae of some prodigious insect and revealed here a cadaverous stone front; here a chestnut tree with all its blossoms riding; and then suddenly the light struck straight at the balcony, and for a second a bright disc shone – perhaps it was a mirror in a lady's hand-bag.

'Look!' Mrs Ivimey exclaimed.

The light passed. They were in darkness again.

'You'll never guess what *that* made me see!' she added. Naturally, they guessed.

'No, no, no,' she protested. Nobody could guess; only she knew; only she could know, because she was the great-grand-daughter of the man himself. He had told her the story. What story? If they liked, she would try to tell it. There was still time before the play.

'But where do I begin?' she pondered.[1] 'In the year 1820? . . . It must have been about then that my great-grandfather was a boy. 'I'm not young myself' – no, but she was very well set up and handsome – 'and he was a very old man when I was a child – when he told me the story. A very handsome old man,' she explained, 'with a shock of white hair, and blue eyes. He must have been a beautiful boy. But queer . . . That was only natural – seeing how they lived. The name was Comber. They'd come down in the world. They'd been gentlefolk; they'd owned land up in Yorkshire. But when he was a boy only the tower was left. The house was nothing but a little farmhouse, standing in the middle of the fields. We saw it ten years ago and went over it. We had to leave the car and walk across the fields. There isn't any road to the house. It stands all alone, the grass grows right up to the gate . . . there were chickens pecking about, running in and out of the rooms. All gone to rack and ruin. I remember a stone fell from the tower suddenly.' She paused. 'There they lived,' she went on, 'the old man, the woman and the boy. She wasn't his wife, or the boy's mother. She was just a farm hand, a girl the old man had taken to live with him when his wife died. Another reason perhaps why nobody visited them – why the whole place was gone to rack and ruin. But I remember a coat of arms over the door; and books, old books, gone mouldy. He taught himself all he knew from books. He read and read, he told me, old books, books with maps hanging out from the pages. He dragged them up to the top of the tower – the rope's still there and the broken steps. There's a chair still in the window with the bottom fallen out; and the window swinging open, and the panes broken, and a view for miles and miles across the moors.'

She paused as if she were up in the tower looking from the window that swung open.

'But we couldn't,' she said, 'find the telescope.' In the dining-room behind them the clatter of plates grew louder. But Mrs Ivimey, on the balcony, seemed puzzled, because she could not find the telescope.

'Why a telescope?' someone asked her.

'Why? Because if there hadn't been a telescope,' she laughed, 'I shouldn't be sitting here now!'

And certainly she was sitting there now, a well set-up, middle-aged woman, with something blue over her shoulders.

'It must have been there,' she resumed, 'because, he told me, every night when the old people had gone to bed he sat at the window looking through the telescope at the stars. Jupiter, Aldebaran, Cassiopeia.' She waved her hand at the stars that were beginning to show over the trees. It was growing darker. And the searchlight seemed brighter, sweeping across the sky, pausing here and there to stare at the stars.

'There they were,' she went on, 'the stars. And he asked himself, my grandfather – the boy, "What are they? why are they? And who am I?" as one does, sitting alone, with no one to talk to, looking at the stars.'

She was silent. They all looked at the stars that were coming out in the darkness over the trees. The stars seemed very permanent, very unchanging. The roar of London sank away. A hundred years seemed nothing. They felt that the boy was looking at the stars with them. They seemed to be with him, in the tower, looking out over the moors at the stars.

Then a voice behind them said:

'Right you are. Friday.'

They all turned, shifted, felt dropped down on to the balcony again.

'Ah, but there was nobody to say that to him,' she murmured. The couple rose and walked away.

'*He* was alone,' she resumed. 'It was a fine summer's day. A June day. One of those perfect summer days when everything seems to stand still in the heat. There were the chickens pecking in the farm-yard; the old horse stamping in the stable; the old man dozing over his glass. The woman scouring pails in the scullery. Perhaps a stone fell from the tower. It seemed as if the day would never end. And he had no one to talk to – nothing whatever to do. The whole world stretched before him. The moor rising and falling; the sky meeting the moor; green and blue, green and blue, for ever and ever.'

In the half light, they could see that Mrs Ivimey was leaning over the balcony, with her chin propped on her hands, as if she were looking out over the moors from the top of a tower.

'Nothing but moor and sky, moor and sky, for ever and ever,' she murmured.

Then she made a movement, as if she swung something into position.

'But what did the earth look like through the telescope?' she asked.

She made another quick little movement with her fingers as if she were twirling something.

'He focussed it,' she said. 'He focussed it upon the earth. He focussed it upon a dark mass of wood upon the horizon. He focussed it so that he could see . . . each tree . . . each tree separate . . . and the birds . . . rising and falling . . . and a stem of smoke . . . there . . . in the midst of the trees. . . . And then . . . lower . . . lower . . . (she lowered her eyes) . . . there was a house . . . a house among the trees . . . a farm house . . . every brick showed . . . and the tubs on either side of the door . . . with flowers in them blue, pink, hydrangeas perhaps . . .' She paused . . . 'And then a girl came out of the house . . . wearing something blue upon her head . . . and stood there . . . feeding birds . . . pigeons . . . they came fluttering round her. . . . And then . . . look. . . . A man. . . . A

man! He came round the corner. He seized her in his arms! They kissed
. . . they kissed!'

Mrs Ivimey opened her arms and closed them as if she were kissing
someone.

'It was the first time he had seen a man kiss a woman – in his
telescope – miles and miles away across the moors!'

She thrust something from her – the telescope presumably. She sat
upright.

'So he ran down the stairs. He ran through the fields. He ran down
lanes, out upon the high road, through woods. He ran for miles and
miles, and just when the stars were showing above the trees he reached
the house . . . covered with dust, streaming with sweat. . . .'

She stopped, as if she saw him.

'And then, and then . . . what did he do then? What did he say? And
the girl . . .' they pressed her.

A shaft of light fell upon Mrs Ivimey as if someone had focussed the
lens of a telescope upon her. (It was the air force, looking for enemy air
craft.) She had risen. She had something blue on her head. She had
raised her hand, as if she stood in a doorway, amazed.

'Oh the girl . . . She was my –' she hesitated, as if she were about to
say 'myself'. But she remembered; and corrected herself. 'She was my
great-grandmother,' she said.

She turned to look for her cloak. It was on a chair behind her.

'But tell us – what about the other man, the man who came round the
corner?' they asked.

'That man? That man,' Mrs Ivimey murmured, stooping to fumble
with her cloak, (the searchlight had left the balcony), 'he, I suppose,
vanished.'

'The light,' she added, gathering her things about her, 'only falls here
and there.'

The searchlight had passed on. It was now focussed on the plain
expanse of Buckingham Palace. And it was time they went on to the
play.

Gipsy, the Mongrel

'She had such a lovely smile,' said Mary Bridger, reflectively. They were talking, the Bridgers and the Bagots, late one night over the fire about old friends. This one, Helen Folliott, the girl with the lovely smile, had vanished. None of them knew what had happened to her. She had come to grief somehow, they had heard, and, they agreed, each of them had always known that she would, and, what was odd, none of them had ever forgotten her.

'She had such a lovely smile,' Lucy Bagot repeated.

And so they began to discuss the oddities of human affairs – what a toss up it seems whether you sink or swim, why one remembers and forgets, what a difference trifles make, and how people, who used to meet every day, suddenly part and never see each other again.

Then they were silent. That was why they heard a whistle – was it a train or a siren? – a faint far whistle that sounded over the flat Suffolk fields and dwindled away. The sound must have suggested something, to the Bagots anyhow, for Lucy said, looking at her husband, '*She* had such a lovely smile.' He nodded. 'You couldn't drown a puppy who grinned in the face of death,' he said. It sounded like a quotation. The Bridgers looked puzzled. 'Our dog,' said Lucy. 'Tell us the story of your dog,' the Bridgers insisted. They both liked dogs.

Tom Bagot was shy at first, as people are who catch themselves feeling more than is reasonable. He protested too that it wasn't a story; it was a character study, and they would think him sentimental. But they urged him, and he began straight off – ' "You can't drown a puppy who grins in the face of death." Old Holland said that. He said it that snowy night when he held her over the water butt. He was a farmer, down in Wiltshire. He'd heard gipsies – that's to say a whistle. Out he went into the snow with a dog whip. They'd gone; only they'd left something behind them, a crumpled piece of paper it looked like in the hedge. But it was a basket, one of those rush baskets that women take to market, and in it, stitched up so that she couldn't follow, was a little scrap of a dog. They'd given her a hunk of bread and a twist of straw –'

'Which shows,' Lucy interrupted, 'that they hadn't the heart to kill her.'

'Nor had he,' Tom Bagot went on. 'He held her over the water and then –' he raised his little grizzled moustache over his upper teeth, 'she grinned up at him like that, in the moonlight. So he spared her. She was a wretched little mongrel, a regular gipsies' dog, half fox terrier, half the lord knows what. She looked as if she'd never had a square meal in her life. Her coat was as rough as a door scraper. But she had – what d'you call it when you forgive a person a dozen times a day against your better judgment? Charm? Character? Whatever it was, she had that. Or why did he keep her? Answer me that. She made his life a burden to him. Put all the neighbours against him. Chased their hens. Worried the sheep. A dozen times he was on the point of killing her. Yet he couldn't bring himself to do it – not until she'd killed the cat, his wife's favourite. It was the wife who insisted. So once more he took her out into the yard, stood her against the wall, and was about to pull the trigger. And again – she grinned; grinned right into the face of death, and he hadn't the heart to do it. So they left it to the butcher; he must do what they couldn't. And then – chance again. It was a little miracle in its way – our letter coming that very morning. A pure fluke, look at it which ever way you will. We lived in London then – we'd a cook, an old Irish body, who swore she'd heard rats. Rats in the wainscot. Couldn't sleep another night in the place and so on. By chance again – we'd spent a summer there – I thought of Holland, wrote and asked him if he'd a dog to sell us, a terrier, to catch rats. The postman met the butcher; it was the butcher who delivered the letter. So by the skin of her teeth Gipsy was saved again. He was glad I can tell you, – old Holland. He popped her straight into the train with a letter. "Her looks are against her",' Bagot quoted again. '"But believe me, she's a dog of character – a dog of remarkable character." We stood her out on the kitchen table. A more miserable object you never saw. "Rats? Why they'd eat her," said old Biddy. But we heard no more of that tale.'

Here Tom Bagot paused. He had come it seemed to a part of his story that he found it difficult to tell. It is difficult for a man to say why he fell in love with a woman, but it is still more difficult to say why he fell in love with a mongrel terrier. Yet that was what had happened evidently – the little beast had exerted over him some indescribable charm. It was a love story he was telling. Mary Bridger was sure of that by something in his voice. A fantastic idea came to her that he had been in love with

Helen Folliott, the girl with the lovely smile. He connected the two somehow. Aren't all stories connected? she asked herself, and thus dropped a sentence or two of what he was saying. The Bagots, when she listened, were remembering absurd little stories that they hardly liked to tell, and yet they meant so much.

'She did it all off her own bat,' Tom Bagot was saying. 'We never taught her a thing. Yet every day she'd have something new to show us. One little trick after another. She'd bring me letters in her mouth. Or, Lucy lighting a match, she'd put it out' – he brought his fist down upon a match – 'so. With her naked paw. Or she'd bark when the telephone rang. "Curse that bell" she'd say as plain as anything. And visitors – d'you remember how she'd size our friends up as if they were her own? "You may stay" – she'd jump and lick your hand; "No, we don't want you" and she'd rush to the door as if to show them the way out. And she'd never make a mistake. She was as good a judge of people as you are.'

'Yes,' Lucy confirmed him, 'she was a dog of character. And yet,' she added, 'lots of people didn't see it. Which was another reason for liking her. There was that man who gave us Hector.'

Bagot took up the story.

'Hopkins by name,' he said. 'By calling a stockbroker. Very proud of his little place in Surrey. You know the sort – all boots and gaiters, like the pictures in the sporting papers. It's my belief he didn't know one end of a horse from the other. But he "couldn't endure to see us with a wretched little mongrel like that".' Bagot was quoting again. The words had evidently had a sting in them. 'So he made so bold as to give us a present. A dog called Hector.'

'A red setter,' Lucy explained.

'With a tail like a ramrod,' Bagot continued, 'and a pedigree as long as your arm. She might have sulked – Gipsy. She might have taken it amiss. But she was a dog of sense. Nothing petty about her. Live and let live – it takes all sorts to make a world. That was her motto. You'd meet 'em in the High Street – arm in arm, I was going to say, trotting round together. She taught him a thing or two I'll be bound . . .'

'Give him his due, he was a perfect gentleman,' Lucy interrupted.

'A little lacking in the upper storey,' said Tom Bagot tapping his forehead.

'But with perfect manners,' Lucy argued.

There is nothing like a dog story for bringing out people's characters,

Mary Bridger reflected. Of course, Lucy had been on the side of the gentleman; Tom on the side of the lady. But the lady's charms had vanquished even the Lucy Bagot who was inclined to be hard on her sex. So she must have had something in her.

'And then?' she prompted them.

'All went smoothly. We were a happy family,' Tom continued. 'Nothing to break the harmony until –' here he hesitated. 'Come to think of it,' he blurted out, 'you can't blame nature. She was in the prime of life – two years old. What's that for a human being? Eighteen? Twenty? And full of life – full of fun – as a girl should be.' He stopped.

'You're thinking of the dinner party,' his wife helped him. 'The night the Harvey Sinnotts dined with us. The fourteenth of February – which,' she added with a queer little smile, 'is St Valentine's day.'

'Coupling day they call it in my part of the country,' Dick Bridger interposed.

'So it was,' Tom Bagot resumed. 'St Valentine's day – the God of love isn't he? Well, people of the name of Harvey Sinnott were dining with us. Never met 'em before. Connected with the firm,' (Tom Bagot was the London partner in the great Liverpool engineering firm of Harvey, Marsh and Coppard). 'It was a formal occasion. For simple people like ourselves a bit of an ordeal. We wished to show them hospitality. We did our best. *She*,' he indicated his wife, 'took no end of trouble, fussed about for days beforehand. Everything must be just so. You know Lucy . . .' He gave her a little pat on the knee. Mary Bridger knew Lucy. She could see the table spread; the silver shining, everything as Tom said "just so" for the honoured guests.

'It was a slap up affair and no mistake about it,' Tom Bagot went on. 'A trifle on the formal side . . .'

'She was one of those women,' Lucy struck in, 'who seemed to be asking themselves "What's it cost? Is it real?" while they talk to you. And rather over dressed. She was saying – dinner half through – what a pleasure it was – they were staying as they always did at the Ritz, or at the Carlton – to have a quiet little meal. So simple, so homely. It was such a rest. . . .'

'No sooner were the words out of her mouth,' Bagot broke in, 'than there was an explosion . . . A sort of under table earthquake. A scuffle. A squeak. And she rose to her feet in all her . . .' he spread his arms wide to show the voluminous lady, 'panoply,' he hazarded, 'and screamed, "Something's biting me! Something's biting me!"' he squeaked in imitation. 'I ducked under the table.' (He looked under the flounce of a chair.) 'Oh that abandoned little creature! That imp of mischief! There on the floor at the good lady's feet . . . she'd given birth . . . she'd had a puppy!'

The memory was too much for him. He lay back in his chair shaking with laughter.

'So,' he continued, I wrapped a napkin round 'em. I carried 'em both out. (Mercifully the puppy was dead, stone dead.) I faced her with the fact. I held it under her nose. Out in the back yard. Out in the moonlight, under the pure gaze of the stars. I could have beaten her within an inch of her life. But how can you beat a dog that grins . . .'

'In the face of morality?' Dick Bridger suggested.

'If you like to put it that way,' Bagot smiled. 'But her spirit! By Jove! She scampered round the yard, the little hussy, chasing a cat . . . No, I hadn't the heart to do it.'

'And the Harvey Sinnotts were very nice about it,' Lucy added. 'It broke the ice. We were all good friends after that.'

'We forgave her,' Tom Bagot continued. 'We said it mustn't happen again. And it didn't. Never again. But other things did. Lots of things. I could tell you one story after another. But the truth is,' he shook his head, 'I don't believe in stories. A dog has a character just as we have, and it shows itself just as ours do, by what we say, by all sorts of little things.'

'You'd find yourself asking, when you came into a room – it sounds absurd but it's true,' Lucy added, 'now why did she do that? just as if she were a human being. And being a dog one had to guess. Sometimes one couldn't. The leg of mutton for instance. She took it off the dinner table, held it in her forepaws, laughing. By way of a joke? A joke at our expense? It seemed so. And one day we tried to play a trick on her. She had a passion for fruit – raw fruit, apples, plums. We gave her a plum with a stone in it. What'll she do with it? we asked. Rather than hurt our feelings, if you'll believe me, she held that plum in her mouth, and then, when she thought we weren't looking, dropped the stone in her bowl of water and came back wagging her tail. It was as if she'd said, "Had you there!"'

'Yes,' said Tom Bagot, 'she taught us a lesson. I've often wondered,' he went on, 'what was she thinking of us – down there among all the boots and old matches on the hearthrug? What was her world? Do dogs see what we see or is it something different?'

They too looked down at the boots and old matches, tried for a moment to lie nose on paws gazing into the red caverns and yellow flames with a dog's eyes. But they couldn't answer that question.

'You'd see them lying there,' Bagot continued, 'Gipsy on her side of the fire, Hector on his, as different as chalk from cheese. It was a matter of birth and breeding. He was an aristocrat. She a dog of the people. It was natural with her mother a poacher, her father the lord knows who, and her master a gipsy. You'd take them out together. Hector prim as a policeman, all on the side of law and order. Gipsy jumping the railings, scaring the royal ducks, but always on the side of the sea gulls. Vagabonds like herself. We'd take her along the river, where people feed the gulls. "Take your bit of fish," she'd say. "You've earned it." I've seen her, if you'll believe me, let one of them feed out of her mouth. But she had no patience with the pampered rich – the pug dogs, the lap dogs. You could fancy they argued the matter, down there on the hearthrug. And by Jove! she converted the old Tory. We ought to have known better. Yes, I've often blamed myself. But there it is – after a thing's over, it's easy to see how it could have been prevented.'

A shadow crossed his face, as if he remembered some little tragedy that, as he said, could have been prevented, and yet to the listener would mean nothing more than the fall of a leaf, or the death of a butterfly by drowning. The Bridgers set their faces to hear whatever it was. Perhaps a car had run over her, or perhaps she had been stolen.

'It was that old fool Hector,' Bagot continued. 'I never like handsome dogs,' he explained. 'There's no harm in them, but there's no character. He may have been jealous. He hadn't her sense of what's fitting. Just because she did a thing, he'd tried to go one better. To cut the matter short – one fine day he jumped over the garden wall, crashed through a neighbour's glass house, ran between an old chap's legs, collided with a car, never hurt himself but made a dint in the bonnet – that day's work cost us five pound ten and a visit to the police court. It was all her doing. Without her he'd have been as tame as an old sheep. Well, one of them had to go. Strictly speaking it should have been Gipsy. But look at it this way. Say you've two maids; you can't keep them both; one's sure of a place, but the other – she's not everybody's money, might find herself out of a job, in the soup. You wouldn't hesitate – you'd do as we did. We gave Hector to friends; we kept Gipsy. It was unjust perhaps. Anyhow, that was the beginning of the trouble.'

'Yes, things went wrong after that,' said Lucy Bagot. 'She felt she'd done a good dog out of a home. She showed it in all sorts of ways, those queer little ways that are all a dog has after all.' There was a pause. The tragedy whatever it was came closer, the absurd little tragedy which both these middle-aged people found it so hard to tell and so hard to forget.

'We never knew till then,' Bagot continued, 'how much feeling she had in her. With human beings, as Lucy says, they can speak. They can say "I'm sorry" and there's an end of it. But with a dog it's different. Dogs can't talk. But dogs,' he added, 'remember.'

'She remembered,' Lucy confirmed him. 'She showed it. One night for instance she brought an old rag doll into the drawing-room. I was sitting there alone. She took it and laid it on the floor, as if it was a present – to make up for Hector.'

'Another time,' Bagot went on, 'she brought home a white cat. A wretched beast, covered with sores, hadn't even a tail. And he wouldn't leave us. We didn't want him. She didn't either. But it meant something. To make up for Hector? Her only way? Perhaps . . .'

'Or there may have been another reason,' Lucy went on. 'That's what I never could decide. Did she want to give us a hint? To prepare us? If only she could have spoken! Then we could have reasoned with her, tried to persuade her. As it was we knew vaguely all that winter that something was wrong. She'd fall asleep and start yelping, as if she were dreaming. Then she'd wake up, run round the room with her ears cocked as if she'd heard something. Often I'd go to the door and look out. But there wasn't anyone. Sometimes she'd begin trembling all over, half afraid, half eager. If she'd been a woman, you'd have said that some temptation was gradually overcoming her. There was something she tried to resist, but couldn't, something in her blood so to speak that was too strong for her. That was the feeling we had . . . And she wouldn't go out with us any longer. She would sit there on the hearthrug listening. But it's better to tell you the facts and let you judge for yourselves.'

Lucy stopped. But Tom nodded at her. 'You tell the end,' he said, for the plain reason that he couldn't trust himself, absurd though it seemed, to tell the end himself.

Lucy Bagot began; she spoke stiffly as if she were reading from a newspaper.

'It was a winter's evening, the sixteenth of December 1937.

Augustus, the white cat, sat on one side of the fire, Gipsy on the other. Snow was falling. All the street sounds were dulled I suppose by the snow. And Tom said: "You could hear a pin drop. It's as quiet as the country." And that of course made us listen. A bus passed in a distant street. A door slammed. One could hear footsteps retreating. Everything seemed to be vanishing away, lost in the falling snow. And then – we only heard it because we were listening – a whistle sounded – a long low whistle – dwindling away. Gipsy heard it. She looked up. She trembled all over. Then she grinned . . .' She stopped. She controlled her voice and said, 'Next morning she was gone.'

There was dead silence. They had a sense of vast empty space round them, of friends vanishing for ever, summoned by some mysterious voice away into the snow.

'You never found her?' Mary Bridger asked at length.

Tom Bagot shook his head.

'We did what we could. Offered a reward. Consulted the police. There was a rumour – someone had seen gipsies passing.'

'What do you think she heard? What was she grinning at?' Lucy Bagot asked. 'Oh I still pray,' she exclaimed, 'that it wasn't the end!'

The Legacy

'For Sissy Miller.' Gilbert Clandon, taking up the pearl brooch that lay among a litter of rings and brooches on a little table in his wife's drawing-room, read the inscription: 'For Sissy Miller, with my love.'

It was like Angela to have remembered even Sissy Miller, her secretary. Yet how strange it was, Gilbert Clandon thought once more, that she had left everything in such order – a little gift of some sort for every one of her friends. It was as if she had foreseen her death. Yet she had been in perfect health when she left the house that morning, six weeks ago; when she stepped off the kerb in Piccadilly and the car had killed her.

He was waiting for Sissy Miller. He had asked her to come; he owed her, he felt, after all the years she had been with them, this token of consideration. Yes, he went on, as he sat there waiting, it was strange that Angela had left everything in such order. Every friend had been left some little token of her affection. Every ring, every necklace, every little Chinese box – she had a passion for little boxes – had a name on it. And each had some memory for him. This he had given her; this – the enamel dolphin with the ruby eyes – she had pounced upon one day in a back street in Venice. He could remember her little cry of delight. To him, of course, she had left nothing in particular, unless it were her diary. Fifteen little volumes, bound in green leather, stood behind him on her writing table. Ever since they were married, she had kept a diary. Some of their very few – he could not call them quarrels, say tiffs – had been about that diary. When he came in and found her writing, she always shut it or put her hand over it. 'No, no, no,' he could hear her say, 'After I'm dead – perhaps.' So she had left it him, as her legacy. It was the only thing they had not shared when she was alive. But he had always taken it for granted that she would outlive him. If only she had stopped one moment, and had thought what she was doing, she would be alive now. But she had stepped straight off the kerb, the driver of the car had said at the inquest. She had given him no chance to pull up. . . . Here the sound of voices in the hall interrupted him.

'Miss Miller, Sir,' said the maid.

She came in. He had never seen her alone in his life, nor, of course, in tears. She was terribly distressed, and no wonder. Angela had been much more to her than an employer. She had been a friend. To himself, he thought, as he pushed a chair for her and asked her to sit down, she was scarcely distinguishable from any other woman of her kind. There were thousands of Sissy Millers – drab little women in black carrying attaché cases. But Angela, with her genius for sympathy, had discovered all sorts of qualities in Sissy Miller. She was the soul of discretion, so silent; so trustworthy, one could tell her anything, and so on.

Miss Miller could not speak at first. She sat there dabbing her eyes with her pocket handkerchief. Then she made an effort.

'Pardon me, Mr Clandon,' she said.

He murmured. Of course he understood. It was only natural. He could guess what his wife had meant to her.

'I've been so happy here,' she said, looking round. Her eyes rested on the writing table behind him. It was here they had worked – she and Angela. For Angela had her share of the duties that fall to the lot of the wife of a prominent politician. She had been the greatest help to him in his career. He had often seen her and Sissy sitting at that table – Sissy at the typewriter, taking down letters from her dictation. No doubt Miss Miller was thinking of that, too. Now all he had to do was to give her the brooch his wife had left her. A rather incongruous gift it seemed. It might have been better to have left her a sum of money, or even the typewriter. But there it was – 'For Sissy Miller, with my love.' And, taking the brooch, he gave it her with the little speech that he had prepared. He knew, he said, that she would value it. His wife had often worn it. . . . And she replied, as she took it, almost as if she too had prepared a speech, that it would always be a treasured possession. . . . She had, he supposed, other clothes upon which a pearl brooch would not look quite so incongruous. She was wearing the little black coat and skirt that seemed the uniform of her profession. Then he remembered – she was in mourning, of course. She too had had her tragedy – a brother, to whom she was devoted, had died only a week or two before Angela. In some accident was it? He could remember only Angela telling him; Angela, with her genius for sympathy, had been terribly upset. Meanwhile Sissy Miller had risen. She was putting on her gloves. Evidently she felt that she ought not to intrude. But he could not let her go without saying something about her future. What were her plans? Was there any way in which he could help her?

She was gazing at the table, where she had sat at her typewriter, where the diary lay. And, lost in her memories of Angela, she did not at once answer his suggestion that he should help her. She seemed for a moment not to understand. So he repeated:

'What are your plans, Miss Miller?'

'My plans? Oh, that's all right, Mr Clandon,' she exclaimed. 'Please don't bother yourself about me.'

He took her to mean that she was in no need of financial assistance. It would be better, he realised, to make any suggestion of that kind in a letter. All he could do now was to say as he pressed her hand. 'Remember, Miss Miller, if there's any way in which I can help you, it will be a pleasure. . . .' Then he opened the door. For a moment, on the threshold, as if a sudden thought had struck her, she stopped.

'Mr Clandon,' she said, looking straight at him for the first time, and for the first time he was struck by the expression, sympathetic yet searching, in her eyes. 'If at any time,' [she] was saying, 'there's anything I can do to help you, remember, I shall feel it, for your wife's sake, a pleasure. . . .'

With that she was gone. Her words and the look that went with them were unexpected. It was almost as if she believed, or hoped, that he would have need of her. A curious, perhaps a fantastic idea occurred to him as he returned to his chair. Could it be, that during all those years when he had scarcely noticed her, she, as the novelists say, had entertained a passion for him? He caught his own reflection in the glass as he passed. He was over fifty; but he could not help admitting that he was still, as the looking-glass showed him, a very distinguished-looking man.

'Poor Sissy Miller!' he said, half laughing. How he would have liked to share that joke with his wife! He turned instinctively to her diary. 'Gilbert,' he read, opening it at random, 'looked so wonderful. . . .' It was as if she had answered his question. Of course[,] she seemed to say, you're very attractive to women. Of course Sissy Miller felt that too. He read on. 'How proud I am to be his wife!' And he had always been very proud to be her husband. How often when they dined out somewhere he had looked at her across the table and said to himself, She is the loveliest woman here! He read on. That first year he had been standing for Parliament. They had toured his constituency. 'When Gilbert sat down the applause was terrific. The whole audience rose and sang: "For he's a jolly good fellow." I was quite overcome.' He remembered that, too. She had been sitting on the platform beside him. He could still see the glance she cast at him, and how she had tears in her eyes. And then? He turned the pages. They had gone to Venice. He recalled that happy holiday after the election. 'We had ices at Florians.' He smiled – she was still such a child, she loved ices. 'Gilbert gave me a most interesting account of the history of Venice. He told me that the Doges . . .' she had written it all out in her schoolgirl hand. One of the delights of travelling with Angela had been that she was so eager to learn. She was so terribly ignorant, she used to say, as if that were not one of her charms. And then – he opened the next volume – they had come back to London. 'I was so anxious to make a good impression. I wore my wedding dress.' He could see her now sitting next old Sir Edward; and making a conquest of that formidable old man, his chief. He read on rapidly, filling in scene after scene from her scrappy fragments. 'Dined at the House of Commons. . . . To an evening party at the Lovegroves. Did I realise my responsibility, Lady L. asked me, as Gilbert's wife?' Then as the years passed – he took another volume from the writing table – he had become more and more absorbed in his work. And she, of course, was more often alone. It had been a great grief to her, apparently, that they had had no children. 'How I wish,' one entry read, 'that Gilbert had a son!' Oddly enough he had never much regretted that himself. Life had been so full, so rich as it was. That year he had been given a minor post in the government. A minor post only, but her comment was: 'I am quite certain now that he will be Prime Minister!' Well, if things had gone differently, it might have been so. He paused here to speculate upon what might have been. Politics was a gamble, he reflected; but the game wasn't over yet. Not at fifty. He cast his eyes rapidly over more pages, full of the little trifles, the insignificant, happy, daily trifles that had made up her life.

He took up another volume and opened it at random. 'What a coward I am! I let the chance slip again. But it seemed selfish to bother him about my own affairs, when he has so much to think about. And we so seldom have an evening alone.' What was the meaning of that? Oh here was the explanation – it referred to her work in the East End. 'I plucked up courage and talked to Gilbert at last. He was so kind, so good. He made no objection.' He remembered that conversation. She had told him that she felt so idle, so useless. She wished to have some work of her own. She wanted to do something – she had blushed so prettily, he remembered, as she said it sitting in that very chair – to help

others. He had bantered her a little. Hadn't she enough to do looking
after him, after her home? Still if it amused her of course he had no
objection. What was it? Some district? Some committee? Only she
must promise not to make herself ill. So it seemed that every Wednesday she went to Whitechapel. He remembered how he hated the
clothes she wore on those occasions. But she had taken it very seriously
it seemed. The diary was full of references like this: 'Saw Mrs Jones. . . .
She has ten children. . . . Husband lost his arm in an accident. . . . Did
my best to find a job for Lily.' He skipped on. His own name occurred
less frequently. His interest slackened. Some of the entries conveyed
nothing to him. For example: 'Had a heated argument about socialism
with B. M.' Who was B. M.? He could not fill in the initials; some
woman[,] he supposed[,] that she had met on one of her committees.
'B. M. made a violent attack upon the upper classes. . . . I walked back
after the meeting with B. M. and tried to convince him. But he is so
narrow-minded.' So B. M. was a man – no doubt one of those
'intellectuals' as they call themselves, who are so violent, as Angela
said, and so narrow-minded. She had invited him to come and see her
apparently. 'B. M. came to dinner. He shook hands with Minnie!' That
note of exclamation gave another twist to his mental picture. B. M. it
seemed wasn't used to parlourmaids; he had shaken hands with
Minnie. Presumably he was one of those tame working men who air
their views in ladies' drawing-rooms. Gilbert knew the type, and had
no liking for this particular specimen, whoever B. M. might be. Here he
was again. 'Went with B. M. to the Tower of London. . . . He said
revolution is bound to come. . . . He said we live in a Fool's Paradise.'
That was just the kind of thing B. M. would say – Gilbert could hear
him. He could also see him quite distinctly – a stubby little man, with a
rough beard, red tie, dressed as they always did in tweeds, who had
never done an honest day's work in his life. Surely Angela had the sense
to see through him? He read on. 'B. M. said some very disagreeable
things about . . .' The name was carefully scratched out. 'I told him I
would not listen to any more abuse of . . .' Again the name was
obliterated. Could it have been his own name? Was that why Angela
covered the page so quickly when he came in? The thought added to his
growing dislike of B. M. He had had the impertinence to discuss him in
this very room. Why had Angela never told him? It was very unlike her
to conceal anything; she had been the soul of candour. He turned the
pages, picking out every reference to B. M. 'B. M. told me the story of

his childhood. His mother went out charring. . . . When I think of it, I can hardly bear to go on living in such luxury. . . . Three guineas for one hat!' If only she had discussed the matter with him, instead of puzzling her poor little head about questions that were much too difficult for her to understand! He had lent her books. Karl Marx. 'The Coming Revolution.' The initials B. M., B. M., B. M., recurred repeatedly. But why never the full name? There was an informality, an intimacy in the use of initials that was very unlike Angela. Had she called him B. M. to his face? He read on. 'B. M. came unexpectedly after dinner. Luckily, I was alone.' That was only a year ago. 'Luckily' – why luckily? – 'I was alone.' Where had he been that night? He checked the date in his engagement book. It had been the night of the Mansion House dinner. And B. M. and Angela had spent the evening alone! He tried to recall that evening. Was she waiting up for him when he came back? Had the room looked just as usual? Were there glasses on the table? Were the chairs drawn close together? He could remember nothing – nothing whatever, nothing except his own speech at the Mansion House dinner. It became more and more inexplicable to him – the whole situation: his wife receiving an unknown man alone. Perhaps the next volume would explain. Hastily he reached for the last of the diaries – the one she had left unfinished when she died. There on the very first page was that cursed fellow again. 'Dined alone with B. M. . . . He became very agitated. He said it was time we understood each other. . . . I tried to make him listen. But he would not. He threatened that if I did not . . .' the rest of the page was scored over. She had written 'Egypt. Egypt. Egypt.' over the whole page. He could not make out a single word; but there could be only one interpretation: the scoundrel had asked her to become his mistress. Alone in his room! The blood rushed to Gilbert Clandon's face. He turned the pages rapidly. What had been her answer? Initials had ceased. It was simply 'he' now. 'He came again. I told him I could not come to any decision. . . . I implored him to leave me.' He had forced himself upon her in this very house? But why hadn't she told him? How could she have hesitated for an instant? Then: 'I wrote him a letter.' Then pages were left blank. Then there was this: 'No answer to my letter.' Then more blank pages; and then this. 'He has done what he threatened.' After that – what came after that? He turned page after page. All were blank. But there[,] on the very day before her death[,] was this entry: 'Have I the courage to do it too?' That was the end.

Gilbert Clandon let the book slide to the floor. He could see her in front of him. She was standing on the kerb in Piccadilly. Her eyes stared; her fists were clenched. Here came the car. . . .

He could not bear it. He must know the truth. He strode to the telephone.

'Miss Miller!' There was silence. Then he heard someone moving in the room.

'Sissy Miller speaking' – her voice at last answered him.

'Who,' he thundered, 'is B. M.?'

He could hear the cheap clock ticking on her mantelpiece; then a long drawn sigh. Then at last she said:

'He was my brother.'

He *was* her brother; her brother who had killed himself.

'Is there,' he heard Sissy Miller asking, 'anything that I can explain?'

'Nothing!' he cried. 'Nothing!'

He had received his legacy. She had told him the truth. She had stepped off the kerb to rejoin her lover. She had stepped off the kerb to escape from him.

The Symbol

There was a little dent on the top of the mountain like a crater on the moon. It was filled with snow, iridescent like a pigeon's breast, or dead white. There was a scurry of dry particles now and again, covering nothing. It was too high for breathing flesh or fur covered life. All the same the snow was iridescent one moment; and blood red; and pure white, according to the day.

The graves in the valley – for there was a vast descent on either side; first pure rock; snow silted; lower a pine tree gripped a crag; then a solitary hut; then a saucer of pure green; then a cluster of eggshell roofs; at last, at the bottom, a village, an hotel, a cinema, and a graveyard – the graves in the churchyard near the hotel recorded the names of several men who had fallen climbing.[1]

'The mountain,' the lady wrote, sitting on the balcony of the hotel, 'is a symbol . . .' She paused. She could see the topmost height through her glasses. She focussed the lens, as if to see what the symbol was. She was writing to her elder sister at Birmingham.

The balcony overlooked the main street of the Alpine summer resort, like a box at a theatre. There were very few private sitting rooms, and so the plays – such as they were – the curtain raisers – were acted in public. They were always a little provisional; preludes, curtain raisers. Entertainments to pass the time; seldom leading to any conclusion, such as marriage; or even lasting friendship. There was something fantastic about them, airy, inconclusive. So little that was solid could be dragged to this height. Even the houses looked gimcrack. By the time the voice of the English Announcer had reached the village it too became unreal.

Lowering her glasses, she nodded at the young men who in the street below were making ready to start. With one of them she had a certain connection – that is, an Aunt of his had been Mistress of her daughter's school.

Still holding the pen, still tipped with a drop of ink, she waved down at the climbers. She had written the mountain was a symbol. But of what?[2] In the forties of the last century two men, in the sixties four men had perished; the first party when a rope broke; the second when night fell and froze them to death. We are always climbing to some height; that was the cliché. But it did not represent what was in her mind's eye; after seeing through her glasses the virgin height.[3]

She continued, inconsequently. 'I wonder why it makes me think of the Isle of Wight? You remember when Mama was dying, we took her there. And I would stand on the balcony, when the boat came in and describe the passengers. I would say, I think that must be Mr Edwardes . . . He has just come off the gangway. Then, now all the passengers have landed. Now they have turned the boat . . . I never told you, naturally not – you were in India; you were going to have Lucy – how I longed when the doctor came, that he should say, quite definitely, She cannot live another week. It was very prolonged; she lived eighteen months. The mountain just now reminded me how when I was alone, I would fix my eyes upon her death, as a symbol. I would think if I could reach that point – when I should be free – we could not marry as you remember until she died – A cloud then would do instead of the mountain. I thought, when I reach that point – I have never told any one; for it seemed so heartless; I shall be at the top.[4] And I could imagine so many sides. We come of course of an Anglo Indian family. I can still imagine, from hearing stories told, how people live in other parts of the world. I can see mud huts; and savages; I can see elephants drinking at pools. So many of our uncles and cousins were explorers. I have always had a great desire to explore for myself. But of course, when the time came it seemed more sensible, considering our long engagement, to marry.'

She looked across the street at a woman shaking a mat on another balcony. Every morning at the same time she came out. You could have thrown a pebble into her balcony. They had indeed come to the point of smiling at each other across the street.

'The little villas,' she added, taking up her pen, 'are much the same here as in Birmingham. Every house takes in lodgers. The hotel is quite full. Though monotonous, the food is not what you would call bad. And of course the hotel has a splendid view. One can see the mountain from every window. But then that's true of the whole place. I can assure you, I could shriek sometimes coming out of the one shop where they sell papers – we get them a week late – always to see that mountain. Sometimes it looks just across the way. At others, like a cloud; only it never moves. Somehow the talk, even among the invalids, who are every where, is always about the mountain. Either, how clear it is today, it might be across the street; or, how far away it looks; it might be a cloud. That is the usual cliché. In the storm last night, I hoped for once it was hidden. But just as they brought in the anchovies, The Rev. W. Bishop said, "Look there's the mountain!"

Am I being selfish? Ought I not to be ashamed of myself, when there is so much suffering? It is not confined to the visitors. The natives suffer dreadfully from goitre. Of course it could be stopped, if any one had enterprise, and money. Ought one not to be ashamed of dwelling upon what after all can't be cured? It would need an earthquake to destroy that mountain, just as, I suppose, it was made by an earthquake. I asked the Proprietor, Herr Melchior, the other day, if there were ever earthquakes now? No, he said, only landslides and avalanches. They have been known he said to blot out a whole village. But he added quickly, there's no danger here.

As I write these words, I can see the young men quite plainly on the slopes of the mountain. They are roped together. One I think I told you was at the same school with Margaret. They are now crossing a crevasse. . . .'

The pen fell from her hand, and the drop of ink straggled in a zig zag line down the page. The young men had disappeared.

It was only late that night when the search party had recovered the bodies that she found the unfinished letter on the table on the balcony. She dipped her pen once more; and added, 'The old clichés will come in very handy. They died trying to climb the mountain . . . And the peasants brought spring flowers to lay upon their graves. They died in an attempt to discover . . .'

There seemed no fitting conclusion. And she added, 'Love to the children,' and then her pet name.

The Watering Place

Like all seaside towns it was pervaded by the smell of fish. The toy shops were full of shells, varnished, hard yet fragile. Even the inhabitants had a shelly look – a frivolous look as if the real animal had been extracted on the point of a pin and only the shell remained. The old men on the parade were shells. Their gaiters, their riding breeches, their spy glasses seemed to make them into toys. They could no more have been real sailors or real sportsmen than the shells stuck onto the rims of photograph frames and looking-glasses could have lain in the depths of the sea. The women too, with their trousers and their little high heeled shoes and their raffia bags and their pearl necklaces seemed shells of real women who go out in the morning to buy household stores.

At one o'clock this frail varnished shell fish population clustered together in the restaurant. The restaurant had a fishy smell, the smell of a smack that has drawn up nets full of sprats and herrings. The consumption of fish in that dining room must have been enormous. The smell pervaded even the room that was marked Ladies on the first landing. This room was separated by a door only into two compartments. On the one side of the door the claims of nature were gratified; and on the other, at the washing table, at the looking-glass, nature was disciplined by art. Three young ladies had reached this second stage of the daily ritual. They were exerting their rights upon improving nature, subduing her, with their powder puffs and little red tablets. As they did so they talked; but their talk was interrupted as by the surge of an indrawing tide; and then the tide withdrew and one was heard saying:

'I never did care about her – the simpering little thing. . . . Bert never did care about big women. . . . Ave you seen him since he's been back? . . . His eyes . . . they're so blue . . . Like pools . . . Gert's too . . . Both ave the same eyes. . . . You look down into them . . . They've both got the same teeth . . . Are He's got such beautiful white teeth. . . . Gert has em too. . . . But his are a bit crooked . . . when he smiles . . .'

The water gushed . . . The tide foamed and withdrew. It uncovered next: 'But he had ought to be more careful. If he's caught doing it, he'll be courtmartialled . . .' Here came a great gush of water from the next compartment. The tide in the watering place seems to be for ever drawing and withdrawing. It uncovers these little fish; it sluices over them. It withdraws, and there are the fish again, smelling very strong of some queer fishy smell that seems to permeate the whole watering place.

But at night the town looks quite ethereal. There is a white glow on the horizon. There are hoops and coronets in the streets. The town has sunk down into the water. And the skeleton only is picked out in fairy lamps.

Notes and Appendices

Abbreviations Used in the Notes

Place and date of first publication have been given

VW   Virginia Woolf

CEI–IV   *Collected Essays*, Vols. I–IV, ed. Leonard Woolf (London: Chatto & Windus, 1966–67)

DI–V   *The Diary of Virginia Woolf*, Vols. I–V, ed. Anne Olivier Bell (London: The Hogarth Press, 1977–84)

HH   *A Haunted House and Other Short Stories*, ed. Leonard Woolf (London: The Hogarth Press, 1944)

JR I–III   The holograph of *Jacob's Room*, Parts I–III, Berg Collection

LI–VI   *The Letters of Virginia Woolf*, Vols. I–VI, ed. Nigel Nicolson (London: The Hogarth Press, 1975–80)

MDP   *Mrs Dalloway's Party: A Short Story Sequence by Virginia Woolf*, ed. Stella McNichol (London: The Hogarth Press, 1973)

MHP   Monks House Papers, B2e, holograph notebook (University of Sussex)

MT   *Monday or Tuesday* (London: The Hogarth Press, New York: Harcourt, Brace and Co., 1921)

NW   *Notes for Writing*, holograph notebook (Berg Collection); transcription of section entitled 'Notes for Stories' published in *Virginia Woolf: To The Lighthouse, The Original Holograph Draft*, trans. and ed. by Susan Dick (Toronto: University of Toronto Press, 1982)

QBI   Quentin Bell, *Virginia Woolf: A Biography*, Vol. I (London: The Hogarth Press, 1972)

Notes

PHYLLIS AND ROSAMOND

The text given here is that of the holograph, which is dated 'Wed. June 20–23rd 1906'. I have supplied the title. Bracketed words followed by a question mark are doubtful readings.

1. Had VW revised this story, she would undoubtedly have clarified the identity of Phyllis and Rosamond's youngest sister.

2. Presumably Sir Thomas has just recounted the story of the Sixth Earl of Mayo, who was appointed Viceroy in India in 1868 and assassinated in the Andaman Islands in 1872.

3. The elegant dresses worn by women whose portraits George Romney (1734–1802) painted, would be out of fashion and certainly out of place at the Tristrams' party.

THE MYSTERIOUS CASE OF MISS V.

The text given here is that of the undated holograph. The story is written with the same sort of pen and ink and on the same type of paper as 'Phyllis and Rosamond' and 'The Journal of Mistress Joan Martyn' and probably also dates from the summer of 1906.

The words within brackets were cancelled but have been included for the sake of clarity.

In the cancelled ending, after the door is opened by the maid the narrator says, 'I walked straight in and saw Mary V. sitting at a table.' This was replaced by the news of Miss V.'s death.

THE JOURNAL OF MISTRESS JOAN MARTYN

'The Journal of Mistress Joan Martyn' was written in August 1906, while VW and her sister were staying at Blo' Norton Hall in East Harling, Norfolk. She describes the Elizabethan house, the countryside, and the manuscript she wrote there in letters to Violet Dickinson (see LI, 233–5).

The text given here is that of the undated, untitled holograph draft. VW's misspellings have been corrected and her ampersands replaced by 'and'. I have retained her use of the contraction 'tho'' and her occasional archaic spellings since these contribute to the characterisation of her narrators. Words within brackets have been added for the sake of clarity.

'The Journal of Mistress Joan Martyn' was published in *Twentieth Century Literature*, 25:3/4 (Fall/Winter 1979), 237–269, edited and introduced by Susan M. Squier and Louise A. DeSalvo, who also supplied the title. I am greatly indebted to their knowledgeable and scrupulous editing of the holograph.

1. *The Paston Letters*: 1422–1509, edited by James Gairdner (London, 1904),

6 vols. See VW's essay 'The Pastons and Chaucer', *Common Reader: First Series* (London, 1925; 1984), reprinted in CEIII.

2. Had VW revised this story, she would undoubtedly have noticed the inconsistencies among the dates in it.

3. As Susan M. Squier and Louise A. DeSalvo point out, VW is probably referring here to John Lydgate's *Temple of Glas*, which she seems to have confused with his *Troy-book*.

MEMOIRS OF A NOVELIST

VW planned to make 'Memoirs of a Novelist', written in 1909, the first in a series of fictional portraits. She submitted it to *Cornhill Magazine*, but the editor, Reginald Smith, rejected it. (See *LI*, 413 and QBI, 153–4).

The text given here is that of VW's typescript with holograph revisions. Words within brackets have been added for the sake of clarity.

Both Miss Linsett and Miss Willatt are imaginary.

1. Christoph Christian Sturm, *Beauties of Nature Delineated* (London, 1800).

2. VW's brackets.

3. William Bright, *A History of the Church* (London, 1860).

4. William Wordsworth, 'Lines Composed a Few Miles Above Tintern Abbey'.

5. A series of novels written by Sir Walter Scott (1771–1832).

6. Harriet Martineau (1802–1876), novelist and journalist, whose advocacy of social reform and expression of anti-theological views the anonymous critic may have in mind.

THE MARK ON THE WALL

'The Mark on the Wall' was published in July 1917, along with Leonard Woolf's short story 'Three Jews', in *Two Stories*, the first publication of the Hogarth Press. It was published (slightly revised) in a separate edition in June 1919; included (with further revisions) in *MT*, and reprinted in *HH*.

The text given here is from *MT*.

The revisions VW made when the story was reprinted in 1919 and 1921 were stylistic ones: she altered some punctuation, reworded a few sentences, and deleted several short passages. The one extensive deleted passage is given in note 1 below.

1. [in *Two Stories* and in the 1919 edition this sentence is followed by:] But I know a house-keeper, a woman with the profile of a police-man, those little round buttons marked even upon the edge of her shadow, a woman with a broom in her hand, a thumb on picture frames, an eye under beds and she talks always of art. She is coming nearer and nearer; and now, pointing to certain spots of yellow rust on the fender, she becomes so menacing that to oust her, I shall have to get up and see for myself what that mark –

But no. I refuse to be beaten. I will not move. I will not recognise her. See, she fades already. I am very nearly rid of her and her insinuations, which I can hear quite distinctly. Yet she has about her the pathos of all people who wish to compromise. And why should I resent the fact that she has a few books in her house, a picture or two? But what I really resent is that she resents me – life being an affair of attack and defence after all. Another time I will have it out with her, not now. She must go now. The tree outside

2. This probably a reference to 'The Peerage of the United Kingdom', which is included in Whitaker's *Almanack*.

3. Many of the popular paintings of Sir Edwin Henry Landseer (1802–1873) were reproduced in steel engravings by his brother Thomas (1795–1880).

KEW GARDENS

Katherine Mansfield appears to be referring to a draft of 'Kew Gardens' in her letter to VW of August, 1917: 'Yes, your Flower Bed is *very* good. There's a still, quivering changing light over it all and a sense of those couples dissolving in the bright air which fascinates me' (quoted in Antony Alpers, *The Life of Katherine Mansfield*, New York, 1980, p. 251). The first reference to 'Kew Gardens' in VW's correspondence occurs in a letter written to Vanessa Bell on 25 July 1918. 'The story seems to be very bad now, and not worth printing, but I'll send it you if you like – I thought perhaps I could rewrite it. I mean to write a good many short things at Asheham and I wish you would consider illuminating them all' (*LII*, 255). She refers again to Vanessa's illustrations for 'Kew Gardens' in letters written on July 1, July 8, and November 7. 'Kew Gardens' was published by the Hogarth Press on 12 May 1919, with two woodcuts by Vanessa Bell. A second edition was published in June 1919, and a third in November 1927. Each of the 22 pages of the third edition contains handsome decorations by Vanessa Bell. 'Kew Gardens' was included in *MT* and *HH*.

The text given here is that of the third edition.

Only one substantive difference exists among the published texts of 'Kew Gardens.' 'Wished' at the end of the second paragraph became 'wanted' in the third edition.

An undated typescript of 'Kew Gardens' with holograph revisions made by VW has survived. The revisions she made before the story was published were mainly stylistic ones: words were rearranged in sentences, phrases were added or deleted, verbs were changed from present tense to past. The most extensive variant is given below. The passage is not cancelled on the typescript and it may have been omitted by mistake.

1. [The following passage precedes the paragraph which begins with, 'The ponderous woman . . .'] They made a mosaic round them in the hot still air of these people and these commodities each woman firmly pressing her own contribution into the pattern, never taking her eyes off it, never glancing at the differently coloured fragments so urgently wedged into its place by her friend. But in this competition, the small woman either from majority of relatives or superior fluency of speech conquered, and the ponderous one fell silent perforce.

She continued: – Nell, Bert, Lot, Cess, Phil, Pa. He says, I says, She says, I says I says I says –

THE EVENING PARTY

Both the style and the appearance of the typescript drafts of this story suggest that it belongs to the period when VW was writing the works she included in *MT*. Her reference in a letter to Vanessa Bell on 26 July 1918 to the story 'about the party' may refer to this one (*LII*, 262). A revised version of the opening, also called 'The

Evening Party', was included in 'Cracked Fiddles' (see Appendix A). The professor in the story may be a forerunner of Professor Brierly, who appears briefly in *Mrs Dalloway*. VW may have considered reworking the story again in 1925; on 6 January she noted in her diary that the stories she was then 'conceiving' included 'the Professor on Milton – (an attempt at literary criticism) & now The Interruption, women talking alone' (*DIII*,3). References in the 'Notes for Stories' she made on 6 and 14 March 1925 to 'Professor Brierly' and to a story that would be 'an exciting conversation all, or almost all, in dialogue' may also refer to this story (*NW*).

There are two undated typescripts of 'The Evening Party', both with holograph revisions, which I have called the A and B drafts. VW incorporates into the B draft most of the holograph revisions made in the A draft. In the A draft, the typed title 'The Evening Party' has been revised to 'A Conversation Party'. The original title appears on the title page of the B draft. Except for the first two pages (the first seven paragraphs), which are missing from the B draft, the text given here is that of the B draft.

    1. P. B. Shelley, 'Stanzas–April, 1814'.

    2. In the A draft, 'correction' is cancelled and 'interruption' written above it.

SOLID OBJECTS

On 26 November 1918 VW described for Vanessa Bell the opening of 'Solid Objects', which she said she had just begun to write (*LII*, 299). The story was published in *The Athenaeum* on 22 October 1920. Soon after its publication VW thanked Hope Mirrlees for praising it and added, 'It was written too quick, but I thought it had some points as a way of telling a story . . .' (*LVI*, 497).

'Solid Objects' was reprinted in *HH*. The text given here is from *The Athenaeum*.

SYMPATHY

Though the typescript (with holograph revisions) of 'Sympathy' is undated, the reference in the story to Tuesday, April 29th, supports my conjecture that it was written in the spring of 1919 (when April 29th fell on a Tuesday). VW used a passage from 'Sympathy' in 'Monday or Tuesday' (see note 3). A much shorter version of 'Sympathy', called 'A Death in the Newspaper', was probably written in January of 1921 (see notes 2 and 4 below). The text given here is that of the typescript.

    1. It is not clear whether in putting brackets around this passage VW intended to cancel it.

    2. See 'A Death in the Newspaper', p. 308.

    3. See Monday or Tuesday', p. 131.

    4. See 'A Death in the Newspaper', p. 308.

    5. [The last two sentences replace the following cancelled ending:] Do you mean to tell me that Humphry is alive after all and you never opened the bedroom door or picked the anemonies, and I've wasted all this; death never was behind the tree; and I'm to dine with you, with years and years in which to ask questions about the furniture. Humphry Humphry you ought to have died! [Before she cancelled the

entire passage, VW crossed out the final sentence and replaced it with:] O why did you deceive me?

AN UNWRITTEN NOVEL

VW's reference to 'An Unwritten Novel' in a diary entry for 26 January 1920 suggests that it was written around that time. (*DII*, 13). It was published in the *London Mercury* in July 1920, included (slightly revised) in *MT* and reprinted in *HH*.

The text given here is from *MT*. The brackets within the text are VW's.

VW's revisions consisted of the deletion of three brief passages which are given in notes 3, 4, and 5 below. The deleted passage appears between the asterisks.

1. The Treaty of Versailles, signed in Paris on 28 June 1919, went into effect on 10 January 1920.

2. Paulus Kruger (1825–1904), leader of the Boers in their 1880 rebellion against Britain and subsequently president of the Transvaal, contrasts sharply with Queen Victoria's beloved Prince Albert (1819–1861) whose earnest Christianity took a far less aggressive form.

3. brim with ribbons *all along the counters.*

4. as if washing helped. *You take the sponge, the pumice-stone, you scrape and scrub, you squirm and sluice; it can't be done – let *me* try; I can't reach it either – the spot between the shoulders – cold water only – why should she grudge that?*

5. opposite *(I can't bear to watch her!)*

A HAUNTED HOUSE

'A Haunted House' was published in *MT* and reprinted in *HH*. The text given here is from *MT*.

A SOCIETY

VW noted in her diary on 26 September 1920 that she was 'making up a paper upon Women, as a counterblast to Mr Bennett's adverse views reported in the papers' (*DII*, 69). No paper has been discovered, but 'A Society' may be in part a fictional response to Bennett's views on the intellectual inferiority of women, put forth in *Our Women*, which was currently being reviewed. VW's two letters of protest to 'Affable Hawk', along with her caustic remarks on the Plumage Bill, also anticipate 'A Society' (see *DII*, Appendices II and III). An incomplete, undated typescript of the story, with holograph revisions, has survived. 'A Society' was published in *MT*, the source of the text given here. It was never reprinted.

1. This is an allusion to the celebrated *Dreadnought* Hoax (February 1910), during which VW and five accomplices disguised themselves as the Emperor of Abyssinia and his entourage and paid a royal visit to the HMS *Dreadnought*. See QBI, 157–161 and Appendix E.

2. Alfred Lord Tennyson, 'Break, Break, Break'.

3. Robert Louis Stevenson, *Underwoods*, 'Requiem', xxi.

4. Robert Burns, 'It was a' for our Rightfu' King'.

5. This may be an allusion to A. C. Swinburne, 'Hymn to Proserpine', 'Laurel is

green for a season, and love is sweet for a day;/ But love grows bitter with treason, and laurel outlives not May.'

  6. Thomas Nashe, 'Spring'.

  7. Robert Browning, 'Home-Thoughts from Abroad'.

  8. Charles Kingsley, 'The Three Fishers'.

  9. Alfred Lord Tennyson, 'Ode on the Death of the Duke of Wellington'.

  10. See 'An Unwritten Novel', note 1.

MONDAY OR TUESDAY

'Monday or Tuesday' was written some time after 31 October 1920 (see LII, 445). The title also occurs in 'Modern Fiction' (1919) in the passage in which VW describes 'an ordinary mind on an ordinary day' (see *The Common Reader: First Series* [London, 1925, 1984] and CEII). 'Monday or Tuesday' was published in *MT* and reprinted in *HH*. The text given here is from *MT*.

  1. This passage originates in 'Sympathy'. See p. 104 and note.

THE STRING QUARTET

On 9 March 1920 VW wrote in her diary that on Sunday 'I went up to Campden Hill to hear the Schubert quintet' and 'to take notes for my story' (DII, 24). A draft of part of the conclusion of 'The String Quartet' is located in *JR*II and appears to have been written in January of 1921. Three pages of a typescript draft with holograph revisions have also survived. 'The String Quartet' was published in *MT* and reprinted in *HH*. The text given here is from *MT*.

  1. See 'An Unwritten Novel', note 1.

  2. [The three brief paragraphs which follow at this point in the published text replace the following paragraph from the typescript:] I draw on my gloves with a sense of drawing on my body. There's very little to be said after a slow movement by Mozart. Together we've been under; together when the last ripple laps to smoothness, wake up, remember, and greet each other. – But I don't know. It's simpler than that; more entire; more intense. Oh much more intense! Aren't all the nerves still thrilling as if the bow had played on them? Isn't one half out of body and mind, beckoned still to release, dance free, caught when the music stops, far from home? But there's only one movement more, so for Heaven's sake look at everything, faces, furniture, pictures on the wall, look through the chink in the curtain and see the branch in the lamp light. Collect every fragment in this lovely and exciting universe. Listen; communicate.

BLUE & GREEN

'Blue & Green' was published in *MT*, the origin of the text given here. It was never reprinted.

A WOMAN'S COLLEGE FROM OUTSIDE

A draft of this story (probably written in July 1920) is located in *JR*I, where it is chapter X. The undated typescript, with holograph revisions, which has *Jacob's Room* written at the top and then cancelled, is also headed X, and the pages numbered 47–52, thus suggesting that VW was still planning to use it in *Jacob's*

Room. The 'chapter' was not included in the novel, however, but was published in November 1926 as 'A Woman's College from Outside' in *Atalanta's Garland: Being the Book of the Edinburgh University Women's Union*. VW's references to Angela as 'Miranda' four times in the holograph and once in the typescript suggest a link between the young woman in this story and Miranda in 'In the Orchard'.

'A Woman's College from Outside' was reprinted in *Books and Portraits*. The text given here is from *Atalanta's Garland*.

1. This sentence also appears in *Jacob's Room* (London: The Hogarth Press, 1976), p. 36.

IN THE ORCHARD

VW referred to 'In the Orchard' as a 'story' in a letter written to Katherine Arnold-Forster on 23 August 1922 (*LII*, 549). 'In the Orchard' was published in *Criterion* in April 1923 and reprinted unchanged in *Broom* (September 1923), and in *Books and Portraits*. The text given here is from *Criterion*. Unfortunately, I have not been able to identify the book Miranda is reading.

MRS DALLOWAY IN BOND STREET

References to this story appear in VW's letters and diary between 14 April and 28 August 1922. On 6 October she made an outline of a book to be called 'At Home: or The Party' in which 'Mrs Dalloway in Bond Street' figured as the first chapter (*JR*III). On 14 October she noted that the story had 'branched into a book' (*DII*, 207). She sent 'Mrs Dalloway in Bond Street' to T.S. Eliott (then editor of *Criterion*) on 4 June 1923, though she noted that 'Mrs Dalloway doesn't seem to me to be complete as she is' (*LIII*, 45). An undated typescript with holograph revisions has survived. 'Mrs Dalloway in Bond Street' was published in *Dial* in July 1923, and reprinted in *MDP*. The text given here is from *Dial*.

1. Here and on pp. 149 and 151, Clarissa recalls lines from stanza xl of P. B. Shelley's 'Adonais', a poem she also quotes in *The Voyage Out* (1915), where she makes her first appearance in VW's work.

From the contagion of the world's slow stain
He is secure, and now can never mourn
A heart grown cold, a head grown grey in vain . . .

2. Edward Fitzgerald, 'The Rubáiyát of Omar Khayyám' (ed. 1, xxi).

3. The hero of R. S. Surtees' novel *Mr Sponge's Sporting Tour* (London, 1853) is called 'Soapey Sponge' by his 'good-natured friends'.

4. In remembering Elizabeth Gaskell's novel *Cranford* (London, 1853), Clarissa brings together the name the boys of Cranford give to the first red silk umbrella they see – 'a stick in petticoats' – and Miss Betsy Barker's cow, who goes about in grey flannel after a fall into a lime-pit leaves her hairless.

5. Here and on p. 152, Clarissa recalls lines from the song in William Shakespeare's *Cymbeline*, IV, ii.

6. The American artist John Sargent (1856–1925) painted many portraits of fashionable women.

NURSE LUGTON'S CURTAIN

A holograph draft of this story is located in volume II of the holograph of *Mrs Dalloway*, pp. 104–106, and was probably written in the fall of 1924. The untitled story interrupts the scene in which Septimus watches Rezia sewing a hat for Mrs Filmer's daughter. On p. 107 of the holograph VW returns to this scene. Wallace Hildick's transcription of the holograph draft of the story was published in *TLS* on 17 June 1965 (as 'The . . .') and by the Hogarth Press in 1966, as 'Nurse Lugton's Golden Thimble'.

An undated typescript draft of the story, with holograph revisions and entitled 'Nurse Lugton's Curtain', was recently discovered by Michael Halls among the Charleston Papers deposited in King's College Library, Cambridge. The typescript is a revised version of the holograph draft of the story and is the text given here.

In his foreword to the Hogarth Press edition, Leonard Woolf says that the story was written for VW's niece, Ann Stephen, when she was visiting her aunt in the country. As Anne Olivier Bell points out, VW's allusion in her diary to one of Nurse Lugton's sayings suggests that she 'may have had a real existence in the Stephen household' (see *DV*, 246 and note 5).

THE WIDOW AND THE PARROT: A TRUE STORY

'The Widow and the Parrot' first appeared in *The Charleston Bulletin*, a newspaper produced by the Bell children at Charleston in the 1920s. The story later reached a wider audience when it appeared in *Redbook Magazine* (July 1982).

VW invested her 'true' story with local colour by placing the widow's brother's house near Monks House, the house in the village of Rodmell where the Woolfs moved when they left Asheham House in September of 1919. The Rev. James Hawkesford, who tries to comfort Mrs Gage, was Rector of Rodmell from 1896 to 1928. He also appears to have contributed to the character of Mr Pember, the rector in VW's later sketch, 'Miss Pryme'.

On the first page of the typescript with holograph revisions, the source of the text given here, VW has drawn a sketch of the widow and her parrot.

THE NEW DRESS

The position of the holograph draft of 'The New Dress' in VW's manuscript book suggests that it was written early in 1925. VW listed it in the 'Notes for Stories' that she made on 6 and 14 March 1925 (*NW*), and she seems to have had it in mind when she wrote in her diary on 27 April 1925, 'But my present reflection is that people have any number of states of consciousness: & I should like to investigate the party consciousness, the frock consciousness &c' (*DIII*, 12). On 5 July 1925 she told H. G. Leach, editor of *Forum* (New York), that she was just finishing the story (*LIII*, 193). An undated typescript with holograph revisions has survived. 'The New Dress' was published in *Forum* in May 1927, and reprinted in *HH* and *MDP*. The text given here is from *Forum*.

1. This is probably an allusion to Anton Chekhov's story 'The Duel': '. . . and it seemed to [Nadyezhda Fyodorovna] that, like a fly, she kept falling into the ink and crawling out into the light again' (*The Duel and Other Stories*, trans. Constance Garnett [London, 1916], p. 115). Mabel could also have in mind Katherine

Mansfield's 1922 story 'The Fly', which features another struggling fly.

   2. See Anton Chekhov, 'The Duel': '[Laevsky] . . . had always tried to assume an air of being higher and better than they. Lies, lies, lies' (p. 142).

   3. Boadicea was the fierce queen of an ancient tribe of Britons who led a revolt against the Romans, was defeated, and took her own life.

HAPPINESS

A holograph draft of the opening pages of 'Happiness', dated Monday, 16 March [1925], follows 'The New Dress' in VW's writing book. It is also listed after 'The New Dress' in the 'Notes for Stories' that she made on 6 and 14 March 1925 (*NW*). The text given here is that of the undated typescript, with holograph revisions, which appears to be made up of pages from two separate drafts.

   1. Mrs Sutton aspires to be as successful as Sarah Kemble Siddons (1755–1831), the most famous English actress of her day.

ANCESTORS

In the notes VW made on 6 October 1922 for a book to be called 'At Home: or The Party', 'Ancestors' is listed as the third chapter (*JR*III). She sketched the subject of 'Ancestors' and listed it after 'Happiness' in the 'Notes for Stories' that she wrote on 14 March 1925 (*NW*). The holograph draft is dated 18 and 22 May 1925. An undated typescript of the opening page with holograph revisions has also survived. 'Ancestors' was published in *MDP*.

   The first five paragraphs of the text given here are a transcription of the typescript; the remainder is a transcription of the holograph. Words within brackets were cancelled but have been included for the sake of clarity.

THE INTRODUCTION

In the 'Notes for Stories' written on 14 March 1925 VW refers to one about 'The girl who had written an essay on the character of Bolingbroke talking to the young man who destroys a fly as he speaks' (*NW*). 'The Introduction' is listed in these notes immediately after 'Ancestors', and a holograph draft of the story follows 'Ancestors' in VW's manuscript book. An undated typescript with holograph revisions has also survived.

   'The Introduction' was published in the *Sunday Times Magazine* (18 March 1973) and in *MDP*.

   The text given here is that of the typescript. Words within brackets were cancelled but have been included for the sake of clarity.

   1. [VW cancelled the following passage at this point in the typescript:] In the direct line from Shakespeare she thought and Parliaments and Churches she thought, oh and the telegraph wires too she thought, and ostentatiously of set purpose begged Mr Brinsley to believe her implicitly when she offered him her essay upon the character of Dean Swift to do what he liked with – trample upon and destroy – for how could a mere child understand even for an instant the character of Dean Swift.

TOGETHER AND APART

VW's characterisation of Roderick Serle probably owes something to her memories of Bernard Holland, whom she first met at his home in Canterbury (see *D*III, 245–7). A holograph draft of this story, entitled 'The Conversation', follows 'The Introduction' in VW's manuscript book. An undated typescript with holograph revisions and with the typed title 'The Conversation' deleted and 'Together and Apart' written above it, has also survived. 'Together and Apart' was published in *HH* and *MDP*. The text given here is that of the typescript.

1. These are the last words of Marmion in Sir Walter Scott's *Marmion*, VI, (XXXII).

THE MAN WHO LOVED HIS KIND

A holograph draft of this story, with the title 'Lovers of their Kind' written above the uncancelled title, 'The Man Who Loved His Kind', follows 'Together and Apart' in VW's manuscript book. A typescript with holograph revisions, entitled 'The Man Who Loved His Kind', has also survived. The story was published in *HH* and *MDP*. The text given here is that of the typescript.

A SIMPLE MELODY

VW's references in the notes she made on 6 and 14 March 1925 to a story about a picture may anticipate 'A Simple Melody' (*NW*). A holograph draft of this story follows 'The Man Who Loved His Kind' in her manuscript book. No typescript has been found. The text given here is that of the holograph. Bracketed words were cancelled but have been included for the sake of clarity. Bracketed words followed by a question mark are doubtful readings.

1. This is probably a reference to the British Empire Exhibition held at Wembley Park (London) from April to October 1924. See VW's essay, 'Thunder at Wembley', *Nation & Athenaeum*, 28 June 1924, reprinted in *CE*IV.

2. Queen Mary was the wife of George V, king from 1910 to 1936.

3. See 'The New Dress'.

4. See 'Happiness'.

5. See 'The Man Who Loved His Kind'.

6. John Crome (1768–1821) was prominent in the Norwich School of Painting.

A SUMMING UP

A three page holograph draft of the last part of 'A Summing Up' follows 'A Simple Melody' in VW's manuscript book. A typescript with holograph revisions has also survived. The holograph contains a final paragraph which is not in the typescript and this suggests to me that the final page of the typescript may be missing. I have included this paragraph in the text of the story. 'A Summing Up' was published in *HH* and *MDP*.

The text given here is that of the typescript with the concluding paragraph taken from the holograph.

MOMENTS OF BEING: 'SLATER'S PINS HAVE NO POINTS'

On 5 September 1926, while revising the final pages of *To the Lighthouse*, VW recorded in her diary that 'as usual, side stories are sprouting in great variety as I wind this up: a book of characters; the whole string being pulled out from some simple sentence, like Clara Pater's, "Don't you find that Barker's pins have no points to them?"' (*DIII*, 106) Her thoughts about 'some semi mystic very profound life of a woman' which might be contained in 'one incident – say the fall of a flower', recorded in her diary on 3 November 1926, may also be linked to this story (*DIII*, 118). On 8 July 1927 she told Vita Sackville-West, 'I've just written, or re-written, a nice little story about Sapphism, for the Americans.' On 14 October she reported, 'Sixty pounds just received from America for my little Sapphist story of which the Editor has not seen the point, though he's been looking for it in the Adirondacks' (*LIII*, 397 and 431). 'Slater's Pins Have No Points' was published in *Forum* (New York) in January 1928. It was printed in *HH* with 'Moments of Being', which appears on the typescript, restored to the title. See the introduction, p. 9, for a discussion of the differences between the two published versions of the story. The text given here is from *Forum*, with the full title restored.

THE LADY IN THE LOOKING-GLASS: A REFLECTION

On 28 May 1929, VW noted in her diary that she felt 'no great impulse' to begin The Moths [*The Waves*]. 'Every morning I write a little sketch,' she added, 'to amuse myself' (*DIII*, 229). The earlier of the two typescripts of 'The Lady in the Looking-Glass: A Reflection' is dated 28 May 1929. (The second is undated.) The story incorporates a scene VW recalled after her July 1927 visit to Ethel Sands in Normandy. On 20 September 1927 she noted in her diary, 'How many little stories come into my head! For instance: Ethel Sands not looking at her letters. What this implies. One might write a book of short significant separate scenes. She did not open her letters' (*DIII*, 157). The final sentence in the first typescript draft is 'Isabella did not open her letters.'

The story was published in *Harper's Magazine* in December 1929, in *Harper's Bazaar* (New York) in January 1930 (as 'In the Looking Glass'), and reprinted in *HH*. The text given here is from *Harper's Magazine*.

THE FASCINATION OF THE POOL

The text given here is that of the typescript with holograph revisions, which is dated 29 May 1929.

1. The Great Exhibition, held in the Crystal Palace in Hyde Park, was opened by Queen Victoria on 1 May 1851.

2. Lord Nelson was killed while defeating Napoleon's fleet in a battle off Cape Trafalgar on 21 October 1805.

3. VW has cancelled 'of the great seer' here.

THREE PICTURES

'Three Pictures' was first published in *The Death of the Moth* (London, 1942), where Leonard Woolf noted that it was written in June 1929. The origin of the third picture is found in 'A graveyard scene' which VW described in her diary on 4

September 1927 (*D*III, 154). The text given here is from *The Death of the Moth*. The word within brackets has been added for the sake of clarity.

SCENES FROM THE LIFE OF A BRITISH NAVAL OFFICER

This sketch was probably written late in 1931. The last title in the following list of 'Caricatures', which VW probably made in January of 1932, appears to be a reference to this sketch: 'The Shooting Party./2. Scenes from English life/The pheasants/Scenes: Life on a Battleship' (MPH). 'The Royal Navy', listed under 'Caricatures' (along with 'Country House Life' and 'The Great Jeweller') in a note dated February 1932, is probably also a reference to this sketch (*NW*). The text given here is that of the undated typescript with holograph revisions. Words within brackets were cancelled but have been included for the sake of clarity.

MISS PRYME

The text given here is that of the undated typescript.

1. Mr Pember, the rector, bears some resemblance to the Rev. James Hawkesford of Rodmell, as VW describes him in her diary on 25 September 1927 (*D*III, 159). Mr Hawkesford appears in person in 'The Widow and the Parrot'.

2. Henry Malthouse, the landlord of the Rodmell pub the Abergavenny Arms, died in the spring of 1933. It is the burial of his son that VW describes in 'A graveyard scene'. See 'Three Pictures' and *D*III, 154.

3. Miss Pryme's resemblance to Florence Nightingale resides in her untiring zeal for reform.

ODE WRITTEN PARTLY IN PROSE ON SEEING THE NAME OF CUTBUSH ABOVE A BUTCHER'S SHOP IN PENTONVILLE

The text given here is that of the typescript with holograph revisions, which is dated 28 October 1934. VW's line divisions have been retained.

Though various London directories list no butchers named Cutbush in Pentonville in 1934, Kelly's does list a florist by that name.

1. George Gordon, Lord Byron's comic poem, 'Written after Swimming from Sestos to Abydos' (1812) commemorates the day he swam the Hellespont.

2. Frederick Leighton (1830–1896), a popular English painter and sculptor, painted many scenes of Greek and Roman life.

PORTRAITS

The title for this group of sketches comes from the third sketch which is headed 'Portrait 3' on the typescript. 'Portraits' and 'Uncle Vanya' which follows them are probably part of a collaborative work called 'Faces and Voices' that VW and Vanessa Bell were discussing in February 1937 (see *D*V, 57 and note 8, 58, 59, 61). The portraits and 'Uncle Vanya' were typed on a mixture of white paper and blue paper, and with what appears to be the same typewriter. Because the typescripts have been preserved in two collections, I have had to guess at the order in which VW would have placed them. I have also supplied the titles of portraits 4 to 8. There are two typescript drafts each of portraits 6 and 8, one on blue paper and one on white; in both cases the white draft (the draft presented here) appears to be a reworking of the blue draft. There are single drafts of the other portraits; all have holograph revisions. The eighth portrait derives from 'The Broad Brow', one of the 'Three Characters' which VW first drafted in 1930. Another version of 'Three Characters', a letter written but not sent to the *New Statesman* in November 1932, was called 'Middlebrow' and was published in *The Death of the Moth* (London, 1942) and CEII (cf. DIV, 129). 'Three Characters' was published in *Adam International Review* in 1972.

1. Author Oscar Wilde (1854–1900) entertained many in London in the 1890s with his engaging wit.

2. In the 1890s pheasants were given to the bus drivers and conductors who passed the Rothschild houses in Piccadilly during the Christmas season. They acknowledged these gifts by decorating their whips and bell cords with ribbons of blue and amber, the Rothschild racing colours. (See Virginia Cowles, *The Rothschilds: A Family of Fortune* [London, 1973], p. 181.)

3. Vernon Lee is the pen-name of author Violet Paget (1856–1935). On 23 August 1922 VW wrote to Katherine Arnold-Forster, 'Oh yes, I remember Vernon Lee, in the dining room at Talland House, in coat and skirt, much as she is now – but that was 30 years ago. . . . I saw her 10 years later, at Florence, . . . and two years ago at the 1917 Club . . .' (LII, 550).

4. Fra Angelico (1387–1455), the great Florentine artist of the early Renaissance, is said to have knelt while he painted a picture of the Virgin Mary.

5. Ouida is the pen-name of Marie Louise de la Ramée (1839–1908), a popular and prolific English novelist who lived most of her life in Italy.

UNCLE VANYA

There are three undated typescript drafts of 'Uncle Vanya', two on blue paper and one on white; all have holograph revisions (see Note on 'Portraits'). The text given here is that of the white draft, which appears to be a revised version of the other two.

On 16 February 1937 VW went to a performance of Anton Chekhov's play, *Uncle Vanya*, the final scenes of which are being watched by the characters in this sketch (see DV, 57). At the end of Act III Vanya fires his revolver at Serebryakov twice, but misses him. In Act IV Serebryakov forgives Vanya and then leaves. The play closes with Sonya telling the unhappy Vanya that at the end of their lives, 'We shall rest.'

In both of the earlier drafts Vanya's missed shots remind the speaker of Countess Tolstoy's melodramatic suicide attempts. 'It reminds me of the Tolstoys,' the speaker says. 'She fired a toy pistol, to try and kill herself. And he drove away' (Draft B). The incidents referred to in the earlier drafts are recounted in *The Final Struggle: Being Countess Tolstoy's Diary for 1910*, trans. A. Maude (London, 1936), pp. 284 and 341, which VW was reading in February of 1937 (LVI, 107).

THE DUCHESS AND THE JEWELLER

The inclusion of 'The Great Jeweller' among the list of 'Caricatures' (along with 'Country House Life' and 'The Royal Navy') that VW made in February 1932, suggests that a first draft of this story may have been written at this time (*NW*). The two undated typescript drafts with holograph revisions that have survived were probably made in August 1937, when VW prepared the story for publication. On 17 August she outlined the plot in a letter to Vanessa Bell (*L* VI, 159). On the same day she noted in her diary that she had 'had a moment of the old rapture – think of it! – over copying The Duchess & the Jeweller . . . there was the old excitement, even in that little extravagant flash . . .' (*DV*, 107). The title on the earlier typescript is 'Passages in the life of a great Jeweller'. The second typescript combines pages from several drafts.

In revising the story for publication, VW removed all direct references to the fact that the jeweller is a Jew, along with some of the details associated with stereotypes of the Jew. In the first typescript, the jeweller recalls his childhood as 'a little Jew boy', while in the second typescript, as in the published text, he recollects himself as simply 'a little boy'. When he says to himself, 'I have won my bet,' in both typescript drafts the narrator adds, '(but he pronounced it "pet").' And his memory of dodging 'in and out of crowds of Jewesses, beautiful women, with their false pearls, with their false hair' in the second typescript, was reduced in the published text to 'in and out among the crowds'. His name, Theorodoric and then Isidore Oliver in the typescripts, became Oliver Bacon in the published text.

VW altered her story at the request of the New York literary agent, Jacques Chambrun, who had approved her synopsis of it, but later wrote to say that his (unnamed) client had rejected the story because, as 'a psychological study of a Jew', it risked offending his readers. After further correspondence between the Woolfs and Chambrun, the story was published in *Harper's Bazaar* (London, April 1938; New York, May 1938). (See *DV*, 107, note 6).

'The Duchess and the Jeweller' was reprinted in *HH*. The text given here is from *Harper's Bazaar*.

THE SHOOTING PARTY

On 29 December 1931, VW wrote in her diary, 'I could write a book of caricatures. Christabel's story of the Hall Caines suggested a caricature of Country house life, with the red-brown pheasants, . . .' (*DIV*, 57). 'The Shooting Party' appears first in the list of 'Caricatures' that she probably made in January of 1932 (quoted on p. 300). Both the holograph draft and the first of two typescripts with holograph revisions are dated 19 January 1932. One page of a draft of 'A Letter to a Young Poet' (published in July 1932) precedes the final page of the holograph of the story. 'Country House Life' appears on the list of 'Caricatures' (with 'The Royal Navy' and 'The Great Jeweller') written in February 1932 (*NW*); 'CARICATURES: Country House Life' appears on the title page of the earlier typescript. The second (undated) typescript appears to be a combination of at least two drafts, neither of which is the final one. The characters and incidents of the final version are present in these drafts, but neither contains the opening and closing paragraphs which provide a frame for the story. On 19 October 1937, while preparing the story for publication, VW wrote in her diary, 'It came over me suddenly last night, as I was reading The Shooting Party, . . . that I saw the form of a new novel. Its to be first the statement of the theme: then the restatement: & so on: repeating the same story:

singling out this & then that: until the central idea is stated' (*D*V, 114).

'The Shooting Party' was published in *Harper's Bazaar* (London and New York) in March 1938 and reprinted in *HH*. The text given here is from *Harper's Bazaar*.

LAPPIN AND LAPINOVA

VW's light-hearted comment to her sister in a letter written on 24 October 1938 that 'marriage, as I suddenly for the first time realised walking in the Square, reduces one to damnable servility. Cant be helped. Im going to write a comedy about it' (*L*VI, 294) can probably be related to this story. On 30 October she noted in her diary that she had been 'asked to write a story for Harpers', and on 22 November she noted that she was 'rehashing Lappin & Lapinova, a story written I think at Asheham 20 years ago or more: when I was writing Night & Day perhaps'. Two days later she complained, 'And then oh the bore of writing out a story to make money!' (*D*V, 183, 188, 189). On 19 December she listed it in her diary among the works she had completed (*D*V, 193). And on 18 January 1939 she noted with pleasure that *Harpers* had taken her story and paid her $600 (*D*V, 200). 'Lappin and Lapinova' was published in *Harpers' Bazaar* (London and New York, April 1939) and reprinted in *HH*. The text given here is from *Harper's Bazaar*.

THE SEARCHLIGHT

The unusually complex evolution of this story has been described in detail by John Graham in 'The Drafts of Virginia Woolf's "The Searchlight",' *Twentieth Century Literature*, 22:4 (December 1976), 379–93. The central incident in the story, the boy watching the couple through his telescope, remains essentially unchanged through the many drafts, though the framing narrative alters considerably. The earliest draft, a typescript called 'What the Telescope Discovered,' is dated 1929. A holograph entitled 'Incongruous Memories' (June 1930) and a typescript draft of this called 'Inaccurate Memories' (8 December 1930), are reworkings of this core incident.

A second group of typescript drafts, called 'A Scene from the Past,' may have been written as late as 1941. In these drafts, VW sets the framing narrative at Freshwater in the 1860s.

'The Searchlight' emerges in a third group of drafts, a holograph dated 31 January 1939, and three undated typescripts (the last of which appears to be a professional one) all with holograph revisions. Page 3 of the third of these typescript drafts is now missing. VW noted in her diary on 31 January, 'I wrote the old Henry Taylor telescope story thats been humming in my mind these 10 years' (*D*V, 204). Vanessa Bell read the story in May 1939 and praised it as being almost 'too full of suggestions for pictures' (Frances Spalding, *Vanessa Bell* [New Haven and New York, 1983], p. 309).

The text given here is from *HH*, where the story was first published, with a few minor changes made on the basis of the third (incomplete) typescript.

1. As John Graham has pointed out, the incident Mrs Ivimey recounts originates in *The Autobiography of Sir Henry Taylor* (London, 1885), I, 44–45. See Graham, p. 382.

GIPSY, THE MONGREL

On 7 October 1939 VW wrote in her diary, 'Chambrun [the literary agent] now demands a dog story: the other [probably the unidentified 'flimsy sketch' she had sent him on 30 August] too sophisticated. So I have that floating about' (*D*V, 232, 241 and note 4). Her 'dog story' was sent to Chambrun on 22 January 1940; on 26 January she noted in her diary that she had 'thrown off those two dead pigeons – my story ["Gipsy"], my Gas at Abbotsford' (*D*V, 260 and note 12). Though she received £170 for 'Gipsy' in March, it was never published (*D*V, 271).

The text given here is that of the undated typescript with holograph revisions, which appears to be made up of pages from at least three drafts.

THE LEGACY

Anne Olivier Bell suggests that VW's visit to Philip Morrell after Lady Ottoline's death during which he showed her his wife's memoirs and pressed her to take some mementoes was the impulse behind this story (see *D*V, 140 and 329, note 6).

On 17 October 1940, VW recorded in her diary that she had had 'an urgent request from Harpers Bazaar for an article or story' (*D*V, 329). *Harper's* acknowledged receipt of the story on 4 November, but then decided not to print it. Though VW wrote them two angry letters (on 23 January and 3 February 1941) in which she reviewed their agreement and described the considerable effort she had made to honour it, she received no satisfactory explanation from them (*L*VI, 463 and 469). One holograph draft, two complete typescripts, and fragments from at least six other typescript drafts of 'The Legacy' (all undated and all containing holograph revisions) have survived. The major change VW made as she reworked the story concerns the identity of 'B. M.'. In neither the holograph nor what appears to be the first typescript draft is he Sissy Miller's brother.

The text given here is that of the final typescript. Words within brackets have been added for the sake of clarity.

THE SYMBOL AND THE WATERING PLACE

Undated holograph drafts of these stories are located at the back of a writing book that VW entitled 'Essays'. The front of the book contains drafts of essays published in 1931 and 1932, and a portion of the holograph of *Flush*. At the back are drafts of five unpublished pieces, only two of which, the first, entitled 'Sketches' ['The Symbol'] and the second, entitled 'The Ladies Lavatory' ['The Watering Place'], appear to be complete. The other three are 'Winter's Night', 'English Youth', and 'Another Sixpence' (perhaps a reworking of the unfinished 'English Youth'). These five sketches may be the last works of fiction that VW wrote. Octavia Wilberforce, VW's friend and a doctor, visited her on 12 March and reported in a letter to Elizabeth Robins that VW was feeling 'desperate – depressed to the lowest depths, had just finished a story' (*L*VI, xvi). VW was probably referring to 'English Youth', a 'portrait' of Octavia Wilberforce that she proposed to write, when she noted in her last diary entry (24 March), 'Octavia's story. Could I englobe it somehow? English youth in 1900' (*D*V, 359). Since I cannot be sure of the order of these last two works, I have followed that of the holograph drafts.

The Symbol

On 22 June 1937 VW noted, 'I wd. like to write a dream story about the top of a mountain. Now why? About lying in the snow; about rings of colour; silence . . . & the solitude. I cant though. But shant I, one of these days, indulge myself in some short release into that world?' (*D* V, 95). On 16 November 1938 she reflected that 'There are very few mountain summit moments. I mean, looking out at peace from a height' (*D* V, 187). Two years later she wanted to 'brew some moments of high pressure. I think of taking my mountain top – that persistent vision – as a starting point' (*D* V, 341). This persistent vision seems to lie behind 'The Symbol'. The alpine setting probably reflects VW's memories of her father's fame as a mountain climber. Lyndall Gordon has pointed out that the name of the proprietor of the inn where the narrator is staying, Herr Melchior, recalls that of one of the three best Alpine guides in Switzerland, Melchior Anderegg, with whom Leslie Stephen always climbed. See Lyndall Gordon, *Virginia Woolf: A Writer's Life* (Oxford, 1984), p. 279, and Noel Annan, *Leslie Stephen: The Godless Victorian* (New York, 1984), p. 90.

The text given here is that of the typescript with holograph revisions, dated 1 March 1941, and typed on the verso side of pages from the later typescript of *Between the Acts* and 'Anon'. The typed title 'Inconclusions' is crossed out and 'The Symbol' written in. The pagination of the typescript suggests that this may be a combination of at least two typescript drafts. In revising this story, VW removed the name of the sister of the woman on the balcony, which was Rosamond, and substantially revised or omitted altogether several passages. The most extensive and significant of these are given in the notes below. Words within brackets followed by question marks are doubtful readings. Most cancelled passages are not recorded.

1. [In the holograph this sentence is followed by:] The virgin peak had never been climbed. [cancelled] It was a menace: something cleft in the mind like two parts of a broken disk: two numbers: two numbers that cannot be added: a problem that is insoluble.

2. [In the typescript this sentence is followed by two cancelled sentences:] There was a cliché at the tip of her pen. The symbol of effort.

3. [In the holograph, after saying that the mountain is a symbol of effort, the woman on the balcony thinks:] But that was unfitting. The other thing that this peak represented was not at all a cliché: in fact it was something that far from running into ink spontaneously, remained almost unspeakable even to herself.

The crater on the top of the mountain registered the changes of the day. Am I enjoying myself, she wrote, with what remained of the ink in her pen? To tell you the truth, I have practically no [emotion?] left. I am writing on a balcony and at one o'clock the gong will sound. I have not cut my nails. I have not done my hair. When I read a book I cannot finish it. I ask myself, why, when I was a young woman, did I refuse the man who wanted to marry me? Why was Papa moved just as I met Jasper? Then there was mama's cancer. I had to nurse her. Everything was lost to me. I mean, it was whisked away.

4. [The holograph version of this passage is followed by:] What is it that makes me write all this? I should I know be entering as they say into your life. That is the

only way in which we can escape. . . . She looked at the mountain . . . There are people who say that's the way to make two and two come together. Am I writing nonsense? I am only trying to tell you what I am thinking on the balcony. I am aware just as they are of the desire to master the height. The most absurd dreams come to me. I think if I could get there, I should be happy to die. I think there, in the crater, which looks like one of the spots on the moon, I should find the answer. It has come over me that, when we regret – say wasted youth – we are only using clichés. The real problem is to climb to the top of the mountain. Why, if that is not [it?], have we the desire? Who gave it us? It is time, she added, that I could buy flowers for the graves of those who have perished: they suffer from goitre too. I could no doubt discover why. But . . . The slopes make me think so many thoughts. [VW's ellipses throughout]

The Watering Place

VW recorded in her diary on 26 February 1941, a conversation that she overheard in a ladies' lavatory in a Brighton restaurant which is very like the one in 'The Watering Place' (*D*V, 356).

The text given here is that of the undated typescript which was typed on the verso side of pages from the later typescript of *Between the Acts*. Besides changing the title and refining the style of 'The Watering Place' when she made the typescript, VW removed all references to the lavatory attendant whose memoirs, the narrator observes, 'have never been written'. 'When, in old age, they look back through the corridors of memory, their past must be different from any other. It must be cut up: disconnected. The door must be always opening: and shutting. They can have no settled relations with their kind.'

'Cracked Fiddles'

'Cracked Fiddles' was probably written early in 1921, when Virginia Woolf was working on the first draft of *Jacob's Room* and on *Monday or Tuesday*. Two of the sketches in it derive from longer pieces which are included in the main body of this collection. 'The Evening Party' is a slightly revised version of the opening of the longer story which is also called 'The Evening Party'. 'A Death in the Newspaper' is made up of passages taken from 'Sympathy' (see 'Sympathy', notes 2 and 4).

On the first of the two undated typescript drafts (all with holograph revisions) of this group of sketches, Woolf has cancelled the title 'ILLUSIONS. Written to the tune of a street violin.' and written above it 'Cracked Fiddles'. The revised title appears on the second typescript.

Holograph drafts of three of the sketches are located in *JR* II, in the following order: 'Romance. written to the tune of a street fiddle' ['Holborn Viaduct'], 'The Telephone', 'A Death in the Newspaper'. An incomplete sketch with three titles, 'Fragment from a letter' [cancelled]/'Written for a picture:'/'A letter to a lady.' precedes 'A Death in the Newspaper'. The latter is followed by a portion of the ending of 'The String Quartet'.

The texts given here are those of the second typescript of each sketch, in which Virginia Woolf incorporated most of the holograph revisions she had made on the first typescripts.

THE EVENING PARTY

Ah, but let us wait a little! The moon is up; the sky open; and there, rising in a mound against the sky, is the earth. The flowing silvery clouds look down upon Atlantic waves. The wind blows soft round the corner of the street, lifting my cloak, holding it gently in the air, letting it sink and droop as the sea now swells and brims over the rocks and again withdraws. The street is almost empty; the blinds are drawn in the windows; the yellow and red panes of the ocean liners cast for a moment a spot upon the swimming blue. The maids linger round the pillar box or dally in the shadow of the wall where the tree droops its dark shower of blossom. So, on the bark of the apple tree, the moths quiver, drawing sugar through the black thread of the proboscis. Where are we? Which house can be the house of the party? All these with their pink and yellow windows are uncommunicative . . . Ah, round the corner, in the middle, there where the door stands open – let us wait. A lady pale and voluminous descends. a gentleman in black and white evening dress pays the driver and follows her. Come – or we shall be late!

On every chair there is a soft mound. Pale whisps of gauze are curled upon bright silks. Candles burn pear shaped flames on either side of the oval looking-glass.

There are brushes of thin tortoise-shell; cut bottles knobbed with silver. Something has dissolved my face. Through the mist of candle light it scarcely appears. People pass me without seeing me. They have faces. In their faces the stars seem to shine through rose coloured flesh. The room is full.

Alas, alas!

'The night is hot.'

'And did you come by train?'

A DEATH IN THE NEWSPAPER

Humphrey Hamond is dead . . . How death changes things! The colours are out. The trees look thin as paper. The traffic sounds across a gulf. The organ peals skeleton music. So from an express train I have seen the man with a scythe look up from the hedge as we flew past, and the lovers lying in the long grass stared – stared. Wheels and cries sound now low, now high; all in harmony. One bee hums through the room and again out – away. The flowers bend their heads in time.

Death, how great you are! Death, how sweet you are! . . . But Hamond has two m's. Humphrey's alive! Oh Death, what a fraud you are!

THE TELEPHONE

London softly surges against the window pane. Innumerable houses, points of light, ribbons of streets have sunk to the bottom or float sprinkled in millions of particles. Like a tethered balloon the mass floats a little this way, a little that. Come nearer – nearer! The telephone rings. Ring – 'The boat sails tomorrow.' Ring – 'The Emperor of China.' Ring – 'Life's a joy.' Ring, ring – But don't answer the telephone.

HOLBORN VIADUCT

This is Holborn Viaduct . . . And there's a pale lawn. Antelopes, sun-dappled, withdraw. Purple, starry flowers climb and hang. All's nodding and waving. Then why, wretched little boy, do you run across the street with your arm crooked against the wind?

Still, still, through the bars of the railings there are caves of redness. The bootboy, lifting the concertina, squeezes out melody. The kitchen table, with its yellow loaf, white aprons and pots of jam, is rooted to the heart of the world. Then why does blood-smeared paper drift down the pavement?

Upstairs, three steps at a time into your drawing-room – Surely, surely, with the firelight red upon the terrier's hind legs, curved pictures in the cheeks of your tea pot and – actually – green dragons on the china – *you* can't be going to kill yourself?

'James'

This untitled story, which I have called 'James', is among the Virginia Woolf papers in the Berg Collection of the New York Public Library. I have placed it in an appendix because I doubt that she wrote it, but cannot prove that it is not by her. The style is unlike that of even Virginia Woolf's earliest stories and the typescript, probably a professional one, does not resemble her other typescripts and contains only one holograph revision, the cancellation of a word. Quentin Bell, who agrees that the story does not appear to be by Virginia Woolf, thinks it *may* have been written by Clive Bell some time before 1914.

'JAMES'

James was a quiet, studious young man. When he left the University he had taken rooms in Bayswater, and, having a modest income of his own, had set himself to write a comprehensive work on the minor poets of the Victorian era. He went every morning to his research in the Reading Room of the British Museum. Sometimes he stayed there the whole day, hardly pausing in his absorbing studies even for lunch: sometimes he returned in the early afternoon to write in his own room. On these occasions he would walk a considerable part, or even the whole of the distance, going along Oxford Street, or down Shaftesbury Avenue and along the more exciting thoroughfare of Piccadilly. For, in spite of himself, the gay-looking shops fascinated him, and still more, the gay-looking people.

He had always preserved a somewhat detached attitude towards people: he had a few close friends, but very few acquaintances; he did not think it worth while. It was not that he was inhuman, or altogether unattractive as a person: merely he preferred to look at people rather than to talk to them. Especially was this the case with regard to ladies; he had never had much to do with them, but he liked very much to look at them carefully if he thought them beautiful.

James had spent one fine summer morning over his piles of books in the Reading Room, but when he went out for his lunch, it seemed so warm and pleasant and the sun made the streets so enticing, that he decided not to return. Instead, he would go for a walk.

He went to Piccadilly Circus, and there he liked so much the look of the fat old women as they sat round the statue with their gay bunches of flowers, that he bought a red rosebud which one of them, a knowing smile on her red face, held out to him. Once he had bought it he did not know what to do with it. It seemed silly to carry it, and too conspicuous for a button-hole, but he dared not throw it away or give it to anyone. So he had to put it in his button-hole. After all, on such a beautiful day, what did it matter even if it did make his clothes look rather shabby? So he continued boldly on his way along Piccadilly, pausing now and then in front of the rich shops, looking at silk shirts and costly foods, for in his way he was a lover of good things. He turned into Bond Street, where he stood looking into a window which contained emeralds and bright diamonds. He could see the reflection of himself in the shop window. He thought his clothes did not look so shabby after all, and now he felt proud of the red rosebud in his button-hole.

Suddenly, out of the corner of his eye, James saw approaching up the street a lady dressed all in white. He turned to look at her and found her to be the most beautiful creature he had ever seen. The street and the other people in it, the bright shops, vanished into nothing as she advanced. James turned and went towards her, his eyes fixed upon her. He knew he had never seen any woman so beautiful: she was as superior to all ordinary women as a white rose to the daisies. As he passed her, almost without knowing what he did he took off his hat. It seemed the necessary and only possible mark of homage and admiration.

After passing the lady James suddenly quickened his step. He bent his head and walked quickly: he blushed deeply as he suddenly realised the enormity of the thing he had done. He hurried on, and blushed again deeply at himself, for having blushed. Ought he to turn back and apologise to the lady, and try to explain? No, that would make it worse, and the shame would be unbearable. He hurried round the corner into Piccadilly and along till he came to the Green Park, feeling like a fugitive from justice. In the Park, in the wide open space, he felt freer again; after all the thing he had done was not so very terrible. Surely he had exaggerated. He sat down on a seat to recover his breath. But perhaps, he suddenly thought, she was a very important lady whom he had insulted, and she had put the police on his track. He looked nervously round, and to his dismay saw approaching him not the police, but, – far more terrifying, – the Lady herself.

James was unable to move as she came towards him. She sat down on the seat beside him, an ingratiating smile on her face. But James dared not look at her and felt himself going red and white by turns.

'What were you in such a hurry for, just now?' she began. 'Why did you run away from me?'

Still James could not look at her. But her voice, he thought, was hardly in keeping with the aristocratic beauty of her bearing.

'Don't be shy, dearie!' she went on, seeing that he needed encouragement. 'What a pretty rose you've got. May I have it?' And she took it neatly from his button-hole, sniffed it and put it in her dress.

James at last turned to her. She winked.

James leapt to his feet and ran at full speed out of the Park, never looking behind him. He jumped into a taxi.

When he got home he felt a little silly. He should have been bolder with her, more at ease, and should not have given himself away in so childish a manner. He should, at all events, have spoken to her. After all, she was extremely beautiful, whatever her other characteristics. He felt he had missed an opportunity, and grew restless. That evening, unable to concentrate on his work, he went for the first time in his life in the front row at a Musical Comedy.

Bibliographical Summary

Besides listing in summary form the information given in the individual notes concerning the drafts and the publication history of each story, this appendix also gives the location of the holograph and typescript drafts. For full information concerning the published stories, readers should consult B. J. Kirkpatrick, *A Bibliography of Virginia Woolf* (Oxford: Clarendon Press, 1980).

The following abbreviations have been used:

MS   holograph draft
TS(S)   typescript draft(s)
MS In/TS In   incomplete holograph or typescript draft
B   The Berg Collection, New York Public Library
MHP   The Monks House Papers, University of Sussex Library
T   Humanities Research Center, The University of Texas at Austin
BP   *Books and Portraits* (1977)
HB   *Harper's Bazaar* (New York and London)
HH   *A Haunted House and Other Short Stories* (1944)
MDP   *Mrs Dalloway's Party* (1973)

Phyllis and Rosamond   MS (MHP)
The Mysterious Case of Miss V. MS (MHP)
The Journal of Mistress Joan Martyn MS (B), *Twentieth Century Literature* (1979)
Memoirs of a Novelist   TS (MHP)
The Mark on the Wall   *Two Stories* (1917), Hogarth Press 1919, *MT, HH*
Kew Gardens   TS (T), Hogarth Press 1919 and 1927, *MT, HH*
The Evening Party   TSS (B)
Solid Objects   *Athenaeum* Oct. 1920, *HH*
Sympathy   TS (MHP)
An Unwritten Novel   *London Mercury* July 1920, *MT, HH*
A Haunted House   *MT, HH*
A Society   TS In (B), *MT*
Monday or Tuesday   *MT, HH*
The String Quartet   MS In and TS In (B), *MT, HH*
Blue & Green   *MT*
A Woman's College from Outside   MS and TS (B), TS (professional) (MHP), *Atalanta's Garland* (1926), *BP*
In the Orchard TS (professional) (MHP), *Criterion* April 1923, *BP*

Mrs Dalloway in Bond Street   TS (B), *Dial* July 1923; *MDP*

Nurse Lugton's Curtain   MS (British Library), TS (King's College Library, Cambridge)

The Widow and the Parrot   TS (Quentin Bell), *Redbook* July 1982

The New Dress   MS and TS (B), *Forum* May 1927, *HH, MDP*

Happiness   MS In (B), TS (MHP)

Ancestors MS (B), TS In (MHP), *MDP*

The Introduction   MS and TS (B), *Sunday Times Magazine* March 1973, *MDP*

Together and Apart   MS and TS (B), *HH, MDP*

The Man Who Loved His Kind   MS and TS (B), *HH, MDP*

A Simple Melody   MS (B)

A Summing Up   MS and TS (B), *HH, MDP*

Moments of Being: 'Slater's Pins Have No Points'   TS (MHP), *Forum* Jan. 1928, *HH*

The Lady in the Looking-Glass: A Reflection   TSS (B), *Harper's Magazine* Dec. 1929, *HB,* Jan. 1930, *HH*

The Fascination of the Pool   TS (MHP)

Three Pictures   *The Death of the Moth* 1942, *Collected Essays,* Vol. 4, 1967

Scenes from the Life of a British Naval Officer   TS (MHP)

Miss Pryme   TS (MHP)

Ode Written Partly in Prose on Seeing the Name of Cutbush Above a Butcher's Shop in Pentonville   TS (MHP)

Portraits   TSS (MHP and Quentin Bell)

Uncle Vanya   TSS (MHP)

The Duchess and the Jeweller   TSS (B), *HB* (London) April 1938, (New York) May 1938; *HH*

The Shooting Party   MS and TS (MHP), TS (B), *HB* March 1938, *HH*

Lappin and Lapinova   TS (professional) (B), *HB* April 1938, *HH*

The Searchlight   MS (B), TSS (MHP), *HH*

Gipsy, the Mongrel   TS (MHP)

The Legacy   MS, TSS, TSS In (B), TS In (MHP), *HH*

The Symbol   MS (B), TS (MHP)

The Watering Place   MS (B), TS (MHP)

Appendix A: Cracked Fiddles:
  The Evening Party   TSS (B)
  Holborn Viaduct   MS and TSS (B)
  The Telephone MS and TSS (B)
  A Death in the Newspaper   MS and TSS (B)
Appendix B: James   TS (professional) (B)

List and Location of Incomplete Stories and Sketches

Monks House Papers

(The number in parentheses is the Monks House Papers Catalogue number of the manuscript.)

The Dog   MS 2 pp.   (A.20)

The Monkeys   MS 3 pp.   (A.23j)

A Dialogue upon Mt. Pentelious [1906?]   MS 1 p., TS 9 pp.   (A.24b)

A Dialogue on a Hill [catalogued as 'Charmides & Eugenia'] [1908?]   TS 2 pp.   (A.24c)

[Untitled] first person narrative spoken by 'Theophile'   TS 2 pp.   (B.4)

[English Youth]   TS 1 p.   (B.5c)

Monday, Tuesday, Wednesday   TS 10 pp.   (B.9e)   (See DIV, 54, entry for 16 November 1931)

The Works of Mrs Hemans   MS 5 pp.   (B.10a)

[Untitled] fragments of scenes mixed in with portions of 'The Telescope' ['The Searchlight']   TS 4 pp.   (B.10f)

Berg Collection

Fragments from a letter [cancelled]/Written for a picture:/A letter to a lady   MS 1 p. (in JRII; see 'Cracked Fiddles' in Appendix A).

The night walk   MS 3 pp.   (in a writing book entitled 'Essays,' which includes a portion of the holograph of Flush.)   The title also appears in MHP B.2e.

Winter's Night   MS 1 p.   (at back of 'Essays' writing book; for this and the next two entries see Note on 'The Symbol' and 'The Watering Place').

English Youth   MS 1 p.   (follows 'Winter's Night')   Relates to TS in MHPB.5c.

Another Sixpence   MS 1 p.   (follows 'English Youth' and may be a part of it.)

Acknowledgements

For permission to transcribe and publish the previously unpublished works included in this edition, I wish to thank Quentin Bell and Angelica Garnett, administrators of the Author's Literary Estate; the Henry W. and Albert A. Berg Collection, The New York Public Library, Astor, Lenox and Tilden Foundations; the University of Sussex Library; King's College, Cambridge University; and Harry Ransom Humanities Research Center, The University of Texas at Austin.

I am grateful to Queen's University, Kingston, Ontario for granting me a sabbatical leave which gave me time to work on the edition and to the Advisory Research Committee of Queen's University and the Social Sciences and Humanities Research Council of Canada for awarding me research grants which gave me financial support for travel and research.

I wish to thank a number of people for their editorial help. Special thanks must go to Elizabeth Inglis, assistant librarian, manuscripts section, University of Sussex Library, who has shared with me her extensive knowledge of the Woolf archive there and whose generous hospitality has helped to make my visits to Sussex extremely pleasant. I am grateful to Lola Szladits, curator of the Berg Collection, and to her efficient staff, for helping me in many ways. I also wish to thank Michael Halls, Modern Archivist, King's College Library, for his aid. S. P. Rosenbaum raised many difficult and important questions during the early stages of this edition; he should not be held responsible for my solutions to them. I am grateful to John Graham for helping me to establish the text of 'The Searchlight' and to Edward Bishop for telling me that 'A Woman's College from Outside' originates in the holograph of *Jacob's Room*. Thanks also go to Mitchell Leaska for his help with 'The Widow and the Parrot'.

I am extremely grateful to Olivier and Quentin Bell for their willingness to answer all my questions. I owe a special debt to Olivier Bell who located three of the unpublished 'Portraits'. I also wish to thank Betty Klarnet of *Harper's Bazaar*; Peter Jovanovich of Harcourt, Brace, Jovanovich; Douglas Matthews of the London Library; the staff of the Records Office in Lewes; Anne Milton of the Libraries Department, London Borough of Islington; the staff of the Douglas Library at Queen's University; Diane Leonard and Jean-Jacques Hamm for helping me with various inquiries.

I wish to thank Carolyn Bond, Edward Lobb, Andrew McNeillie, Duncan Robertson, S. P. Rosenbaum, and Douglas Spettigue for reading and commenting on my introduction, and A. C. Hamilton, Catherine Harland, Claudette Hoover, Barbara Robertson, Catherine Smith, and, as always, my parents, for their interest and encouragement.

I would finally like to thank Hugo Brunner, of The Hogarth Press, for his knowledgeable, enthusiastic, and consistently good-humoured support of this project.

SUSAN DICK, *Kingston, Ontario, February 1985*

VINTAGE CLASSICS

Vintage launched in the United Kingdom in 1990, and was originally the paperback home for the Random House Group's literary authors. Now, Vintage is comprised of some of London's oldest and most prestigious literary houses, including Chatto & Windus (1855), Hogarth (1917), Jonathan Cape (1921) and Secker & Warburg (1935), alongside the newer or relaunched hardback and paperback imprints: The Bodley Head, Harvill Secker, Yellow Jersey, Square Peg, Vintage Paperbacks and Vintage Classics.

From Angela Carter, Graham Greene and Aldous Huxley to Toni Morrison, Haruki Murakami and Virginia Woolf, Vintage Classics is renowned for publishing some of the greatest writers and thinkers from around the world and across the ages – all complemented by our beautiful, stylish approach to design. Vintage Classics' authors have won many of the world's most revered literary prizes, including the Nobel, the Man Booker, the Prix Goncourt and the Pulitzer, and through their writing they continue to capture imaginations, inspire new perspectives and incite curiosity.

In 2007 Vintage Classics introduced its distinctive red spine design, and in 2012 Vintage Children's Classics was launched to include the much-loved authors of our childhood. Random House joined forces with the Penguin Group in 2013 to become Penguin Random House, making it the largest trade publisher in the United Kingdom.

@vintagebooks

penguin.co.uk/vintage-classics